RAPTURE
BECOMES HER

Books by Shirlee Busbee

Scandal Becomes Her

Seduction Becomes Her

Surrender Becomes Her

Passion Becomes Her

Rapture Becomes Her

Whisper to Me of Love

Desire Becomes Her

Lovers Forever

For Love Alone

Published by Kensington Publishing Corporation

RAPTURE BECOMES HER

SHIRLEE BUSBEE

ZEBRA BOOKS
KENSINGTON PUBLISHING CORP.
http://www.kensingtonbooks.com

ZEBRA BOOKS are published by

Kensington Publishing Corp.
119 West 40th Street
New York, NY 10018

All Kensington titles, imprints, and distributed lines are available at
special quantity discounts for bulk purchases for sales promotion,
premiums, fund-raising, educational, or institutional use.

Special book excerpts or customized printings can also be created
to fit specific needs. For details, write or phone the office of the
Kensington Special Sales Manager: Attn.: Special Sales Depart-
ment. Kensington Publishing Corp., 119 West 40th Street, New
York, NY 10018. Phone: 1-800-221-2647.

Zebra and the Z logo Reg. U.S. Pat. & TM Off.

First Zebra Books Trade Paperback Printing: July 2011
First Zebra Books Mass-Market Paperback Printing: April 2014
ISBN-13: 978-1-4201-1843-8
ISBN-10: 1-4201-1843-9

First Zebra Books Electronic Edition: July 2011
eISBN-13: 978-1-4201-3619-7
eISBN-10: 1-4201-3619-4

10 9 8 7 6 5 4 3 2 1

Printed in the United States of America

Chapter 1

He was going to die, Barnaby thought incredulously. He was going to drown in the middle of the night, in the midst of a storm sweeping across the English Channel, and no one would ever know what had happened to the most recent holder of the title Viscount Joslyn. He would have simply vanished.

A crackling bolt of silver lightning snaked across the black night sky, and through the heavy rain, Barnaby glanced desperately around, trying to get his bearings, searching frantically for something to use to save himself, but all that met his gaze was roiling seas. There was no land or sign of rescue to be seen. He was going to die, he thought again as the brightness from the lightning vanished and he was left alone in the blackness. Fighting to keep afloat in the churning water, he admitted that there would be some in London who would rejoice at his passing, and heading that list would be his newly met English cousin, Mathew Joslyn.

Mathew had been furious that the title, long considered his, was going to an American and with it the Joslyn family fortune and estates. "A bloody, half-breed colonist, Viscount

Joslyn? It is an insult!" Mathew snarled at their first meeting three months ago in October in the London solicitor's office.

Barnaby didn't blame Mathew for being angry. In Mathew's shoes he might have felt the same way, but he wasn't about to allow the slur to pass. "You are mistaken," Barnaby drawled. "It was my grandmother who was half-Cherokee." He smiled, showing his excellent teeth. "But I warn you— you would be wise not to use that term again in my hearing. As for being a colonist . . ." His black eyes full of mockery, he continued. "I think you forget that America gained her independence from Britain a decade ago. I am a citizen of the United States."

"Very well," Mathew snapped, his cheeks faintly flushed, "but it is insupportable that someone like you should think to step so easily into command of my great-uncle's estates. Good God, man, you don't know the first thing about running an estate like Windmere. You're little more than a backwoods upstart!"

Barnaby held on to his temper with an effort, thinking that it wouldn't help his cause any if his first act as Lord Joslyn was to throttle his cousin. He took a deep breath and, letting that last comment ride for now, said curtly, "I would remind you that I am not *un*educated and that I have been overseeing my own plantation in Virginia for a number of years. I'll grant you that Green Hill is not as vast as Windmere—there will be differences, but I'm quite capable of managing Windmere."

Mathew's lips tightened. "Perhaps, but you are a fool if you think that someone with a grandmother who is a half . . . uh, part savage will be eagerly accepted by the *ton* as Viscount Joslyn."

"Considering the situation with France, you should be more worried about the fact that my grandmother's father was a Frenchman," Barnaby retorted. The expressions of horror on the faces of those present at this new abomination

For a pair of people who do, truly, make my
life a little less complicated—thanks!

MICHELLE SHARROCK—my patient Web designer who
is doing her best to drag me screaming and kicking into
the twenty-first century. She deserves *great* sympathy.

AND

JERRY MUNN—my favorite blackberry picker,
the kind you eat, and my main man when it comes
to delving into the mysteries of my computer.
He deserves some sympathy, too!

AND

As always, HOWARD, truly the love of my life.

had Barnaby biting the inside of his cheek to keep from grinning. His gaze swept the handsome room, and with his foes momentarily silenced, he rose to his impressive height and walked to the door. His hand on the knob, he looked back at Mathew and said softly, "Upstart I may be, but I've never lived in the backwoods and you, sir, can go hang—and for all I care, take the damn title with you!"

It had been a pleasurable moment, but as he lifted his face above the next wave and the cold seeped deeper into his bones, Barnaby tried to remember the events leading up to his present predicament, but his thoughts were sluggish and erratic. Like a serpent curling around its prey, the icy water was inexorably draining the life from him and with every second, his will to survive wavered.

It would be so easy, so simple, he thought, to let the storm have its way, so easy to stop fighting and allow himself to be pulled down into the depths. . . . A wave slapped him in the face, startling him and shattering the seductive song of death that crooned in his head.

With a curse, he renewed his struggle to stay afloat in the darkness—if only for a few seconds longer. Ignoring the stinging pain at the back of his head, he vaguely remembered freeing his knife fastened at his ankle and then jettisoning his boots and heavy greatcoat, along with his jacket, within minutes of hitting the water, knowing they would only weigh him down. He'd held on to the knife for a while, until he realized it was hampering his ability to swim and then reluctantly he'd let the waves take it. Those memories did him little good because he still had no idea how he had ended up in the Channel, yet oddly enough he knew he *was* in the English Channel. But where, or how he had gotten there, he had no inkling. His mind was blank—as much from the lethal cold as the blood he had lost from the wound on the back of his head.

He frowned. How the devil did he know he had a wound?

And how did he know that the wound had bled? Again he had no answers, and as his head slipped beneath the onslaught of another wall of water, the urge to end it, to let the cold and the Channel have its way, was nearly impossible to resist.

But as his friends often pointed out, he could be stubborn as a mule, and with a powerful kick of his long legs he surged up above the waves. He wasn't, he swore, with a fierce grin, going to make it easy for anyone or anything to kill him. Another streak of lightning lit the black sky and in that moment, Barnaby spied something that made his heart leap: several planks linked together bobbed in the water not six feet from him. He half recognized them as being a section of the floor of the yacht he had inherited along with everything else owned by the late Seventh Viscount Joslyn. Fighting his way toward that beacon of hope those boards represented, he struggled to think where the yacht had been moored and then it came to him: near Eastbourne on the Sussex coast. But what in the hell had he been doing there?

He had no time for further thought—all of his focus was on surviving—and though it seemed that it took him hours to reach those planks, in mere minutes, his fingers brushed against the slippery wood. Getting himself out of the water took longer, the tossing waves and the shifting, slick surface of the planks thwarting his efforts, but finally, he was able to heave himself aboard the makeshift raft.

Gasping for breath, he rolled over onto his back and with his face pelted by rain, he stared up at the black sky. He was freezing, his teeth chattering, his body shaking from the cold, and he suspected he had traded one form of death for another. Exposure would kill him as sure as a hangman's noose, but he wouldn't die, he consoled himself grimly, by drowning. And that, he thought as he drifted into unconsciousness, was a victory of sorts.

* * *

"Is he dead?" asked Jeb Brown ghoulishly above the shrieking wind and rain whipping around outside the best room at The Crown. It was a pleasant room with high, open-beamed ceilings and a gleaming oak floor covered here and there with cheerful rag rugs, the space dominated by a huge bed, impressively draped with a rich green silk canopy. A fire glowed orange and gold on the brick hearth; soft yellow light from several candles lit by Mrs. Gilbert, the widowed owner of The Crown, flickered about the room and, despite the snarling storm, cast a cozy spell.

Mrs. Gilbert, her liberally streaked gray hair half hidden beneath a muslin cap, gave a sharp shake of her head. "No, he's not dead. Half drowned and near frozen, but not dead."

Jeb looked to the other occupant in the room, a tall, fair-haired youth wearing breeches, boots and a leather jerkin over a billowy long-sleeved shirt. Looking beyond the boy's garb, closer inspection revealed that the slim shape and finely etched features belonged to a young woman, her thick silvery-blond hair pulled back into a queue tied with a bit of black ribbon.

"I tell you, Miss Emily, it was pure luck I spied him," Jeb said, his wrinkled fisherman's face full of wonder. "With the storm and all, it's black as midnight out there, and if it hadn't been for this bloody big bolt of lightning at the very second I was looking in his direction, I never would have seen him." He shook his head. "Good for him that we had a run tonight else we'd be finding his body washed up somewhere along the shore—if we found it at all."

Emily Townsend nodded and walked closer to stare down at the man Jeb had pulled from the waters of the Channel. "He was indeed lucky," Emily said, her gaze running over the man who lay still and silent beneath Mrs. Gilbert's examination. His hair was black, his skin so dark it was almost swarthy—except for the worrisome blue cast to his lips. From what she could see, he was an exceptionally tall, fit man—and a stranger to all of them.

Mrs. Gilbert muttered, "He had the devil's own luck, I'd say." Looking up from her examination, she added briskly, "And most likely will recover with no ill effects." Her hand on the cold, damp blankets that Jeb had wrapped the stranger in once he'd dragged him on board his boat and stripped off the wet clothes, she glanced over her shoulder. "Miss Emily, you need to leave the room now," she ordered, "and let Jeb and I put this nightshirt on him and get him into a warm bed."

When Emily hesitated, Mrs. Gilbert's plump face softened and she said, "I know you have dozens of questions to ask Jeb, but go fetch those hot water bottles I left in the kitchen." When Emily's jaw took on that mulish cast they all knew so well, Mrs. Gilbert said firmly, "It wouldn't be proper for you to stay. By the time you return, we'll have him snug and warm between the sheets. Now go."

Emily snorted at Mrs. Gilbert's determination to treat her like some gently born miss just out of the schoolroom. It was true, she was gently born—her father had been the local squire until his death seven years ago—but she'd turned six and twenty months ago and was no child. And, she reminded herself, if it weren't for her, Jeb wouldn't have been running a load of contraband from France tonight and the stranger wouldn't have been found. She had every right to remain, but from past experience she knew that there was no arguing with Mrs. Gilbert and reluctantly she left the room. Never one to brood, by the time she reached the inn's kitchen she was smiling. No one, she admitted ruefully, as she picked up the hot water bottles and accepted the heated brick thrust into her hands by Flora, the middle Gilbert daughter, no matter what age or standing, disobeyed Mrs. Gilbert. Even her cousin, the dissolute Squire Townsend, was known to scamper away like a schoolboy to escape a tongue lashing by Mrs. Gilbert.

When she had returned, the stranger was decently garbed in an old nightshirt that had belonged to Mrs. Gilbert's deceased husband and tucked beneath the quilts. The heated brick was placed at his feet; the water bottles snuggled up against his sides. Mrs. Gilbert shooed Jeb from the room and after taking one last look around, said to Emily, "I'll send Mary up with some warm water and a cloth—you can clean that nasty gash on his head." With a meaningful look at Emily, she added, "We've wasted enough time as it is—the others need to be on their way."

Emily opened her mouth to protest but Mrs. Gilbert shook a finger at her. "I know," said Mrs. Gilbert, "you think you should be the one down there dealing with them, but for once act like the lady you were raised to be and stay up here out of sight. Please."

Emily hesitated. "Keep an eye out for anything out of the ordinary," she finally said. "My cousin has been acting strangely lately and I think he is spying on me." She took a deep breath and confessed in a rush, "Every night for the past week or so someone, and I suspect it is my cousin, has tried the knob to my room." At Mrs. Gilbert's quick intake of breath, she said quickly, "Don't worry. I keep the door locked and a chest of drawers pushed against it—as does Anne—so whoever it was goes away. But it would not be good if my cousin found me gone from my bed." She swallowed. "If he were to discover what we are about—"

Mrs. Gilbert looked grim. "You don't think he saw you leave tonight and followed you when you left the manor, do you?"

"I don't believe so, but I've had the feeling ever since I slipped from my room that something wasn't right, that something was wrong." She glanced at the stranger. "First him and then . . ." She shivered. "I feel like a goose, but I still haven't been able to stop myself from looking over my shoulder all night. I keep feeling as if someone is watching me . . . us." Wearily, she added, "If the door to my bedroom was forced and Jeffery discovered my room was empty this is probably the first place he'd look."

Mrs. Gilbert's lips thinned. "Well, he won't find you. We'll have you on your way back to the manor quicker than a cat can lick its ear!" Giving Emily a fond pat on the shoulder, she said, "You worry too much, my dear—you always have. The stranger's arrival has put us all in a dither, but I'm sure that's all it is." She looked around the room one last time and said, "And now I must go and see if Jeb and the others are loaded up and ready to leave. I'll send Mary to you with those rags and the warm water. She can keep you company while I'm gone."

Mrs. Gilbert bustled from the room and shortly Mary showed up with the cloths and bowl of water. At seventeen, Mary was the youngest of the five Gilbert daughters, and her blue eyes wide with excitement she approached the bed and stared at the stranger.

"Coo!" she exclaimed. "He isn't dead, is he?" she asked, echoing Jeb's earlier question.

Emily smiled faintly and said, "No. He just looks dead, but your mother says he will recover." Her smile became a grin. "And we all know your mother is never wrong."

Mary grinned back at her. "You can wager your last guinea on that!"

Taking the clean, white cloth and dipping it into the bowl of water, gingerly Emily began to clean the ugly wound, wincing when the man groaned at her ministrations. Just as well he's unconscious, she thought, as she dipped and rubbed the length of the gash.

Mary shuddered as another violent gust of wind slammed into the walls of the inn. "Ma says it's a miracle he's alive.

Not many survive a dip in the Channel on a night like tonight."

Concentrating on the task at hand, Emily nodded and murmured, "I wonder what he was doing out there. And who he is."

Mary paled as a thought struck her. "Oh, miss! You don't think he's a revenuer, do you?"

Having cleaned the wound as good as it was going to get under her hands Emily dropped the bloodstained rag in the water and studied the man's features, noting the broad forehead, the high cheekbones and the generous mouth. She had nothing to base it on, but revenuer would be the last occupation she would have guessed this man to ply. There was something about his face . . .

Emily shook her head. "No, I don't think he's a revenuer." Lifting the quilts, she looked down at his hand, studying the long, elegant fingers and the clean and trimmed fingernails. She frowned and glanced over at Mary. "Did Jeb bring the clothes the man was wearing with him to the inn? Or leave them on board the boat?"

Mary's pretty face grew animated. "They're downstairs drying by the fire in the little private room at the back. Do you think they'll tell us who he is?"

Emily spared the stranger one last look. He seemed to be resting easier and the faint blueness around his lips was fading. There was nothing more she could do for him for now. Rising to her feet, she said, "I think we'll know more about him than we do right now, if we take a look at what he was wearing when Jeb pulled him out of the Channel."

The clothes told Emily quite a bit. Though damaged by salt water, the frilled white linen shirt was expensive and sewn by an expert seamstress and the cream-and-fawn patterned silk waistcoat was something only a wealthy man would own, as was the ruined pocket watch and the gold chain and fob. The water-stained cravat, like the shirt, was of the best linen and the finely knitted pantaloons also would have belonged to a man of means. When he'd gone into the water, to avoid the extra weight, she assumed his boots and coat had been wisely discarded.

Staring at the items draped over a pair of chairs near the roaring fire, Emily considered what she'd learned. The stranger was apparently a wealthy man. Not a revenuer, that much was certain.

Leaving his clothes behind, Emily dismissed Mary and returned upstairs. Resuming her seat beside the man on the bed, she stared at him, as if willing him to wake and tell her who he was and how he'd gotten into the Channel.

Being the daughter of the previous squire and having lived all of her life near a small village nestled in the Cuckmere valley she was intimately familiar with the local inhabitants. Her mouth twisted. And since her cousin had stepped into her father's position, she had, unfortunately, become familiar with several randy, young bucks and widows of questionable morals from London who made up her cousin's circle of friends.

This man was a complete stranger, but he wasn't just any bit of flotsam tossed up from the belly of the Channel either. He was wealthy and his hands told her that he was a member of the gentry, perhaps even a member of the aristocracy.

Her expression puzzled, she continued to stare at him. There'd been no gossip about someone of his description visiting any of the great houses in the surrounding countryside. . . . So who was he? And why was he found drifting in the Channel on a wicked night like tonight?

As if to punctuate her thoughts, a shaft of wind suddenly shrieked down the chimney, making her jump. Amused at her reaction and noting that the fire was dying, Emily got up and walked over to poke at the fire, sending a shower of sparks flying upward. From the neat stack nearby, she threw on several more pieces of wood and only when the fire was crackling and snapping to her satisfaction, did she take a seat in the high-backed tapestry-covered chair near the fire.

She looked over at the stranger and was pleased to see that there was a faint flush to his cheeks and that his lips were a more natural color, the blueness having faded as his body warmed. Mrs. Gilbert was right: he should recover.

With the stranger's most immediate needs taken care of, she dismissed him from her mind and turned her attention to what Mrs. Gilbert and Jeb were doing at this very minute. And she wondered again, if she had made the right decision four years ago. . . .

She'd resisted the idea in the beginning and for the first few years following her father's death, despite the unpleasant intrusion of her cousin and his drain on the family estates, she'd managed to keep her great-aunt, Cornelia, and her stepmother, Anne, fairly insulated and comfortable. Once her cousin had frittered away the bulk of the tidy fortune her father had amassed and began to ravage the estate for money to squander at the gaming tables and brothels in London, she'd had no choice.

With the Sussex coast only a few miles away, Emily had grown up hearing all the stories about the local smugglers and so it wasn't such an outrageous decision. For as far back as she could remember, Cook, and even their butler, Walker, had filled her head with legendary tales of the smugglers' bravery and cleverness in outwitting the custom officials and the hapless riding officers. When feeling mellow, even Cornelia had been known to tell a rollicking good story about the smugglers who plied their trade just off the coast. Many in the area, while not smugglers themselves, were relatives of smugglers or were aligned with the smugglers.

By the time she was ten, Emily could have named several known smugglers and a dozen or more villagers and farm laborers who helped transport the contraband goods to the outskirts of London. Her father had not been above accepting without comment the packet of tea, the cask of French brandy or the bolt of fine silk that periodically appeared in his stables—usually the morning after several of his horses were found standing in their stalls, muddy and exhausted.

Realizing that she had to do something to save them all from ending up destitute or nearly as bad, at the complete mercy of her cousin, turning to smuggling had been a simple step. And, she admitted with a clenched jaw, there'd been another reason: her little smuggling operation kept several villagers in their homes and saved them from the work house or being reduced to homeless beggars.

The sudden death of her father from a broken neck when his horse had balked at a fence and thrown him while he had been fox hunting in Leicestershire had stunned the family and the neighborhood. Anne, her stepmother, only two years her senior, had been shattered by the news of her husband's death and had lost the baby she had been carrying.

It had been a terrible time. Not only had the little family suffered the devastating loss of nephew, father and husband, but Jeffery Townsend, the son of the old squire's younger brother, had gleefully stepped into his shoes and took up the position as head of the family. It wasn't a good fit. The new squire was as different from the old squire as chalk to cheese. Certainly Jeffery was no family man and had no time or patience for a cantankerous old woman, a weeping widow who'd just lost her husband and stillborn child and a fierce-eyed Emily. Only grudgingly had he accepted their presence in the lovely manor house that had housed the Townsend family for over two centuries.

The stranger stirred, groaning, and pushing aside her unpleasant memories, she hurried to his side. Hovering over him, she brushed back a strand of salt-stiffened black hair from his forehead.

She watched him for several more seconds, but he gave no further indication that he was coming awake. Staring intently at the dark face and noticing the thick black brows, the ridiculously long lashes of his eyes, she wondered again who he was and why he had been in the Channel. Did he have a family worried about him? A mother? A wife? Children?

The wound bothered her. It looked to her as if something . . . or someone had brought something very hard and very heavy down on the stranger's head. Not that she was an expert, but in the four years since she had undertaken to rescue them all from destitution by smuggling, she had cleaned and patched and sewn up her share of wounds. Some were simply the result of the dangers faced at sea; others from clashes with the revenuers or with the vicious Nolles's gang that claimed this part of Sussex as their own. She'd seen this kind of wound before and the cause was usually a blow to the back of the head.

Faith, at twenty-eight the eldest Gilbert daughter, opened the door and peeked inside. Seeing Emily standing beside the bed, she came into the room and stood by her side. "Whoever he is, he's quite handsome, isn't he?"

Emily shrugged. Thinking of her cousin, she muttered, "Handsome is as handsome does." She glanced at Faith. "Has your mother returned?"

"No, but young Sam slipped by to say that she wouldn't be long."

"Did he say why they're delayed?" Emily glanced at the painted china clock on the mantel. It was approaching two o'clock in the morning. "The ponies should have been loaded and on their way by now."

"I expect the storm is the reason they're running late."

"There's always a storm, Faith," Emily said impatiently. "It shouldn't have made a difference."

"Well, that's true, but with the stranger and all . . ."

Emily sighed. Faith was right. The stranger had played havoc with their schedule. Not having access to the easy landing at Cuckmere Haven like the Nolles gang, her intrepid little band of smugglers was forced to derrick their contraband goods up the steep, chalk face of the Seven Sisters. Without dashing him to death, getting the unconscious stranger up those same cliffs had been a slow process.

"Do you want me to bring you some soup or something hot to drink?" Faith asked.

Emily shook her head, and with her eyes on the stranger, she replied, "I'm fine and until he wakes, there's no reason to prepare anything for him either. You can go help your sisters in the kitchen."

Uncertainly Faith eyed her. "Miss," she began hesitantly, "shouldn't you be riding home? You've been away from the manor longer than usual. What if the squire misses you?"

With more confidence than she felt, Emily said, "Don't worry. My cousin thinks that I am tucked safely in my bed. Before I left, I checked on him and he was deep in his cups with Mr. Ainsworth—his foppish friend he means for either Anne or myself to marry."

Her eyes full of sympathy, Faith nodded, and since there was nothing else for her to do, she left for downstairs.

Emily stared at the door Faith shut behind her and sighed. There were few secrets in the village and it was common knowledge that Townsend wanted Emily, her great-aunt and her stepmother out of the manor. The late squire's will prevented Jeffery from tossing them out of their home with only the clothes on their backs, but if he could marry off the two younger women . . .

Short of murder or marriage, Emily thought wryly, he was stuck with them—just as they were stuck with him. The former squire's will had stipulated that Cornelia, Emily and Anne were allowed to live in the manor for their lifetimes— unless, of course, they married. Her lips twitched. But Jeffery would never be rid of Great-Aunt Cornelia, Emily thought with relish—at her age, no one expected Great-Aunt Cornelia to leave The Birches any other way than in a coffin.

Not only had the old squire ensured the women of his family a home for as long as necessary, he had also placed a nice sum in the funds to ensure that they would never be needy. Emily's eyes hardened. Unfortunately, her father's will hadn't gone far enough. Jeffery, acting as head of the family and their trustees, had overseen the account and the money had vanished.

He may have gotten his hands on the money, Emily acknowledged, but he couldn't budge them from the manor. Only by marriage or murder would they leave their home behind. But Jeffery wasn't ready to murder them yet, she admitted with a curl of her lip, thinking of Mr. Ainsworth.

Mr. Ainsworth was the latest in a line of *unsuitable* suitors Jeffery had dredged up and forced under their noses, but Ainsworth was different and he worried Emily. She and Cornelia had managed to send the others packing, but Ainsworth was proving difficult to discourage and she wondered if it had been he who had tried the knob to her bedroom this past week.

Ainsworth had a compelling reason to want a wife: due to turn five and thirty in a matter of a few months, if he was not married to a "respectable" woman by his thirty-fifth birthday, he would lose a handsome fortune. It was well known for the last year or so that Ainsworth was hanging out for a wife, but since his reputation was reprehensible there were few respectable ladies willing to entertain his suit.

And that despicable creature, Emily thought furiously, is the man Jeffery thinks one of us should marry! Her hands tightened into fists. By heaven, she'd like to run the pair of them through.

A sudden awareness sent a trickle of unease down her spine and she glanced over to the man in the bed. Her heart skittered in her chest when she saw that the stranger was awake and staring at her.

Forcing a smile, she walked over to the side of the bed.

"You've had a miraculous escape, sir," she explained. "If Jeb hadn't spied you when he did, I fear it would have gone badly for you."

Eyes black as midnight studied her face. "Where am I?" he asked flatly. One hand shot out from beneath the pile of quilts and fastened like an iron vise around her slender wrist. "And who the hell are you, boy?"

With a swiftness Barnaby admired, a small knife appeared in the boy's other hand and a second later the blade was pressed against his throat. The boy smiled fiercely and said softly, "I think, sir, that should be my question. Who the hell are *you*?"

Chapter 2

The moment his hand closed around that slender wrist, Barnaby had a sensation of wrongness, but that feeling vanished in a flash, and he was left looking at the boy's tense features. A very pretty boy, he thought frowning.

They stared at each other for a long moment, Barnaby's black eyes boring into the boy's gray ones. Neither was giving an inch and, reading the cool determination in the boy's gaze, Barnaby decided, considering his dip in the Channel, that he might be wise not to find out precisely how handy the boy was with the knife.

Slowly letting go of the boy, he muttered, "Forgive me. I fear that I am not at my best at the moment."

Her breathing ragged, Emily prudently put several feet between them. Keeping her knife handy, she said levelly, "Indeed, I would agree—especially if that is the way you greet someone who is trying to help you."

The boy was insolent and Barnaby liked his pluck, but staring hard at the boy, he was nagged by the sensation that he was missing something, and that feeling of wrongness swept over him again. Unable to determine its cause but assuming it was a leftover effect from his ordeal, Barnaby glanced around the room and asked again, "Where am I?"

"In the best room at The Crown."

He shot the boy an impatient look. "And where is The Crown located?"

"In Broadhaven." His gaze narrowed and Emily added quickly, "It is a small village not far from Alfriston in Sussex. We are only a few miles inland from the coast."

Barnaby recognized the name and relaxed slightly. The events of the night were hazy, but he remembered that he'd been told that Windmere, the Joslyn country estate, was situated near the village of Broadhaven. His memory wasn't clear, but he rather thought that he'd been on his way to Windmere when he'd ended up in the Channel. "And someone named 'Jeb' pulled me from the Channel?"

Emily nodded. His speech was not that of an Englishman, but had a soft cadence that she found attractive. She frowned, trying to place it. It wasn't French or Spanish. . . . A bit of gossip she'd heard recently flitted through her mind and she gasped, "You're the American."

The sound of raised, angry voices and a sudden crash below distracted them, preventing Barnaby from answering. The boy's gray eyes widened and the already fair skin paled as the boy swung to face the door, the slender body braced.

Not liking the boy's reaction or the noise of a violent altercation filtering up through the floorboards, Barnaby struggled to sit up. A sharp burst of pain lanced across the back of his head and he groaned, falling back against the pillows. Dizzy and afraid he was about to cast up his accounts, Barnaby fought to gain control over his body.

Footsteps pounded up the stairs and a second later, the door burst open. It was Flora, the middle daughter, her cheeks flushed and her expression grim and frightened at the same time.

"He's here!" Flora exclaimed, hurtling into the room. She

slammed and locked the heavy oak door behind her before turning to look at Emily. "My sisters and Sam can only hold him for a few minutes. You have to leave. *Now.*"

Emily hurriedly stuck her knife in her boot and started toward the lone window on the far side of the room. It was a two-story drop, but it was her only way out.

Flora grabbed her arm and cried, "Not that way. Here. Open the wardrobe. There's a hidden door at the back— you'll be able to escape out the secret passageway. Hurry!"

Hearing the shrieks from Flora's sisters and the sounds of furniture crashing below her, Emily flung open the door to the massive wardrobe on the wall opposite the bed and dived inside. Hovering behind her, as Emily pawed her way through some quilts and odds and ends hanging inside the ancient oak wardrobe, Flora said, "Reach up to the top at the back. There's a small lever. Pull it and the door opens away from you. Be careful you don't fall down the stairs."

With shaking fingers, Emily found the lever and, despite Flora's warning, nearly tumbled down the narrow stairs that appeared at her feet when the concealed door at the back of the wardrobe suddenly gave way.

Both women stiffened as the sound of a desperate struggle came nearer. From the curses and noise, it was clear the fight had moved to the bottom of the stairs. They had only seconds.

Flora fairly shoved Emily down the hidden staircase. "Go. *Go!*" Flora hissed. "He must not find you here." As Emily disappeared, Flora shut the concealed door and dragged the quilts back into place. With a practiced move that told Barnaby she had done this more than once, Flora fastened the outer door to the wardrobe.

Flora's sisters, with young Sam's valiant assistance, had done their best, but they were no match for a full-grown, furious male, and Flora had hardly turned around when there was a thunderous banging on the door to the room.

"Emily!" shouted a man's angry voice. "I know you're in there. Open up. Open up, I say."

Flora glanced at Barnaby. She placed a finger to her lips and at his nod she took a deep breath, straightened her muslin cap and walked calmly over to the door.

Confronted by utter blackness, Emily wasn't certain how she made it down the unfamiliar steps. Leaning against the rough wooden walls on either side of her, she half stumbled, half fell down the narrow, twisting staircase. Reaching the bottom, she stood indecisively for a second, not certain of her next move. As she fumbled around in complete darkness, the best she could tell was that she was in a very small space, hemmed in by three walls with the stairs at her back. Remembering how the door had worked in the wardrobe, she reached up and ran her hand along the top of the wall in front of her, her heart leaping when her fingers found the lever. She gave it a pull and nearly hit herself in the face when the door swung open.

The full force of the storm buffeted her the instant she stepped outside. Rain lashed down on her and the wind screamed around her as she pulled the door shut. There was a click and the door locked behind her, leaving her alone in the dark.

It took her a moment to find her position, but the faint light from the candles burning in the main room of the inn told her that she was at the side of the inn with the stables behind her. Fighting against the wind and the rain, she ran to the stables and a moment later was on one of The Crown's horses on her way home.

It was difficult going, the storm having turned the road to muddy slush, the darkness, wind and rain adding to the difficulty, but eventually Emily turned the lathered horse down the long, curving drive that led to her home, The Birches.

Jumping from the horse, she tied the reins to the saddle and with a slap on the animal's haunch sent it lumbering back in the direction of The Crown.

Her cousin had replaced many of their old, trusted servants with men who were loyal to him, and upon meeting the new stableman, Kelsey, that he had installed several months ago, Emily immediately took precautions to keep her activities secret. She stopped using her own horses and made arrangements with Mrs. Gilbert for Sam to bring her a mount on the nights they had a run. When their work was done Sam would accompany her this far and take the horse back, but tonight that hadn't been possible.

She closed her mind to what might be happening at The Crown and concentrated on accomplishing the reason Flora and the others were risking themselves for her. When her cousin returned to The Birches, she *had* to be home and safely in her bed. Her lips twisted. She also needed an innocent excuse to explain why he did not find her there when he had obviously come looking for her tonight.

Her stride lengthened and she broke into a run, oblivious to the rain and the wind shrieking through bare limbs of the birch trees that lined the half-mile driveway. The squire must never learn what they had all been up to because Emily didn't doubt for a moment, far from being outraged, he would immediately take over the operation and reward himself with the lion's share of the profits. The villagers, Mrs. Gilbert, her daughters, the blacksmith, Jeb and the others—all those who desperately depended on the money they made from smuggling would suffer.

The torches at either side of the heavy double front doors of the big house gleamed in the darkness and Emily veered around to the back. If she'd gone to the front door, Walker, most likely pacing anxiously, would have whisked her away in an instant, but she didn't want to involve him any more than he was already. As for Flora and the others . . .

Guilt smote her. Had she done the right thing abandoning

them to her cousin's rage when he discovered his prey had escaped him? Reminding herself that it had been for their protection that she had fled didn't ease her conscience. Wearily, she admitted that too many people were dependent upon her to bring them to a safe harbor for her to have remained, but oh, how she would have enjoyed confronting Jeffery and telling him precisely what she thought of him—and his friend, Mr. Ainsworth.

Thoroughly soaked, her teeth chattering, her breath coming in great gulps, Emily finally reached the trellis fastened to the wall at the rear of the house. Avoiding the thorns of the climbing rose that would be covered in fragrant pink blooms in a few months, she dragged herself up the trellis to the window from which she had exited hours ago.

Pulling open the unlocked window, she slowly, gratefully climbed inside. As the warmth from the fire burning on the hearth hit her, she spared another thought for her companions she'd had to leave behind at The Crown, hoping her wretched cousin had not done them any harm. As she stripped out of her wet clothing, her jaw clenched. By God, if he'd hurt one of them she *would* run him through!

Squire Townsend had not inflicted any damage upon the Gilbert daughters and young Sam, but the opposite was true for the determined defenders at The Crown. Faith had broken a pitcher of ale over Townsend's head, cutting him above his right eye, and Molly, next to her in age, had been able to use the broom with great effect. The squire was going to walk with a limp for several days from the fall Molly had caused when she had stuck the broom handle between his legs, and Sam had added insult to injury by biting his calf and drawing blood. Harriet and Mary had pelted him with several, heavy pewter tankards, and by the time Townsend had staggered through their gauntlet and started up the stairs, in addition to his other wounds, he was sporting the beginnings of an impressive bruise on one cheek and his chin was bleeding.

It was a thoroughly enraged and disheveled gentleman that charged into the room only seconds after Emily had disappeared into the wardrobe. His once-immaculate cravat was askew, his dark blue coat and formerly pristine cream-colored waistcoat were splattered with ale and blood and his chestnut curls were in disarray.

Limping into the room, once Flora had unlocked the door, Townsend looked around wild-eyed, and seeing only Flora standing there and the dark-skinned stranger in the bed, he demanded, "Where is she? I know she is here. Emily, show yourself at once!"

Faith and Molly were right behind Townsend and hands on her hips, Faith said, "How dare you force your way into the room of a gentleman who has just escaped death. Wait until the constable hears of this!"

Townsend turned on his tormentors and snapped, "I think it is you, Faith, who should fear the constable." His voice rising in outrage, he said, "You and Molly and the others attacked me! I shall bring charges against the whole parcel of you and we'll see how you like that."

"I'm sure that there is some misunderstanding," Flora said calmly. "And if my sisters 'attacked' you—a great exaggeration I'm sure—there was probably a good reason for it."

Townsend's face purpled. "You doubt my word! May I remind you, Flora, that I *am* the squire and you would be wise to show me proper respect!"

Barnaby, who had watched the scene with great appreciation, felt it was time to make his entrance and said idly, "Perhaps if you acted more like a squire instead of a brawling bully, you might garner some, ah, proper respect."

Townsend's fulminating gaze swung to this new foe. "Who the hell are you?"

With an American's innate scorn of titles and trappings of aristocracy, Barnaby's title hadn't impressed him much, but he perceived in this situation a title might actually be useful. Ignoring the dizziness movement caused, he sat up in the bed and said coolly, "I am Joslyn, the, ah, Eighth Viscount Joslyn. And you are . . . ?"

Townsend gasped and took a backward step. "Never say so!"

Out of the corner of his eye Barnaby caught Flora's astonished expression and his lips twitched. Behind Townsend, Faith and Molly stared at him slack-jawed and Barnaby didn't know whether to be amused or annoyed at everyone's reaction to a mere title. Deciding the entire situation was something out of a farce, he chose to be amused, but not with Townsend. . . .

Mimicking Mathew's reaction when offended (which occurred frequently in Barnaby's company), Barnaby's brow lifted arrogantly, and looking as if he smelled rotten fish, he said, "I would indeed say so. Who the devil are you that you dare question my identity?"

Recovering from her shock, her eyes alight with wicked enjoyment, Flora murmured with relish, "My lord, allow me to introduce Squire Townsend to you. He lives nearby at The Birches—not far from Windmere."

Upon learning the gentleman's identity, the angry flush died from Townsend's handsome face. Despite his battered appearance, he smiled affably and with practiced grace bowed and murmured, "As Flora said, I am the local squire, Jeffery Townsend—we are neighbors. While I wish the circumstances were different, it is my pleasure to meet you, my lord." Straightening, he added, "I do apologize most sincerely for my unseemly intrusion, but you see I am searching for my missing cousin, Emily." He glanced around the room as if he expected Emily to suddenly appear. Turning back to Barnaby he said, "I have it on good authority that my cousin is here."

"You think that I am hiding her?" Barnaby asked incredulously, his mind reeling. The boy, a girl? Emily?

Townsend didn't know what to believe, but he was as certain as he stood here that Emily had been at The Crown tonight and that the perfidious Gilbert clan was hiding her from him. Kelsey had told him as much. There'd been no sign of Emily downstairs and well aware of the pride Mrs. Gilbert took in her best room and the respect and affection she held for Emily, this room had seemed the likeliest place Mrs. Gilbert would have put Emily. The fierce battle waged by the Gilbert vixens and that hell-brat, Sam, only confirmed his certainty that Emily was cowering in this very room.

When he'd entered the room, Jeffery had been positive he'd find his quarry and for once have his bloody insolent cousin at a grave disadvantage. There was no plausible excuse she could offer that would explain what she was doing here at this time of night in the best room at The Crown—especially when she was supposed to be angelically sleeping in her own bed at home.

He'd suspected she was up to something for months, but so far he had not been able to discover precisely what it was. Despite the spy he'd set on her, beyond the fact that his cousin slipped from the house on certain nights and disappeared into The Crown, he had learned nothing. Undecided whether Kelsey was simply inept or, more likely, withholding information, upon learning she had once again sneaked out of the house tonight, full of fuming impatience, he had determined to confront her.

A lover had seemed the most plausible reason for her furtive trips to The Crown, but Jeffery could think of no logical reason for her to be secretive about it. The Lord knew he'd have welcomed a suitor—respectable or not. *Anyone* who would rid him of his aggravating cousin he would have greeted with delight.

Finding a male abed hadn't been such a surprise, but the identity of the man dumbfounded him and Jeffery was perplexed about the role the viscount played in tonight's doings. Well aware, as was nearly every member of the *ton,* of Mathew Joslyn's stunning reversal of fortune last spring when news of the American heir had been announced, like everyone else, Jeffery had been curious about the new viscount, but until now their paths had not crossed.

Not for a moment did Townsend believe that the viscount was the reason for Emily's late-night excursions: she'd been sneaking away from The Birches long before the new viscount's arrival in Britain in October. Never one to let an opportunity to gain his own ends pass him by though, Jeffery wondered how he might be able to turn this unfortunate set of events to his own advantage.

He shot Joslyn a speculative look. While there was no sign of Emily at the moment, he'd swear on his mother's grave that she had been here tonight. And if, for whatever reasons, Emily *had* been here with the viscount, she'd be thoroughly compromised. Good God, the man was nearly naked in the bed right before him and it didn't take much imagination to put Emily beside him. Hmmm. . . .

Jeffery eyed the viscount again. The Joslyns were known to be very plump in the pocket, with the new viscount having the plumpest pocket of all. . . . Visions of breathtaking wealth dazzling him, he began to calculate how best to rid himself of his cousin and get his hands on some of the Joslyn gold.

Barnaby didn't trust the sudden gleam in Townsend's eyes and he said, "You have barged into my room uninvited and as you can see for yourself, there is no 'Emily' here. I suggest you leave."

Ordinarily Jeffery would have done his best to ingratiate himself with the viscount, but the idea of getting his hands on some of that Joslyn gold made him bold. "I do apologize for the manner of our meeting," Jeffery said, "but it cannot divert me from discovering the whereabouts of my cousin." His gaze settled on the big wardrobe and his heart leaped. It was a very large wardrobe; large enough to conceal a full-grown man, let alone a baggage like Emily.

Convinced he knew precisely where his cousin was hiding, startling everyone, in swift strides he crossed the room and flung open the doors to the wardrobe. The sight of the big empty interior with only a few quilts hanging there filled Jeffery with embarrassment and dismay.

Flushing, Jeffery slammed the doors shut and stepped back from the wardrobe. Meeting the sardonic stare of the viscount, he muttered, "Well, she could have been hiding in there."

Fighting against the pounding in his head and the waves of dizziness rolling over him, Barnaby said, "Unless you are blind, it is obvious that your cousin is not here."

Not finding Emily in the wardrobe had been a setback, but seduced by the possibilities of engineering a union between Emily and the viscount, he pressed forward. "Perhaps not at the moment, but how do I know she wasn't here before I entered the room?" He flashed a look of dislike at Flora. "The Gilberts certainly did their best to prevent me from seeing for myself."

Unable to fight the dizziness any longer, Barnaby sank back against the pillows and, closing his eyes, asked wearily, "Are you just naturally rude or are you an imbecile?"

Dropping any pretence of politeness, Townsend snarled, "Damn it all—I know she was here! You are hiding her from me."

"Shame on you!" cried Flora. "His lordship is not well and here you are badgering him about Miss Emily." Taking a step closer to him, she asked furiously, "Perhaps you would like to look under the bed? Or would you prefer to throw his lordship out of his bed and shake out his sheets?" Through clenched teeth, she said, "Miss Emily is not here."

Jeffery's confidence faltered. Could Kelsey have been wrong? Had he just made a ghastly mistake? Yet instinct, and a good dose of stubbornness, told him he was right: Emily had been here. Unable to conceive a reason why Lord Joslyn would side with the Gilberts and with no sign of Emily's presence in the room, common sense told him a prudent man would retreat in good order.

Jeffery looked longingly at the big bed where Joslyn lay. He would have liked to have called Flora's bluff and looked underneath the bed, but he wasn't that brave—especially after making a fool of himself with the wardrobe.

Chagrined and resentful, Jeffery muttered, "I apologize, my lord. There has obviously been a mistake."

Barnaby opened his eyes and muttered, "Obviously."

The patter of feet on the stairs alerted everyone to the arrival of a newcomer and Barnaby perked up, wondering who the next player in this farce would be. A short, plump, apple-cheeked woman, wisps of salt-and-pepper hair escaping from her neat muslin cap, sailed into the room. Arms akimbo, she stopped just inside the doorway and surveyed the room. Barnaby settled back against his pillows to watch the show.

"I step out to visit with a sick neighbor," the newcomer said in a no-nonsense voice, "and what do I find upon my return? The main room downstairs a shambles and the lot of you dithering around up here!" Pointing a finger at the three women, she said, "Downstairs with you—I want that mess cleared up before I am much older."

The three women vanished as if by magic. Her bright blue gaze locked on Townsend and Barnaby almost felt sorry for him.

"And you, Squire? What is the meaning of this? Mary

and Harriet have informed me that you are the cause of the destruction I find below. What have you to say for yourself?"

Under that unblinking gaze, Jeffery's rumpled cravat suddenly felt as if it were choking him. "Ah, I assure you, it was all an unfortunate misunderstanding, Mrs. Gilbert," he said lamely.

Her brows rose. "Really? Perhaps you would like to explain it to me?"

Reminding himself that he *was* the squire, he said with an edge, "I have it on good authority that Emily was here tonight. I came to discover for myself just what sort of mischief she was up to."

"And you think that gives you the right to lay waste to my inn and barge into a private room and disturb the gentleman who has rented it?" Mrs. Gilbert snorted. "And just what is this 'good authority'?"

His face reddening, Jeffery snapped, "That's none of your business."

Mrs. Gilbert advanced into the room and, stopping only when her nose was inches from Townsend's, she said, "You are mistaken. Any 'authority' that spreads malicious lies about dear Miss Emily and is the cause of my guests being disturbed and considerable damage done to my inn is definitely my business."

Eager to escape, and feeling more and more like a fool, Jeffery mumbled, "I'll pay for the damages and I've already apologized to his lordship."

Mrs. Gilbert looked over at Barnaby and Barnaby smiled and wiggled his fingers at her. He caught the barest shadow of amusement that flashed across her face before she turned back to the squire.

Fixing Townsend with a steely look, she said, "Very well. I shall have a bill for you tomorrow and I expect it to be paid in full." She stepped back and said, "Now I would appreciate it if you would leave the premises before I am forced to send for the constable and lay a complaint against you."

Barnaby watched Jeffery struggle to control his temper in the face of this new insult. It was a near thing, but in the end, the squire nodded curtly and with as much composure as possible, bowed in Barnaby's direction and departed—hastily.

With Townsend gone, Mrs. Gilbert closed the door and locked it. A friendly smile on her lips, she walked over to stand beside the bed. "A lord, are we?" she asked lightly.

"Uh, yes, I'm afraid it's true," Barnaby answered. A flush on his cheeks, he muttered, "Viscount Joslyn."

Mrs. Gilbert nodded. "Ah, yes, the American. We'd heard that someone from America had inherited the title." She laughed. "Mr. Mathew was quite incensed, I can tell you."

"I'm well aware of it," Barnaby answered drily. "He has taken great pains to see that I know of his displeasure."

Mrs. Gilbert smiled. "Oh, don't pay attention to Mr. Mathew's hoity-toity manner. He's a decent sort—a bit high in the instep now and then, but once he gets over his disappointment, you'll find him a good friend." Her lips tightened. "Unlike that chuckle-headed coxcomb that just left the room."

He agreed with her about the squire, but Barnaby was doubtful about her reading of his cousin. So far, Mathew hadn't struck him as a friendly sort—quite the opposite. And he didn't think that Mathew was going to offer him the hand of friendship anytime soon—if ever. Which bothered him not a whit. Until he'd arrived in London in October he'd never laid eyes on any of the Joslyns. In fact, he had only the haziest idea about the English branch of the family—for all he cared, the lot of them could go hang. They'd certainly done nothing to endear themselves to him. He grimaced. There was fault on his side, too; he'd let them get his back up and couldn't deny that he'd gone out of his way to irritate them.

Seeing his grimace, Mrs. Gilbert asked, "Are you in pain? Is there something I can do for you?"

Barnaby shook his head, wincing when the room spun. "No," he said, "I'm fine. Just a spot of dizziness." He sent her a charming smile. "You and your family have already done a great deal and I am grateful for it. I owe my life to you."

A gust of shrieking wind slammed against the stout walls of the inn and the rain beat hard against the windows, reminding both of them of the storm that still snarled its fury outside.

Speculation in her eyes, she asked, "How was it that you were at sea in this weather? Jeb said you could have knocked him over with a feather, when he spied you in the Channel."

"No one would be happier than I if I could tell why I was in the Channel or how I came to be there," Barnaby answered. "The last thing I remember is leaving London, planning to stop briefly at Eastbourne where I was told the Joslyn yacht is anchored."

She studied his face for a long time and Barnaby was on the point of squirming when her eyes dropped and she began to fiddle with the quilts on his bed. "Well, it certainly wasn't a night to go sailing, I can tell you that," she said.

"I agree." Watching her closely, he said carefully, "It isn't a night for man or beast to be abroad, let alone at sea, and that makes me curious about your Jeb's arrival just in time to save my neck. What was he doing out there?"

She glanced up and half smiled. "With all that has gone on tonight, Jeb's presence in the Channel is what arouses your curiosity?"

"That and the girl-dressed-as-a-boy, Emily, and her amazing disappearance into the wardrobe," he answered, an amused gleam in his black eyes.

"Ah, and here I was hoping that you had still been unconscious during Miss Emily's escape," she said in a rueful
tone.

Barnaby laughed. "No. We had not quite made our, er, introductions when, Flora, I believe her name is, dashed into
the room with the news that the squire was below."

Mrs. Gilbert nodded. "Yes, Flora is my middle daughter
and the most sensible one—although they are all good girls."
With quiet pride she added, "I have five daughters—Faith,
the eldest, and Molly, next to Faith in age, are the other two,
along with Flora, that were up here when I arrived. Harriet
and Mary, my two youngest, met me when I returned and
warned me what was afoot."

A timid tap on the door caused Mrs. Gilbert to look in
that direction. "Yes?" she asked.

"It is me, Ma," answered Flora through the door. "I have
some hot broth for his lordship."

Mrs. Gilbert chuckled and said to Barnaby, "I think it is
curiosity rather than mere kindness that is behind Flora's arrival." Crossing the room, she unlocked the door and opened
it. Flora slipped into the room carrying a large pewter tray
covered with several items. Locking the door behind her
daughter, Mrs. Gilbert said, "Set it on the small table by his
lordship's bed."

Flora did more than that. After placing the tray on the
table, she piled even more pillows behind Barnaby's back
and offered him a mug of the broth. Smiling encouragingly,
she said, "This will make you feel better."

To his surprise it did. It was more than just broth; minced
bits of chicken and carrots, cabbage and onions floated in
the salty hot liquid and Barnaby sipped it appreciatively. He
was, he discovered, hungry and finished the mug of soup in a
few long swallows, along with a thick slice of bread.

Flora refilled the mug from the covered green china
tureen she had brought along and offered him more bread,

and by the time he had finished two more mugs of soup and another large chunk of bread, the worst of his hunger had abated. From the tray, Flora offered him his choice of ale or wine and he settled on a tankard of ale.

Not only had the food and drink revived him, but the dizziness, while still there, had also receded. Smiling at the two women, he said, "Thank you. For the first time since I found myself in the Channel tonight, I feel as if I might actually live."

"Which brings us back to what you were doing out there in the first place," said Mrs. Gilbert, her eyes fixed on his face.

"No," said Barnaby gently, not willing to be sidetracked, "it brings us back to Emily and what she was doing here dressed as a boy and what Jeb was doing out in the Channel tonight."

Chapter 3

Mrs. Gilbert's friendly air vanished and her lips thinned as she and Barnaby stared at each other, neither giving an inch. Flora glanced from one face to the other and sighed. Touching her mother's sleeve, she muttered, "Ma, we can trust him. He saw Emily go into the wardrobe and he never said a word to the squire."

"Just because he didn't give Emily away to the squire doesn't mean we can trust him," Mrs. Gilbert said grimly. Her eyes never leaving Barnaby's dark face, she added, "How do we know he didn't keep his mouth shut *just* to make us trust him? And I'll remind you that we only have his word that he is who he says he is." Her voice hard, she concluded, "He doesn't need to know our business. For all we know he's a revenuer informer or someone from the Nolles gang sent to spy on us."

Flora hadn't considered that and some of her friendliness faded as she considered Barnaby. "Ma's right," she said. "This could just be a trick just to make us trust you."

"Don't you think it was a little foolhardy on my part to get myself nearly killed in order to ingratiate myself with you?" Barnaby asked. "What if your Jeb hadn't seen me? I'd have drowned."

"Perhaps it's a shame you didn't," Mrs. Gilbert snapped. "Especially if you mean to go poking about in something that is none of your business."

"*Ma!* You don't mean that," Flora exclaimed, shooting Barnaby an anxious look, clearly torn between taking his side or her mother's.

Mrs. Gilbert held her ground for a moment and then sagged. Tiredly, she said, "No, I don't mean it—at least not about drowning. It's been a long night and I am not as young as I used to be." Sinking down on a chintz-covered chair near the bed, she studied Barnaby for another long moment. "What goes on in here is none of your business," she finally said. "I don't see why you want to know more than you do already—unless it is merely to have a grander tale to tell your fancy friends." When Barnaby would have objected, she raised a hand silencing him and said, "If you are who you say you are, tomorrow you'll ride away to your fine house and go back to your fine life. A life, I might add, that is vastly removed from ours and, except for the rare times you might stop in here for a tankard of ale, our paths will not cross." Unhappily, she added, "It would be best if you forgot everything you've seen or heard here tonight and just be grateful that you're alive."

Barnaby hesitated. Mrs. Gilbert had a point, but she was wrong in her estimation of him. He owed them his life and that was a debt he could never repay. Aware of how very much he owed them, he wasn't, he admitted, going to be able to ride blithely away tomorrow just as if nothing had happened. As for his fine house and fine life—he was quite positive that he would be more comfortable amongst the inhabitants of The Crown than he would be mingling with the likes of Cousin Mathew. The last thing, however, that he wanted to do was upset and alienate the very people who had just saved his life. He could wait to have his questions answered.

Smiling crookedly at Mrs. Gilbert, he said, "Very well, I will follow your wishes. I am grateful for all you've done for me and while I can't promise that I'll forget everything about tonight, I owe you too much to continue bedeviling you."

Relief spread across Mrs. Gilbert's features. "Spoken like a true gentleman," she said, rising to her feet. "Now if you'll excuse me, I must go below and see how things are faring down there." She nodded toward her daughter. "If you need anything else Flora will see to it. Good night, my lord."

Her expression thoughtful, Flora gathered up the things from his meal and once the door had shut behind her mother, she said apologetically, "Ma didn't mean any disrespect, it's just that . . ."

"She has enough to do running a smuggling operation without having to deal with me," Barnaby said.

Flora gasped and stared round eyed at him.

Barnaby laughed in spite of himself. "Why else would Jeb have been crossing the Channel tonight?" he asked reasonably. "I may be a newcomer to your shores, but I've heard tales of the smuggling trade going on in certain parts of England—in particular this area. My youngest cousin, Simon, already warned me not to make a, er, fuss if I find some casks of brandy left in my stables." Flora remained mute and he went on calmly. "I've thought about Jeb's rescue of me tonight and smuggling is the only logical explanation for him being where he was when he saw me."

His words did not reassure Flora. If anything, they made her even more wary and she took a step back, eyeing him uneasily. "Very well," he said. "Don't tell me anything, but I've figured out the smuggling part of it already, but Miss Emily now . . ."

Gripping the tray as if she thought about hitting him with it, she said fiercely, "You leave Miss Emily out of this! She has enough troubles as it is."

"I'm not trying to get her or you into any trouble. I'm simply trying to understand what is going on here." Gently, he said, "I'm on your side, Flora."

"That may be," Flora said sharply, "but until *Ma* says you're on our side, I'm not telling you anything—so don't try to charm me." Nose in the air, she swept from the room, slamming the door behind her.

Barnaby glanced around the empty room. "That went well," he muttered.

Having stripped off her wet clothing and scrambled into the long, flannel nightgown and woolen robe that one of the servants, probably Sally, had left warming by the fire for her, Emily thought that things had gone very well. Especially when one considered how badly events could have turned out, she admitted tiredly. At least Jeffery hadn't caught her at The Crown.

Out of her cold and wet clothing, the flannel nightgown and woolen robe did much to drive away the chill she had suffered during the mad ride home. Weary in every bone in her body, she stared down at the pile of sodden clothes, knowing that she had to hide them before Jeffery came home and stormed into her room. Once he discovered she was not at The Crown, this would be the first place he would look.

Too tired to be clever, she kicked the wet clothes and muddy boots under her bed and twitched the ruffled blue silk bed skirts back into place. She didn't think that Jeffery would bother to look under the bed and she half smiled, picturing him down on his hands and knees peering under her bed. No, her cousin wouldn't look under the bed—it would be beneath him. Not that much else was, she thought disgustedly.

Turning away from the bed, she pushed back a strand of silvery-fair hair that had come loose from the queue. Reminded that Jeffery didn't need to find her with a wet head or her hair worn in such a masculine manner, she undid the black silk ribbon that held the queue in place and shook the mass free. The pale tresses hung in wet clumps and she knelt before the fire and finger combed through the bright tendrils as they dried, waved and curled in wild abandon about her head.

A tap on the door had her stiffening, even as she realized that Jeffery would have just barged into her room. "Yes?" she called.

The door opened instantly and, framed by a multitude of dusky curls, Anne's pretty little face, tense with anxiety, appeared around the edge. Seeing Emily before the fire, she glanced back over her shoulder and said to someone behind her, "It's all right, she's home." Pushing the door wider, the edges of her pale rose robe flying, Anne rushed into the room, crying, "Oh, thank God! You are back. Jeffery was looking for you and he is in a terrible state."

Emily nodded. "I know—he nearly found me at The Crown. It was only by luck that I escaped."

Wearing a heavy, puce woolen robe, Great-Aunt Cornelia followed Anne, her carved walnut cane thumping loudly as she half walked, half limped into the room. "It wasn't just luck," Cornelia snapped in her deep voice. "If you couldn't outwit that mackerel-brained jackass then you're not the woman I raised you to be."

In spite of the situation, Emily grinned at her great-aunt. The widow of her grandfather's only brother, Cornelia was the only mother Emily remembered clearly. Her own mother had died during her birthing and it was Cornelia who had swept up the squalling infant and carried her away. It was

Cornelia who hired Mrs. Gilbert as wet nurse for Emily and much to her father's guilty relief, taken over the household and the raising of little Emily—leaving him to pursue his horses and hounds.

Outspoken and irascible, Cornelia was both the joy and bane of the family. Built on Amazonian lines, at eighty-nine years old, she carried herself as erect as a woman half her age and even now a look from her hazel eyes had been known to drop grown men to their knees. Emily had always loved her outspoken, gruff great-aunt, but never more than when Cornelia fixed Jeffery with that eagle-eyed stare and caused him to pale and stammer and retreat at a gallop.

"I did have some help from Flora," Emily admitted, smiling. Cocking her head to one side, she asked, "Did you know about the hidden staircase in the big wardrobe in the best room at The Crown?"

Seating herself in a yellow chintz wing-backed chair near the fire, Cornelia cackled with glee. "Lord, yes! I had to use it once myself."

Staring at Cornelia, astonished, Anne blurted, "Never say that you ran a smuggler ring, like Emily?"

The old squire's marriage to a young woman only a few years older than his daughter had been the talk of the neighborhood when he had married a twenty-year-old, Anne Farnham, nearly a decade ago. Emily had been aghast at the marriage—Anne was only two years her senior and until the old squire had presented his bride to her, she had never laid eyes on her or guessed he was contemplating marriage. Cornelia had been openly scornful of the new young wife, grumbling in her carrying voice, "Nothing like an old fool, blinded by a lovely face."

It had been peculiar welcoming such a young bride, but it would have taken a harder heart than Emily or Cornelia possessed not to warm to the little brown-eyed sprite the old squire had married. Full of laughter and sunshine, a smile always on her lips, Anne had danced into their lives and enchanted them all. Emily decided years ago that it was those huge, heavily lashed brown eyes of Anne's that melted the coldest heart. Certainly none of them, she admitted fondly, had been able to resist Anne when she fixed those speaking eyes on one and oh, so, meekly suggested some modification to a routine or décor that hadn't been altered in forty years.

But even if Anne hadn't been a darling, Emily and Cornelia would have welcomed Anne into their hearts for one simple reason: Anne had been deeply in love with her much-older husband. Even if she had been a harpy, rather than the delight she was, Emily and Cornelia would have forgiven her much for being a doting wife to her not-always-considerate husband.

Looking at these two women who meant so much to her, Emily knew that the risks she had taken tonight had been worth it. And she would continue, she thought with a clenching of her jaw, to take those same risks until they were all safe and out from under Jeffery's thumb.

"Smuggling?" Cornelia said in reply to Anne's question. "Good gad, no!" A sly smile curved her lips and her hazel eyes gleaming, she murmured, "My husband had discovered I was meeting Lord Joslyn there, and Flora's great-grandmother came running up the stairs to warn me."

Since it was well known that Cornelia's marriage to her husband had been an arranged match and that they both loathed each other, neither Emily nor Anne was particularly shocked by her words. It was precisely the sort of explanation they expected from her.

But the identity of Cornelia's long-ago lover startled a gasp from Emily. "Lord Joslyn?" she exclaimed.

"Hmm, yes, the sixth viscount . . ." She tapped her lip and looked thoughtful. "Or was it the seventh?" She shrugged. "Probably both of them—the Joslyns are very handsome men."

At Anne's expression, Cornelia snorted. "Oh, get that die away look off your face. It was a long time ago."

"Um, I think I met the eighth viscount tonight. There was a man . . . an American. Who else could it be?"

The object of two pairs of intent eyes, Emily flushed and muttered, "Jeb found him drowning in the Channel and had no choice but to rescue him." Briefly, she related the sequence of events.

"Oh, my! How exciting!" exclaimed Anne, picking up a silver-backed brush from the dressing table nearby. Walking up to Emily, she began to brush the heavy locks. "Did you find him handsome?"

Emily grimaced. "No. I was too worried about how much trouble he was going to cause us to pay much attention to him." Thoughtfully, she added, "He's a big man, dark-skinned and black-haired but without a strong resemblance to the Joslyns." She cast her mind back to the man in the bed and admitted, "I suppose one would say he was handsome in a rough, rugged sort of way. His features are harder, less chiseled than say, Mathew Joslyn's." She shrugged. "Of course, he wasn't at his best either."

"Were you frightened when he grabbed your wrist?" Anne asked, big eyed. "I would have been."

Cornelia snorted. "You're frightened of your own shadow, poppet," she said not unkindly. "Of course, you'd have been frightened."

When Anne nodded a bit wistfully, Cornelia looked at Emily and said, "What I'd like to know is how Jeffery knew you were at the inn."

Nearly purring from Anne's steady brush strokes through her hair, Emily shrugged. "Obviously, someone told him," she muttered.

"Most likely that rascally bailiff, Daggett, he hired after your father died," Cornelia sniffed. "The man is robbing him blind and because he simpers and fawns over him, your cousin believes him to be wonderful. Bloody fool!"

"Well, I think it is that horrid man, Kelsey," Anne said fiercely.

Cornelia's brow rose and Emily twisted away from the blissful strokes of the brush to look over her shoulder at her.

"What?" Anne asked, puzzled by their reactions.

"You rarely have anything bad to say about anyone or anything," Emily said carefully. "Yet Kelsey appears to have aroused your dislike."

Anne flushed. "I've always thought it cruel that Jeffery turned out poor old Hutton and replaced him with Kelsey." Her jaw set, she added bitterly, "He's rude, a boor a-a-and a wretched stableman. He doesn't know the first thing about horses and Hutton had such a wonderful touch with them."

Emily and Cornelia didn't disagree with her. They'd been outraged when Jeffery had let go servants who had served the Townsend family for years, generations, and had put in his own people—men that were lazy, insolent and had much to do with the decreased revenues of the estate. What Jeffery didn't squander, they lost through poor management or pilferage.

Emily studied Anne's face for another moment. "He hasn't overstepped himself, has he?" she asked.

Red roses bloomed in Anne's cheeks and told the story.

Emily stood up, towering over the elfin Anne. Her eyes stormy, she demanded, "What did he do?"

Anne swallowed and glanced down at her feet. "H-He touched me," she whispered. At Emily's snarl of fury, she said hastily, "Please! It isn't so very terrible . . ." She swallowed. "It isn't what you're thinking . . . it—it—it's only that he looks at me in a certain way and his hands linger on me longer than polite. I don't like it."

"And you've said nothing?" demanded Cornelia, even her steel-gray hair seeming to bristle with outrage.

"I—I've told him repeatedly," she admitted in a low voice, "that I don't need his help mounting and dismounting

my horse, but he just ignores me and h-h-helps me anyway."
That usually smiling face full of misery, she looked at Emily
and said, "I didn't want to bother you—you have enough on
your plate. I complained to Jeffery about him." Tears simmered in her eyes. "He just *laughed*."

A red mist of rage swirled in front of Emily and for a moment, she could not breathe, she was so angry . . . and
frightened. How far would Jeffery go to drive them away?
Would he dare allow Anne to be ravished by one of his men?
It was unthinkable, but she would put nothing past him.

Her hands clenched into fists, she stared down into
Anne's miserable face. That *Anne* had been subjected to the
unwanted advances of a *stableman* and Jeffery had done
nothing . . . Rage choked her.

"That yellow cur!" spat Cornelia, her eyes glittering with
fury, her grip on her cane so tight, the knuckles of her hand
gleamed white through the skin. "To think that a relative of
mine would condone such behavior. Shameful!"

The door to Emily's bedroom slammed open and Jeffery,
his greatcoat dripping from his ride home in the storm, stood
in the doorway.

"So here you are, cuz," he growled as he walked into the
room and confronted the three women. "I've been looking
for you."

"And I for you," Emily shot back. "What sort of a craven
creature are you that you subject the women of your household to the pawing of a servant?"

"I don't know what you're talking about," he blustered,
taken aback by the unexpected attack.

"Oh, you know nothing about Anne's complaint against
Kelsey?" Emily demanded. "You have no idea that he has
pressed his attentions on her—despite her objections?"

Jeffery cleared his throat and said, "There must be some
mistake. I assure you if I knew that Kelsey acted inappropri-
ately with her, I would naturally have sent him packing."

"I *told* you!" Anne declared hotly, glaring at him. "And you laughed and said I was imagining things."

"I must have misunderstood you," he hedged.

"Well, just so there is no misunderstanding this time," said Cornelia, the hazel eyes narrowed and hard on his face, "Anne is complaining to you *again* about the actions of Kelsey. We are witnesses to her complaint." She lifted a brow. "And of course, I know as a gentleman that your word is your bond, so I will expect Kelsey to be dismissed first thing in the morning." Cornelia smiled at him, showing her teeth, and Jeffery blanched. "I do have your word, don't I," she purred, "that you will no longer employ Kelsey? And that he will be gone in the morning?"

Jeffery swallowed and his gaze not meeting Cornelia's, he muttered, "Yes."

"Your word as a gentleman?"

He nodded and ground out, "Yes, my word as a gentleman."

Cornelia turned and smiled gently at Anne. "Well, there you are, poppet. Kelsey will be gone tomorrow and you no longer have to fear him."

Sally, Emily's occasional maid, holding a heavily laden tray, hesitated in the doorway and, catching Emily's eye, took a deep breath and stepped into the room. Beyond a swift, speaking look at Emily, she ignored everyone and walking over to a small table near where Cornelia sat, she set down the tray. In the silence that greeted her appearance, she fussed a moment with the silver-covered tureen, before turning around to face Emily.

Her eyes meekly lowered, Sally murmured, "If you will give me your wet things, I'll see that they are washed and dried."

An expression of smug satisfaction on his face, Jeffery smiled and waited for Emily's answer. He'd known the bitch had been out and Sally had just confirmed it.

"Uh, that's not necessary," Emily said, horrified that Sally was giving away the fact that she had been anywhere but safely at home. She trusted Sally. What the devil was she up to?

"Will that be all then?" Sally asked.

"Ah, yes, thank you," Emily replied, wary and uncertain. Betrayal from within had always been a possibility, but that Sally would be the one . . .

Sending Emily a wink only she could see, Sally added brightly, "Cook thought you would enjoy something hot after your long night in the lambing shed." Shaking her head, she added, "Leave it to old Nappy to choose a stormy night like tonight to lamb. Loren said it was a real pleasure to watch your sure hand with a difficult birthing. All of us think it was just wonderful that you were able to save old Nappy and deliver all three of her lambs."

Jeffery's satisfaction evaporated and he glanced suspiciously from Sally to Emily. "*That's* where you were tonight?" he demanded incredulously. "Helping that old shepherd, Loren, with the lambing?"

Sally had tossed her a lifeline and Emily grabbed on to it for all she was worth. She flashed him a wide-eyed innocent look. "Where else would I be at this hour and on a terrible night like tonight?" she asked reasonably.

Jeffery stared at the four women. Instinct told him that they were lying, but there was just enough of a ring of truth about the tale to give him pause. Even though it was a major source of income to him, Jeffery knew little about the sheep raised at The Birches, but he vaguely remembered Emily and Cornelia mentioning something a few days ago about lambing season not being far away. While he was convinced Emily had been at The Crown tonight, it was possible that she had indeed been helping some smelly old ewe push three more lambs into the world.

Furious, frustrated and feeling like a fool for the second time that night, he snarled, "I will speak with Loren in the morning . . . and that bloody old ewe had better have three woolly lambs jumping around her."

"Oh, she will have," Cornelia said serenely, smiling at him. "You can go see for yourself . . . right after you dismiss Kelsey."

Jeffery muttered something under his breath and, turning on his heel, tramped from the room.

The door shut and locked behind his departing form by Sally, the four women looked at each other. Emily and Sally both grinned, Anne stifled a giggle, but it was Cornelia who laughed aloud.

"By gad!" she hooted. "I've not enjoyed myself so much in a decade. Did you see his face? He looked like he had swallowed a muddy boot."

Sinking back down to the floor by the fire, Emily nodded. "He certainly wasn't very happy."

"Well, I am," said Anne firmly. "Tomorrow that horrid Kelsey will be gone."

Sally looked curious and Emily explained the situation. "That'll make several of us very happy," Sally commented when Emily finished speaking. "He, along with that Daggett fellow have not made themselves very well liked amongst the staff—anywhere on the estate." She made a face. "He's been making up to my sister, Rosie, at The Ram's Head and I can't say I'll be sorry if he has to leave the area."

Glancing from Cornelia to Sally, Emily asked, "Whose idea was it to have me helping at the lambing shed?" To Sally, she said, "I nearly fainted when you mentioned my clothing. I couldn't imagine what you were up to."

Cornelia chuckled. "We have fate to thank for that. When Jeffery came looking for you and obviously you were not to be found, we knew something had to be done to explain your absence. As luck would have it, Loren showed up to warm himself by the fire and drink some hot soup, not ten minutes after Jeffery stormed out of the house on his way to The Crown." She smiled. "Once Loren learned of our dilemma, he explained that he had just come from the lambing shed and that dear old Nappy had given birth to the first lambs of the season—all three of them."

Sally grinned and nodded. "It was the perfect excuse. Everyone knows that you always help with the lambing and we just had to, uh, add some urgency to Nappy's lambing."

"I hope that Loren gave her some extra grain," Emily said. "She certainly saved the day."

Eyeing Emily's pale features and knowing of the long night she'd had, Cornelia stood up and tamped her cane a few times on the floor. "It's been a long night for everyone. I don't know about anyone else, but I'm for my bed." She hobbled over to Emily and pressed a kiss to the top of her head. "You eat your soup and go to bed. We can discuss this further tomorrow," she said gruffly.

Anne and Sally followed her lead and within minutes, Emily was alone. The strain of the night had taken its toll and after only a few swallows of the rich beef and barley soup, Emily crawled thankfully into her bed.

Despite everything, it had been a successful night. The contraband was on its way to London and Jeffery had been thwarted. Kelsey's dismissal was a side benefit and she smiled when she recalled the way Cornelia had nailed Jeffery's feet to the floor on that matter. Her smile faded though when she considered the impact Lord Joslyn might have on tonight's events. If the man had been Lord Joslyn . . .

She felt again the force of those black eyes and the strength in the hand that had clamped around her wrist, and she shivered. Nerves, she told herself, pushing aside the unwanted reaction. But she could not dismiss him entirely from her mind. If he was indeed the newest Lord Joslyn, she thought wearily, he could cause them untold difficulties. Difficulties, she admitted with a huge yawn, I shall have to overcome if I am to save us all.

Barnaby had no intention of causing anyone any difficulty. He had enough problems of his own to worry about, and while the events at The Crown were intriguing, his main focus was finally reaching Windmere and discovering, if possible, how he had ended up in the Channel.

Since he'd awoken, when he hadn't been being distracted by the antics going on in his bedroom, he thought with a smile, he'd been racking his brain seeking an explanation for what had happened tonight. Lying in bed, he stared into the darkness, mulling over what he knew.

Someone had tried to kill him. He already knew that unpalatable fact and the why was obvious: the Joslyn wealth and title. Barnaby sighed. The most logical culprit was his cousin, Mathew, but Barnaby couldn't quite convince himself that Mathew had been behind what had happened to him.

Leaving him to drown in the Channel just didn't seem like Mathew. Mathew would be far more likely to run him through with a sword or shoot him dead in a rage than coldly plan his death by drowning. Barnaby grimaced. None of his cousins, including Mathew and his two younger brothers, Thomas and Simon, held any love for him, but there was a calculating cowardice about tonight's doings that made it difficult for him to believe they were behind his near drowning.

He made a face. But then he didn't know his Joslyn cousins very well either. On the surface, Mathew, if one put aside his natural reaction to having a fortune and title snatched away from him, seemed a decent enough fellow. Under different circumstances, Barnaby admitted they might even have been friends . . . perhaps.

Thomas, the middle brother, he'd only seen twice, and

Simon, the youngest, appeared to be a happy-go-lucky young scamp—certainly not the type to arrange his drowning in the Channel.

He might not know precisely what had happened, but he didn't doubt that someone had gotten him on board the Joslyn yacht, and then either blown it up or ensured that it sank—with him lying unconscious on it.

The one thing he did know for certain: he'd left London in a hooded gig, driving a big bay gelding, having planned a swift side trip to Eastbourne to inspect the yacht before traveling on to Windmere. Beyond that knowledge, events grew hazy.

Barnaby frowned, concentrating hard. He'd sent his man, Lamb, along with the majority of his luggage ahead to Windmere. He remembered that much. Remembered, too, that he'd told Lamb he'd arrive in a day or two. It seemed an innocent enough itinerary. He snorted. Innocent or not, if not for the fisherman, Jeb, he'd be feeding the fishes in the Channel right now.

He moved his head and winced with pain. Gingerly he reached up and probed the back of his head. Swearing at the burst of pain he felt when his fingers found the deep gash, he left off exploring his wound, but in the darkness, he smiled wolfishly. At least he had discovered why he didn't remember much. Someone had given him a vicious blow to the back of the head and if they'd struck harder, he admitted grimly, he wouldn't have had to worry about drowning.

A yawn took him and as he drifted off to sleep, the features of the girl-dressed-as-a-boy floated through his mind. He'd thought her a pretty boy. . . . When he had time, it might be amusing to discover how she cleaned up.

Chapter 4

Barnaby woke the next morning and, despite the faint throbbing in the region of his head where he had suffered the blow he was convinced had been meant to kill him, he felt surprisingly well. Until he sat up and swung his long legs over the side of the bed. The room swam and for a moment he feared he'd black out.

He didn't, but only by sheer stubborn effort was he able to stand up. Granted, he hung on to one of the bedposts for several moments and fought off the dizziness, but by God! He was standing on his own two feet.

With an unsteady gait, he walked to one of the chairs by the fire and sank gratefully into it. He was as weak as a newborn and he scowled at the fire on the hearth as if the exuberant red and yellow flames were at fault.

He heard a knock on the door but before he could reply, the door swung open and Flora, with a tray in her hands holding a pewter coffeepot, a white pottery mug and a plate heaped with fat golden biscuits, came tripping into the room. Catching sight of him sitting by the fire, she stopped abruptly.

"And what do you think you're doing?" she demanded in

a scolding tone, setting down the tray on the small table next to his chair. Hands on her slim hips, she declared, "You should still be abed. And you should let me dress that wound of yours. Ma says it probably should be wrapped."

"Probably," Barnaby agreed, feeling foolish sitting there swathed in yards and yards of cotton nightshirt that barely covered his knees. The deceased Mr. Gilbert, may God rest his soul, had been far rounder than he'd been tall.

Since Barnaby remained precisely where he was and the jut of his formidable chin told her he wasn't going to climb meekly back into bed—or let her touch his head—after a moment Flora snorted and poured him a cup of black coffee. The rich scent of the coffee tickled his nose as she handed the steaming cup to him. Giving him a stern look, she said, "Stubborn, that's what you are."

Taking the cup, Barnaby smiled. "I see that in our short acquaintance you already have a correct reading of my character."

She shook her head and grinned at him. "It's a male trait. Now drink your coffee."

Barnaby obeyed, taking a long swallow. Setting down the cup, he asked, "Is there someone you could send to Windmere for me? My man, Lamb, should have arrived and he will have a change of clothes for me." He grimaced. "I assume what I was wearing is ruined."

Nodding, Flora said, "Young Sam can take a message for you." She shook her head. "As for your clothes . . . the shirt might be salvageable, but the sea water shrunk everything else." She giggled. "Your pants might fit Sam and he's only eleven."

Barnaby half smiled. "You can give him everything—with my compliments." He looked around. "Do you have quill and paper? I'd like to get the message to Lamb as soon as possible."

* * *

John Lamb arrived some three hours later and her cheeks pink, a flustered Flora showed him into Barnaby's room. Barnaby wasn't surprised at Flora's reaction. John might be his servant, and Barnaby often wondered who served whom, but women of all stations found his manservant *most* attractive.

As tall as Barnaby, he was a strikingly handsome man, the dark gold of his skin and the crisp curl of his black hair revealing an African ancestry not too far away in his background. But even more stunning were his azure eyes set against the deep gold of his complexion—that and his cat-like grace and elegance.

After Flora reluctantly left, watching Lamb as he unpacked the valise he had brought with him, Barnaby asked, "And how was your journey?"

Lamb glanced over his broad shoulder at his employer and grinned, showing a gleaming set of even white teeth. "From your note, far less exciting than yours, it appears."

"Be glad of that," Barnaby growled as he rose to his feet. Taking the pair of breeches Lamb handed him, he proceeded to dress. The initial dizziness and weakness had passed and by the time he was pulling on his boots, other than a slight headache, he was feeling more himself.

The valise emptied, Lamb turned and sent Barnaby a sharp look. In a voice no servant ever used to his master, he asked, "Do you want to tell me what happened?"

John Lamb was the result of a liaison between Paxton, Barnaby's grandfather, and a quadroon mistress he'd taken under his protection while in New Orleans on business for several months some thirty-six years previously. Paxton had died three years later, never knowing, or caring for that matter, that he had sired a son while in New Orleans. No one ever questioned that Lamb was his son. John's build and facial features, especially those azure eyes, told their own story: he looked more Joslyn than did Barnaby.

When Lamb was six years old, at the urging of his mother's latest protector, she had sent him to Virginia. Bewildered and frightened, the little boy with the stunning blue eyes in the dark gold face was shown into the grand library at Green Hill. It wasn't until years later that he learned that the tall, handsome man regarding him so unhappily was actually his half brother.

One look at the boy and Lyndon had no doubts that John Lamb was indeed his father's by-blow. Unable to turn his back on the boy, but unwilling to acknowledge him as his half brother, he banished the boy to his overseer's care but saw to it that the boy was educated. Lamb wasn't raised as the child of a wealthy planter or taken to the bosom of the family, but he wasn't put in the fields to work either.

As Lamb put it to Barnaby one night when they were both very drunk, "Neither fish nor fowl, that's me." He scowled at his tankard of ale. "Sometimes, I wish your father *had* sent me to the fields. This half life . . ."

"Remember it is your own damn choice these days," Barnaby said. Equally drunk, Barnaby spoke carefully, struggling not to slur his words. "After he died, I offered to set you up on your own land. You're the stiff-necked jackass who refused."

Lamb had grinned at him. "That's because, as your ser-servant, I like watching you squirm. I couldn't prick *his* conscience, but I sure as hell can yours."

Which, unfortunately, was true, Barnaby thought, sighing. Neither Paxton nor Lyndon had been particularly evil: both men just ignored or brushed aside anything unpleasant or that interfered with their pursuit of pleasure.

Lamb interrupted his thoughts. "You're thinking of them, aren't you?"

"And if I am?"

"Stop it. I made my choices and for now"—Lamb flashed him a dazzling smile—"it pleases me to play your servant."

Barnaby snorted. "Servant," he muttered, "doesn't even

begin to describe you. Anyone less servile I've yet to meet. Or arrogant, now that I think of it."

"True," Lamb agreed fairly, "but I think you're straying from the subject at hand. What happened?"

Briefly Barnaby told him what he knew, leaving out only the farce that had been played out in his bedroom after his rescue. For reasons that escaped him, he wanted to keep Miss Emily to himself—and that The Crown was rife with smugglers. At least for the present.

Lamb tried to examine the wound, but Barnaby hastily waved him away. "I'm fine—or at least I'm fine enough to ride away from here without my head wrapped in bandages."

Frustrated, but knowing him of old, Lamb asked, "So who was it that hit you on the head and left you to drown in the Channel? Mathew?"

Barnaby studied his boots. "It doesn't feel like Mathew." He glanced up at Lamb, frowning. "You met him. Did he seem like the sort of fellow who would use such an elaborate and uncertain method? Knocking me on the head and I'm pretty certain, blowing up, certainly sinking the family yacht?"

"No. Your cousin Mathew would take no chances. If he'd clouted you on the head, you wouldn't be sitting here—he'd have made certain you were dead before he put you on the yacht. But like you, it doesn't feel like Mathew to me—if your esteemed cousin Mathew wanted you dead, dead you would be."

Barnaby nodded. "My thoughts precisely."

"So who?"

"That's the devil of it!" Barnaby declared angrily. "I don't know! Beyond leaving London for Eastbourne, I have no clear memory. It could have been anyone."

Lamb shook his head. "Not anyone. You're a stranger here and"—John grinned at him—"while you can be infuriating, you haven't been here long enough to drive anyone to murder. Your death only benefits Mathew . . . and his family."

Unable to argue with Lamb's logic, Barnaby picked up the jacket Lamb had laid on the bed. Shrugging into an expertly tailored jacket of brown superfine, Barnaby said, "At least I have you to watch my back."

"That you do," Lamb said and, reaching into the valise, he took out a long-bladed knife. Handing it to Barnaby, he watched as Barnaby examined the lethal instrument. Nodding his head in satisfaction, Barnaby bent and deftly slid the knife into a specially constructed sheath in the side of his boot.

Straightening Barnaby said, "I know I wrote you that I lost my knife in the Channel. How the devil did you find another one so soon?"

The corners of Lamb's lips twitched. "Must I remind you—I am a *most* superior servant."

After leaving a generous sum of gold for Mrs. Gilbert and his sincere thanks for their efforts, a few minutes later Barnaby and Lamb were riding away from The Crown. In addition to his own horse, John had brought along a fine black gelding for Barnaby to ride.

The weather was still fretful, but since the worst of the rain and wind had abated, it wasn't an unpleasant day. Riding through the open, rolling countryside broken only by the occasional stand of trees, Barnaby felt a pang for the green meadows and forests of Virginia.

"It is very different than home, isn't it?" Barnaby said after they'd traveled a few miles.

"This is your home now," Lamb said quietly. "Unless, of course, you mean to turn your back on the title and all that comes with it and return to Virginia."

"I wonder if English law would allow me to do so? I suppose I could do something like abdicate, couldn't I? Mathew would certainly be elated." Barnaby sighed. "Life was simpler when I only had Green Hill to worry about."

Lamb looked at him, one brow raised. "Are you seriously considering doing something that harebrained? Whistling down a fortune and running back to Virginia?" Bluntly he added, "I think perhaps you suffered a harder blow than you realized."

Barnaby stared glumly between the ears of his horse. Did he really want to return to Virginia? He could do it. England had not been very welcoming; his cousins clearly wished him at Coventry and one of them might have tried to kill him last night; he had no reason to stay. . . . The features of the boy who was not a boy floated through his mind. Well, he reminded himself, there was no reason to leave *immediately*.

More cheerful, Barnaby glanced at John and asked, "And how was your arrival at Windmere? Pleasant? Or hostile?"

Lamb frowned at him but realizing he would get no more out of him on this subject, he shrugged. "Somewhere between the two. Some of the servants were obviously delighted that they were finally going to meet the new master; others were sitting out in judgment. No one was rude."

"And Windmere itself? Your impression?"

A slow grin spread across Lamb's face. "I think you should see it for yourself."

Barnaby's first sight of Windmere left him breathless. Half castle, half manor house, the place was huge and stunning. Dominating a hill with the Cuckmere River flowing far below, on two sides of the original castle massive turrets rose up to meet the sullen gray skies. Woodland of birch, white willow, oak and beech planted by a Joslyn over two centuries ago fanned out around the massive stone, wood and brick house. Large, gray slabs of Horsham stone covered the multileveled roof; mullioned windows gleamed and numerous brick chimneys speared skyward.

Barnaby gaped like a bumpkin at a fair seeing a two-headed pig for the first time. He'd always been proud of his stately home in Virginia with its flowing verandas, tall windows and graceful lines. The three-storied house at Green Hill was considered one of the largest and most elegant houses in the surrounding area, but *this!* Barnaby swallowed. Good God! He'd wager that Green Hill and three or four houses of that ilk could be swallowed up within the walls of Windmere as if they'd never been.

Lamb chuckled beside him, saying teasingly, "And to think that a simple planter from Virginia is now lord of all of this."

"Christ! No wonder you didn't want to tell me about the place," Barnaby said, a note of awe lingering in his voice. He shook his head, bemused. "I never expected anything like this. It's magnificent! But I'm going to need a guide to find my way from the bedroom to the dining room."

"You'll have that—I think the staff numbers around thirty." Lamb grinned. "And that's not counting your stablemen and shepherds and bailiff and—"

"Stop! My head is spinning." He shot Lamb a pitiful look. "You forget the night I just passed and that I am a wounded man. Remember my poor head."

Lamb guffawed. "You are too hard-headed to be slowed by that little bump you took last night." His laughter fled and he said softly, "Whether you like it or not, this is your destiny . . . unless you intend to run like a coward back to Virginia."

Barnaby shot him a glance almost of dislike. "You just had to say it, didn't you?"

"Been waiting for just the right moment."

* * *

Dismounting in front of the arched and pedimented three-story porch in the middle of the building, Barnaby was unprepared for the commotion his arrival caused. The pair of molded and paneled oak doors, dark with age, swung open the moment his foot touched the bricked driveway and a half-dozen servants, some wearing dark green livery, spilled out to greet him. Like arriving majesty he was gently wafted through the doors, and upon entering the house, to his stunned gaze, it appeared as if the grand hallway was filled with a crowd of people, bobbing and bowing, all of them seeming eager to meet him. Or catch their first sight of the American, he thought drily.

The house steward down to the smallest, shiest scullery maid came forth to be introduced to the new master and most passed in a blur before Barnaby. Raised as the son of an aristocratic wealthy planter in Virginia, he was used to servants and elegant surroundings, but he was still a bit startled at the size of the staff. Did he really need six scullery maids?

The introductions over, leaving word with the butler to bring up a tray, Lamb hustled Barnaby upstairs to the quiet of his suite of rooms. When the door shut behind him, Barnaby looked at Lamb and muttered, "And that was just the house servants?"

"Most of them—there were probably a half dozen you might have missed, and I thought I recognized one or two of the gardeners and a few stable folk that had finessed their way inside."

"Good God! It's like a small city." He glanced around the sitting room in which they were standing. Taking in the bronze damask upholstered sofas, leather-covered chairs and satinwood tables, the large mahogany desk near the bow window and the long sideboard against the far wall, he estimated that the room was large enough to hold a ball. An equally large bedroom decorated in the same shades lay be-

yond. His gaze was met with the same luxurious gold and tobacco silk-covered walls, and similar rugs in shades of fawn,
cream and amber lay scattered across the gleaming expanse
of parquet flooring. He peeked into the dressing room and
almost laughed. It was barely smaller than his sitting room
in Virginia.

Wearier than he realized, he sank down into one of a pair
of channel-backed chairs of brown mohair, positioned at either end of a small sofa in front of the fire that blazed in the
marble fireplace. Looking at Lamb, he said simply, "Big
house."

Lamb laughed. "Indeed. And this is just one of several
properties you own."

"No wonder Mathew was put out when I inherited," Barnaby said, staring moodily at the fire. "I wouldn't have taken it
well either to have something like this place snatched out
from beneath me—let alone the fortune that goes with it."

Lamb's eyes traveled over the richly furnished room. "It's
certainly a motive for the attack on you." When Barnaby
continued to stare at the fire, he said softly, "Lest you feel
too guilty, I would remind you that all of the Joslyn family is
very wealthy—you may have inherited the jewel in the
crown, but Mathew and his brothers, Thomas and Simon, are
hardly paupers. Gossip has it that Mathew's home, Monks
Abbey, is nearly as large and impressive. And I've heard that
Thomas, especially, has an impressive fortune of his own."

Barnaby leaned his head back, wincing when his wound
came in contact with the back of the chair.

Lamb muttered an oath and crossed quickly to his side. "I
want to take a better look at that gash of yours." When Barnaby objected, he said fiercely, "Enough! I can see that it is
bleeding from here. Now let me tend to it."

Before they had left Barnaby's room at The Crown Lamb
had heard the story Barnaby and Mrs. Gilbert concocted
about Barnaby's unfortunate "illness" to explain his unex-

pected arrival at the inn and had gone along with the story. Lamb agreed that there was no need to announce to the countryside that the previous night someone had tried to murder the newest Viscount Joslyn. And the illness would give Barnaby an excuse to remain in his bedchamber should it prove necessary.

Lamb's lips thinned as he examined the deep laceration at the back of Barnaby's head. Probing the bleeding wound, he decided the viscount was going to suffer relapse of his illness and retreat to his bed for a few days.

Leaving off his examination, Lamb said, "It needs stitching, but for now, I'll do a quick cleanup and get rid of the obvious blood. After Peckham arrives with the food and drink I ordered, I'll see to it. For the present you just sit here and don't move."

Barnaby grimaced, but agreed. Lamb disappeared into the dressing room, only to reappear a few moments later with a strip of clean linen. With less-than-tender care, and ignoring Barnaby's jump, he pressed the linen to the cut and held it there for several minutes. Removing the pad of linen, he took another look at the cut. Blood was still seeping out, but satisfied for the time being, he tossed the blood-soaked linen into the fire.

"That'll do until I can sew it up."

"Do I thank you or curse you?" Barnaby asked, the cut throbbing from John's ministrations.

"You may thank me now and curse me later," Lamb snapped.

They both heard the butler's approach through the sitting room and John hissed at him, "Remember, just sit there. Look bored."

Peckham, a small, middle-aged man with thinning blond hair and shrewd blue eyes, entered the room. Carrying a huge tray with a domed silver cover, he set the tray down on the carved mahogany table behind the sofa.

"Would you like me to serve you now, my lord, or would you prefer to wait?" Peckham asked.

"Oh, ah, I'll wait. Thank you, er, Peckham." Giving him a languid wave, Barnaby added, "You may go."

Lamb accompanied Peckham from the bedroom and as they were crossing the sitting room, he murmured, "His lordship is not feeling himself—we think it was something he ate on his journey."

Peckham glanced at him. "Nothing serious I hope?"

"Oh, no, I expect in a few days he'll be up and about and eager to see the estate," Lamb said easily. "But he'd prefer not to have any visitors for a while."

"I shall see that he is not disturbed," Peckham replied, and exited the sitting room.

Returning to the bedroom, Lamb took a deep breath. Now to sew up Barnaby and get him in bed—even if he had to wrestle him to do it.

An hour later, thinking of various tortures he'd inflict upon his "servant," Barnaby's head was neatly stitched and, despite his bitter protestations, he was in one of his own nightshirts—something he rarely wore—and enthroned in the huge, velvet draped bed which sat upon a dais in the middle of the room. Brooding, he watched as Lamb poured him some coffee—tepid after sitting so long—and served up a slab of smoked country ham, chunks of bread and thick slices of yellow cheese. Adding butter, mustard, pickles and an apple to the plate, he brought it over to the side of the bed.

"Eat half of this and I'll leave you alone for a few hours," Lamb said, setting it down on the mattress.

Balefully, Barnaby regarded him. "I am not an invalid, you know."

"And I intend to make certain you don't become one."

There was no arguing with Lamb when he was in one of his mother hen moods and admitting, at least to himself, that he really wasn't feeling up to snuff, Barnaby ate as directed.

To his surprise and Lamb's satisfaction, it appeared that his appetite was excellent and he demolished the plate of food. Leaning against the pillows, he watched as Lamb whisked away all signs of his meal.

Barnaby bit back a yawn, and reluctantly he confessed, "You know, mayhap a few hours in bed won't come amiss."

Lamb smiled and, picking up the tray, prepared to leave the room. Reaching the door to the sitting room he glanced back at Barnaby. Gruffly, he said, "Get some rest."

"I intend to," Barnaby answered. When John would have turned away, he added quietly, "Thank you."

Lamb smiled, nodded and walked through the doorway, leaving him alone.

Lamb was able to keep him abed that first day, but by Thursday, Barnaby, ignoring his furious objections, rose from his bed, bathed and dressed as usual. Leaving Lamb to sulk in the dressing room, he left his rooms and walked down the curving staircase to the black-and-white marble tiled foyer. A young man Barnaby remembered being introduced as his house steward, Tilden, was standing in front of a black japanned cabinet, shuffling through several envelopes, a faint frown on his face. Hearing Barnaby's step on the stairs, he looked up.

A smile replaced the frown and he bowed and said, "My lord."

"Ah, good morning, Tilden, isn't it?"

Pleasure gleamed in the young man's steady gray eyes. "Yes, my lord. I am happy to see that you have recovered from your indisposition."

"No more than I," Barnaby said. He glanced around. From the foyer doorways appeared to beckon in all directions and, looking at Tilden, he asked with a smile, "Now, if I wanted breakfast, where would I find it?"

Tilden laughed and said, "If you will allow me, my lord, I shall show you into the morning room. And perhaps, after you have eaten, I could give you a short tour around the house?"

"Excellent!"

The morning room with its slightly faded green-and-cream rug and blue-and-ivory chintz-covered chairs was surprisingly cozy and Barnaby felt more at ease since he had first laid eyes on Windmere. Pale sunshine leaked into the room from the narrow windows and, finishing a fine breakfast of stewed fruit, bacon, coddled eggs, toast and marmalade at the oval oak table, Barnaby was ready for Tilden's tour.

During the following days with Peckham, the housekeeper, Mrs. Bartlett, or Tilden, Barnaby toured the seemingly endless rooms of the house, then handed over to the head gardener, Hervey, he tramped over the extensive, manicured gardens, the greenhouses and the huge kitchen gardens at the rear of the house. He met the head stableman, the bailiff, the coachman, the head shepherd, listening and observing intently as each one of them explained the workings of the great estate. At night when he retired, his head was abuzz with all that he had learned that day, but with every passing hour, the mantle of responsibility, while heavy, felt more and more familiar.

On a Wednesday afternoon, two weeks to the day that Barnaby had first set foot in Windmere, young Sam, the blacksmith's son, appeared at the kitchen door, telling an astonished Peckham that he had a message from Mrs. Gilbert for my lord. Reluctantly, Peckham delivered the news of Sam's arrival to Barnaby in the library, where he was going over some paperwork with Tilden, who was proving, along with his other duties, to be an excellent secretary.

Barnaby threw down the page of accounts he had been

studying and standing up, scandalized Peckham by saying, "Take me to him."

Peckham coughed delicately. "I think, my lord, that it would be better if I brought the, er, young man to you."

"Nonsense," said Barnaby. He glanced around the elegant room. "Believe me, Sam would be more comfortable in the kitchen."

The cook was flustered to have his lordship stroll into her bustling kitchen. But Barnaby put her at ease with a friendly smile. "Mrs. Eason, I believe?" he said, and at her nod, continued, "I remember you from that first day." And made her his adoring slave when he added, "May I compliment you on the poached salmon steaks and the pullets with chestnuts that were served with dinner last night? I enjoyed the entire meal, but the salmon and pullets were exceptional."

Mrs. Eason, short, buxom and round as a plump pigeon, wisps of curly brown hair escaping her white cap, dropped a curtsy. "Thank you, my lord," she murmured, her cheeks pink with pleasure.

Young Sam was sitting at a scrubbed heavy oak table, a small plate of just-from-the-oven cinnamon biscuits and a tall glass of milk before him. Feeling Barnaby's eye on him, he hastily swallowed the biscuit he'd been eating, swiped his lips clear of crumbs and jumped to his feet. Brushing back a lock of dark hair from his forehead, his equally dark eyes on Barnaby's face, he said, "My lord, Mrs. Gilbert is most wishful for you to visit her at the inn. She says that"—he frowned, trying to remember her exact words—"you'll find it worth your while."

Sam had been sent back to the inn with word that his lordship would be arriving within the hour, and despite Lamb's argument to the contrary, Barnaby rode away from Windmere alone. His blue eyes worried, Lamb said, "I would

remind you that this time two weeks ago, someone tried to
kill you."

"True," Barnaby agreed mildly as he swung up into the
saddle. "And I will be on my guard." He half opened his dark
blue jacket, partially revealing the ivory handle of a pistol. "I
am armed with both a pistol and my knife—I will not be
such easy prey again." Lamb opened his mouth to continue
his protest but Barnaby held up a silencing finger. "I have no
intention of locking myself away within the confines of
Windmere—or having you following me about like a hen
with one chick." Effortlessly controlling the restive black
stallion beneath him, he said, "I would remind you that I still
have no memory of what happened to me that night—I may
never remember. And I agree that the most likely explanation is that someone tried to murder me, but it is possible
that there is another less dramatic explanation. Perhaps what
happened was some sort of ridiculous accident—and all my
own fault."

Lamb glared helplessly at him, but seeing the determined
line of Barnaby's jaw, he knew there was no swaying him.
Spinning on his heel, he snarled, "I'll enjoy dancing on your
grave."

Laughing, Barnaby rode away.

Arriving at the inn, Barnaby dismounted. Holding the
reins of his horse in one hand, he slowly walked toward the
two-storied plaster-and-brick building and tied his horse to
one of the short sturdy posts scattered across the front of the
place.

Barnaby was almost to the front door when a muscular
man with dark hair and eyes, a large smithy's hammer held
carelessly in one hamlike hand, appeared around the corner
of the inn.

"I thought I heard someone ride up," the newcomer said,

a friendly smile on his lips. "The inn is closed this afternoon. Mrs. Gilbert and her daughters will be back soon. They are gone to market, but she warned me to keep an ear open for you in case you arrived before their return."

From the heavy leather apron he was wearing over his jerkin and breeches and the hammer, Barnaby instantly guessed his identity. "You're the blacksmith. Young Sam is your son."

Nodding, he said, "I cannot deny it." He half bowed and said, "I'm Caleb Gates, my lord. Sam said you wouldn't be far behind him."

Barnaby grinned. "I could hardly ignore a summons from Mrs. Gilbert."

Caleb laughed. "Few of us can. If you will follow me, I can show you what she thought you would find so interesting."

They walked around to the back of the inn and crossing a large gravel-and-mud yard behind the building they approached a long, low stable. The deserted air to the inn and Mrs. Gilbert's absence made Barnaby uneasy and his hand wasn't far from his pistol as he followed Caleb into the stable.

Shafts of weak sunlight crowded through the wide, double doors of the stable and, stepping inside, Barnaby paused to let his eyes adjust to the shadowy interior of the building. Was it a trap? Another attempt on his life? His hand strayed closer to his pistol as he moved deeper into the stable.

Caleb walked past several empty stalls and stopped at the next to the last one on the right. Reaching Caleb's side, Barnaby glanced warily inside the stall. The big bay gelding with the distinctive blaze face that had been hitched to the hooded gig he'd been driving when he'd left London over two weeks ago stood in the center of the stall looking back at him.

Chapter 5

The sound of approaching feminine voices alerted Barnaby to Mrs. Gilbert's return. Her gray hair caught up in a neat bun at the back of her head, a few girlish curls dangling near her cheeks, she hurried into the barn.

"I must apologize, my lord, for not being here when you arrived," she said breathlessly when she reached him. "I thought I'd be back sooner."

Flora accompanied her mother. "Good afternoon, my lord," she said with a dimpled smile and a quick curtsy. "Ma wasn't sure you would even come."

An easy smile on his face, Barnaby said, "Refuse an invitation from your mother? After all your kindness to me, what sort of a craven would that make me?" To Mrs. Gilbert, he said, "I've only been here a few minutes and Caleb has taken very good care of me."

Her eyes on the bay gelding, Mrs. Gilbert asked, "Is that your horse, Blazer Boy? Faith swears that he is."

Barnaby nodded. "Yes, that's Blazer, all right. I was driving him when I left London." He frowned. "How does she know him? And where did you find him?"

"Faith has loved horses all of her life and notices them—

especially the fine ones like your Blazer there. Blazer was the old viscount's favorite driving horse and he used to drive him with his curricle all over the place. Your great-uncle stopped here whenever he came to the village and Faith was quite familiar with Blazer." She smiled. "Blazer was a favorite of hers, too. As to where she found him . . ." Her smile vanished. "She and Molly were coming back from Eastbourne and passed a horse trader with six or seven horses in tow. Faith recognized Blazer right away—his face marking is quite distinctive. When she stopped the man and demanded to know what he was doing with Viscount Joslyn's horse, the fellow claimed all innocence. Said he'd found him running loose several days ago farther up the coast." Mrs. Gilbert's lips thinned. "I know horse traders, and from the hasty way he handed over Blazer to her without an argument—or payment—I suspect there is more to the story, but Faith and Molly were alone and they didn't want to question him too closely. Faith was just glad to get her hands on Blazer."

"It seems my debt to your family is only increasing," Barnaby said.

Mrs. Gilbert snorted. "As long as you keep your tongue behind your teeth about certain events you observed the other night, you owe us nothing."

"What things?" Barnaby asked with big-eyed innocence.

Mrs. Gilbert chuckled. "I see we understand each other. Now come along. I'm sure you want to question Faith about the horse trader yourself."

"I'm sorry, my lord," Faith told Barnaby when he asked her to describe the horse trader to him. "I didn't pay him any mind." A faint flush rose in her cheeks. "All my interest was in Blazer and I was more concerned about getting my hands on him than the horse trader."

"Beyond being a stranger, there's not much else you can tell me about him?"

"I think he was an older man," she offered, trying to be helpful. Her pretty blue eyes distressed, she said unhappily, "I'm sorry."

Molly, who had accompanied Faith to Eastbourne, had little more to add to her sister's tale. Barnaby did a swift examination of Blazer and, beyond having lost a small amount of weight and having a slight cut on one shoulder, he appeared in fine shape. Temporarily leaving the horse in the stall, he walked with Mrs. Gilbert and Flora to the inn.

Mrs. Gilbert and her lively daughters provided good company and he had the opportunity to meet some of the locals. After having introduced him to a few fishermen and laborers drinking ale at the long counter, her expression bland, Mrs. Gilbert marched him over to a table where a young gentleman in military garb sat alone. "My lord, allow me to introduce Lieutenant Deering. He is our local riding officer." She smiled grimly. "Lieutenant Deering has been sent here to stamp out all those nasty smugglers that abound in the area."

Deering flushed and Barnaby felt sorry for him. "Revenue service, are you?" he asked in a friendly voice, as the lieutenant rose to his feet to meet him.

"Yes, my lord," Deering replied, standing almost at attention.

Barnaby liked the look of him. Brown haired and of a medium build with intelligent blue eyes, from the neatness of his attire, it was clear he took his job seriously and had not fallen into the slovenly ways of some of the men in the revenue service.

"Do you mind if I join you?"

Astonished at being singled out, the young officer stammered, "If y-y-you wish, m-m-y lord, I—I—I'd be honored."

As Barnaby sat and drank a tankard of ale with the young man, he was aware of the narrow-eyed glances sent their way. It wasn't an easy job the lieutenant faced. Forced to live amongst the very people he was trying to apprehend, Barnaby imagined that most of the locals treated Deering with suspicion and wariness. Certainly none of them would have joined him in drinking a tankard of ale.

"A thankless task you have," Barnaby said.

Deering nodded. "I'll not pretend otherwise—or that half my men aren't being bribed to look the other way." He sighed. "But I took on the job and I mean to uphold the law—even if it makes me an unpopular man around here— and my own men think I'm a fool for trying to stop the smuggling."

They conversed for a few minutes longer and, finishing his ale, Barnaby rose to his feet and said, "I do not envy your task, but I wish you well in it." Provided, he thought to himself as he walked away, you stay away from Mrs. Gilbert . . . and Miss Emily.

Barnaby was taking his leave of Mrs. Gilbert when an older fisherman, his dark hair grizzled and his face worn and burned by the elements, wandered in and settled at a small round table in the far corner of the oak-beamed room.

Mrs. Gilbert spied the newcomer and said to Barnaby, "That's Jeb Brown."

"The man who pulled me from the Channel?"

Mrs. Gilbert nodded.

Barnaby walked to the table where Jeb Brown sat and said quietly, "Mr. Brown, I am Lord Joslyn. Mrs. Gilbert tells me that you saved my life the other night. Thank you." He hesitated, then added, "A mere thank-you seems a scant reward for what you did. If there is anything I can do . . ."

Jeb stood up and cautiously took the hand Barnaby stretched out. "Truth is, my lord, I thought you was dead when I pulled you on board," Jeb said. "Almost jumped out of my boots when you groaned and I found you was alive." He studied Barnaby a long moment, then said meaningfully, "As long as you prove to be a good friend to Mrs. Gilbert and them girls of hers, that's thanks enough for me."

Barnaby inclined his head in perfect understanding. "None of you have anything to fear from me." His eyes met Jeb's. "It would be an honor to be considered your friend, and should you ever have need of my friendship, you know where to find me."

Sharp gray eyes studied him a moment longer, then Jeb nodded. "Thank you, my lord. I'll remember that . . . and take you at your word."

With Blazer following on a lead rope behind his horse, Barnaby rode away from the inn. The weather was worsening and he noted that during the time he'd been inside the skies had darkened to a surly gray and the wind had picked up. The scent of rain was in the air and dusk wasn't far away. Not liking the idea of finding his way home through unfamiliar territory in darkness *and* rain, Barnaby kicked the black into a fast trot, Blazer responding obediently to the quickened pace.

Not more than a mile later, the first raindrops fell. Within minutes Barnaby and the horses were drenched and an ugly wind nipped at them, adding to the general discomfort. Cursing himself for not paying attention to the time and weather, he spurred his horse to a faster clip, Blazer keeping pace behind the black. It was a miserable wet and cold ride.

Barnaby was delighted when he recognized a straggling row of beech trees and realized that he was just over a mile from Windmere. Around the next bend lay the entrance to Windmere and once he'd traversed the half mile or so of driveway that led to the great mansion, warmth and shelter awaited him. Intent on reaching his goal, he rounded a broad bend in the road at a dead gallop. Without warning, his horse skidded to a halt and reared in fright, nearly throwing him from the saddle. Blazer following behind shied and snorted and shuddered to a halt at the side of the road alongside Barnaby's plunging horse.

Bringing his mount under control and keeping Blazer on a shorter lead, Barnaby searched for what had frightened his horse and caused it to rear. Through the blowing rain, on the opposite side of the road, he spied a small black buggy leaning drunkenly in the ditch. The woman driver, concentrating on convincing her horse to move, hadn't noticed Barnaby and his horses.

As he slowly angled across the road and walked his horses toward the buggy, the driver gently urged the horse forward and the little animal made a valiant effort, plunging against the breast strap of the harness. Beyond a rocking motion, the buggy didn't move. "It's no use, Emily," the woman cried. "I'm afraid she's lame."

From behind the buggy a feminine voice answered. "Blast it! I cannot budge the wheel by myself. It is mired too deeply in the mud. Hell and damnation!"

"Oh, Emily, you know you shouldn't swear like that," scolded the driver. "What if someone should hear you?"

"Bloody hell! I wish there was someone to hear," Emily said bitterly. "At least we'd have help."

Barnaby's lips twitched. The name and the voice identified the hidden speaker. Emily Townsend. Suddenly he was no longer worried about being wet and cold or in such a hurry to reach home.

Unaware of Barnaby's presence, Emily said fiercely, "I'll strangle that wretched Kelsey if I ever lay eyes on him again—he deliberately ran us off the road. And if he's caused real damage to Sunny, I'll have his liver."

Barnaby neared the buggy and, trying not to startle the occupant, he called out softly, "Hello. I am Lord Joslyn of Windmere. May I be of service to you?"

The rain and the deep shadows created by the curved top of the buggy didn't allow him to see much, but as the driver looked in his direction he was left with the distinct impression of very large dark eyes in a pretty face.

"Oh!" the driver exclaimed. "I didn't see you. Emily, come quick! Someone is here."

From behind the buggy a tall, female form appeared and climbed nimbly onto the road and stalked toward him. The hood of her mud-stained cloak hid her features from him, but Barnaby was certain even without having heard her name or her voice that he would have recognized the challenging set to the head and shoulders and the defiant stride of his boy-who-was-not-a-boy.

Stopping in front of his horse, Emily recognized the big man immediately and decided that fate hated her. Lord Joslyn. How bloody wonderful.

She'd known they'd meet again, and while she hadn't wasted time thinking about him, she'd hoped when their paths next crossed it would be under more flattering conditions. But no, she thought acidly, she had to be wearing her oldest clothes, mud-splattered now after her fight with the recalcitrant wheel, and she was soaked to the skin.

Hoping he didn't connect her to the youth at the inn, Emily said coolly, "I am Emily Townsend. My cousin, Jeffery Townsend, is the local squire." Indicating the driver with a wave of her arm, she added, "This is my stepmother, Mrs. Anne Townsend." Some imp pushed her to ask, "And you are?"

Quashing the urge to laugh, he replied, "As I told your stepmother, I am Lord Joslyn." A mocking gleam in the black eyes, he added, "And I'm sure you know that I live at Windmere."

"It is a pleasure to meet you, my lord," said Anne hastily. She smiled shyly. "Even in such uncomfortable circumstances."

Swinging from his saddle, Barnaby said, "I think the circumstances are rather providential, don't you?" Holding on to the reins and Blazer's lead rope in one hand, ignoring Emily, he bent down and examined the mare hitched to the buggy. A long jagged cut along her rear leg was seeping blood, but it didn't appear to be deep or dangerous. A good cleaning and a stitch or two and some rest and the horse would be fine. But the little chestnut mare was decidedly lame and if he was any judge, was not going to be pulling the buggy out of the ditch tonight.

Ignoring the rain, he asked Emily, "How far do you have to travel?"

"Only about four miles." Testily, she added, "If you will help us free the wheel, we can be on our way."

He looked at the horse, the obviously wet and miserable woman before him and the small huddled driver and made a decision. "Windmere is less than a mile away. It will be far better if you take refuge there for the time being." He thought a second and aware of the treacherous roads, added, "Once you are warm and dry, I shall send you home in one of my carriages. Meanwhile your horse can be stabled and seen to. She is welcome to remain in my stables until her lameness is gone."

"Oh, thank you, my lord!" exclaimed Anne before Emily could say a word. "Sunny is a good little mare and would do her best to get us home, but I fear we might cause her great harm. You are too kind to not only shelter us, but to think of our dear Sunny, too." And when Emily remained silent, she prodded gently, "Don't you agree that it is very kind of his lordship, Emily?"

Emily didn't know why she was so reluctant to accept his offer or why he aroused the contrary urge within her to do just the opposite of what he proposed. It was a sensible solution and if it had been anyone else other than Lord Joslyn she wouldn't have thought twice about accepting his hospitality. Ashamed and a little surprised by the stubborn desire to defy him simply because of who he was, Emily muttered, "Yes, it is very kind."

"Since that is settled," Barnaby said, "I think, for your

mare's sake, that it would be better if my Blazer were harnessed to your buggy. He's an excellent driving horse and I suspect he will be able to free the wheel by himself."

He got no argument from Emily. She knew Blazer of old and she was more worried about Sunny than she cared to admit. Having a common goal, Emily and Barnaby worked quickly together and in minutes, Blazer was in harness and Sunny, her head hanging low, was standing at the side of the road, wearing Blazer's large halter and lead rope.

At Anne's command, Blazer leaned into the harness and with one powerful lunge freed the wheel and pulled the buggy back onto the roadway.

Emily squeaked when Barnaby's hands closed around her narrow waist and he tossed her into the buggy beside Anne. Flustered and breathless, she stammered, "T-t-thank you."

He grinned at her, his teeth gleaming in the shadows. "Entirely my pleasure."

After mounting his horse, holding Sunny's lead rope, he looked at the two women in the buggy and said, "You go on ahead and alert my butler that I shall be arriving shortly behind you." He glanced back at the mare. "Your, er, Sunny and I shall travel a bit more slowly."

His thoughtfulness toward the mare touched Emily and, her voice far warmer than it had been so far, she said, "Thank you, my lord. I'm very sorry we are causing you such inconvenience."

"It is my pleasure, Miss Townsend. Now be on your way. I shall be right behind you."

Barnaby with Sunny in tow arrived at Windmere ten minutes after the ladies. By the time Barnaby rode out of the darkness and into the flickering light from the torches at the front of the house both women had already been whisked inside by Peckham. Of Blazer and the buggy there was no sign and he assumed rightly that they had been taken to the stables. A pair of stableboys waited under the magnificent porch for him and ran out into the rain to take both horses from him the instant he dismounted.

Inside the grand foyer, Peckham and Tilden hovered like lightning bugs around him. "The ladies are upstairs in the blue bedroom," Peckham said, taking Barnaby's soaked greatcoat. "Mrs. Bartlett is seeing to their needs." He hesitated. "I thought perhaps it would be easier if they were served in the morning room rather than the formal dining room."

Barnaby nodded. "Excellent choice! If they are down before I am, tell them not to wait for me. I doubt any of us wish to stand on ceremony tonight."

"I have warned Lamb that you would be arriving any moment and would be in need of a change of clothing," chimed in Tilden. He coughed behind his hand. "I took the liberty of sending one of the footmen to The Birches with a note explaining the ladies' delay and warned John Coachman to have the smaller coach readied for travel tonight."

Nodding his approval, Barnaby took the marble steps two at a time and upon reaching his rooms, the instant the door shut behind him, began stripping off his wet clothes. His cravat, jacket and shirt had been discarded by the time he strode into the dressing room.

Lamb awaited him and as he continued stripping, Barnaby related the events of the afternoon. A brisk rub with a towel and he was stepping into the pair of breeches Lamb handed him and a second later slipping into a fine linen shirt—both mercifully dry and warm.

"I saw the two ladies as they came up the stairs," Lamb said idly, but the expression in his azure eyes was anything but idle. "A sprite and an Amazon," he continued. "Which one has caught your fancy?"

"Neither," Barnaby replied, tucking in his shirt. "Consid-

ering the situation, offering them shelter seemed the gentle-
manly thing to do."

"And that's all that prompted your actions? Politeness?"

Barnaby grinned at him. "Why, what else could it have
been?"

Lamb snorted and handed him a freshly laundered cravat.
"There is certainly a bevy of females in your life lately. First
those Gilbert women and now these two damsels."

"Happenstance. But don't forget I owe the Gilberts a
huge debt. Not only for nursing me, but now they've helped
me recover Blazer."

Watching critically as Barnaby hastily tied his cravat in a
simple arrangement, Lamb asked, "Do you believe this
Faith's story? That she just happened to find your horse in
the hands of a horse trader?"

Barnaby glanced over his shoulder. "It makes sense. I
think whoever tried to murder me sold Blazer at a bargain
price to the horse trader. And I don't doubt that my gig is in
various pieces scattered between here and London or has
been repainted and refurbished and is being driven around
London by a new owner thrilled with the exceptional buy he
made. So to answer your question, yes, I believe Faith's
story." His eyes gleamed. "You've not yet had the privilege
of meeting any of the Gilberts. I think you will find Mrs.
Gilbert, er, impressive and her daughters charming."

"You trust them?"

Barnaby nodded as he sat down and began pulling on a
pair of gleaming black boots. "I do." Standing up, he
shrugged into the bottle-green jacket with brass buttons that
Lamb handed him. "And since you seem to doubt my judgment," he added with a grin, "you should meet them and
form your own opinion."

Following Barnaby as he walked from the room Lamb
muttered, "I intend to do just that."

                              *   *   *

The previous squire and the seventh viscount had been good friends and both Anne and Emily had been frequent visitors to Windmere. Aware of the many grand rooms housed within the huge mansion and despite having repaired the worst of the damage from their ordeal, feeling worn and bedraggled, both ladies were relieved when Peckham showed them into the morning room.

A cheery fire burned on the old brick hearth and the soft shades of the rugs and chintz-covered furnishings created a cozy atmosphere. A teapot and a silver urn full of hot coffee sat at one end of the golden oak sideboard and several plates covered with a variety of meats, cheese, breads, pickles and relishes were laid out along its length. An oyster stew prepared for milord's return this evening filled a big tureen at the opposite end of the sideboard.

Peckham hovered over them. After seating them at the table and pouring cups of coffee, he filled two bowls of oyster stew and placed them with a flourish before the women. Without asking their preferences, he piled two plates high with items from the sideboard and set them on the table.

He would have continued to wait on them, but longing to be left alone, Emily said firmly, "Thank you. We can see to ourselves."

He bowed and murmured, "If you are sure . . . ?"

"No, thank you," Anne said politely. "We'll be fine."

After he left the two women exchanged glances. "I must say, he seems very . . . *efficient,*" Anne said kindly.

"I much preferred Bissell," Emily said, taking a sip of coffee.

"He is a dear man, isn't he?" Anne said. "I still don't understand why Mathew thought he should be replaced after his great-uncle died. I would have thought that should have been the new heir's decision."

"You forget—Mathew thought he *was* the heir. And it

wasn't Mathew who suggested that Bissell retire—it was Thomas."

Anne frowned slightly. "Isn't Thomas the middle brother? Or is he the youngest one? They all look so much alike I can never remember which one of the previous viscount's great-nephews is which."

"Tom is the middle one. Simon is the youngest—and my favorite," Emily answered. "Probably because he was kind to me when I was a child and I used to tag after him when he and his brothers came to visit their great-uncle. Mathew and Tom ignored me, but Simon . . ." She smiled warmly. "Simon always stuck up for me."

The viscount walked into the room and the smile still curving her lips, Emily glanced in his direction.

Barnaby had known that he was intrigued by his boy-who-was-not-a-boy, but he was stunned by his visceral reaction when he caught his first real sight of Emily Townsend. Hair the color of moonlight framed an arresting face that made his heart thud like a war drum. She wasn't pretty, a part of him acknowledged, but by God, he'd swear she was the most attractive woman he'd ever seen in his life. Her features were intensely feminine, yet strong and spirited, her jaw stubborn and her mouth too wide and full for true beauty, but he was only aware that he'd probably kill to feel those lips soften beneath his, and that smile . . . That smile filled him with a fervent zeal to do whatever it took to keep her looking at him precisely as she was at this moment.

As the seconds passed, Emily's smile faded and as her long-lidded, gray eyes widened and fixed on his, something powerful and fierce sprang to life within him. It was all he could do not to stride across the room and sweep her into a crushing embrace. Dazed, feeling as if he'd been poleaxed and not very pleased about it, Barnaby wrenched his gaze away and looked blankly at the small dark-haired woman seated next to Emily.

Her pansy-brown eyes smiling, Anne said, "My lord, we cannot thank you enough for your kindness."

Anne's voice cleared his head and putting aside his primitive response to Emily Townsend, he forced a smile and advanced into the room. Once more in command of himself—at least he hoped to hell he was—he said, "I trust that my staff has treated you well and seen to all your needs."

"Indeed," replied Anne, "everyone has been most kind."

Avoiding looking at Emily yet vibrantly aware of her, he said to Anne, "But you've hardly touched your food! Isn't it to your liking? If you wish, I can have Cook prepare something more to your liking."

Emily heard their voices, but the sound was like bees buzzing around in her head. She was conscious of her surroundings, but the world had tipped on its axis the second her eyes had fallen upon Lord Joslyn. She was dizzy, her chest felt tight and she fought against an insane desire to leap to her feet and run as fast as she could. But which direction? she wondered faintly. To him or away from him?

He was very tall, but so much bigger, darker and formidable than she remembered. Entering the room, he dominated it and she could not drag her eyes away from that dark, harsh-featured face and those powerful shoulders and arms. He looked nothing like a Joslyn, she thought stupidly. The Joslyns were handsome, polished men, but this man . . . She swallowed. This man looked like a savage—a brigand—and perfectly capable of swinging a woman up into his arms and carrying her away, to do what he willed. An odd sensation curled low in her stomach at the idea of being at his mercy.

She buried her nose in her cup, taking a long swallow, appalled and angry at her reaction to him. Good God! She didn't even like him. Through lowered lids she judged him, trying to decide what there was about *him* that had the power to rock her world. He was not traditionally handsome, she decided, but he possessed an undeniable virility, an unmistakable attractiveness that women would find hard to resist. Staring at that bold face, watching the mobile mouth as he smiled at Anne and hearing the lazy drawl of his voice, she shivered.

She was afraid of him, Emily realized with a start. Instinctively, she knew he wasn't a bully and a braggart like Jeffery, or a poseur and a fop like Ainsworth, nor was he a doting, if indifferent man, like her father. She thought of kindly Vicar Smythe puttering about in his garden and nearly laughed. No, Lord Joslyn was *nothing* like Vicar Smythe. She glimpsed the arrogance of Mathew Joslyn in him, but standing next to this man, Mathew would fade into the background. No, heaven help her, Lord Joslyn was like no man she had ever met in her life.

"Miss Townsend? Are you all right?"

His words jolted her and she looked up to realize that both he and Anne were staring at her.

"Emily? Is something wrong?" asked Anne worriedly. "Lord Joslyn has asked you twice if you're certain there's nothing else you need."

Emily flushed. "I'm sorry. I—I—I guess that I'm a trifle wool-headed after today's events." With an effort she forced herself to look at him, her heart plunging right to her toes at the narrowed expression in those black eyes. Her gaze dropped to her bowl of oyster stew. "I'm fine," she said. And picking up her spoon, babbled, "Doesn't this stew look delicious? I've always enjoyed Mrs. Eason's cooking."

Barnaby looked surprised. "You know my cook, Mrs. Eason?"

"Oh, yes," Anne answered. "Your Mrs. Eason and our cook, Mrs. Spalding, are sisters, and our butler, Walker, is your housekeeper Mrs. Bartlett's uncle. Bissell, who used to be the butler here, is married to Mrs. Bartlett's oldest sister."

He shook his head. "I have had a hard time just remembering everyone's name, much less that of their relatives."

"It must be difficult for you," Anne said sympathetically,

"being amongst strangers and in a different country than you were born."

"Not so different, and I have my man, Lamb, with me." He smiled at Anne. "I'm adjusting and at least the language is the same."

Interested, Emily looked at him and asked, "Do you think you'll like living in England?"

His gaze seemed to reach out and caress her and he said softly, "Since I have met you two charming ladies, I find that I am liking it more and more by the minute."

"Oh, that was prettily done," cried Anne, clapping her hands together in delight. "I can hardly wait for you to meet Great-Aunt Cornelia! She is going to flirt outrageously with you."

"Great-Aunt Cornelia . . . ?" Barnaby asked with a lifted brow.

Despite the flutter in her chest that his look had caused, Emily couldn't help smiling as she pictured Cornelia's reaction to Lord Joslyn. "She'll have you dancing to the tune of her piping in no time," Emily said, a teasing gleam in her eyes.

"That's if she doesn't eat you for dinner," Anne added, grinning. "At eighty-nine, she is a remarkable woman. She'll like you—especially if you stand up to her."

Having helped himself from the sideboard, he took a seat across from the ladies and motioning them to their food, joined them at the table. Conversation was scant and general as everyone concentrated on the food, but Barnaby learned a great deal about the neighborhood during the course of the meal. Vicar Smythe grew the most exceptional roses, Anne informed him. Sir Michael, his house steward's father, was a dear, dear old man; Mrs. Featherstone, widow of a wealthy landowner, was a darling but a great gossip with a quiver full of daughters to marry off and by all means, Emily warned, never buy a horse from Lord Broadfoot.

"I shall look forward to meeting all of them," Barnaby said untruthfully as they finished up their meal and settled back to enjoy a final cup of coffee. He looked rueful. "I suspect it will be months before I meet all my neighbors and even longer before I can put faces with names. I am not even familiar with the staff at Windmere—let alone my neighbors."

Anne smiled kindly at him. "I wouldn't be at all surprised if Lord and Lady Broadfoot don't come to call soon." Her eyes twinkling, she murmured, "Cornelia says that Lady Broadfoot is already planning a soiree to introduce you to the neighborhood—her good friend, Mrs. Featherstone, has promised to help."

"Not the Mrs. Featherstone with the quiver full of hopeful daughters?" Barnaby asked, looking alarmed.

"The very same," Emily said, smiling. "And there are three Broadfoot daughters. While you have been hiding away here at Windmere, the ladies of the neighborhood have been all atwitter knowing that the American Lord Joslyn was finally in residence. According to Cornelia they have been badgering their husbands unmercifully to call upon you. Only a fast, fading sense of decency has kept them from your door but I expect within the next day or two you will have callers. . . ." She giggled. "And most of them with marriageable daughters."

Barnaby groaned and both women laughed.

There was a tap on the door and Peckham popped his head inside the room. "My lord," he began, "you have—"

"Get out of my way, Peckham," Mathew Joslyn said irritably from behind the butler. "It will be a cold day in hell before my brothers and I have to be announced to our cousin."

Chapter 6

Mathew Joslyn, reputed by many to be one of the handsomest men in the country, stalked into the room. Thomas, favored by some to be even more handsome than his older brother, followed him. Trailing in the rear was Simon, the youngest and in the opinion of the largest contingent, truly *the* handsomest man in England.

All three men possessed the Joslyn charm and attractiveness and had inherited the stunning azure eyes, black hair and the tall athletic bodies for which the family was known. There were, of course, differences; Mathew was the tallest, Thomas the shortest, though not more than two inches separated the three brothers. All had the same similarly chiseled features, but Thomas's face was a trifle narrower than his brothers, giving him, Emily always thought, the look of a most handsome fox. Mathew's chin was classical perfection, but Simon had the squarest jaw—and in Emily's opinion, the best smile. That smile and a quick wink were flashed her way as he entered the room behind his brothers.

Mathew was surprised to find that Barnaby had company. His annoyed expression immediately changed. Smiling po-

litely at Anne and Emily, he said, "I beg your pardon, ladies.
I did not realize my cousin had visitors."

"We are not visitors exactly," Anne said after acknowledging the newcomers. "Lord Joslyn rescued us when our
buggy was stuck in a ditch and our mare went lame. After
helping us free the vehicle, he graciously offered us shelter."
She smiled at Barnaby. "He was most gallant."

Mathew, looking as if he had swallowed a hedgehog,
murmured, "Really? How, er, heroic of him."

Barnaby, lounging at one side of the table, his long legs
stretched out in front him, grinned. "Even we crude Americans know how to do the right thing, cousin."

"I don't believe that my brother," said Tom Joslyn aus-
terely, "ever called you crude."

"No," said Simon, walking over to help himself to a cup
of coffee, "Matt never called him crude, but I seem to remember"—he smiled wickedly and looked at his eldest
brother—"that you once referred to him as that 'uncouth
barbarian.' "

"Uncouth?" Barnaby asked, a gleam in his black eyes.
"Surely not."

Mathew flushed and said testily, "You know we have had
our differences, cousin, and in a moment of anger I may
have allowed my tongue to run away with me." Under Barnaby's calm gaze, he almost fidgeted. Stiffly, he added, "I
apologize."

Emily's eyes went from one man to the other searching for
the family resemblance. She could find little beyond the *impression* that Lord Joslyn and Mathew had a shared ancestry. Lord
Joslyn was big and tough looking, his features lacking the
Greek perfection of Mathew's and, as she had thought earlier,
even seated, Lord Joslyn commanded the attention of everyone
in the room. She bit her lip to keep from smiling. Compared to
Lord Joslyn, Mathew, a noted Corinthian, more resembled a

pretty Pink of the *ton*. While Lord Joslyn . . . She swallowed. Lord Joslyn looked like a lazy tiger sizing up prey . . . very large, very powerful and dangerous. . . .

"Oh, for God's sake, climb down off your high horse and help yourself to something to eat and sit down," Barnaby said without heat. "I'm sure if positions were reversed, I would have called you a great many worse names."

"Handsomely done," murmured Simon.

"Yes, it was," Barnaby agreed. Smiling at Simon, he added, "And you need to quit throwing the cat amongst the pigeons."

Simon looked crushed. "But how else shall I find amusement?" he asked mournfully, the blue eyes dancing.

"Oh, stop trying to act like a court jester and behave yourself," Tom said, approaching the sideboard. After pouring himself some coffee, he took a sip and made a face. "Good God! This is colder than yesterday's porridge. Ring for Peckham and order us some hot coffee."

Barnaby's brow lifted, his eyes, their expression unreadable, on Thomas, but he said nothing. As the seconds passed, Thomas's cheeks deepened to a hard red. Barnaby let him dangle for a moment longer, then breaking the growing tension said softly, "You know where the bell rope is . . . With my permission you may ring for him."

"I d-d-didn't mean t-t-to be rude," Tom stuttered. "It is just that . . ."

"I know," Barnaby said wearily, "until a few months ago, your brother was considered the heir to all of this and all of you were used to running tame through the place and treating it as your own."

Her sympathy aroused, Anne said, "This must be very hard for all of you."

"Not for me," Simon said cheerfully, making himself comfortable beside Emily at the table. He grinned at Emily. "I was never in the running for the title."

Emily grinned back at him. "I know that, you fool, and so does everyone else."

"Fool?" Simon clutched his chest. "Fair maiden, how can you be so cruel? Your words have cut me to the quick. I shall never recover."

Barnaby's eyes narrowed at the easy intimacy between Emily and Simon. He hadn't missed the smile or the wink Simon had sent her when he walked into the room either. He liked Simon. He hoped he wasn't going to have to show the impudent cub his punishing right.

Not at all amused by Simon's antics, Mathew's lips tightened. "Must you always jest? It is entirely inappropriate."

"Matt is right," said Thomas, having recovered his aplomb. "You should mind that wayward tongue of yours."

Simon's teasing manner vanished. "Now why am I not surprised that you agree with our godlike sibling? Tell me, brother dear, have you ever had an original thought of your own?"

"Oh, for heaven's sake," Mathew said, "cease this childish baiting."

Innocently, Simon said, "Well, I have wondered. All he does is parrot you."

Thomas's fists clenched and he stepped toward Simon.

Simon, an expression of gleeful anticipation on his handsome face, stood up.

Barnaby had observed the dissension between the brothers previously and he was tempted to let the scene play out, his money on Simon sending Thomas crashing to the floor, but deciding that a dust-up in the morning room wasn't proper entertainment for the ladies, he intervened. "Er, all of this is most amusing, but is there a reason for this unexpected visit?" he asked. "Other than your enjoyment of my company?"

Simon grinned at him and sat back down. Thomas swung

away and gave a violent yank on the black velvet bell rope hanging at one end of the sideboard.

Mathew glared at Simon a moment, before turning to Barnaby. "Actually there is," he began. His eyes fell upon Emily and Anne's rapt faces and he muttered, "But it can wait until your guests have departed."

Peckham's entrance into the room provided a timely interruption. The butler smiled warmly at the newest arrivals. Barnaby ordered fresh coffee and more food. Before Peckham hurried away, he said, "And please see that rooms are prepared for my guests and any servants they have brought with them."

Mathew smiled at Barnaby, the smile transforming his haughty features and giving a glimpse of the great charm for which he was famous. "I wasn't certain you'd allow us to stay."

Barnaby shrugged. "It's an unusual situation for all of us—there is no reason to make it worse." A slow smile curved his mouth. "Whether we like it or not, we are, after all, family."

"Well!" exclaimed Anne, a short while later as she and Emily were driven away from Windmere in the comfortable coach Lord Joslyn had provided. "That was most interesting, wasn't it? I was certain that Tom and Simon would come to blows."

"Which isn't the least unusual for them," Emily answered. "Even as children the three of them were always at each other's throats—especially Tom and Simon. I cannot count the number of times one or both of them gave the other one a bloody nose or a black eye." She frowned. "But I wonder what brought them to Windmere."

"Perhaps Mathew is trying to be kind."

"To the man who has just snatched a title and an estate

like Windmere out of his grasp?" inquired Emily with a lifted brow. "I'd be more inclined to think he came to murder him."

"*Emily!* Never say such a thing!" Anne cried, shocked.

"You forget the circumstances under which I first met Lord Joslyn. He was more dead than alive and you'll never convince me that someone hadn't gone to a great deal of trouble to arrange for him to die that night. If Jeb hadn't spied him, he *would* be dead."

"I'd forgotten that," Anne admitted. Unhappily, she added, "And of course, it would be to Mathew's benefit if Lord Joslyn were to die."

Barnaby was very aware that of everyone, Mathew had the most to gain by his death, but he couldn't quite put the face of a murderer on him. Having bid the ladies good-bye, the four gentlemen wandered into the study and, covertly studying Mathew's features as he poured him brandy, Barnaby still didn't see his oldest cousin in the role of murderer.

Once the gentlemen had been served brandy, or port in the case of Thomas, and were scattered around the elegantly masculine room, Barnaby asked, "So to what do I owe this honor?"

"Lord Padgett," Simon said.

Mathew, standing near one end of a massive black gold-veined marble fireplace, threw Simon an annoyed glance. At the opposite end of the fireplace from his two brothers, Simon was sprawled comfortably in a black leather chair trimmed in small brass buttons and he grinned back at his brother.

Barnaby frowned. "Lord Padgett? I'm afraid I do not recognize that name."

"I don't believe you've met—he is a friend of mine," said Tom, standing to the side of Mathew. "I happened to pass Padgett on the street in London and he mentioned that he'd just returned from Eastbourne, where he keeps his own yacht, and had noticed that the Joslyn yacht was missing from her berth. Said she'd been gone for several days. Naturally, I thought Mathew should be informed."

"Naturally," said Barnaby, deciding that he much preferred Simon's irreverence to Thomas's self-righteous tale bearing.

"As you are aware," Mathew said carefully, "this is not precisely the yachting season. . . . Thomas was concerned you may have taken the boat out and . . ."

"Drowned?" Barnaby asked drily from his position at the other end of the fireplace, not far from where Simon sat.

Simon snickered and Mathew looked pained.

Thomas glared at Simon. "Must you always act the fool?"

When Simon would have risen to the challenge, Barnaby turned his head and stopped him with a look. Slightly abashed, Simon sank down deeper into his chair. "Better a fool than a prissy old maid," he muttered into his brandy so lowly only Barnaby heard him.

Barnaby agreed with Simon and he hadn't missed the fact that they'd divided themselves into two camps. At one end of the fireplace stood Mathew and Thomas almost shoulder-to-shoulder and he and Simon had taken up positions at the other end. To anyone viewing the scene it would appear that Simon was aligned with him. . . . But dare he trust Simon?

"I cannot pretend," Mathew said from between gritted teeth, "that your death wouldn't be to my advantage or that I would shed tears over your grave, but dash it all! Give me some credit." Mathew took a deep breath, throttling back his temper. "Knowing the yacht was missing, it seemed appropriate to find out if all was well with you . . . and the yacht. Since Simon was already staying with me at Monks Abbey when Tom brought me the news of the yacht being missing, it seemed reasonable that the three of us come to call. None of us," he half snarled, "came here in the guise of vultures."

The pale blue eyes flashing, he said tightly, "And I resent the implication that we did!"

Barnaby believed him. His cousin was clearly offended by the notion that Barnaby thought him capable of taking pleasure in another man's death—even if he didn't like him. Mathew would meet him head-on in a fair fight—of that much Barnaby was convinced. "I acquit you of that," Barnaby said quietly. "And I apologize for implying your actions were anything less than those of an honorable man."

"Thank you," Mathew said stiffly.

"Did you know about the yacht?" Simon asked, looking at Barnaby closely.

Barnaby considered telling them the truth about the night he was dragged from the Channel, but decided against it for several reasons. Except for a handful of people no one else knew the truth and he'd just as soon keep it that way—just thinking of explaining why he and the others had lied about the cause of his indisposition made him wince. Worse yet, if Emily and Anne were to be believed, just his mere presence at Windmere had caused enough gossip in the area as it was. A near brush with death would be a nine days' wonder in the neighborhood and he'd just as soon avoid enduring that, thank you very much!

Blending what he thought to be true with fiction, Barnaby said, "The yacht was in Eastbourne two weeks ago last Tuesday. I saw it when I passed through on my way here. If it has gone missing, it had to be after that."

Thoughtfully, Simon said, "I'll wager it's that bloody Nolles gang." He shook his head. "And if they stole her, most likely she's at the bottom of the Channel . . . or so disguised she'll never be recognized."

Knowing full well that the yacht was indeed at the bottom of the Channel, Barnaby asked, "The Nolles gang? That's the second time I've heard that name . . . who are they?"

Mathew sighed. "They're a vicious band of smugglers

and rule this area. The revenuers and Customs have been trying to break their back for years—to no avail. Nearly everyone for miles around here, and Monks Abbey for the matter,
belongs to the gang or is related in some manner to the
members of the gang . . . or terrified of them."

Thomas took a dainty swallow of his port. "Gossip has it
that they have a wealthy London backer and that enables
them to snare the largest share of the smuggling market. The
amount of contraband they move is said to be phenomenal."

Mathew nodded. "That they've had a wealthy financier
behind them for the past six to eight years isn't a secret. Before that, Will Nolles and his brethren were like any other
gang in the area, but with a great deal of money behind
them, they've become quite powerful—a force to be obeyed
and feared."

"Seems to me that if the authorities exposed this, er,
backer, the problem would be solved," Barnaby said.

"Yes, of course, but no one seems to know anything about
him—he's like a ghost." Mathew looked unhappy. "And, unfortunately, he supplies the Nolles gang with the funds to
buy larger and larger shipments of contraband and enables
them to hire more men and gives them more influence and
power." Mathew sighed. "The revenue service pay is so mea-
ger that many of the men stationed here to stamp out smuggling are quite willing to accept bribes and live comfortably
ignoring what is right under their noses."

"Smuggling is a way of life along our coastal areas—especially here in Sussex and Kent," Simon stated wryly.
"You'll be hard-pressed to find anyone who isn't touched by
it one way or another." He cocked a brow. "Did you know
that decades ago, one of our less illustrious ancestors was a
smuggler?" He grinned. "It's said that most of the family
wealth is based on his enterprising use of the tunnels and
cellars beneath Windmere. Legend has it he'd store enor-

mous amounts of contraband until it was safe to make a run to London."

Barnaby sat up. "Tunnels? Underneath Windmere?"

"The old place is full of them," Simon said.

Thomas chuckled. "When we were children, Matt, Simon and I used to play in them every time we came to visit. It was a favorite place for all of us to gather and pretend we were dangerous smugglers. Miss Townsend, Faith Gilbert and Miss Broadfoot and even from time to time, Jeffery Townsend joined us. There were some others, but I've forgotten their names at the moment. It was great fun, I can tell you that."

A reminiscent smile on his lips, Mathew said, "Oh, Lord, the grand times we had chasing those screaming girls or acting as their defenders against the wicked smugglers."

"So having people around like the Nolles gang is common?" Barnaby asked, filing away the information about the tunnels.

Simon shook his head. "Most of the smuggling is done by small groups of fishermen desperate to help their families, but the Nolles gang—they are not to be trifled with. They're vicious."

"Indeed, I've been hearing gossip of a small gang operating in this neighborhood for the past few years," Tom said. Adding almost with relish, "But they won't last much longer—Will Nolles and his friends will take care of them. They don't tolerate competition . . . of any kind." He glanced at Mathew. "Remember four or five years ago when they—"

"I don't think that our cousin needs to be regaled with tales of the antics of violent criminals," Mathew said.

Barnaby was very curious about the Nolles gang and his curiosity had much to do with the distinct possibility that they represented a danger to Emily and the Gilberts. He would have liked to press for more information, but decided there was no reason to reveal his interest to the Joslyns. There were other ways of finding out what he needed to know. The information about the tunnels and their connection with smuggling was interesting, he reminded himself, and would bear looking into sometime in the following weeks.

The gentlemen parted for the evening and Barnaby was thoughtful as he entered his bedroom and walked into the dressing room. Entering the dressing room, he spied the emerald-and-gold embroidered black robe that Lamb had laid across the chair for him and began to undress.

He rang for Lamb and finished stripping out of his clothes, then shrugged into the robe. When Lamb arrived, he was in the sitting room adjoining the bedroom looking down at the yellow and orange flames gleaming on the hearth of the big stone fireplace.

Waving a hand toward the array of liquors kept on the top of the long sideboard on the other side of the room, he said, "Help yourself and pour me a brandy while you're at it."

After pouring both of them snifters of brandy, Lamb walked back and handed Barnaby one of the snifters. Taking a seat, he stretched his legs toward the fire and looked inquiringly at Barnaby.

"I want you to find out what you can about a fellow named Kelsey," said Barnaby. "He may have been here this afternoon."

John shook his head in amazement. "How in the hell did you know about him and that Jamieson, your head groom, sent him away with a flea in his ear?"

"I didn't know about that, but I did know that he was the cause of the Townsend ladies ending in the ditch," Barnaby replied. "I overheard Miss Townsend say something to her stepmother about that 'wretched Kelsey' running them off the road. Since the accident occurred outside the main gate to Windmere it seemed probable that he had been here."

"Well, I can tell you that Kelsey showed up at the stables when I was visiting late this afternoon with Jamieson, excellent man, by the way, and was looking for a job. Jamieson already knew him—until recently, Kelsey was Squire Townsend's head stableman. Kelsey was drunk and belligerent and not at all the sort of person you would want on your staff—even if you were looking to hire someone. Jamieson tried politely to turn him away, but Kelsey would have none of it and grew abusive." John grinned. "The upshot was that Jamieson gave him as pretty a right uppercut as I have ever seen and after Kelsey had picked himself up off the ground, ordered him from the estate."

Barnaby considered the situation, wondering if he should pursue it further. No permanent harm had been done and the accident had given him a chance to spend time with Emily Townsend. . . . He'd let it go for now, he decided, but Kelsey had best not come to his attention again.

"Do you want me to find out more about him?" John asked.

Barnaby shook his head. "No. Let it go for now. But tell me, have you heard anything about a gang of smugglers called the Nolles gang? The leader is someone called Will Nolles."

Lamb nodded. "My first day here one of the footmen took far too much pleasure in telling me all about Will Nolles and his gang." Lamb swirled his brandy around in the snifter. "I think he thought to frighten me."

"And did he?" Barnaby asked, grinning.

Lamb snorted. "Hardly. But why are you interested in a gang of smugglers?"

Barnaby hesitated. Lamb knew about his brush with death in the Channel and that the fisherman, Jeb Brown, had pulled him to safety, but nothing about Emily Townsend or the fact that he suspected that Jeb Brown and the Gilberts were smugglers. And he'd wager a pocketful of gold guineas that they were the same small gang that Thomas had alluded to tonight. He seldom kept secrets from John and he saw no reason not to tell him the whole truth.

Pulling on his ear, Barnaby said, "Uh, there's a bit more to my near drowning than I told you."

"I knew it!" Lamb exclaimed, sitting upright. "You've always been a bad liar and there was something . . . So what really happened?"

Succinctly Barnaby relayed the sequence of events that had occurred that night at The Crown.

When he finished speaking, Lamb was grinning from ear to ear. "So it's the smuggling Amazon who caught your interest. I suspected it was more than just kindness that prompted your actions tonight."

"No, I am not interested in either of the Townsend ladies—except as my neighbors," Barnaby lied, and almost swore at the knowing look Lamb slanted him. "But I owe Emily Townsend and the Gilberts a debt of gratitude," he continued doggedly, "and if keeping them from harm at the hands of this Nolles gang helps repay some of their kindness, then I am more than willing to do it." He grimaced. "And out of the sights of Lieutenant Deering—the young man is everything the revenue service needs most desperately—honest, dedicated and determined. I'm willing to help him in any way I can to stop the Nolles gang, but he'll need to be guided away from the Gilbert group."

Lamb shrugged, but there was a mocking gleam in his eyes. "Of course," he purred. "You are being good and noble and doing nothing more than repaying a debt. How very, very lord of the manor."

"Tell me what you know about the Nolles gang," Barnaby said in a voice that even Lamb obeyed.

His teasing air left him and frowning, Lamb said, "The

footman hasn't been the only person to mention them since I arrived at Windmere. From things I've overheard, it appears that several of your staff are related to them either by blood or marriage—or work with them upon occasion." He shook his head. "Almost to the man . . . or woman, they're on the side of the smugglers and aligned against the revenuers and custom officials."

Barnaby sighed. "I was afraid you were going to say that. How many of my staff have ties to the gang?"

Lamb hesitated. "While they talk freely in general terms, I am not privy to anything specific—and upon occasion conversations come to an abrupt end when I enter the room, but I've come to some conclusions on my own. I think your coachman's youngest son is part of the gang and that the cook's daughter is married to a fellow who sometimes helps the gang move their goods. One of the scullery maids let something drop that leads me to believe that her father does the same and Mrs. Bartlett has some connection to the gang, but I don't know what it is."

"But what do you know of the gang itself?" Barnaby asked, frowning.

"Not a lot, and how much is true and how much is exaggerated to impress or intimidate the American newcomer I have no way of knowing," he warned. When Barnaby motioned for him to continue, Lamb said, "It's a large gang— over sixty members, if what I've heard is true, and Will Nolles is the leader. From being a lowly member of a fishing crew eight years ago, he has risen to be the captain of a small fishing fleet and owns the largest inn in the area, The Ram's Head." Lamb grimaced. "Quite the success story—and I gather that nearly every lad in the area aspires to follow in his path."

"And where would I find this Nolles?"

"At The Ram's Head—your Mrs. Gilbert's competition." His eyes met Barnaby's. "There were questions about her husband's death four or five years ago one night after he visited The Ram's Head to object to Nolles accosting several regulars of The Crown and implying that it would be better for their health if they changed their allegiance to The Ram's Head. It appears that anyone who opposes him comes to an unfortunate end."

"Nasty-sounding fellow, our Nolles," Barnaby murmured.

"Not someone to be trifled with if gossip is to be believed."

Barnaby took a long swallow of his brandy. "I think," he said slowly, as he set the snifter down on the mantel "that I shall have to see for myself if The Ram's Head holds as much charm for me as The Crown."

Not liking the expression on Barnaby's face, Lamb said, "Did I mention that several members of the gang regularly frequent The Ram's Head and that Nolles is seldom without a half dozen or so of his men around him?"

Barnaby shrugged. "I doubt they'll attack me in broad daylight in a public place."

"I worry less about them attacking you than I do you starting a rumpus, thinking to champion your Amazon and the Gilberts!"

Barnaby looked innocent. "What a ridiculous notion—as if I would lower myself to such vulgar actions as brawling in a tavern! But as a member of the aristocracy," he said, twinkling at him, "and one of the largest landholders in the district, it is my civic duty to see to it, if the gossip is true, that a nefarious fellow like Nolles doesn't continue to flout the law."

"I don't suppose I can convince you that it would be unwise to antagonize Nolles?"

His expression bored, Barnaby examined his nails. "Antagonize? Now why would you think such a thing?"

Lamb's gaze narrowed. He knew that deceptively bored

expression of old and knew that no matter what he said that there was no stopping Barnaby from visiting The Ram's Head one day soon . . . and no doubt, he thought viciously, wreaking havoc in the place.

"Christ!" Lamb swore. "At least let me accompany you."

Barnaby smiled sunnily at him. "But of course. Surely you didn't think I was fool enough to stick my head in the lion's den without you beside me?"

Chapter 7

Emily hoped she and Anne could arrive home without having to face Jeffery or Mr. Ainsworth, but fate failed her. The Joslyn coach hardly pulled to a stop in front of the gracious old manor house before Jeffery, braving the rain, appeared at the side of the coach and swung open the door with a flourish.

Smiling, he glanced inside. His smile vanished when he realized that the coach held only two occupants, Emily and Anne. Peevishly he asked, "Lord Joslyn did not accompany you home?"

"No," replied Emily, stepping from the coach, followed by Anne. With Jeffery trailing behind them the two women hurried to the house.

Inside, Walker, the Townsend family butler, met the two ladies and efficiently whipped away their outer clothing and directed them to the small blue sitting room, where, he said, a fire and a nice pot of tea awaited them. His blue eyes amused, he murmured into Emily's ear, "Your great-aunt is most desirous of hearing every moment of your time with Lord Joslyn." He coughed delicately. "You know how fond she is of the family."

Emily choked back a laugh. "Yes, I seem to recall something to that effect."

Cornelia wasn't the only person waiting for them in the blue sitting room; posed negligently against the cream marble fireplace stood Mr. Ainsworth.

There was nothing particularly notable about Mr. Ainsworth. He was neither short nor tall, neither lean nor fat and if not precisely handsome, not unattractive. His eyes were a clear gray, his hair a soft brown and his build neither muscular nor flabby, but somewhere in between. He was in Emily's opinion eminently forgettable and she longed for the day he was but a memory—one that never crossed her mind.

Neatly garbed in a dark blue jacket, dove-gray pantaloons and black kid pumps, he lifted his quizzing glass and ogled the ladies as they walked into the room. When his gaze fell upon her, Emily felt as if her gown's modest neckline fell to somewhere down around her waist and left her breasts naked. From the pink in Anne's cheeks as her stepmother greeted Cornelia and drifted toward the tea tray in the middle of the room, she knew her stepmother had the same reaction.

When he first arrived at The Birches, Emily and the other ladies had started out being polite to Mr. Ainsworth—he was, after all, a guest—but they soon had his measure . . . as did everyone else in the household. The majority of the inhabitants at The Birches heartily despised Mr. Ainsworth only marginally less than they did Jeffery. Once they realized they had an out-and-out rake on their hands, Emily and Cornelia saw no reason to endure Mr. Ainsworth's offensive leers and ribald comments and wasted no time in treating him to the sharp side of their tongues. Anne, being of a more retiring nature, avoided him when she could and suffered in silence when forced into his company—which was seldom, thanks to Emily and Cornelia's watchful eye.

In no mood to put up with his lecherous appraisal, Emily

asked with interest, "Are you aware, Mr. Ainsworth, how hideous that quizzing glass makes your eye look?" She shuddered. "The sight of that huge orb bearing down on one is enough to cause those of a delicate nature nightmares." Smiling like a shark, she added, "Fortunately, I am not one of them, but you would be wise upon whom you bend your glass."

Mr. Ainsworth dropped the quizzing glass as if it scalded him and glared at her.

"Emily!" Jeffery thundered, entering the room behind her. "Will you mind your manners? Mr. Ainsworth is a guest."

"Not mine," Emily said sotto voce, walking over to sit beside Cornelia, who was taking in the scene with a smile. Patting Emily's hand where it rested on the arm of the chair, Cornelia murmured, "That's my gal! Don't hold your fire."

Jeffery's face darkened and he took a threatening step forward, only to be brought up short when Anne thrust a cup and saucer at him. "Tea?" she asked brightly.

Jeffery fought to recover his equanimity. Except to Ainsworth, he'd never mentioned his unfortunate meeting with Lord Joslyn that night at The Crown and hoping to redeem himself, he'd been elated when he learned that Lord Joslyn had rescued Emily and Anne. He'd been certain that the viscount would accompany the ladies home, and he'd looked forward to the opportunity to show himself in a more flattering guise . . . and the privilege of being the first in the neighborhood to entertain his lordship. That his lordship had not escorted the ladies home had been a blow, and now his accursed cousin was behaving to his guest with her usual disregard for anything remotely resembling civility. By God, if he didn't break her neck one of these days it would be a miracle. Breathing heavily through his nose, he brushed aside the cup and saucer and muttered, "No, thank you. I am in no mood for tea."

Anne hid a smile and turned away, sitting near the other two women. Looking at Cornelia, she asked, "May I get you something? Some tea? Or would you like a few of those lovely lemon biscuits Mrs. Spalding baked for us?"

Cornelia waved away the offer of refreshment and glancing expectantly from Anne to Emily demanded, "Well? Now that you have had an opportunity to spend some time in his company, what do you think of the newest Lord Joslyn?" She shook a finger at them. "And don't be coy."

"Oh, for heaven's sake," Jeffery burst out as he poured himself some port from the same tray that held the tea things. "I'm sick of the way all the ladies in the neighborhood are in a titter over Lord Joslyn." He sniffed. "Believe me, he's merely a man like any other. To listen to you tabbies, you'd think the fellow walked on water."

"I seem to recall that you strutted around here, all cock-a-whoop over the notion that he would escort Emily and Anne home tonight," Cornelia observed. "One might have been mistaken in believing that you were most anxious to meet him yourself."

Jeffery ignored her jab and took a swallow of his port, imagining the expression on the old harridan's face when he made his announcement. Looking superior he declared, "I *have* met him."

Since the three ladies had been privy to a blow-by-blow description of that meeting from Flora some time ago, they were to be congratulated on their expressions of surprise.

After a moment's pause, while Jeffery congratulated himself on the effect of his announcement, Cornelia demanded with just the correct amount of amazement in her voice, "And you've never said anything before now?"

"Oh, my," said Anne, her eyes very big and innocent, "how very exciting! When did you meet him?"

"Yes," murmured Emily, her skepticism striking the right note, "tell us when you met him." She took a sip of her tea.

Looking over the rim of her cup, she asked, "Was it recent? Why have you not told anyone?"

Ainsworth cleared his throat and murmured, "He mentioned it to me a few weeks ago."

Cornelia favored him with a glance that made him step back before returning her attention to Jeffery. "Please do tell us about your meeting with him," urged Cornelia. She fluttered her lashes and came as close to simpering as she dared. "You know how much we will appreciate hearing a gentleman's impression of him."

Jeffery shot her a suspicious look, but Cornelia kept her face perfectly composed. Airily, Jeffery said, "I met him a fortnight or so ago, while he was staying at The Crown."

Emily frowned. "But wasn't he ill when he was staying there? Surely, I remember Mrs. Gilbert saying something about the poor man being so sick he never left his room." Appearing as if something had occurred to her, she looked at him askance. "Oh, Jeffery, do not tell me," she protested, "that you were so determined to be the first to meet him that you forced yourself upon him while he was ill."

"I didn't *force* myself upon him," he replied through gritted teeth. Resentment scorched his breast. This was all *her* fault! If she'd been in her bedroom where she was supposed to have been when he checked that night, he wouldn't have had a damned uncomfortable ride through the storm to The Crown in search of her and burst into Lord Joslyn's private room. Wishing he'd never brought up the subject, Jeffery complained, "The fellow didn't impress me much and I do not understand why everyone is so eager to make his acquaintance."

"Then you're a bigger fool than you look," Cornelia said tartly. "Good gad, man! Use your head." Ticking the points off on her bony fingers, she said, "He's not married. He has an old and notable title. He's wealthy. He owns one of the largest, grandest estates in the area. No wonder every marriageable woman or those with marriageable daughters are dying to meet him." She smiled at Emily and Anne. "And just think our darlings have beaten them all to the march."

Emily and Anne looked at each other and then at Cornelia. "Uh, you're not suggesting that one of us would . . ." Emily began uneasily.

"Would make him a suitable bride?" asked Cornelia.

Liking the trend of the conversation, Jeffery perked up. If he could marry Anne off to Ainsworth and Emily to Lord Joslyn . . . He almost crowed aloud in delight. The Birches would be his without the pesky presence of these wretched females. Even Cornelia would be gone—she would go live with either Emily or Anne or . . . or, he thought viciously, she'd suffer a fatal fall down the main staircase if he had to push her himself.

"Excellent idea!" Jeffery said. Smiling benignly at Emily, he said, "You'd make an outstanding viscountess, my dear— and just think how proud such an honor would have made your father."

Emily glowered at him. She knew precisely what he was thinking—force Anne into marriage with Ainsworth and then, somehow engineer her own marriage to Lord Joslyn. Remembering her reaction to Lord Joslyn when he had entered the morning room at Windmere, an odd sensation rippled through her at the idea of being married to him. It wasn't an unpleasant sensation, but neither was it pleasant. Mostly, she decided, it was unsettling . . . and perhaps, just a trifle exciting?

Ignoring the flutter in her stomach, Emily said, "What utter nonsense! I wish Lord Joslyn well in the marriage stakes, but I am *not* in the running!"

Standing up, she shook her gown and remarked, "And now, if no one minds, I am for bed. It has been a long and tiring day."

"Indeed it has," agreed Anne, rising gracefully to her feet, following Emily's lead. She smiled at the gentlemen. "The hour is late and I'm sure you gentlemen understand."

Cornelia gave a cackle of laughter. "Don't matter if they do. Townsend women always do as they please." She rose from her chair and her cane thumped on the floor as she limped to the door.

Before Jeffery or Ainsworth could protest, the three women were out of the room and gone.

Left alone, Ainsworth stared hard at Jeffery. "I would remind you," Ainsworth said in a cold tone, "that time is running out. If I do not have a bride in less than two months, I shall lose a large fortune and your vowels that I hold will come due and you will lose the tidy sum I have promised you." His expression ugly, he said, "My time here so far has been wasted. I could have looked elsewhere and I could have made arrangements with someone else, but you swore I'd have my bride."

"It ain't my fault you haven't settled things with the little widow," Jeffery argued. "You're a man of the world—you can't expect me to do your courting for you."

"But I can hardly court the charming Mrs. Townsend if she is never around," Ainsworth snapped. "I have done my damnedest but that long Meg cousin of yours or that old witch is always hovering around her." Accusingly he said, "You've been telling me for weeks that you would arrange everything, but so far I have seen no progress."

"I can hardly seduce her for you!"

"I can do my own seducing," Ainsworth drawled, "but you need to create the opportunity when I *can* seduce her." He glanced around the room and sniffed. "With servants always popping in and out and your female relatives nearly inseparable, it is hardly likely to happen anywhere in this house. I need time alone with the lady to accomplish my, ah, seduction."

Jeffery would not meet his gaze, knowing full well that

they were not talking about seduction but rape. He hadn't wanted it to come to that, but Anne's persistent repulsion of Ainsworth's advances made it clear that she wanted nothing to do with him and had left them with no other choice.

Thank God, Jeffery thought, that Ainsworth's choice had fallen upon his uncle's widow and not that termagant, Emily. It boggled the mind imagining Emily's reaction to, er, forced seduction. She'd not submit tamely and Jeffery wasn't positive that even facing ruin that she wouldn't spurn Ainsworth's offer of marriage. He shuddered. Emily was far more likely to go after Ainsworth with a knife, but Anne . . .

Anne was a sweet thing and once Ainsworth had compromised her, there was no question in Jeffery's mind that she'd meekly marry her seducer. Guessing correctly that Emily would not be to Ainsworth's liking, despite having offered his friend his choice of the two women, from the beginning he'd assumed that Anne would suit Ainsworth's purpose beautifully. Really, it was a pity, he decided, that Ainsworth had not caught Anne's fancy. It would have made things so much simpler for him. He sighed, resigned to it, but not happy about his part in arranging for Ainsworth to thoroughly compromise his uncle's widow. But needs must when the devil drives, he reminded himself self-righteously. He desperately needed Ainsworth to return those ruinous vowels he'd so foolishly offered after a night of drunken gambling, and as vital, if he was to bring himself about and get out of dun territory, he must have the other money his friend had promised him.

Staring down at his glass of port, Jeffery said, "It can't be at the house."

"I know that, you fool!" Ainsworth's fist banged on the mantel. "I am not familiar with the area. You are. Surely, you know of some place I can be private with her long enough . . ." He smiled, his gray eyes cold and calculating, "Long enough to accomplish my task."

"I know of a place," Jeffery admitted. He cleared his throat. "I've used it upon occasion myself. There's a deliciously willing little widow in the village who visits me there from time to time."

At Ainsworth's look of interest, Jeffery said, "It's a small, comfortable farmhouse on the outskirts of the village. Kelsey's woman, Rosie, from The Ram's Head keeps it clean and stocked for me . . . and she's discreet."

Ainsworth frowned. "How near the village? It must be private. . . ." An unpleasant smile crossed his lips. "I'm sure the lady will protest, perhaps loudly, and I do not want any interruptions."

"You have nothing to worry about," Jeffery assured him. "The house is a mile or so from the edge of the village and sits a good half mile back from the road. In fact, if you didn't know the house was there, you'd ride right past it. The driveway leading to it is partially overgrown and hedges and trees surround the house itself. There's even a stable at the rear where you can hide your horse and vehicle." Uncomfortable, Jeffery muttered, "You don't have to worry that you'll be disturbed."

"Excellent," said Ainsworth, rubbing his hands together. "How soon can you make arrangements?"

Within a few minutes a plan was arranged.

"It's a shame that you let Kelsey go," said Ainsworth as the two men prepared to leave the room and adjourn to the gaming room at the rear of the house. "He might have been of help to us—certainly we cannot rely on any of the other servants—not even our valets."

"I didn't have any choice," Jeffery growled, resentment again stirring in his breast. "Cornelia forced my hand." Bitterly, he added, "But it is Kelsey's own fault. I warned him not to overstep his bounds with Anne, but he ignored me."

"She is a tempting armful, isn't she?" Ainsworth said as they strolled down the hall, passing Walker as they did so.

Blind to the butler, as he was to servants in general, Ainsworth murmured, "I quite look forward to furthering my acquaintance with your uncle's widow." He laughed low. "Especially without interruption—I'm relying on you to arrange it, my dear friend." His voice hardened. "I'm not wasting any more time. Willing or not, I will be married to her within a fortnight or it will go ill for you."

Walker didn't hear Jeffery's reply, but his expression was alarmed as he entered the blue room and gathered up the tea tray and the various glasses and cups and saucers scattered about. Returning to the kitchen where Mrs. Spalding was busy putting some dough near the small fire to rise in time to bake fresh bread in the morning, he set down the tray and said, "I fear that Master Jeffery and Mr. Ainsworth are up to no good."

The few other servants still employed at The Birches had gone to bed and it was only the two of them in the pleasant kitchen. While not related, the butler and the cook had been in service with the Townsend family since they were children, both of them stepping into positions once held by their parents.

They were easy in each other's company and spoke freely to one another. Wiping her hands on her flour-dusted apron, Mrs. Spalding snorted. "If you ask me, those two are always up to no good! A more disreputable pair, I've never met. The old squire would roll over in his grave if he knew the sort of riffraff Master Jeffery invites here these days." She shook her head. "We've known Master Jeffery since a boy and I don't know about you, but he's never been a favorite of mine—nor the old squire's I might add. That boy was always into trouble and then whining and blaming everyone else when caught doing something he shouldn't." Her face softened. "Now his brother, young Master Hugh—as different as cheese is to chalk." She sighed. "It's a shame that Master Hugh didn't inherit—how different things would be."

Walker nodded unhappily. "I agree. If Master Hugh was here, even the master wouldn't dare allow Ainsworth to act so outrageously around the ladies."

"That's not likely to happen. Master Jeffery doesn't want him around and unfortunately, The Birches is his and he can say who comes and who goes."

When Walker continued to look worried, Mrs. Spalding cocked a brow and asked, "Is there something specific that has you concerned?"

Walker related the bit of conversation he'd overheard as he had passed the two men in the hall.

Her lips pursed, Mrs. Spalding admitted, "I don't like the sound of that at all." Moving efficiently about her kitchen as she put away a few items, she said, "You talk to Miss Emily or Miss Cornelia in the morning. They'll warn the missus to be careful and they'll be on the lookout for any tricks."

Walker nodded, relieved that Mrs. Spalding agreed with him.

Walker waited impatiently the next morning for the ladies to descend from the upper reaches of the house. Knowing the gentlemen had imbibed heavily the night before as was their wont, and that they'd not gone to bed until the hour had struck four, he felt confident that Mrs. Townsend was safe— for the moment. Still, he breathed a sigh of relief when the three ladies came down the stairs and entered the slightly shabby, but dearly familiar breakfast room.

He allowed the ladies to serve themselves from the old oak sideboard and settle around the table, before he spoke. He gave a polite cough and when the three women looked at him, he murmured, "You know it is not my habit to gossip or spy, but I overheard a bit of conversation between the two gentlemen last night that I feel you must know."

"Spill it," barked Cornelia, setting down her cup of coffee

and staring hard at the butler. She'd known Walker all his life
and his father before him and knew that something important must have occurred for him to break protocol.

"What is it, Walker?" Emily asked softly, anxiety seizing
her. "Is it something to do with the . . . uh, our business
arrangement? Has Jeffery discovered what we are about?"

Walker was one of the investors in their smuggling oper-
ations and he knew precisely what she meant by "business
arrangement." Walker smiled fondly at her, but his smile
faded almost as quickly as it had appeared. His face somber,
he said, "No, miss. It has nothing to do with our business."
He glanced at Anne who was watching him as closely as the
other women. Apologetically, he said, "I fear that Master Jeffery and Mr. Ainsworth have some evil plan for Mrs.
Townsend." Succinctly, he told them what he had heard as he
had passed the two men in the hallway.

None of the women needed explained to them what Jeffery and Ainsworth planned if they meant to force Anne into
marriage with Ainsworth.

"Those devils!" Emily exclaimed, her eyes nearly silver
with fury.

Anne's face was white with fear and her fingers shook as
she set down her cup of coffee. "You think they mean to kid-
nap me and . . ." Her throat closed up, she could not say the
ugly words aloud.

"Mean to compromise you one way or another," said Cornelia, looking older and wearier than Emily or Anne had
ever seen her.

Walker nodded unhappily. "Yes, this is what I fear." He
tried to smile reassuringly at Anne as he said, "We shall keep
you safe. Mrs. Spalding, Jane, Sally and the other servants
we can trust will see to it that you are never alone."

It was some comfort, but they all knew that keeping Anne
continually under surveillance was going to be nearly impossible. Despite their loyalty to Emily, Anne and Cornelia,

Jeffery had to be obeyed unless they wished to lose their positions and there were dozens of ways he could arrange for many of the servants that remained at The Birches to be away from the house. There were always errands to be run; trips to the village for supplies and the like. Even with the servants on her side, Anne's best hope lay with Cornelia's eagle eye and Emily's fierce presence.

Emily touched Anne's hand. "We will protect you."

Anne took a deep breath. "I know you will." She smiled wanly at Walker. "And I know that you and the others will do your best." Her shoulders straightened and she said, "We will all be on our guard . . . and pray that we can outwit these scoundrels."

After Walker bowed and walked from the room, it was a very quiet trio of ladies who sat around the breakfast table. No one had any appetite, and after nibbling at a piece of toast, Emily pushed it away.

Her expression dangerous, she swore, "By God! This is intolerable! Anne is being driven to slaughter like any lamb and we are near helpless to prevent it." Emily had never resented her sex more than she did at this moment, and tears of frustration and fury filled her eyes. "Oh, if only I had been born a man! My dreadful cousin would never have inherited and we'd not be on the brink of ruin."

"No use repining for what cannot be," said Cornelia, her gaze soft as it rested on Emily's tight features. "Don't fret, my pet, we will plan our defenses and we will come about— even if I have to stab Ainsworth with a carving knife where it will do the most good."

Both Anne and Emily chuckled weakly. "And if you don't," Emily said, "then I shall." Her eyes darkened. "And Jeffery, while I am at it."

Since no one had any appetite, the three ladies left the breakfast room a few minutes later. Anne and Emily retired to the small room off the kitchen that Emily had taken over as her office to go over the depressing account books. Usually, Cornelia returned upstairs to her room to write or answer some letters from her network of far-flung friends. This morning, however, upon reaching her rooms, she rang for Walker.

He arrived a few minutes later to find Cornelia settled behind her cherrywood desk, ink nearby, a sheet of paper before her and quill in hand.

"How soon," she asked bluntly, as soon as the butler shut the door behind him, "do you think we have before they strike?"

Walker shrugged, helpless. "Ainsworth mentioned marriage within a fortnight."

"Or it would go ill for Jeffery . . ." Cornelia muttered. "I wonder what that lecher has on that twit? Jeffery is a weak fool but I've never known him to be vicious." She brooded over Jeffery's deficiencies a moment before unknowingly repeating Mrs. Spalding's words of the previous evening, "If only Hugh had inherited! Now there's a fine young man!"

Walker didn't disagree, but there was nothing to be gained from speculation about how different everything would be if Hugh had been the elder brother instead of the younger. Dismissing the butler, Cornelia said, "I would not normally ask you or any of our servants to spy . . . but in this case, I would urge you to keep your eyes and ears open—Mrs. Townsend's safety will depend upon it."

Walker nodded grimly and left. Alone in her room once again, Cornelia stared out the window for a long time. The day was gray and gloomy and fit her mood perfectly, she thought sourly.

She didn't like growing old, she admitted, but she had never chafed against it, nor felt as weak and helpless as she did now. She was an old woman. Old and useless. Pushing aside her descent into pity, she considered how best to save the two people that meant the most to her in the world. No matter the cost. It didn't matter what happened to her—her time had come and gone. Cornelia grinned. And by gad! She'd *lived*. But Emily and Anne . . . Her smile faded and she scowled. If that damned nephew of hers had been a better father and a better husband, Emily would be happily married now and Anne would have had a child or two (if the squire had stayed home from the hunt long enough) and one of them might have been a boy. An heir.

Fiddling with the quill, she sighed. The previous squire hadn't been a bad father or a terrible husband, she conceded, just an indifferent one. With her prodding, he'd seen that Emily was launched into society and he'd rented a fine town house and spent lavishly on Emily's wardrobe for not one but two Seasons in London. Emily had been just seventeen that first Season, but even then, her great-niece had decided notions about the character of any man who might wish to marry her. None of her suitors, and there had been more than one young man and an old roue or two who had been enchanted by the fair-haired, gray-eyed slender beauty, that first year or the second had aroused anything but amusement or contempt in her breast.

Always spirited and strong-willed, and Cornelia admitted guiltily that she was as much to blame for that as her father's indulgence, when they'd come home from London after that second Season, Emily had announced that she would not endure being paraded through London like a prize filly again. There would be no third Season for her. Cornelia had been appalled, but nothing she could say swayed Emily. Her heart heavy, she resigned herself to the knowledge her lovely girl would die a spinster, knowing that if several eligible London bachelors found no favor with Emily, it was unlikely that she'd find a match buried in the country. Shortly afterward the squire had gone looking for his own bride.

Cornelia's wrinkled face softened. Dear sweet little Anne. She'd forgiven her nephew long ago for springing an unknown bride on them and she could not love Anne any more than she did Emily or a daughter of her own. They *are* my daughters, she thought fiercely, and I will move heaven and earth to save them.

If only that dratted Jeffery weren't such a buffle-headed coxcomb! Or more like his younger brother, Hugh . . . If he knew what his brother was up to, welcome or not, he'd be on the steps of The Birches before the cat could lick her ear. Hugh would send that obnoxious Ainsworth packing and most likely give Jeffery a sound thrashing. . . .

An arrested expression on her face, she stared down at the paper before her. Hugh . . . Hmmm . . . A gleeful smile on her lips, she began to write.

Chapter 8

The day was tense, but to everyone's relief, when Jeffery and Ainsworth arose late in the afternoon, the two men departed almost immediately for The Ram's Head—Jeffery's favorite haunt. The Crown was too staid and respectable for him.

Emily was convinced the gentlemen had left to set in motion their nefarious scheme, and not for the first time she wished they still had a house full of trusted servants—she wouldn't have thought twice about sending one to spy on her cousin and his friend. Anne's future was at stake and Emily wasn't the least bit squeamish about the methods used to keep her safe.

The gentlemen gone, the three ladies retired to Cornelia's bedroom to discuss the situation.

"Night is most likely when they'll strike," Cornelia said. She banged her cane on the floor in frustration. "By God, if only I were younger!" Glancing at Emily she said, "Most of the responsibility falls on you, and certainly it will be best if you are the one to be with Anne at night." Her lips twisted. "I sleep too soundly and I would be of little use in a fight." She smiled bitterly and thumped her cane on the floor again. "I could get in a good blow or two, but that would only delay them for a few minutes."

Her pretty face distressed, Anne said, "Oh, Cornelia, do not blame yourself! Just knowing you are near is a comfort to me and I'm sure your cane would prove an able weapon." She smiled shakily. "I confess I'm relieved that Emily will be with me tonight—I wouldn't be able to sleep a wink if I was alone in my room."

"I don't think we should sleep in your room," said Emily. "That's the first place they'd look for you." She sighed. "I'm afraid that until the danger is passed that you and I shall be sharing my room."

"Which means we should move as many of her things as we can into yours this afternoon while the cowards are gone," said Cornelia.

"But won't they be suspicious when they learn I have moved in with Emily?"

Cornelia snorted. "Don't intend to tell them. The servants won't give away the change and the only way they will discover you are not asleep like a little lamb in your own bed will be if they come to your room—where they have no business being."

"They'll know we're on to them if they are bold enough to attempt to snatch you from your bed," Emily admitted. "But finding your room empty will disrupt their plans—and give us more time."

They had no illusions about the precariousness of the situation. The servants would help, but Anne's best protection lay with Emily and Cornelia, with most of the responsibility for keeping Anne safe falling on Emily.

Her face grim, Emily rose to her feet. "I'll speak with Sally and Walker. We need to get your belongings moved to my room as soon as possible."

Walker and Mrs. Spalding already knew what was afoot and, with Emily's consent, the two senior servants had shared that information with the remaining trusted members of the household staff.

The presence of Jeffery's and Ainsworth's valets presented a problem. Despite Jeffery's and Ainsworth's rooms being in another wing of the house, Emily worried that one of the valets might stumble across them in the midst of the move. The two valets were both strangers and Londoners and had not proven any more popular with the inhabitants of The Birches than their masters. It must be assumed, Emily warned everyone, that either man would betray them in a flash.

"The last thing we want," she said to Walker, "is for one of them to discover what we are about and carry tales back to Jeffery or Ainsworth." Emily nibbled her lip. "We'll have to have someone keep an eye on them," she said, "while we're moving Anne's belongings."

Luck was with them—both the valets had been given the afternoon off and not a half hour after their masters had ridden away, the two valets departed.

The coast clear, everyone sprang into action, with Agatha, Cornelia's longtime maid, remaining downstairs to sound the alarm should the gentlemen or their valets return. Despite the small number of willing hands, within a matter of hours, Anne's belongings, including a large, unwieldy mahogany wardrobe and a tall chest of drawers, were moved down the hall from her room and into Emily's. The heavy work completed, except for Sally, the other servants hurried back to their duties.

As Anne folded and put away some of her things in the chest of drawers shoved against the wall next to a similar chest that Emily used, she said, "Thank goodness, everything is moved. I was terrified the whole time. How could we have explained what we were about if we had been discovered?"

Helping Sally hang a few of Anne's gowns in the wardrobe, Emily said over her shoulder, "Don't think about it. It didn't happen and that's the main thing."

Cornelia nodded. "No doubt about it—fate was—"

The opening of the door halted her words and all four women turned alarmed faces in that direction. There was a general sigh of relief when they realized that it was only Agatha.

Aware her sudden appearance had startled everyone, Agatha slipped around the door and into the room and murmured, "Oh, my, I am so sorry for giving everyone a fright." Shutting the door behind her, she added, "With everything that is going on, I simply forgot to knock."

Agatha Colby had served Cornelia for forty of her fifty-eight years and over that time had evolved from personal maid to trusted companion. She was a slight woman with gentle blue eyes and dark hair now liberally frosted with silver. There were no secrets within the Townsend family that she wasn't privy to and her loyalty to the family was as fierce as it was quiet.

"Don't give it a thought," Emily said, her gaze on the door. "You just revealed a precaution we should have taken." Handing the yellow frock in her hands to Sally, she crossed the room and carefully turned the key in the lock. Looking back at the others, she said, "From now on this door is to be kept locked—it may provide only a moment's warning, but we'll need it."

Only the ladies were at dinner that night and they spent a strained evening starting at every sound and bracing for Jeffery's and Ainsworth's return. As the hour grew late, there was no sign of the gentlemen and grateful for the reprieve, the ladies retired for the night.

Bidding good night to Cornelia, Emily and Anne disappeared into Emily's bedroom, Emily locking the door behind them. Not satisfied with that, she grabbed a small chair and wedged it under the doorknob.

Anne stared at the chair for a long moment, then sighed and, picking up her nightgown, disappeared behind the blue silk dressing screen in one corner of the room.

Listening to the rustle of Anne's clothes as she changed into her nightgown, Emily prowled about the changed confines of her room. She smiled as she took in the added pieces of furniture standing cheek by jowl against the wall. The space was crowded, but at least they didn't have to climb over furniture to get to the door.

Though she was pleased with this afternoon's work, she knew the precautions they had taken were only a temporary measure. The only advantage they had was that they knew what Jeffery and Ainsworth were up to—but not the how or the when. She stopped, struck by a thought. Ainsworth had to have his bride by a certain date and if they could keep Anne safe until after that date . . . If they could spirit Anne away and hide her until it was too late . . .

Because she had never considered they'd be in this predicament, Emily hadn't paid attention to the actual date by which Ainsworth must have his bride and she resolved to find out that vital bit of information tomorrow. Cornelia would know.

Anne appeared from behind the screen and Emily took her place, quickly stripping off her gown and scrambling into her nightclothes. Still considering the idea of hiding Anne she walked over to the bed.

Looking terrified, Anne wrung her hands together. "I am such a silly goose! I know that I am safe with you, but oh, Emily, I cannot help being frightened." She looked beseechingly at her. In a voice filled with horror, she asked, "What if they break down the door?"

A savage smile curved Emily's mouth. From beneath the folds of her nightgown, she brought forth a pistol. "Well, then, we'll see how they like finding this shoved up their noses."

Tuesday morning dawned bright and clear and cold. Following their routine, the three ladies met in the breakfast room for a light breakfast.

After greeting Cornelia and dropping a kiss on her forehead, Emily asked, "Do you know the exact date that Ainsworth must be married or lose his fortune?"

"March first," Cornelia said. "Why?"

"Because it tells us how long we have to keep Anne out of his clutches."

"That's nearly six weeks away," Anne said woefully. "A very long time."

Walker entered with a bowl of piping hot scones right from the oven and Emily asked him, "What time did my cousin and his friend come home last night?"

"The gentlemen haven't returned yet," Walker replied, "but the valets are back and upstairs in their rooms."

Walker departed and the three ladies stared uneasily at each other.

"I do not know how I am to pretend that all is well," Anne said, "when I am frightened to death. How are we to act normally for the next six weeks?"

Emily leaned forward, her gaze intent. "There is a solution. You must go away."

Her voice quivering, Anne asked, "You are throwing me out?"

"Don't be a goose!" Emily said. "I mean that we have to find a safe place for you to stay until after the first of March. Someplace where Jeffery won't think to look for you or a place from which he wouldn't dare try to abduct you."

Anne's face cleared. "Of course!" Her expression fell. "But where?" she asked anxiously, her big brown eyes fixed on Emily's face. "My parents are dead. I have no brothers or sisters. You and Cornelia are my family—there is no one else." Looking even more miserable she added, "How will I live? Thanks to Jeffery, I have very little money of my own . . . and what we receive from the, uh, um, you know."

Anne's "you know" referred to the smuggling profits, and those, Emily thought bitterly, were erratic and never a sure thing. "I have to think about it," she muttered.

A few hours later, Emily was still brooding over where to hide Anne and how to finance it, when Walker found the three ladies in the blue sitting room. Handing Emily a note, he said, "Sam just delivered this from Mrs. Gilbert."

After quickly reading the note, Emily looked up. "I must go to The Crown. Our, ah, friend, has returned from London with, um, gossip that I should hear."

Everyone knew precisely what she meant. The contraband goods had been safely delivered and sold in London and it was time to discover how well they had done and divide the profits.

A scant half hour later, garbed in a decade-old sapphire riding habit adorned with gold braid, Emily was riding to the village. She was hatless, but her moonlit-fair hair was caught up in a black snood at the back of her head and the cold brought roses to her cheeks and a sparkle to her gray eyes. For late January the day was almost pleasant, but she was glad of her black leather gloves and the warmth of the heavy velvet riding habit.

Surreptitiously she approached the inn, halting her horse when she reached the stables where Caleb waited for her. He helped her from her horse.

Smiling, Caleb said, "You know where to go. Go ahead. I'll hide the mare away and join you in a few minutes."

Emily hurried across the area that divided the inn from the stables and slipped inside the back door. Mary was there to greet her. "Ma and the others are waiting for you," she said, waving an arm in the direction of the private sitting room Mrs. Gilbert kept for family and friends.

Almost as familiar with the inn as her own home, Emily walked quickly down the hallway to the rear of the building. After giving a warning rap on the door, she opened the door and stepped inside.

It was a friendly sort of room. Large enough to hold several people easily with whitewashed walls and golden oak floors. A faded amber-and-brown woolen rug covered the floor in the center of the room and a fire burned in the brick fireplace. Crisp cream-and-green calico curtains draped the brace of windows that overlooked the herb-and-vegetable garden at the side of the inn. In the center of the room was a big table with several wooden chairs placed around it. Overstuffed chairs selected for comfort rather than style, a pair of small unremarkable tables and a massive gothic cabinet across from the fireplace comprised the rest of the furnishings.

The inhabitants were gathered around the big table and Emily joined them. Taking the seat they'd left for her at the head of the table, she smiled warmly at everyone.

Except for Caleb, the people seated around the table represented Emily's intrepid band of investors. It had been to these people that she had turned when she had first conceived her desperate scheme.

Mrs. Gilbert had been the first person Emily had solicited to join her in the dangerous venture. Mrs. Gilbert hadn't hesitated. Emily had barely laid out her proposal and Mrs. Gilbert was in. Her husband's death, suspected at the hands of the Nolles gang and the harassment of her clients by the Nolles gang, had pushed her to a precarious position. Without the money earned from the smuggling, she would have lost the inn and she and her five daughters would have been homeless.

Jeb Brown had been essential to the scheme and once he

was on board, Emily and Mrs. Gilbert had looked around for other possible investors.

Emily's eyes rested on the worn features of little Miss Martha Webber and her widowed sister, Mrs. Gant. Once Miss Webber had been a needlewoman much in demand, but age had twisted her once nimble fingers and she had fallen on hard times. She and Mrs. Gant lived together, barely scraping by, taking in wash and whatever chores the two old women could still do. Emily had hesitated to approach them, but Mrs. Gilbert had urged her to do so. "They're worse off than I am," Mrs. Gilbert had said. "I know that Martha and her sister don't have much between the pair of them, but I suspect they'd be willing to risk a few pounds. Ask them." Emily had and Miss Webber and Mrs. Gant had eagerly added their mite.

Mrs. Goodson, the widow of a laborer left to fend for herself with a family of starving children, had followed Miss Webber and Mrs. Gant. James Ford, the shoemaker, and Caleb Gates, the blacksmith, had been drawn in next. Mr. Meek, a retired law clerk, had been the last to join the investors.

Mr. Meek had been an excellent addition to their little group. He kept the account books and traveled with the goods to London and oversaw the selling of the contraband to the eager buyers.

Being novices they'd made some mistakes in the beginning—fortunately none that had put an end to their risky enterprise. It had taken time for Jeb to make contacts in France that could be trusted to give them good value for their investments and not cheat them. The same was true for Mr. Meek when he had first attempted to market the contraband in London. These days there were several shopkeepers in London who bought regularly from them and a trio of tavern owners who purchased any spirits they smuggled into the country. For the past two years or so the little group had been making steady profit.

Caleb joined them and Mr. Meek cleared his throat and reported, "We made our best profit yet on this last run—which was also our largest to date." Looking over his round spectacles perched at the end of his nose, he declared happily, "And some of our clients have already placed orders for our next run. There is a demand for silk, net and French point lace from one of the dressmakers and as usual, our tavern owners have indicated they would take any and all brandy we can transport to London."

Mr. Meek brought forth a plump leather bag and over the next few minutes the chink of coins could be heard as he dispersed the contents. Counting out the coins before Emily, he added, "Before you is proof of just how splendidly we did." He set a small bag beside the coins and murmured, "And here is everyone's share for the next shipment. Keep it safe."

Emily nodded, and put the bag, which had a nice feel to it, in the deep pocket of her riding habit. From the beginning, she had been the banker and from every run, they'd kept out a portion of the profits, when there was a profit, to pay for the next trip to France to buy contraband goods. She hid it, along with her own profit, in a false baseboard in her bedroom at home.

The bag filled with money for the next run already forgotten, Emily looked at the remaining pile of coins before her and the knot of anxiety that seemed her constant companion loosened. Mrs. Spalding and Walker and the other servants would be paid a bit more this quarter than the paltry sum Jeffery deemed adequate. The old stableman, Hutton, so unfairly let go when Jeffery had hired Kelsey, wouldn't be penniless and the head shepherd, Loren, would be able to hire a few men to help him during the height of the lambing season—not far off. And Anne . . . Emily eyed the coins, wondering if salvation wasn't piled right in front of her.

"Another storm should be blowing up before much longer," Jeb said slowly, interrupting Emily's thoughts. "Might

be a good time for me to make another run to Calais. I can fill
our orders and then wait for a storm to return."

During the storms that lashed the coast, most of the revenue officers would be found huddled inside, nursing a tankard of ale near the fire. Though dangerous, stormy weather
gave the smugglers their best chance for a run and to move
their goods inland unobserved and unhindered. They routinely braved the raging waves of the Channel to bring their
contraband from the French ports of Calais or Boulogne to
England.

It was agreed that Jeb should prepare for another run and
after a few minutes the group dispersed, leaving Emily and
Mrs. Gilbert alone.

Eyes narrowed, Mrs. Gilbert studied Emily. Despite the
charming flush in Emily's cheeks and the jeweled clarity of
her eyes, it was obvious something was preying on her mind.
Having nursed Emily at her breast, there wasn't much the
younger woman could hide from her and Mrs. Gilbert asked,
"What is wrong? And don't fob me off with some silly tale
that you ate something that disagreed with you."

Emily hesitated only a moment before telling of the danger to Anne.

Mrs. Gilbert sighed. "Your poor father would turn over in
his grave if he knew what a scoundrel that cousin of yours is.
We shall help you in any way that we can—just say the word
and we shall descend upon The Birches armed with only
brooms and mops if necessary."

Emily choked up at her words, touched by the generous
loyalty. "I know," she said when she had command of herself.

Flora, her eyes bright with excitement, stuck her head
around the door and exclaimed, "Ma, Lord Joslyn is here!
Coo! His manservant, Lamb, is with him."

Ignoring the flutter in her stomach at the mention of Lord
Joslyn's name, Emily rose to her feet. Pouring her share of

the profits into a small silk bag and placing it in her opposite pocket, she said, "I must be off." She grinned at Mrs. Gilbert. "Go see to your distinguished guest. Who knows? Perhaps his patronage will tear clients away from The Ram's Head and bring them to your door."

Mrs. Gilbert smiled back at her. "Perhaps, you are right. Run along with you now . . ." Slyly she added, "Unless of course, you'd like to see Lord Joslyn yourself?"

The faintest shade of pink bloomed in her cheeks, but Emily shook her head. "No. My stepmother and great-aunt will be anxious to hear Mr. Meek's news."

Hurrying through the kitchen to the back door of the inn, Emily was waylaid by Molly and Harriet, both in a dither over Lord Joslyn's presence. "Oh, miss," cried Harriet, at eighteen, the next to youngest daughter, "did you know that Lord Joslyn is here? And his man, Lamb?" Pretty face full of mischief, she added, "Now that Mr. Lamb is the handsomest man I've ever seen—I wouldn't mind a tumble with him."

Molly fluttered her lashes. "I may be a happily married woman, but I can tell you that just one look from Lord Joslyn and I came near to swooning."

Despite her problems, Emily laughed. Molly was madly in love with her sailor husband and Harriet had been keeping company with a young farmer she was besotted about— everyone expected a wedding before too many more months went by.

"Shame on the pair of you!" Emily teased. "What would your Billy say?" she asked Molly. "And would you," she said, pointing a finger at Harriet, "throw away Hampton's heart for a brief romp?"

Molly smiled and Harriet giggled.

The kitchen was warm and cozy and the Gilbert daughters were hard to get away from, and it was several minutes later before Emily was able to leave.

Halfway across the muddy yard she heard someone say

her name. Turning a startled face in the direction of the voice, her heart unaccountably leapt when she recognized the big man leading his horse around the corner of the inn. Lord Joslyn.

She smiled politely and said, "Milord! I did not expect to see you here."

Leading his horse, Barnaby strolled up to her. "That's probably," he said with a smile, "because you have a habit of slipping away at the first opportunity."

Her chin lifted and a belligerent sparkle in her eyes, she said, "I do not know what you are talking about."

"What a rapper! But I'm too much a gentleman to argue with a lady."

"Thank goodness for that," Emily muttered, not certain whether to be pleased or offended when he laughed. Edging toward the stables, she added, "Now if you will excuse me, I must be on my way."

"Yes, I know. Mrs. Gilbert mentioned something to that effect."

Her head whipped around. "Mrs. Gilbert told you I was here?" she demanded incredulously.

He nodded. "Yes." Eyes twinkling, he added, "And she suggested that since you were unescorted that I might do nicely as your groom."

Torn between amusement and embarrassment at Mrs. Gilbert's flagrant matchmaking, Emily set off with determined strides toward the stables. "I appreciate your offer," she said politely, "but I have no need of a groom—I have roamed this countryside all my life and I'm quite capable of finding my way home by myself."

"And leave me to face Mrs. Gilbert with my mission unaccomplished?" Barnaby asked in tones of horror.

Emily fought back the laugh that bubbled up in her throat and walked faster. The man was irrepressible and handsome and attractive and she feared that with very little effort he could charm her into acting like a foolish green girl. And she wasn't about to let that happen, she reminded herself. She had too many people dependent upon her to lose her head over Lord Joslyn.

Caleb had heard their voices and appeared in the doorway of the stable with her horse. Relieved that the creaking of the saddle and the rattle of her horse's bit covered the muted clink of the coins concealed on her person, a moment later, Emily was mounted and with Barnaby riding by her side was on her way home.

As the inn receded behind them, Emily asked, "Your man, Lamb? Where is he?"

"Ah, so you *did* know I was there," he commented, watching the delightful blush spread across her cheeks.

"As I was leaving one of the Gilberts may have mentioned it," she mumbled, keeping her gaze fixed between her horse's ears and damning herself for the slip.

"Yes, I'm sure they did," Barnaby agreed. "As for Lamb, he is a great favorite amongst the females—of any age—and I left him charming Mrs. Gilbert and Faith."

Seeking a polite topic of conversation, Emily inquired, "Are your cousins still visiting at Windmere?"

"Yes. Mathew has been manfully suppressing the urge to murder me in order to step into my shoes; Tom has been annoying both myself and Simon by echoing Mathew's pronouncements and Simon continues to throw the cat amongst the pigeons to see what will result." He shook his head, a smile lurking in his eyes. "I sought refuge at The Crown before I did one of them harm."

"Your presence at the inn will be a boon for Mrs. Gilbert," Emily said. "The Ram's Head has managed to, er, lure many of her clients away. Perhaps when they hear that Lord Joslyn patronizes The Crown some of them will return."

"I intended to sample the charms of The Ram's Head later this afternoon," Barnaby admitted. "But Lamb wanted to reacquaint himself with The Crown and Mrs. Gilbert and her daughters first."

Emily looked at him, astonished. "Do you usually allow your manservant to decide what you do?"

Barnaby laughed. "I've known Lamb all of my life and he is hard to persuade differently when his mind is made up."

"But he's your servant!"

"I wouldn't tell him that," he replied. "I'm quite certain he'd take great offense."

His reply baffled her. Lord Joslyn did not appear to be a man who allowed others to direct him, yet he had deferred his own plans because of the wishes of his manservant. She tried to envision Jeffery accommodating his valet, Bundy, in such a manner, or even her father changing his plans to suit one of his servants, *any* servant, but she could not. It was unthinkable, yet Lord Joslyn apparently had done just that and thought nothing of it.

She eyed him, noting the strong features, the firm chin and hard jaw, the powerful build. A big man, he sat his horse with a careless grace that she admired and she was, she admitted, far, far too aware of him in ways that alarmed her. Her gaze dropped down to the masculine hands holding the reins, a curious thrill racing through her as she remembered the warmth of those hands around her waist when he had tossed her into the buggy the other night.

Ignoring her silly reaction to him, she concluded that there was nothing about him that indicated a weak nature. Quite the contrary, he exuded strength and confidence and gave the impression that this was a man used to having his own way.

She looked up and realized he had been watching her as she studied him. Embarrassment flooded her and, jerking her eyes away from him, she babbled, "It's a lovely day for January, isn't it? Oh, you wouldn't know, would you—this is your first January in England. Is the weather here comparable to that in, in . . . Virginia, isn't it?"

Barnaby suppressed a laugh. She was enchanting—even when trying to keep him at a distance. He enjoyed fencing with her and seeing the vivid color come and go in that lovely face, and he had discovered that provoking that flash of temper in those long-lidded gray eyes delighted him. Emily Townsend amused, intrigued and fascinated him, and he suspected uneasily that she always would. And then there were all those fierce emotions she evoked within him, and that wasn't counting the allure of her long, supple, luscious body. . . . She was, he admitted, a great temptation to a man that had never thought to marry. . . .

Not quite certain what he was going to do about her, he followed her lead and said, "Virginia is warmer and perhaps not as wet as England."

Feeling on safer ground, Emily glanced at him. "Do you like it here?"

Barnaby shrugged. "I don't *dis*like it and as time goes by and I become more familiar with the land and the people, I assume that it will feel like home."

Emily steered the talk away from anything personal and kept the conversation firmly on neutral topics. Lord Joslyn seemed perfectly agreeable, but now and then she had the unsettling sensation that he knew precisely what she was doing and was laughing at her.

The ancient birches that marked the driveway and gave the house its name came into view and Emily barely suppressed a sigh of relief. Lord Joslyn aroused emotions she'd never felt before and she was having a difficult time dealing with them. Her heart was behaving in a most unseemly manner and she was experiencing all sorts of other strange physical reactions to his presence. Her entire body tingled, and when she risked a glance at his face, her gaze was irresistibly drawn to his mouth. . . . What would it be like to kiss him? she wondered. Or to feel those strong arms curl around her and crush her against that hard body . . . ? Unsettled by the trend of her thoughts, she was anxious to get away from him.

"We'll turn off the main road where you see those big birches," she said brightly, grateful that escape was close at hand. She cleared her throat. "You, um, don't have to escort me the whole way. I can ride alone from here."

"And deny me the pleasure of furthering my acquaintance with your charming stepmother and, perhaps, meeting your great-aunt, Cornelia?"

She pulled her horse to a stop. "Jeffery will most likely be there," she warned. "And no doubt will fawn all over you."

"Well, it'll certainly be a novel experience to have someone in your family appreciate me," Barnaby drawled, stopping his horse beside hers.

Emily's lips twitched but she managed not to laugh. This man confounded her. She wanted nothing to do with him, and yet . . .

Their horses were side by side, Barnaby's leg brushing against her. He bent forward, his hand capturing her chin. With his face only inches from hers, he said softly, "I promise to be on my best behavior."

As she fumbled for a reply, the angry sound of a shot exploded through the cold winter air. She jumped. "Now that was too close—" she began, only to stop in horror as blood gushed from Barnaby's head and he fell forward into her arms.

She struggled to hold him, but he was too heavy and he tumbled to the ground. Leaping from her horse, she sank to the muddy ground and cradled his head in her lap. Staring down at his bloodstained features, with shaking fingers, she gently touched his forehead. Merciful heavens, she thought wildly, someone just shot Lord Joslyn.

Chapter 9

Furious and frightened, Emily shouted, "Hold your fire, you fool! There are riders on the road."

Guessing the shot had been fired by a poacher, she didn't expect anyone to appear and as the seconds passed, the only sound she heard was the ghostly whisper of the freshening wind in the bare branches of a nearby scraggly stand of trees. They were alone, she realized uneasily. Whoever had fired that shot had vanished. No one was coming to help them.

Her gaze dropped to Barnaby's bloodied head and anguish ripped through her. Was he dead? Please dear God, no! Her heart thumping in her breast, Emily examined him, almost bursting into tears when she realized that he was alive. She couldn't determine how dangerous the wound was, but two things were clear: he was alive and he needed a physician.

She gnawed her lip, looking around. The Birches was over a mile away but she dared not leave him here alone. This wasn't a main road and traffic was never heavy, and late on a winter afternoon the possibility of a farmer or even a servant on an errand coming along was unlikely.

The day was fleeing, the air growing colder by the minute and aware she was wasting time, Emily reluctantly laid his head down and staggered to her feet. She glanced frantically around for the horses: without the horses there would be no hope of moving Lord Joslyn or of her riding for help.

The animals had not gone far and she quickly caught them up and tied them to a pair of saplings at the edge of the road. Hurrying back to where Barnaby lay so still and pale, she struggled to drag him out of the mud to the grassy verge adjacent to the road. She was strong for a woman, but he was a big man and she despaired of being able to move him. Yet inch by precious inch she made progress until at last he was stretched out on the sparse brown grass, with the white flannel petticoat she'd worn beneath her habit tucked under his head.

He was still unconscious and that worried her more than anything else did. Staring down at him, she shivered in the wind, wondering at her next move. If he was awake, even wounded he would have been able to help her and she might have been able to get him on his horse, but that wasn't an option. The wound had bled copiously and that added to her anxiety. The severity of the damage done by the bullet had to be assessed by someone with more knowledge than she possessed and that meant a physician *had* to see him and soon.

Fighting panic, she bit her lip. How bad was the wound? It was still bleeding sluggishly. She looked around again. No one in sight. Her gaze swung back to him. She watched the rhythmic rise and fall of his chest and that encouraged her. Perhaps the wound wasn't serious. . . . She swallowed. There was only one way to find out.

Dropping to her knees beside him, after stripping off her gloves, she ripped off a small piece of the soft flannel petticoat and gingerly wiped away some of the blood. She worked cautiously, fearful of making a bad situation worse, and after she had removed most of the blood, she could see that the bullet had dug a deep furrow across the side of his head, the thick black hair hiding the extent of the wound. Her heart shook. The wound was serious, but if the bullet had been an inch or two lower . . .

With shaking fingers she caressed the lean cheek and the wide mouth. This man, this stranger, could so easily infuriate her and just as easily make her laugh. And with a desperation that surprised her, she wanted him awake, teasing and mocking her. Until this moment, she hadn't realized how much she looked forward to seeing him—even if he made her want to comb his hair with a stool! Lord Joslyn had become in some indefinable way, she admitted dazedly, vitally important to her. . . .

Fighting back tears and terror, she leaned forward and hissed in his ear, "Don't you dare die on me! I will never forgive you if you do!" She shook his shoulder. "Do you hear me? Don't you dare die!"

He remained motionless and, feeling silly, she lifted her head and went back to soaking up the blood that trickled from the wound. The bleeding appeared to be slowing and she took that as a good sign.

She cast an anxious glance up and down the road, her heart leaping when she saw a horseman riding in their direction. In one bound she was on her feet, and picking up the skirts of her riding habit she ran down the road toward the approaching horseman.

Still some distance from the horse and rider, she shouted, "Sir! Oh, please hurry! I beg you lend us assistance. Lord Joslyn has been shot. Come quickly!"

The man heard her words because he reacted instantly, kicking his horse into a gallop and nearly knocking Emily down as he sped by. Emily spun on her heels and stared astonished as the man, a stranger to her, sprang from his horse and knelt by Lord Joslyn's side.

"God damn you, Barnaby, I warned you to be careful,"

the newcomer snarled, confidently examining the wound. "But do you listen to me? Oh, no. Someone may be trying to kill you and you have to do things your way—and just look where the bloody hell it gets you. I've a mind to murder you myself."

His words alarmed Emily. Good God! Was the man mad? Was he about to do Lord Joslyn more harm? Ready to intervene, although what she could do against a brute this size escaped her, she ran back to Lord Joslyn's side. Seeing the gentleness of the big man's hands as they moved over Barnaby's head, the idea that he meant Lord Joslyn harm vanished. She knelt beside the stranger, only to gasp when she looked into his face. His resemblance to the members of the Joslyn family was stunning, but he was no Joslyn she had ever met. It occurred to her that this impressively big and exceedingly handsome man looked more a Joslyn than Lord Joslyn himself did and that he could have passed for Mathew, Thomas or Simon's brother. His skin was darker and the black hair possessed a tighter curl, but the stunning Joslyn azure eyes and the chiseled cast to his face smacked of Joslyn ancestry.

Aware of her reaction, Lamb said testily, "Yes, yes, I know, I look like the rest of that pack of Joslyns, but tell me what happened to Barnaby."

Emily swallowed and quickly related the events. The whole time she was talking, the stranger was busy assessing the extent of the wound, his hands moving quick and sure over Barnaby's head.

Sinking back on his heels, he frowned. "I want to get him cleaned up and comfortable. Where can we take him?"

"Uh, my home, The Birches, is not more than a mile away," Emily said, bowled over by the way the newcomer had taken command. Hesitantly, she asked, "Are you Lamb?"

He smiled a singularly dazzling smile and she blinked.

"Yes, I am Lamb and I apologize for my rudeness. You are Miss Townsend."

"Er, yes," Emily said, beginning to have a glimmer of understanding of the relationship between Lord Joslyn and his servant.

Barnaby groaned and both Lamb and Emily looked down at him. Barnaby's eyes fluttered and he groaned again. "My head," Barnaby muttered, reaching up to touch the wound. "Christ!" he swore, and with Lamb's help struggled upright. "What the devil happened?"

"Someone accidentally shot you," Emily said, relief flooding through her at his return to consciousness.

She saw the look that Barnaby and Lamb exchanged. Glancing from one grim face to the other, she asked, "What?"

Ignoring her, Lamb said, "How do you want to handle this? Do we return to Windmere? Or are you going to try to keep this attack a secret too?"

Emily's breath caught. Attack? Too?

Frowning at Barnaby, she demanded, "What do you mean 'attack'? Are you saying that this wasn't an accident?" When Barnaby remained silent, she said slowly, "You think that someone deliberately shot you. That they tried to murder you." The idea that Lord Joslyn had just missed being murdered was incredible to her, but he and Lamb seemed to have no trouble believing it. Thinking over Lamb's outburst and recalling the night they had first met, how close he had come to death, her eyes widened. "You don't believe that it was an accident that you nearly drowned in the Channel either, do you?"

Barnaby shot her a glance almost of dislike. "Sometimes you are too damned clever for your own good."

"Better to be clever than jackass stubborn," she snapped. "Lamb is right: if someone is trying to kill you, you should listen to him."

Barnaby glared at Lamb.

Lamb shrugged his shoulders and murmured, "I may have, ah, allowed my tongue to run away with me when I came upon you lying bloodied and lifeless on the ground."

Emily didn't understand everything, but it was obvious that both men were convinced that Lord Joslyn's dip in the Channel had been no accident, or that this afternoon's shooting had not been a chance incident. They believed that someone was trying to kill him. Her heart sank, knowing who would be their leading suspect.

Like everyone else, Emily knew that Mathew had been furious at having the title snatched from his hands. Was he attempting to murder his winning rival? Mathew Joslyn could be arrogant and autocratic and when aroused he had a vile temper, but did that make him a murderer? Ordinarily she would have laughed at the notion, but seeing the expressions on the faces of the men before her, she admitted that as far as they were concerned, it was not a subject for laughter.

She shivered and looked around at the few winter-bare trees that dotted the undulating countryside, uneasily aware of the easy targets they made standing here at the side of the road. If Lord Joslyn had, indeed, been marked for murder, whoever had shot at him could still be out there. . . .

"We have to get him to the house," Emily said abruptly. "If someone is trying to kill him, standing out here with no protection will only make the task easier." When neither man made a move, in a voice laced with sarcasm she added, "It's a simple decision. Either remain here like grouse before a scenting hound or follow me home. Which is it?"

Barnaby sighed. "She has a point." He glanced at Emily, and despite the seriousness of the situation and the throbbing pain in his head, he smiled. She looked, he decided whimsically, as she stood before him with her eyes flashing and her challenging stance, very much like the Amazon Lamb had called her. *His* Amazon, Barnaby thought possessively, and he was very sure that she was wreaking havoc with every plan he'd ever had for a long and exuberant bachelorhood.

Dizziness washed over him. He fought it off and when he felt more in command of himself, he said, "She's right—we cannot stand around here."

"My home is not far. Do you think you can ride that far?" Emily asked. "Or shall I go and get a farm cart to carry you?"

Thinking of the brutal jostling of a cart and his aching head, Barnaby replied, "Let's try the horse first."

It was no easy task, even with Lamb's great strength and Barnaby's willingness to get himself on his horse, but they managed it. By the time they had him firmly in the saddle, Barnaby's face was even whiter and his wound was bleeding more heavily.

Dizzy, and fighting off nausea, Barnaby swayed in the saddle. Through gritted teeth, he said to Emily, "This is your parade, so lead the way."

They proceeded slowly, Emily in front, Lamb keeping his horse close to Barnaby's to ensure Barnaby stayed in the saddle.

They turned at the two huge birches Emily had indicated marked the drive to her home. Though she was riding ahead of them, she was aware of the low-voiced and vehement conversation being held between the two men. They were arguing and she suspected that it had to do with her and their belief that someone was trying to murder Lord Joslyn. The first attempt, and she wasn't entirely convinced there had been an attempt, had been passed off as an accident, so it was apparent they were trying to keep their suspicions a secret. Until Lamb's unwise comments when he had first come upon Lord Joslyn and the later exchange between them, she assumed today's incident had been an accident. But now . . .

They traveled about a half mile when conversation be-

tween the two men abruptly ceased and Barnaby called a
halt.

Emily wasn't surprised. They'd come to some conclusion,
she guessed. Swinging her horse around to face him, she
asked, "What?"

Barnaby was in no condition to be clever and he muttered, "I'd appreciate it if you'd keep Lamb's unfortunate
words to yourself and forget any mention of murder. I'd prefer that everyone think that this afternoon was simply an accident."

He looked awful. A trickle of blood crept down one side
of his face and his color was so pale, she was alarmed—and
angry that he felt he had to ask her not to reveal their suspicions. Her mouth tightened. Good God! Did he think she was
so addle-brained she'd gossip about what they suspected?

Under different circumstances Emily would have given
him the sharp side of her tongue and probed deeper, but getting Lord Joslyn safely abed and having a physician examine
him took precedence over everything else. Nodding curtly,
she said, "I know how to keep my mouth shut. You don't
have to fear that I shall blurt out anything that was said between the three of us this afternoon. As far as I know, what
happened was a dangerous accident."

Barnaby dredged up a smile, faint and pale though it was.
"Thank you."

"Now, before you tumble out of the saddle," she grumbled, "can we continue?"

After taking one look at Lord Joslyn and hearing Emily's
hurried explanation, within minutes of their arrival at the
gracious old manor house, Walker had seen to it that Barnaby was ensconced in the second best guest bedroom—
Ainsworth, unfortunately, occupied the best guest room. To
her frustration, Emily had been banished from further pro-
ceedings by Lamb.

Barring her entrance and grinning at her, Lamb said, "Let me get him cleaned up before you start badgering him." He glanced down at her bloodstained riding habit. "I suggest that while I'm working on him that you change your clothes." Taking great liberty, he tugged on a long strand of her blond hair that in all the confusion had come loose from the black snood and his eyes twinkling, he murmured, "Go and pretty yourself—Barnaby will like that."

Emily came as close to flouncing away as she ever had in her life. The gall of that man! It was obvious, she thought, torn between exasperation and amusement, that the servant was every bit as audacious as the master was!

With Emily out of the way, Lamb turned back to Barnaby. Despite Barnaby's objections, together he and Walker stripped him and bundled him into a nightshirt hastily absconded from Jeffery's things.

"Why do I always seem to end up wearing someone else's nightshirt?" Barnaby complained from the bed.

"You have only yourself to blame," Lamb said brutally, the image of Barnaby lying motionless on the ground still fresh in his mind. "Next time you get shot, do it at Windmere and you won't have to worry about wearing someone else's nightshirt."

Walker kept his face expressionless at this exchange, but it startled him. No more, however, he admitted, than Lamb's undeniable resemblance to the Joslyn family. Mrs. Spalding would find it all quite interesting.

"Some warm water and clean cloths would be next," said Lamb, breaking into Walker's thoughts. "I need to get a good look at the wound and dress it."

Diffidently Walker asked, "Perhaps, you'd like me to send Thomas, our footman, to the village for the physician?"

Smiling with great charm, Lamb murmured, "That won't be necessary. I have tended milord through worse events than this. If you could have someone bring me my saddle-bags though, I would appreciate it."

Walker bowed. "I shall see to it myself."

Having forgotten that the door to her room was locked, Emily slammed painfully into the unyielding surface. Swearing under her breath, she pounded on the door and demanded, "Anne, are you in there?"

The door opened and taking in the sight Emily presented with her disheveled hair and bloodstained habit, Anne cried, "*Emily!* Merciful heavens! Are you hurt?"

"I'm fine," Emily said, pushing past her. "Would you ring for Sally? I'm filthy and need to wash."

Anne shut and locked the door behind her. "But what has happened to you?" Anne asked as she trailed Emily across the room.

Cornelia was sitting in a chair by the fire. Taking in Emily's tattered and bloody appearance, she declared, "Good gad, girl! Never say that you were attacked!"

Sitting on the edge of the bed, Emily dragged off her boots. "No, I wasn't attacked," she said. "Lord Joslyn was—he is presently being tended by his manservant, Lamb, in our second best bedroom."

"Lord Joslyn, here? Under our roof?" demanded Cornelia, a spark of interest in her eyes.

Anne's hand went to her breast and she gasped. "But what happened?"

Rifling through her wardrobe and chest for a change of clothing, Emily related the sequence of events, leaving out any reference to the possibility of someone attempting to murder Lord Joslyn, not once but twice.

"Never say that a poacher shot at Lord Joslyn!" exclaimed Anne, her eyes huge in her little face.

"That's exactly what I'm saying," Emily said impatiently,

turning away from her raid of the wardrobe with a mulberry gown made of fine wool.

A tap on the door heralded Sally's presence. Once Sally had been sent away to fetch some water for Emily, Cornelia said thoughtfully, "A poacher, you say? Odd time and place for a poacher to be about, don't you think?"

Emily kept her head down, apparently fascinated by the lace-trimmed shift she'd added to the items of clothing she carried over her arm. "Hmmm. Yes, it is odd, but how else would you explain it?"

Cornelia's eyes narrowed and she studied Emily's down-bent head. There was, she decided, a bit more to the tale than her niece was telling her. . . .

"Well, of course, it was an accident!" Anne declared roundly. "There's simply no other explanation."

Emily grabbed a dressing robe and disappeared behind the screen. Eager to change the subject, as she removed her clothing, Emily told them about the meeting with the investors and she was able to waste several minutes telling them what had transpired at The Crown. "We made an excellent profit," she said, taking the silk bag from her one pocket. She handed it over the top of the screen to Anne to place in the hiding place in the baseboard. "Oh, and here is the other one, nicely filled with money for our next run." Stripping out of the riding habit, her voice was muffled by the heavy fabric as she added, "I suspect Jeb will be leaving within days for Calais, so I don't think we'll be holding it long." Tossing aside the riding habit, she said, "We did well on this run and after we pay out the necessary expenses," Emily said, "I think the remainder should be used to hide Anne somewhere."

Anne's first instinct was to refuse. Guilt consumed her at the idea that the profits from Emily's dangerous scheme should be squandered on her, but Emily and Cornelia soon convinced her that she was acting like a ninny.

"What use is having money," Cornelia pointed out, "if we cannot use it as we see fit? Emily and I have no objections, so neither should you, you little goose!"

Sally returned with the warmed water and the next several minutes passed with Emily washing away the signs of her ordeal and scrambling into fresh clothing. A quick brush of her flyaway hair and she tied back the heavy mass with a wide green velvet ribbon.

Stepping out from behind the screen, Emily walked over and sat down in one of the chairs near the fire. She was tired, yet strangely energized, and she pushed aside the ridiculous notion that her condition had anything to do with the knowledge that Lord Joslyn was in the house . . . or that she would see him again very soon. Not that *she* was about to suggest they intrude into his sickroom.

Emily could have kissed her great-aunt, when Cornelia asked, "I wonder how long before Lord Joslyn will be well enough for visitors? I'd like to meet the fellow." She grinned and arched a brow. "The sixth viscount was a fine figure of a man. Be nice to see how this new pup compares to his great-grandfather."

The ladies of The Birches were not the only ones considering presenting themselves to Barnaby's sickroom. Walker had kept the news from Jeffery as long as he dared, but eventually he'd had no choice but to inform the squire of his guest.

Jeffery and Ainsworth had been indifferently playing cards in the game room when Walker informed him that Lord Joslyn lay wounded upstairs in the second best guest room.

Jeffery gaped at him. "Joslyn *here*? In my house?"

Walker nodded and explained the circumstances.

When Walker departed, Jeffery turned to Ainsworth, excitement blazing in his blue eyes. "By Jove! What a stroke of luck! Joslyn here!"

"How so?"

Jeffery bent forward eagerly. "I told you I thought there was something between that fellow and Emily. I'm convinced of it now."

"Because he got shot?" drawled Ainsworth. "I'm afraid I don't see the connection."

"No, not because he got shot," Jeffery said impatiently. "Because he was with Emily again! They were together when he was shot. What does that tell you?" When Ainsworth shrugged and looked bored, Jeffery went on. "I tell you, there is something going on between the pair of them. Though he denied it, I know she was at The Crown that night and it must have been to meet Joslyn."

"You forget, he'd just arrived in the area—they'd never met."

But Jeffery wasn't about to let a little thing like that puncture the never-quite-discarded-glorious image in his head of marriage between Emily and Joslyn. "That we know of," said Jeffery with satisfaction, nodding wisely. "That we know of."

Jeffery rose to his feet. "If you'll excuse me, I'm going to see for myself how Joslyn is doing."

Leaving Ainsworth sitting at the gaming table like a day-old crumpet, Jeffery strode from the room.

Having delivered the news that Lord Joslyn was in the house, Walker hastened upstairs to warn Lamb. Knocking on the door, at Lamb's "Enter," he slipped inside.

Barnaby was sitting up in the bed, his eyes closed, a big bank of pillows at his back. A white cloth was draped rakishly across one part of his head; his lordship looked pale but rallying. The tray of refreshments Walker had delivered just after carrying away the bowl of bloody water and the bloodied rags Lamb had used to clean the wound, sat on a round marble-topped table next to the bed.

Lamb stood nearby, repacking the saddlebags Walker had brought him earlier. Approaching the bed, Walker murmured, "My lord, Squire has been told of your presence and will, naturally, want to see for himself that you are well taken care of."

Barnaby opened his eyes. "Thank you for holding him off as long as possible."

Walker bowed. Straightening, the butler asked, "Shall I send a message to Windmere?"

Barnaby started to nod, then winced as his newly stitched scalp, courtesy of Lamb, made itself felt. "Yes, I'd appreciate that."

Walker would have left the room but Lamb stopped him. "Wait," Lamb said. Glancing at Barnaby he asked, "Shouldn't you send for your coach?"

Barnaby looked pitiful. "Oh, I am far too weak to travel," he said in a low voice. Smiling bravely at Walker he murmured, "Perhaps you could tell my people to send over the necessary things I shall need for the next few days." He slid his eyes to Lamb. "And for my manservant, Lamb."

Walker departed.

Putting away the needle and the silk thread in his saddlebag, Lamb said, "I don't think it's a good idea to stay here. You can be better cared for at Windmere."

"Hmm. I suppose, but I find The Birches charming."

Dryly, Lamb observed, "She has a ring in your nose already."

His hands behind his head, Barnaby grinned. "Ah, but it is a very handsome ring, don't you think?"

* * *

Once he had sent Tom the footman off to Windmere, Walker scampered up the stairs to Emily's bedroom. Hearing his voice, Emily opened the door and whisked him inside, locking the door behind him.

Walker quickly relayed the news that Lord Joslyn would be staying at The Birches for a few days. An arrow of fright went through Emily at the news. Was the wound worse than she had thought? "How bad is he?" she asked, her eyes worried.

Walker coughed delicately. "Not as bad as one would think." His gaze slid to Cornelia who was watching him with avid interest. "I think there is some reason he wishes to remain here."

Cornelia smothered a cackle of glee. She smelled a romance. Rubbing her hands together, she remarked, "Excellent! Run along now, but when you see his lordship next, would you inform him that we would very much like to visit when he is feeling better. Tomorrow morning, perhaps?"

Walker bowed. "I shall do so, Madame."

The ladies may have given Barnaby a respite, but Jeffery wasn't to be denied the pleasure of seeing his guest. Ushered into the room by a stoic-faced Lamb, Jeffery rushed forward, saying, "Milord! Walker has just informed me of your presence. Have your needs been met? If there is anything I can do to make your stay at The Birches more pleasant, just say the word and it shall be done."

"Your staff has been most kind," Barnaby said. "In particular, ah, Walker, has been exceedingly helpful."

"Yes. Yes," Jeffery said, dismissing Walker's efforts. Approaching the bed, he said, "I must tell you that I am very happy to have this opportunity to correct the mistaken impression you may have of me based on our first, unfortunate meeting."

"I had already forgotten about it," Barnaby replied politely, wishing Jeffery to purgatory.

Jeffery beamed. "I cannot tell you how relieved I am." He chuckled. "You must have thought me a madman bursting into your room that way and making those wild accusations."

"The idea crossed my mind."

Jeffery's smile slipped a little. "Well, it is good that I can now put to rest any reservations you may have harbored about the Townsend family."

Wanting the fellow gone before he said something he would regret, Barnaby sighed heavily and closed his eyes. Weakly, he said, "Lamb, my cordial. I feel faint."

Lamb bustled forward. Smiling with a great many teeth down at Jeffery, he said, "I must ask you to leave now. His lordship suffered a grievous wound only hours ago and is not yet ready to receive visitors."

"Oh, er, yes, of course," Jeffery muttered, taken aback by Lamb's intimidating size and the unmistakable resemblance to the Joslyn family. "Uh, didn't mean to intrude." He glanced back at Barnaby slumped against the pillows. "If there is *anything* you need, milord, just say the word."

"My cordial," Barnaby moaned. "I must have my cordial."

Lamb's hand at his elbow propelled Jeffery across the room and out the door quick as a cat pouncing on a mouse. Hearing the door shut, Barnaby opened one eye. Seeing only Lamb, the other eye opened and he sat up. "You know," Barnaby said, "that fellow wears me out."

"Just remember he's her cousin—and if you continue down the path you are treading, your heir could be just like him," said Lamb, grinning.

*   *   *

Barnaby's and Lamb's things were delivered from Windmere that evening by an alarmed Mathew who was accompanied by Thomas and Simon, and Barnaby spent a long evening convincing his cousins that he was in no danger of dying. It was difficult to tell, but he sensed that all three men were genuinely concerned about him and appalled at his brush with death. "They may be," Lamb said, when he was finally able to banish them from Barnaby's room, "but that doesn't mean that one of them isn't behind what happened."

Lamb's words echoed Barnaby's own thoughts. But which one? he wondered.

After enduring a dose of laudanum forced down his throat by Lamb, Barnaby fell asleep. He woke Wednesday morning to a gray, showery day.

Bringing in a tray of coffee and an array of tidbits prepared by Mrs. Spalding to tempt the invalid's appetite, Lamb examined him critically. "Your color is better," he said as he placed the tray on the table next to the bed. A sly smile curved Lamb's mouth. "And the ladies have requested permission to visit the sickroom at eleven o'clock—if that meets with my lord's approval."

Barnaby brightened and sat up in bed. "Now that's the best thing I've heard since I arrived here."

Emily was anticipating the visit to Barnaby's room with far more pleasure than she cared to admit. Worse, she found herself paying far more attention to her gown and hair. What does it matter how I look? she wondered irritably. He's already seen me looking like a hag.

When the ladies finally descended for a light breakfast, Emily was wearing a round-necked gown of cashmere, her hair bouncing in soft curls near her face. Cornelia was pleased with Emily's appearance, the thought that the chit would drag out her oldest gown just to be contrary having crossed her mind more than once. It boded well that Emily had chosen to wear something presentable.

The three ladies had just served themselves and settled around the table in the breakfast room, when they heard a great commotion coming from the front of the house. Hearing voices and more clatter they looked at each other.

"What in the world—!" Emily exclaimed as the door to the breakfast room was thrown open and a gentleman in a mud-splattered greatcoat strode into the room.

Emily recognized the laughing blue eyes in an instant and started to her feet. On light steps she rushed across the room and immediately was swept up in a warm embrace. "Hugh!" she cried happily, grinning into the lively features of her favorite cousin.

Chapter 10

Pandemonium reigned as the ladies bombarded Hugh with hugs, kisses and excited questions. Walker appeared and swiftly divested Hugh of his greatcoat and hurried away with the garment on his way to the kitchen to inform Mrs. Spalding of the newest arrival.

At thirty-one years old, Hugh Townsend was four years Jeffery's junior and a world away from his older brother's profligate lifestyle. Although a handsome man in his own right, he did not possess Jeffery's classic handsomeness or height, standing less than an inch above average height, but he possessed something in abundance that Jeffery lacked—charm and kindness.

Both those attributes were displayed, when after bussing Emily and Anne on the cheeks, he crossed to where Cornelia sat observing the scene with a satisfied gleam in her eyes. Dropping to one knee before her, Hugh lifted her hand and pressed a kiss onto the wrinkled skin. "And how," he asked gently, his blue eyes searching her face, "goes the woman who holds my heart?"

"Very prettily done," Cornelia said, reaching out and caressing his cheek. "You have a way about you, boy, and if I was fifty years younger . . ."

"At any age," Hugh declared, "you will always hold my heart."

Cornelia burst out laughing. "Doing it far too rare and brown, my boy." Despite her words, everyone could tell that she was pleased. Indicating the empty chair next to hers, she said, "Now sit and tell us how your mother is. And Parkham House? All is well there?"

Jeffery and Hugh's widowed mother lived with Hugh at Parkham House. The widow of Emily's father's younger brother, William, Mrs. Althea Townsend, at fifty-five still bore a marked resemblance to the pretty little widgeon she had been when she had first married. Hugh had inherited his mother's kind heart and easygoing nature—if not her flighty tendencies. To Jeffery's chagrin, at twenty, Hugh had inherited Parkham House, a small estate less than a day's ride away, and a respectable fortune from his godmother. In his cups, Jeffery was known to complain about the unfairness of fate. His godmother had never left him anything, he would state bitterly, but the care of her smelly lapdog—which he had promptly thrust into his mother's arms.

Nearly ten years ago, when Jeffery and Hugh's family home had been sold to cover their father's gambling debts, Althea had been left homeless and with little money. Hugh instantly had her comfortably installed in a suite of rooms at Parkham House. The pair of them rubbed along together very well, Althea happily pottering about the gardens and overseeing the household, when she remembered, and Hugh living the life of a gentleman with means enough to please himself.

Obeying Cornelia's command, Hugh sat down beside her, saying, "Mother is well. I left her busy pruning the roses." Glancing around the table, he added, "She sends all of you her love."

There were a few moments of general conversation before the news of their prominent guest was relayed to Hugh and the circumstances behind Lord Joslyn currently being housed upstairs.

Hugh was aghast. "Good God! Lord Joslyn shot! Monstrous!" He looked at Emily. "You were unhurt?"

Emily nodded. "It was terrifying and I was never so thankful as when Lamb arrived on the scene. Fortunately, Lord Joslyn was not seriously wounded."

"What sort of fellow is he?" Hugh asked. "I've been hearing gossip about him—all of London was agog when he arrived last fall. No one could stop talking about him." He grimaced. "Or how furious poor Mathew Joslyn was at losing such a fortune . . . and title. Half of London was appalled that some half-savage colonial had snatched away Mathew's inheritance, the other pitied him."

Cornelia sniffed. "Mathew Joslyn is wealthy enough in his own right. No need for anyone to pity him."

"Oh, pooh!" said Emily. "I don't want to talk about Mathew." She bent an inquiring gaze on Hugh, asking, "But what brings you here this time of year? Are you staying long?" She grinned at him. "I certainly hope so—Jeffery will be put out."

Hugh chuckled. Trust Emily not to wrap his relationship with Jeffery in clean linen. He and Jeffery could barely tolerate each other and he had to admit that while he would have heeded Cornelia's request for his presence at The Birches under any circumstances, the prospect of tweaking Jeffery's nose added a certain . . . stimulation to the trip. But how to answer Emily's main question?

Cornelia had not sworn him to secrecy, but it was obvious she had not told the others she had sent for him. Until he had a private word with his great-aunt, Hugh didn't want to reveal that it was her urgent missive that had brought him posthaste to The Birches. So why was he here?

"Winter doldrums!" he said, inspired. "London is deserted; most of the best hunting is behind us and I was in need of a change of scenery." His blue eyes teasing, he murmured, "The thought of your lovely faces brought me here."

Anne blushed, but Emily snorted. "Humbug!" She smiled. "Whatever the reason, we are happy to see you."

The painted clock on the mantel rang the hour and Emily glanced at it astonished. "How can it be eleven o'clock already? It seems we just sat down." Apologetically she said to Hugh, "We are to see Lord Joslyn now—will you mind being on your own for a little while? I would ask you to accompany us . . . but he *was* shot just yesterday and might not be up to meeting strangers."

Hugh waved her away. "No. No. You go ahead. If you will just tell me which room you want me in, I shall have Walker take my things up there and get settled in."

Rising to her feet and leaning heavily on her cane, Cornelia asked, "Barnett with you?"

Hugh nodded. "Yes, my valet is with me."

"Have Walker see that he is quartered near you—in the same wing with us," she said, stumping from the room. Her gaze boring into his, she added, "I want you nearby."

Anne hurried to follow Cornelia, and after dropping another kiss on Hugh's cheek, Emily stared at him. "She wrote you, didn't she?"

Hugh grimaced. "Yes, but she didn't tell me why I was needed here so urgently. I gather things are very bad with my brother?"

Emily glanced over her shoulder, and seeing that Anne and Cornelia were not waiting for her, she turned back to Hugh. In a rush, she said, "Jeffery and that bounder, Ainsworth, mean to abduct Anne and ruin her in order to force her to marry Ainsworth. I suspect that Aunt Cornelia wants you to take Anne to Parkham House—where Jeffery would not dare try to snatch her."

Having dropped that explosive round at Hugh's feet, Emily vanished in the direction of the other women.

Unwilling to receive visitors in bed like an invalid, though he was quite capable of playing one when it suited him, when the three ladies were ushered in by Lamb, Barnaby was enthroned in a large overstuffed chair centered near the fire burning on the gray stone hearth. He was garbed in a gold embroidered burgundy silk robe, black silk slippers on his feet and a tastefully arranged white scarf of fine wool around his throat. The bandage around his head had disappeared, and except for the appearance of a growing purple-and-black bruise near his hairline marking the beginning of the bullet's path and faint blue shadows beneath his eyes, he looked remarkably healthy.

And handsome, Emily thought with a jump of her pulse when their eyes met as he stood up to greet them. Her gaze shied away from the warm glint in his and she hung back, wondering if everyone else heard the mad thumping of her heart.

With Emily struck dumb, it was left to Anne to introduce Barnaby and Cornelia.

"You've your great-grandfather's size and broad shoulders," Cornelia observed bluntly after the introductions were made and all of them had been seated, "and the look of him about the mouth when you smile, but there's not much else to mark you as a Joslyn, is there?"

"No, I'm afraid not," Barnaby replied meekly. "I take after my mother's side of the family." A smile lurking in his dark eyes, he asked, "Does that put me totally beyond redemption?"

Cornelia grinned. "With those shoulders? And your title and fortune? Don't be silly, boy! You could look like a two-day-old dead lizard and the ladies would still flock around you."

Lamb, who stayed in the background, turned away to hide a smile, but Barnaby laughed. "That certainly put me in my place, didn't it?" he replied good-naturedly.

Walker entered and refreshments were served. Sipping tea and nibbling lemon puffs and Savoy fingers, Emily did more listening than talking, most of the conversation being between Barnaby and Cornelia. They enjoyed each other, Emily thought, as she watched them. Her great-aunt was in high fettle, clearly basking in the attention of a handsome man, and Barnaby smiled and laughed often at Cornelia's quips. Cornelia and Anne flanked Barnaby with Emily sitting quietly on the other side of Cornelia. She was in a good position to study Barnaby's features as he effortlessly charmed her great-aunt and her stepmother. Now and then his gaze would flicker over her and each time his eyes touched her, Emily was conscious of an unwelcome spurt of excitement.

Despite having looked forward to seeing Lord Joslyn again, Emily was now eager to escape from his presence. She needed time to think, to understand why he had such an effect upon her, and to come to grips with the new emotions he aroused within her. Watching that hard, dark face, she reluctantly admitted that she was attracted to him in a way that she had never been to any man before him, and that knowledge disturbed her and made her wary.

Love or marriage had never held the allure for Emily that it did for other women. Tales of Cornelia's bitterly unhappy marriage and her father's kind indifference to her young stepmother had not precisely engendered a fondness for the state of marriage in her breast. Jeffery's conduct and that of the raffish friends he filled the house with had certainly not enamored her of the male of the species. Quite the contrary, and if it had not been for Hugh and to a lesser extent, Simon, she might have been forgiven for thinking that all men were either careless curs or predatory beasts. Ainsworth definitely fit that latter category, she thought with a curl of her lip.

Barnaby Joslyn was in a completely different category than any man she had ever met. He confused her, or rather, her reaction to him confused her. Not once, not even during her two Seasons in London, had she ever wondered what a man's kiss would be like or been so physically aware of a male as she was Lord Joslyn. His seductive attractiveness and its effect upon her were definite causes for alarm. The very last thing she wanted, especially at this time, was the added complication of fighting the forceful pull of his virile personality. She was not, she reminded herself sharply, some country milkmaid to be bowled over by a handsome face. Risking a glance at him and finding his eyes on her again, she buried her nose in her teacup, conscious of a breathless anticipation rushing through her body. Bloody hell! He wasn't even that handsome—at least not in the traditional sense.

When Cornelia brought the visit to an end, Emily couldn't get out of Lord Joslyn's room fast enough, but as luck would have it, she was the last to leave. Barnaby gallantly escorted Cornelia to the door and he remained there bidding his guests good-bye. Emily flashed him a polite smile and tried to scoot past him only to have Barnaby's hand capture her elbow, halting her escape. She glanced up at him, her gray eyes wide and wary, her rosy mouth parted.

Barnaby bent down, his breath warm and tingly against her ear, and something twisted deep within her. "Running away from me, sweet?" he whispered. "I thought you were braver than that."

Her eyes darkened and a flush stained her cheeks. Her chin lifted and she muttered, "I have no idea what you're talking about, my lord."

"Don't you?" he teased, his black eyes moving warmly across her face. He let go of her arm and ran a caressing finger down her nose. "I think you know very well what I'm talking about."

Helplessly, her eyes fastened on that smiling masculine mouth only inches above hers, her heart beating so fast she thought she would strangle. She could not drag her gaze away and unaware of it, she swayed toward him. His breath caught, his eyes darkening and for one wild moment she thought he was going to kiss her. And dear God! She wanted him to . . . desperately.

Trapped in the same web, Barnaby caught her upper arms, pulling her against his big, lean body. Lamb coughed discreetly from inside the room, the sound stopping him in his tracks. Recalled to his senses, Barnaby's hands dropped and, stepping away from her, he said softly, "Run along, my gray-eyed dove. We'll finish this next time. . . ."

Appalled at how close she had come to letting him kiss her in the doorway of his room where anyone could have come upon them, Emily tore her eyes away. Furious with herself and his arrogant assumption that there *would* be a next time, she threw him a fulminating look and shot out of the doorway like a scalded cat. To her further discomfort, Barnaby's chuckle followed her down the hall as she dashed away. Damn him!

Smiling with satisfaction, Barnaby shut the door and leaned back against it. The attraction was not only on his side. She was aware of him. And curious. Splendid!

Lamb regarded him sourly. "What were you going to do? Ravish her in the doorway?"

Barnaby made a face. "Now that would have been rather ungentlemanly of me, don't you think?"

Lamb snorted. "Just be glad that obsequious cousin of hers didn't see the pair of you. I don't like him and I don't trust him. I suspect that if you're not careful he'll have you leg-shackled to her before you can say your name."

"I can't say that I disagree with you," Barnaby admitted, sitting down in the high-back chair and closing his eyes. He'd enjoyed the visit of the ladies, but he was aware that it had tired him. His lips twisted. He was weaker than he cared to admit and he wondered if the wound was more serious than first thought.

Lamb frowned and walked over to stand next to him. Examining Barnaby's paler-than-usual complexion, he said, "I told you that you should stay in bed."

Barnaby opened his eyes and sighed. "I suppose you'll be more insufferable than normal if I tell you that in this case, I think you're right."

"Of course, I was right! Now are you going to go back in bed by yourself or do I have to carry you?"

Barnaby stood up, grateful he didn't sway. "Thank you, no," he said grandly and walked toward the bed.

Only when Barnaby was settled in bed and dozing, did Lamb leave him. Time, Lamb decided, as he shut the door behind him, to see for myself, the lay of the land.

Ordinarily, Hugh's uninvited arrival would have affronted Jeffery, but with Anne's abduction on the horizon, Lord Joslyn residing in his upstairs bedroom and the dazzling possibility of engineering a match between Emily and Lord Joslyn, his younger brother's presence caused only the barest ripple of irritation. After Walker had delivered the news about Hugh's visit, Jeffery thought it over and, reminding himself that Hugh was decidedly plumper in the pocket than he was, Jeffery decided having his brother here was another sign that Lady Luck was with him. His younger brother was no gambler and Jeffery was anticipating several hands of cards in the evening. Some of Hugh's gold, he decided, was going to be in his pocket before they were much older.

Under questioning, Walker had also relayed to Jeffery the news of the visit by the ladies to Lord Joslyn's room this morning—which pleased him enormously. It was encouraging that Emily and Lord Joslyn were circling each other's orbit. He frowned. But it would have been better, Jeffery thought, if he could have arranged for Emily to be discovered in Lord Joslyn's room, without a chaperone, even better in his lordship's bed. . . . Hmmm. Smiling, Jeffery set about concocting various scenarios that would see Lord Joslyn's ring on Emily's finger . . . whether either one of them wanted it or not.

The only person not happy with the current situation was Ainsworth. He was annoyed by the excited reaction of the household to Joslyn's arrival; even that cretin Jeffery, he thought annoyed, was over the moon about it. With the abduction of Anne in the offing, Ainsworth viewed Joslyn's presence in the second best bedroom as a complication they didn't need. Hugh's sudden appearance was equally displeasing, and though certain of the outcome, he was aware that Jeffery's younger brother might provide some competition for the fair Anne's hand. It would be such a pity if her fancy fell upon young Hugh. . . . A cruel expression crossed his face. Ainsworth wasn't about to let a fortune slip through his fingers because of a recalcitrant female—even if her heart was given to another. He was determined that the young widow was going to be his bride. And soon, he thought, pleasurably aware of a thrumming in his loins when he pictured her naked and helpless before him.

Lamb was able to stall a visit with Barnaby from Jeffery until late afternoon and inevitably Jeffery brought along his friend Mr. Ainsworth. Refreshed after a nap and a meal of rare sirloin, yellow farm cheese and chunks of bread still warm from the oven, all washed down with some excellent ale, Barnaby insisted upon meeting his guests while seated in the high-back chair in front of the fireplace. Jeffery introduced Ainsworth and each man took a chair on either side of Barnaby.

Barnaby disliked Ainsworth on sight, recognizing him for the Captain Sharp he was. He may not have spent many months in London, but Barnaby had seen more than one loose fish like Ainsworth during his stay in the capital city. Creatures like Ainsworth might have some claim to respectability, but they spent their days in the gaming halls and whorehouses, looking to pluck the unwary or hanging about the fringes of the *ton* hoping for notice.

Jeffery's manner grated on Barnaby, but Ainsworth's superior air, as if he knew a special secret not shared with lesser mortals, made Barnaby want to plant him a facer.

"I'm pleased to see you looking better, my lord," said Jeffery. "I assume that my staff is treating you well?" He tittered. "Of course, my servants are not the caliber of those you have at Windmere, but I trust that you will overlook their shortcomings."

Barnaby stared at him long enough to make Jeffery squirm in his chair, before saying coolly, "I could not ask for better service. Walker has been most helpful and your Mrs. Spalding is an excellent cook." Barnaby smiled, showing a great many teeth. "If you don't appreciate them, be careful—someone might steal them away from you."

"That's not likely," Jeffery said carelessly. "They'd never leave my cousin. Devoted to her." He looked arch. "Speaking of my cousin, I understand that she paid you a visit this morning. I hope you found her company agreeable."

Barnaby inclined his head politely. "Yes, I did—as I did that of your great-aunt and young Mrs. Townsend who accompanied her."

"Taking thing, the little widow, ain't she?" Ainsworth commented, entering the conversation for the first time. Not wanting Joslyn to get any ideas and determined to make the situation clear, he added, "We mean to make a match of it."

Barnaby hid his astonishment. Good God! Emily's charming stepmother married to this bounder? It was inconceivable.

"Er, is this a recent development?" Barnaby asked, grappling with the idea that the gentle young woman he'd met and liked enormously would stoop to marry someone of Ainsworth's stamp. "I'm surprised she made no mention of an impending wedding."

An unattractive flush marred Ainsworth face. "Nothing's settled yet," he admitted. Stiffly, he declared, "I mean to make her my bride within the fortnight."

Jeffery jumped in, saying airily, "There are only a few details to work out before the announcement. My aunt Anne is being quite shy about the whole thing." He winked at Barnaby. "You know women. She doesn't want anyone to know just yet, so let it be our secret."

Looking from one man to the other, Barnaby had the ugly suspicion that the marriage to Ainsworth was also a secret from the intended bride. There was mischief afoot here or he was a blind man. Aloud he merely said, "Your cousin and your great-aunt will undoubtedly be sad to see Mrs. Townsend leave. They appeared to be quite fond of each other."

Jeffery waved a dismissing hand. "Oh, naturally, but I'm sure they'll be happy to see her settled and in her own home."

Ainsworth smirked. "I'm coming into a great deal of money before long—it's time I set up my nursery. I intend to keep my wife busy filling it."

Finding the conversation increasingly distasteful, and already weary of this pair of jackals, Barnaby lifted a hand, summoning Lamb, who hovered in the background. "My cordial, if you please, Lamb. My head is aching."

Ainsworth took the hint and rose to his feet saying, "It has been a pleasure meeting you, my lord." He paused and ever hopeful of an easy mark, he added, "When you are feeling more the thing, if you like, we can play some cards to help you pass the time. I'm sure it is quite boring being confined to the sickroom."

The black eyes unreadable, Barnaby murmured, "Thank you for the offer, but I don't care much for cards."

Ainsworth shrugged and took his leave.

Once Ainsworth was gone, Jeffery bent forward and said confidingly, "Good thing you don't play—Ainsworth is well known in all the best clubs in London and devilishly lucky when it comes to cards."

Barnaby doubted that Ainsworth had entrée into any respectable club, much less the "best" ones, but he kept that thought to himself. "Really? Then I shall congratulate myself on a near escape," he said drily. Lamb handed Barnaby a small glass filled with a red liquid. After sipping it, Barnaby sighed and closed his eyes.

Reluctantly, Jeffery rose to his feet. "I shall leave you now, my lord, but if there is anything you wish for, you have only say the word. . . ."

Not opening his eyes, Barnaby said, "Thank you. You and your family have been most kind to a stranger. If not for your gallant cousin, I'm certain I would not be feeling as well as I do. I am indebted to her . . . and you."

"Think nothing of it! Emily is an, ah, unusual woman," Jeffery said. "Getting a bit long in the tooth," he added, "but if she caught the fancy of the right man . . ."

"Indeed." Barnaby should have left it there, but since he was curious about Emily, he wasn't above pumping her cousin for information. Hoping Jeffery would take the hint and reveal more about his enticing cousin, he murmured, "I'm surprised that she is not married."

Encouraged, Jeffery sat back down. "Surprises me, too,"

Jeffery said mendaciously, suppressing the thought that only a fool would marry a strong-willed, sharp-tongued shrew like his cousin. While the idea dazzled him, Jeffery didn't truly believe that a man of Joslyn's wealth and standing would willingly lower himself to marry the penniless daughter of a country squire. Joslyn could look as high as he wanted for a bride, but even knowing that it was a desperate dream, Jeffery wasn't ready to give up on it. Dreams did come true and who was to say this one wouldn't? Stranger things had happened. But his lordship, he admitted bitterly, would have to be tricked into offering Emily marriage. If only he could get Emily into Joslyn's bed. . . .

A calculating glitter in his blue eyes, Jeffery said carefully, "Of course, I doubt these days that Emily longs for marriage." He stared down at his gleaming boots and said, "Speaking man to man, at her age, I wouldn't be surprised if she wouldn't be willing to settle for something else . . . something of a more temporary nature—if she caught the fancy of the right man, I could persuade her . . ."

It was a good thing that Jeffery wasn't looking at Barnaby or he'd have realized he'd just blundered, badly. Barnaby's whole body stiffened, disgust and fury raging through him. He could hardly believe his ears. Emily's cousin, the man entrusted with her protection, was offering her to him with all the finesse of a pandering whoremonger! Blinded by rage, it wasn't until he felt Lamb's hand pressing down urgently on his shoulder that Barnaby realized he had half risen to his feet.

Only when he was certain that Barnaby had some command over himself did Lamb remove his hand. His eyes on Jeffery, Lamb coughed and murmured, "My lord wearies easily. I think it would be best if you left and allowed him to rest."

Oblivious to having just escaped with his life, Jeffery looked up from his contemplation of his boots. "Oh, what?

Yes, yes, of course." Standing, Jeffery smiled at Barnaby, not seeing the dangerous glitter in the black eyes. "I have enjoyed our visit, my lord," he said politely. Meaningfully, he added, "And as I said earlier, should you desire *anything*, you have only to say the word."

"Thank you," Barnaby said from between clenched teeth, struggling against the savage urge to get his hands around Jeffery's throat. "I won't forget our conversation."

Shown to the door by the intimidating Lamb, Jeffery hummed to himself as he walked away. That went rather well, he thought. If Joslyn wanted Emily in his bed, if Jeffery had to drug her, she'd damn well be there. He giggled. And won't Joslyn be surprised, after it is too late, when I appear and demand he marry her . . . ? Things were definitely looking up.

The door had hardly shut behind Jeffery before Barnaby swore. "Christ! Did you hear that weasel? Just as if she was a harlot in his stables, he did everything but name a price for her services."

"Hmmm. Yes, he was rather, ah, blunt in his approach, wasn't he?" Lamb murmured, deftly guiding Barnaby with his hand under his elbow toward the bed.

Barnaby threw off his hand and snarled, "I am *not* an invalid! I only wanted to get rid of the piece of offal before I killed him."

"There is a positive side to all of this," Lamb said, watching Barnaby stride over to stand in front of the fireplace.

A dangerous expression on his face, Barnaby swung around and stared at him. "Be careful, dear Lamb," he warned, in a voice Lamb seldom heard. "I am in no mood to hear one of your quips." When Lamb shrugged and would have turned away, Barnaby sighed and said in his more usual tones, "Oh, out with it!"

Relieved that the worst of Barnaby's temper had abated, he said lightly, "I was just thinking after that most enlightening conversation with her cousin, when you ask for her hand, you have no fear of being denied."

Barnaby laughed without amusement. "Yes, there is that," he agreed. Staring moodily down at the fire, he said, "You were right—staying here wasn't such a good idea." Ruefully, he added, "I can hardly court the elusive baggage when I am confined to my room, and if I am well enough to wander through the house there is no reason to remain here."

"But?"

Scowling, Barnaby admitted, "I had thought of returning to Windmere tomorrow, but after meeting Ainsworth and hearing that he means to marry the younger Mrs. Townsend, I am uneasy." His lips tightened. "And Jeffery's ugly offer makes me disinclined to leave Emily to his tender devices. Either woman for that matter."

"So what are we going to do?"

Wearily, Barnaby said, "Stay where we are for the time being." He cast Lamb a questioning look. "During your, er, travels in the house, did you learn anything?"

"Actually, I did. Apparently, there is another guest in the house—Hugh Townsend, Jeffery's younger brother."

"Oh, God! Never tell me she's related to two of those despicable creatures?"

Lamb smiled. "No. Hugh appears to be very different from his older brother and is held in high esteem by the staff. He's also a great favorite with the ladies. The universal opinion amongst the staff is that it is a shame that Hugh hadn't been the older of the two brothers."

"And he's here now?"

"Yes. Arrived just before the ladies came to visit you."

"Anything else?"

"Not much more, I'm afraid. I'm a stranger, so no one shared any intimate details with me," Lamb admitted. "I got the impression, though, that they tolerate Jeffery, but to the man, or woman, they would die for the ladies of the house."

Lamb frowned. "Some things didn't need explaining. For a house this size, there is a minimal staff employed. Signs of obvious penury are not yet obvious, but it's clear that nothing has been done to the house in perhaps a decade."

"Jeffery's stewardship?"

Lamb nodded. "In a matter of seven years or so, the new squire has gone through a respectable fortune and now teeters on the brink of ruin—that much Mrs. Spalding was blunt about." He grinned. "She was far more forthcoming than Walker, having taken a liking to me. Other than that, I overheard a few disapproving comments about someone named Daggett. He's the bailiff Jeffery hired when he inherited the estate. I gather the man has been pilfering off funds and putting them in his own pocket." Lamb looked thoughtful. "There's something else going on, but I'm not certain precisely what it is. What I do know is that your Amazon has found a way to provide the servants with extra funds. The scullery maid let something slip that brought a sharp rebuke from Walker and the conversation was changed rather hastily. Despite some expert wheedling on my part, even Mrs. Spalding wouldn't give me a hint."

Barnaby let out a deep breath. "You learned a great deal and Hugh's presence may be helpful. Knowing that the staff is in Emily's camp eases my mind somewhat."

Lamb had given Barnaby a great deal to think about and long after Lamb had left the room to see what else he could learn, Barnaby stood staring down into the fire. He liked little of what he had learned, but it explained things and he now knew why the cousin of the local squire was involved with a band of smugglers. She was risking her reputation and possibly her life to keep her small band of loyal followers and Anne and Cornelia from utter ruin. He suspected the same applied to Mrs. Gilbert and her charming daughters and Lord knew whom else.

Barnaby smiled. Lamb was more right than he knew in

calling Emily an Amazon. And all I have to do, he told himself, is convince her that I am not the enemy . . . and a worthy mate. He shook his head, ruefully suspecting the latter was going to be the most difficult task of all. But the rewards . . . the rewards would make it all worthwhile.

Chapter 11

While Lamb was reporting to Barnaby, Hugh was tapping on the door to Cornelia's rooms. They'd decided upon meeting in Cornelia's rooms because unlike Emily, she had a suite, comprising a large sitting room and bedroom.

The three ladies were waiting for him and once the door shut behind him and was locked by Emily, Cornelia wasted no time in laying out her plan.

Hugh had hardly taken a seat beside her on the ivory-and-rose tapestry-upholstered settee before she said, "I want you to take Anne with you to Parkham House and keep her there until it is safe for her to return here."

Ignoring Anne's shocked gasp, and not as surprised as he would have been without Emily's warning, Hugh nodded. "Emily told me what Jeffery and Ainsworth plan. She suspected you wanted me here in order to take Mrs. Townsend away. When do you want us to leave? Tomorrow?"

"Am I the only one who didn't know what was planned?" Anne asked in a small voice, feeling just the slightest bit hurt that she had been excluded from plans that intimately involved her. Even if their intentions were good, she hadn't even been consulted and that stung. Suppose, she thought resentfully, she didn't want to go to Parkham House?

Anne and Emily were sitting directly across from Cornelia and Hugh on an identical settee and Emily clasped Anne's hand and said quickly, "I didn't know either, but Hugh's arrival was too timely for me not to suspect something of this sort. Once I thought about it, there was only one conclusion: Cornelia had sent for him and there could be only one reason why she wanted him here."

"Oh!" Anne's hurt and resentment vanished, but she wasn't so certain that she wanted to be thrust into the home of someone she knew only slightly. Although Anne had met them upon more than one occasion, Hugh Townsend and his mother had not been frequent visitors to The Birches, and after Jeffery inherited, she could remember only once or twice that his brother had stepped a foot in the place. At no time had he remained long. Mostly what she knew of Hugh and his mother came from Cornelia and Emily.

Anne risked a glance at Hugh and finding him smiling warmly at her, she blushed and dropped her gaze. He was more handsome than she remembered . . . and she decided he had kind eyes.

Not looking at him, Anne asked, "I don't want to impose upon you. Are you very sure you won't mind? And your mother, what will she think when you arrive home with me?"

Hugh laughed. "My mother will fall on your neck with delight! She says often that it would be pleasant to have some female company. I am often gone to London and visiting my friends and I fear she is lonely. As for me . . ." His eyes traveled over her sweet little face. "How could I possibly object to the presence of such a charming young woman in my home?"

Anne's blush deepened.

From under lowered lids, Cornelia watched the pair of them, thinking things were going very well, indeed. Two birds with one stone, she thought complacently. Two birds with one stone. Anne safe and placed right under Hugh's nose. . . .

Emily looked at her great-aunt through narrowed eyes, then back at Hugh and Anne. If she didn't know better, she'd swear that while Cornelia had come up with an excellent solution, there was also an ulterior motive in her great-aunt's scheme. Cornelia had more tricks up her sleeve, she reminded herself, than a family of foxes.

"I take it then," Cornelia said, glancing around the room, "that no one has any objections to Hugh taking Anne to Parkham House as soon as we can arrange it?"

His face grim, Hugh said, "I am more than willing to lend my services. This scheme of theirs is despicable!" An angry flush crossed his face. "I've half a mind to call Jeffery out! Putting a bullet through the scoundrel would be a fitting end to him."

"Under no circumstances are you to act so foolishly!" snapped Cornelia. "Aside from not wanting you to risk your life, we don't want them to be aware that we know of their plans. Anne's visit to your house will raise suspicions, but they won't be certain that the visit isn't the innocent trip it appears." She glared at Hugh. "Getting yourself killed or wounded will do us no good."

Hugh nodded, but his fist was clenched and he muttered, "That my brother would be so low and base . . ."

"But how are we to get Anne away?" Emily interrupted quickly, giving Hugh something else to think about other than challenging his brother to a duel. "She can hardly just walk out of here under Jeffery's and Ainsworth's noses. Jeffery will never allow it."

"Of course, he wouldn't," Cornelia said testily. "Don't intend for him to know until Anne is safely away." She looked at Hugh. "Drove your phaeton, did you?"

"Precisely as you ordered."

Cornelia gave him an approving look before saying, "Jeffery and Ainsworth have plans to ride to Newhaven tomorrow to look at a horse for sale that Jeffery likes—they'll be gone until late evening. Long enough for us to have you on your way." Her gaze fell upon Anne and she said, "Tonight, missy, you will pack what you need for a few days' stay at Hugh's house, but don't pack more than one valise—a phaeton ain't a coach. Once you are at Hugh's, we can send your other things to you. Agatha will go with you, but I want her back when you're safely installed." She bent an inquiring eye on Hugh. "I assume you have servants enough to provide a lady's maid for Anne during her visit?"

"I'm sure my mother will be able to suggest someone from the staff to serve Mrs. Townsend," Hugh replied.

"If we're lucky," Cornelia said, "with Jeffery and Ainsworth gone most of tomorrow and unlikely to rise before noon the next day, they won't know that Anne is gone until the day after tomorrow, hopefully late in the day. By then she'll be safe." Cornelia glanced around at the others. "Any questions? Objections?"

"What reason will we give for Anne's departure?" Emily asked, frowning.

Cornelia smiled. "Hugh said it himself—Althea is lonely. Longs for the comfort and conversation of another female. Anne, being the kindhearted creature she is, upon hearing that Althea was pining for feminine company, offered her services. Not wanting to leave his mother alone for longer than necessary, Hugh insisted they leave immediately for Parkham House."

"Thank you for that," Hugh said drily. "Blame it on me."

"Your shoulders are broad enough," Cornelia said, her eyes twinkling, "and you'll enjoy shouting Jeffery down— assuming he is foolish enough to descend upon your doorstep and demand an explanation."

Finding no flaws in the plan, Emily nodded. "It is a good

solution. Jeffery can hardly argue against Anne's actions and he certainly cannot object to her visiting his own mother." She cast an anxious eye at Hugh. "You do know that you will have to take care that there is no opportunity for Jeffery or Ainsworth to snatch her from your house? Don't let her wander about alone and *never* let her go anywhere by herself."

Hugh sent Emily an offended look. "I am not a dunce! I'll be on my guard. She'll be safe enough at Parkham, but I wouldn't put an attempted abduction past him—or that disreputable friend of his." He glanced at Anne and smiled. "I will guard you well, my lady. You will have nothing to fear while you are in my care."

"T-t-thank y-y-you," Anne said, her heart full of gratitude. "You are very kind to go to all this trouble for someone who is almost a stranger."

Hugh stared into her big pansy-brown eyes and something warm and powerful slid through him. His voice huskier than he realized, he said, "I'm sure that people find it very easy to be kind to you."

Emily and Cornelia exchanged glances, Emily's brow rising and Cornelia grinning. Very pleased with herself and the situation, Cornelia said, "It's all settled then. As soon as Jeffery and Ainsworth are gone from the house tomorrow, you and Anne will leave for Parkham."

The plan unfolded without any problems. Jeffery and Ainsworth didn't leave as early as anyone would have liked, but once they had ridden off, keeping in mind that Bundy and Temple were upstairs in their masters' rooms, Hugh's phaeton was pulled discreetly to the side of the house and the valises were loaded. Minutes later, after several hugs and fond admonitions, Anne, Agatha and Barnett, Hugh's circumspect valet, were settled in the phaeton and Hugh set his pair of grays off at a spanking pace.

The house felt very empty after their departure, but Emily was aware of a lifting of her spirits. Anne was safe. Jeffery was going to be furious, she admitted thoughtfully, and the next several days were going to be decidedly unpleasant, but the main thing was that Anne was beyond his reach. And for that she could put up with Jeffery's rages and dark looks.

Her hand under Cornelia's elbow, as they walked toward the green salon, Emily said, "Jeffery is going to be mad as fire."

"I know," Cornelia said, "but there is little he can do but bluster and sputter." She eyed Emily. "If I'd thought you would go, I'd have sent you too."

Astonished, Emily stared at her. "*Me?* Why?"

"Because denied their prey, their sights may turn on you," Cornelia said wearily.

"That's true," Emily admitted. She smiled nastily. "But I am not Anne, and even if they were stupid enough to try such a thing, they'd not find me easily intimidated." Her gray eyes fierce, she said, "No matter what Ainsworth did to me, I would never marry him! And I'd shout his perfidies from the village pulpit. Everyone would know him and Jeffery for the villains they are."

Cornelia wouldn't have expected any less from Emily, but it was obvious Emily hadn't realized all the ramifications. Hadn't stopped to think how much her life would change if Ainsworth were to succeed in destroying her reputation.

"I know, but don't forget, you'd be ruined," Cornelia said softly, her eyes on Emily's face. The young were so confident, so certain they could overcome any obstacle, she thought heavily, but if Ainsworth was able to implement his wicked plan and Emily spurned marriage to him, she would face social ostracism and become a pariah, an outcast. Cornelia's heart shook at the very idea of her lovely, spirited niece having to deal with the ugly rape she would endure if Ainsworth had the opportunity and then being denied the homes and the company of people she had known all her life. Oh, there would be those that would rally around her— Mrs. Gilbert, Jeb Brown and Caleb Gates to name a few. But once it was known that Emily had been seduced, willing or not, by Ainsworth, she would never again be invited or welcomed into the homes of those people who were her equal in station, Lord and Lady Broadfoot, Mrs. Featherstone and others. Emily's ruination would make her prey to creatures like Kelsey, and Cornelia, always strong, nearly wept at the lonely and shameful future her beloved niece might face if Ainsworth was to proceed with his wicked plan, only substituting Emily for Anne. And he would be cruel, Cornelia acknowledged bitterly, cruel and vicious, punishing Emily for denying him Anne.

Not considering the bleak future that would be hers should the worst happen, Emily snorted. "As if I would care."

Cornelia stopped and glared at her. "You should care!" she said angrily. "Stop and think how you will feel when you find you are no longer welcome in the vicar's home, or when Mrs. Featherstone and Lady Broadfoot deny you entrance to their homes. How will you feel when people you have known and liked all your life cross the street to avoid meeting you? Or another Ainsworth accosts you or someone like that disgusting Kelsey. You haven't *thought*, girl! If you fall into their hands, this won't be something you can *fix*."

Emily's face went white and she swallowed hard. Cornelia painted a grim picture and Emily was conscious of the faintest quiver of fear. She fought it back and her chin lifted. "Then I'll just have to make certain Ainsworth doesn't get his hands on me, won't I?"

It wasn't precisely the answer Cornelia wanted, but at

least Emily was thinking of the consequences and not thinking rape by Ainsworth would be something she could just
brush off.

The two ladies spent a tense, uncomfortable day together.
Neither one was much for conversation and when the invitation to visit Lord Joslyn late that afternoon was delivered via
Walker, Emily would have turned it down, but before she
could, Cornelia said, "Tell Lord Joslyn we would be most
happy to visit with him."

Walker departed and Emily shot her great-aunt a dark
look and demanded, "Why did you accept? I am in no mood
for polite chatter."

Standing up and shaking out the skirts of her dove-gray
gown, Cornelia said, "Neither am I, but it'll be something to
distract us." She smiled at Emily. "I've always found that the
company of a handsome man lifts me from the doldrums."

The moment Emily entered his room, Barnaby knew that
something was amiss. He studied the faces of the women, as
Walker moved about serving tea and offering a plate of
sliced currant cake. He was most aware of Emily's de-
meanor, but even Cornelia seemed subdued. Knowing that
Ainsworth intended to marry Anne and he strongly suspected, whether the lady was willing or not, Anne's absence
alarmed him.

He waited until everyone was served and Walker departed before he did any probing. The minute the door shut
behind Walker, keeping a bland expression on his face, he
inquired, "And where is the delightful young Mrs. Townsend?
Hopefully, she is not indisposed?"

Cornelia smiled, though not, he decided, with her usual
roughish vigor. "You probably haven't heard: Jeffery's younger

brother, Hugh, was here for a lightning visit. Arrived yesterday and has already departed for his home, Parkham House—less than a day's ride from here. Took Anne with him to keep his mother company. Hugh is busy with his own affairs and his mother, who lives with him, is lonely."

"Hugh was very sorry he didn't have the opportunity to meet you," chimed in Emily. Her face full of affection, she added, "You would like Hugh." For a second amusement flickered in her eyes. "He is *nothing* like my cousin Jeffery."

Barnaby laughed. "Actually, I did know about Hugh's arrival. The servant grapevine is very efficient, but I hadn't yet heard that he had left and that your stepmother had gone with him." He hesitated, thinking of Ainsworth's declaration. Something wasn't adding up. Unable to help himself, he asked, "Ainsworth didn't have a problem with her leaving at a time like this?"

Emily's eyes narrowed. "What do you mean, 'at a time like this'?"

"Why only that Ainsworth led me to believe that an engagement between them was imminent."

So angry she forgot herself, Emily declared hotly, "That lying, yellow snake! *Nothing* could be further from the truth! Anne cannot abide him. In fact," she said, "it was to escape Ainsworth's odious attentions that she decided it would be prudent to leave The Birches for several weeks."

Barnaby glanced at Cornelia, but she made no attempt to smooth over Emily's outburst. Anne was safely away, but Cornelia had one more chick to protect—and if she had to lie down with the devil to do it, she would. She didn't think Lord Joslyn was the devil—quite the opposite. Cornelia was a good judge of people and instinctively she trusted him. They needed help and having taken his measure during that first meeting and noted the way his gaze strayed to Emily, she decided that perhaps it was time for some plain speaking.

Bluntly she said, "Ainsworth will come into a great deal

of money if he marries a respectable woman by the first of March. His reputation is such that few responsible parents or guardians would countenance a match between him and their daughters or wards. He has been hunting for months for a woman foolish enough to marry him. Time is running out for him and he is rather desperate to find a bride."

"And Jeffery brings him here," Barnaby drawled, "where he thinks he has, not one, but two likely prospects?"

Cornelia nodded, her face tight and grim.

Barnaby picked up the cup of tea they'd been served earlier and took a sip in order to give himself a moment to control the fury clawing at his breast. He was very good at deciphering what Cornelia had left unsaid. There was wicked mischief in the air and the one person who should have the care of the two women under his protection foremost in his mind was aiding Ainsworth. Now why would Jeffery . . . The answer came to him even as the thought formed. Money.

Setting down his cup in the saucer, he said, "Your Jeffery is an enterprising gentleman, isn't he? Not only does he introduce a varlet like Ainsworth into a respectable household with two eligible young women, but he's willing to accept Ainsworth's money to ensure he has his bride. Rather like shooting fish in a barrel." He raised a brow. "Do I have the correct reading?"

Again Cornelia nodded, delighted with his quick grasp of the situation . . . and the dangerous gleam in his black eyes.

Barnaby's fingers formed a steeple, and looking at them he said to no one in particular, "With Anne . . . I trust you have no objections to my familiarity?"

"At this point, no," said Cornelia. "In fact, I would prefer it. You may call me Cornelia, and you already know Emily's given name."

Barnaby showed that singularly attractive smile of his. "In that case, I insist that you call me Barnaby." The smile became a grin. "I've been Barnaby Joslyn for far longer than

I have been Lord Joslyn and I find myself a bit weary of 'milord this' and 'milord that.'"

"Are all Americans like you?" Emily asked curiously, finding it astonishing that he would so easily discard his title and offer them such easy familiarity. She tried to picture Mathew Joslyn doing so, but she could not.

Barnaby shrugged. "Just as not all Englishmen are alike, the same is true of Americans. Believe me, we have our villains, too." A scowl creased his forehead. "But none, I don't think, as villainous as the pair of scoundrels you have underfoot."

"I agree," said Cornelia. "It would be hard to find their equal."

Bending forward, Barnaby asked, "With Anne out of the way, is it your belief that they will turn their attention to Emily?"

"I cannot say for certain," Cornelia admitted, "but even with Anne beyond his grasp, Ainsworth still needs a wife . . . and only Emily remains."

Both Barnaby and Cornelia looked at her and Emily made a face. "Most likely Ainsworth will turn his attention onto me, but I am not Anne! I'm stronger and I'm certainly not easily intimidated nor very biddable or frightened."

"You may be all of those things, but you would be no match for a determined man," Barnaby said grimly. "Especially if he had you in a place where no one would hear your screams . . . or anyone who did would ignore them."

Emily swallowed. "We don't know that Ainsworth will settle for me." Her lip curled. "He doesn't like me very much and I've made my aversion to him plain."

"As apparently has Anne, but that didn't deter him, did it?" Barnaby growled, the very thought of Ainsworth touching Emily arousing every protective and possessive instinct he possessed. I'll kill him if he dares lay a finger on her, he admitted savagely. And enjoy doing it.

"So what are we to do?" Cornelia asked practically, her gaze fixed on Barnaby's dark features.

Barnaby rose to his feet and stalked around the room, his lithe grace making Emily think of the big lion she'd seen in the royal menagerie in the Tower of London. He didn't, she decided, look much like a man who had come so near death only a few days ago. The heavy black hair hid the wound site and there was no outward sign of debilitation. He exuded power and purpose and she was ashamed to admit she was grateful he was on their side.

He stopped and stood before Emily, that inescapable feeling of possession riding him hard. This woman was his, realizing with no little astonishment that he meant to marry her. And by God! He'd not leave her in danger. The expression in the dark eyes hidden, he said, "You are not safe here. You and your aunt must come with me to Windmere—I can protect you there, as I cannot here. Within Windmere's stout walls you will have no fear that Ainsworth or your cousin will touch you."

It wasn't exactly what Cornelia wanted, but it would do, she decided thoughtfully. Certainly, their sudden removal to the home of the viscount would cause gossip and more than a little speculation, but it didn't worry her. If she read the signs right—and she rather thought she did; she was, after all, a wise old bird who'd observed more than one moonstruck pair—it wouldn't be many weeks before the engagement between Emily and Lord Joslyn was announced. It would do. Emily would be safe and Joslyn could do his wooing without interference. She half smiled. And Jeffery would be furious.

Barnaby glanced at Cornelia and breathed a sigh of relief at the slight nod of her head. Splendid! He had one ally now, he thought, turning his attention back to Emily. He just needed to convince the gray-eyed virago before him.

Aware of nothing but Barnaby's harsh-featured face above

hers, his startling words ringing in her ears, Emily gaped at him. Chaotic thoughts whirled through her brain, but she was finally able to catch one and demanded incredulously, "Are you mad? Good God! The countryside would be aflame with gossip." Her eyes narrowed. "Or don't you care for your reputation as well as mine?"

Lamb stuck his head inside the room, preventing Barnaby's reply. "Mathew is here to see you," announced Lamb. "Shall I have Walker show him up?"

Bad timing, Barnaby thought, but it changed nothing. No matter what argument the lady put forth, she and her aunt would be installed in Windmere. It was, he told himself virtuously, for her own good.

Mathew was shown into the room and it was obvious that this was no formal visit; Mathew's handsome features were grim above his elegantly tied cravat.

Never one to stand on ceremony, Cornelia said, "You are obviously big with news. Do you wish us to leave you in private?"

"No, that's not necessary," said Mathew. "You will soon hear it." Looking at Barnaby he said quietly, "I received a letter this morning from a friend of mine staying in London. Word has arrived from France that Louis the Sixteenth was guillotined on Monday in Paris."

There was a concerted gasp from the ladies, but beyond a tightening around his mouth Barnaby betrayed no emotion. The death of the King of France was stunning news, no less so than the knowledge that he had been condemned to death by the revolutionaries who had taken over France, but Barnaby's most immediate concern was the whereabouts and safety of Lucien, his bastard half brother. Lucien was known to be in France and, knowing Lucien, he'd be up to his ears in intrigue. Something sick curled in his belly. Damn you, Lucien! he thought angrily. If you get yourself killed . . .

Cornelia leaned forward and asked anxiously, "The Queen? Marie Antoinette? She lives?"

Mathew nodded curtly. "At least at the writing of my friend's letter."

"What of the dauphine?" Barnaby asked in a hard voice. "Have they taken to killing children?"

Mathew shook his head. "According to my friend, the rest of the royal family remains imprisoned at the Temple and all of them are still alive . . . for now." He glanced meaningfully at Barnaby. "France is no place to be at this time. We shall be at war with her within weeks, if not days."

Barnaby flashed him a dark look. "Don't you think I know that!" His face set in grim lines, he muttered, "I warned him, but no one can tell Lucifer what to do when he gets an idea in his head."

"Lucifer?" questioned Emily, big-eyed.

"My half brother, and if ever there was a hell-born babe . . . and not to wrap it in clean linen, one born on the wrong side of the blanket," Barnaby answered. "His mother was French— she died years ago, but when the current madness overtook France, Lucien—Luc—took it in his head to see if any of the family had survived the Revolution." His lips twisted. "Since her family was a member of the minor nobility, I doubt that anyone is left alive, but if there is someone, Luc will find them—and get them out of the country . . . if he doesn't lose his own head in the process."

Shaken by news of the king's terrible fate, Cornelia rose to her feet. "We shall leave you, gentlemen. I'm sure there is much you wish to say in private." She glanced at Barnaby who was already opening his mouth to argue. "After your cousin has left, we can continue our conversation." Her voice full of meaning, she said, "I shall see to it that everything is in order for your departure to Windmere."

As the ladies left the room, Mathew asked Barnaby, "You're coming back to Windmere? Do you think that is wise? I assure you that there is no need, I have things well in hand." A note of resentment crept into his voice and he added, "I think you forget that I have known Windmere all my life and oversaw the day-to-day operation of the estate during the last several months of our great-uncle's life. I am quite familiar with what is needed."

"I could hardly forget those facts," Barnaby said, ringing for Lamb, "when you remind me of them so often." His gaze narrowed, he murmured, "It's time I returned to my home—I wouldn't want you to get too comfortable in my absence."

Mathew flushed and his lips thinned. "Damn you! I am no carrion eater! I cannot wish you well, but I do not wish you evil." He stared daggers at Barnaby. "I did not deserve that remark—if anyone else had uttered it, I'd have demanded they name their seconds."

Barnaby sighed and waved an apologetic hand. "You're right. It was uncalled for and I am sorry for it." He smiled ruefully. "I'm afraid that you bring out the worst in me."

Mathew hesitated, then muttered bitterly, "And you in me." His azure eyes met Barnaby's watchful black ones. "I doubt we will ever be friends, but I hope that we can learn to deal with each other without animosity."

Lamb's entrance precluded further comment. Mathew stiffly took his leave.

"Ruffled his feathers, did you?" asked Lamb.

"Yes, and unnecessarily—especially when I believe he was trying to do me a favor." Briefly, Barnaby told him the news Mathew had relayed.

Like Barnaby, Lamb's first thought was of Lucien. "That damned Lucifer! If he escapes from France with his head intact it will be a miracle."

"I agree," said Barnaby in a calmer tone, although his worry for Lucien did not escape Lamb. "Unfortunately, there is nothing we can do to help him," Barnaby admitted heavily. "We have no idea where he is . . . even if he is still alive, and I see no way we can even begin to mount a rescue." He eyed Lamb. "Your thoughts?"

His own face reflecting the same deep concern on Barnaby's, he said bitterly, "I see nothing we can do with what we know at the moment, but wait and hope the lucky devil's luck holds." He forced a smile. "Knowing Lucifer, he'll rise to the top of the dung heap—just as he always does."

Emily's protestations hissed into Cornelia's ear as they hurried through the house toward Emily's bedroom made absolutely no impact. Reaching her bedroom, the door slammed shut behind them, Emily growled, "For the last time, I am not going to be hustled off to Windmere like a trussed-up chicken going to market." Arms crossed over her chest, she said childishly, "And you can't make me go."

Cornelia rounded angrily on her and, shaking a bony finger in Emily's face, she said grimly, "Girl, if I have to hit you over the head or truss you up *exactly* like a hen for market, I damn well will! And if you think Walker and the rest of the servants won't help me, you're sillier than I thought." She caught her breath and said more gently, "Emily, it is the only way you will be safe from Ainsworth and that wretched cousin of yours. You might think that his dislike of you will keep Ainsworth away, but that's folly. He wants that fortune and you have to get it through your head that he will do anything to get it—even marry a woman he detests."

Shaken by Cornelia's vehemence, Emily's resistance crumbled. Unhappily, she admitted that her beloved great-aunt obviously believed that she was in danger, and if for no other reason than to ease Cornelia's fears, she should accept Lord Joslyn's offer of refuge. "Very well," Emily said in a low voice. "We'll go."

More relieved than she cared to admit, Cornelia said, "We

have no time to pack very much. Just take what you will need for a few days. The rest of our things can follow later."

"If Jeffery doesn't burn them in a rage," Emily said drily. Despite having accepted that they would go to Windmere, she couldn't help asking, "You really believe that Ainsworth would take me as a substitute for Anne?"

Cornelia nodded. "He wants that fortune—at any cost. We are lucky that Anne is on her way to Parkham and that Ainsworth and Jeffery are unaware of it. It will be even better if *we* are gone before they return. For once we can be happy that Jeffery is in Newhaven squandering money he doesn't have on a horse he doesn't need."

Jeffery and Ainsworth were *not* in Newhaven and there never was any horse. The trip to Newhaven had been a ruse to disguise their real destination—the farmhouse where Jeffery met his mistresses. The two men were spending that day seeing that all was in readiness for Anne's abduction and ravishment. Unfortunately, the news that Anne had slipped from their grasp had already come to their ears. . . .

Chapter 12

It was simple happenstance that Jeffery and Ainsworth learned of Anne's departure for Parkham House. As she did frequently, Rosie Perrin, Sally's sister, visited at The Birches that Thursday afternoon. Seated at Mrs. Spalding's scrubbed table in the kitchen, drinking tea and laughing and chatting with Sally and the others, Rosie heard in passing that Mrs. Anne Townsend had left that morning to stay for several weeks at Parkham House.

Returning to the village in the late afternoon, she stopped at The Ram's Head to see if she was needed for work that evening. She wasn't, but she spied Kelsey sitting at a small table in the corner and joined him.

The two of them talked desultorily for several minutes before Rosie mentioned her visit to The Birches and the news that Mrs. Anne Townsend had gone to stay with the squire's mother at Parkham House. Kelsey immediately perked up and wondered how best to use the information Rosie had so innocently passed on to him.

While not privy to the plans of the squire and Ainsworth, he was aware that the two men were up to no good and that whatever they were scheming to do involved Anne Townsend. Knowing of the fortune in the offing for Ainsworth once he had secured a respectable bride, and being of a like mind, Kelsey had long ago guessed the method Ainsworth would use to gain the hand of a woman who spurned his suit.

A natural-born snoop, Kelsey had known for months about the farmhouse used for Jeffery's assignations. Since his dismissal, with scant money, except the pittance Jeffery passed him now and then, he had broken into the place and had been sleeping in one of the bedrooms. This morning he'd been startled awake by the arrival of Jeffery and Ainsworth and had barely managed to escape undetected out of the bedroom window at the side of the house. Finding the horses concealed in the stables and noting the saddlebags bulging with wine and foodstuff and other items, Kelsey had chosen a hiding place nearby and hung around watching. Clearly they were preparing to use the house and he didn't think that it would be Jeffery meeting a willing wench for a night of frolic. Ainsworth's presence was particularly telling.

After Rosie left the tavern, Kelsey sat back and considered what he knew and how best to use it. It was a good bet that the squire and Ainsworth had no idea that Anne Townsend had slipped away and he wondered how grateful they'd be to learn of her departure. Only one way to find out, he decided, rising to his feet.

Neither Jeffery nor Ainsworth was happy when Kelsey strolled into the old kitchen at the farmhouse some time later. Kelsey observed that little had been done in the kitchen, but there were now several bottles of wine set out and food and plates, utensils and glasses scattered across the dusty table against the far wall. The bedroom, he thought with a tingle in his privates, was most likely to reveal the majority of their efforts, such as clean sheets on the well-worn mattress; Ainsworth was fussy that way.

"What are you doing here?" demanded Jeffery. "I told you to lay low and that I'd see that all was right with you as soon as I could."

Kelsey shot him a look of dislike. "And in the meantime, I'm reduced to damn near beggary. I'm tired of waiting! I want some money and I've discovered something that should fill these hands with gold." Glancing at the items on the table, he smiled nastily and added, "Especially, if all these preparations are in anticipation of the arrival of the young Mrs. Townsend."

Jeffery stiffened. "What do you mean?"

"Why, only that I have news that you might like to hear . . . for a price."

His eyes cold and considering, Ainsworth asked, "And what makes you think that we are interested in the activities of Mrs. Townsend?"

"Do you take me for a fool?" Kelsey snarled. "The lady doesn't want to marry you, but you need a bride and there's only one sure way of gaining her consent—if you have a stomach strong enough for it."

Ainsworth studied his fingernails. "Suppose you are right," he drawled. "Why do you think what you know will help us?"

Kelsey grinned, showing yellowed and missing teeth. "Because I can save you wasted effort."

"How?" asked Jeffery.

"Pay me and you'll find out."

Ainsworth studied Kelsey for a long minute and then, reaching into his vest pocket, he extracted a gold coin. He tossed it at Kelsey who caught it in one smooth movement. "If what you have to say is valuable," Ainsworth said, "you can keep that, but if it is not . . ."

"It's worth it," Kelsey said, the coin disappearing under his clothing. Only after he had hidden the gold away did it occur to Kelsey that Miss Emily, or that old witch, Mrs. Cornelia, might have been willing to pay much more to know about Jeffery and Ainsworth's activities at the farmhouse. He brightened, realizing that there was nothing to stop him from leaving here and taking his chances with the ladies. . . .

"I'm still waiting to learn if I get good value for my money," said Ainsworth impatiently, walking toward the old stone fireplace. Stopping just a few paces from Kelsey, he asked, "What do you know?"

Kelsey repeated what he'd learned from Rosie, enjoying the consternation and dismay that flooded Jeffery's face. Ainsworth's expression revealed nothing.

"Good God!" burst out Jeffery despairingly. "What are we to do? If they left this morning, we have no chance of overtaking them."

"And I wouldn't even try if they left only minutes ago," snapped Ainsworth. "Not unless you want to put a bullet through your brother's heart and attempt an abduction in broad daylight on a public road."

No longer interested in Ainsworth and Jeffery now that he had some money, and eager to reach The Birches, Kelsey said, "Think I'll be on my way."

"Wait!" said Ainsworth. "You've earned this." He tossed another coin in Kelsey's direction, deliberately miscalculating the distance. The coin fell and danced across the worn stone floor. Kelsey bent to pick up the coin and Ainsworth moved with the speed of a viper, snatching up a hefty piece of firewood from the neat stack on the hearth and swinging it down viciously on the back of Kelsey's head.

Kelsey fell facedown without a sound. Ignoring Jeffery's horrified gasp, Ainsworth kicked Kelsey over onto his back. Kelsey was still breathing and Ainsworth bent over and coolly and methodically hit him several more times with the heavy piece of wood. Only when Kelsey was dead, did Ainsworth straighten and toss the wood onto the hearth.

Jeffery took one look at what had once been Kelsey's face

and his stomach lurched. He ran out of the kitchen, barely making it outside before he was violently ill. Only when he was certain his stomach was empty did he return inside. Wiping his mouth and keeping his eyes averted from Kelsey's body, he asked in shaken tones, "Was that necessary?"

"Yes," replied Ainsworth, not even breathing hard after his exertions. "I wasn't willing to run the risk that he would run to your cousin and great-aunt with news of our activities." Prodding the body with the toe of his boot, he said maliciously, "I'll leave it to you to dispose of the body."

Jeffery opened his mouth to protest, but the look on Ainsworth's face stopped him. Swallowing his gorge he approached Kelsey's body and, gingerly taking hold of one arm, began to pull the body from the room. Kelsey hadn't been a big man, but he was deadweight and it was several minutes before Jeffery had the body out of the house and hidden beneath some brush behind the stables.

Returning to the kitchen, still pale and shaken, he found Ainsworth sitting in one of the rickety wooden chairs, sipping a glass of wine from one of the bottles they'd brought with them.

Helping himself to a glass, Jeffery tossed it off in one swallow. "What are we to do now? All is lost."

Ainsworth flashed him a contemptuous glance. "No, all is not lost." His eyes went dark with fury. "She will not be the bride I wanted, but I'm afraid that your cousin, Emily, will just have to do."

Jeffery gaped at him. "You're mad if you think you can force Emily to do anything."

"She will fear ruin," Ainsworth said carelessly, "as much as the next woman."

Jeffery looked doubtful. "That may be, but she's going to make you an intolerable wife."

Ainsworth looked at him and Jeffery was chilled at what

he saw in Ainsworth's eyes. "She only has to live," Ainsworth said softly, "long enough for me to gain my fortune. After that . . ." He took a sip of his wine and smiled. "After that, I fear my bride will suffer a fatal accident."

Jeffery's eyes dropped. He wasn't, he told himself a *bad* man, and if it hadn't been for some unfortunate losses at the gaming tables, the majority to Ainsworth, he wouldn't have found himself in this situation. He had been perfectly willing to help Ainsworth marry Anne, but Kelsey's death wasn't something he would ever have condoned—if his opinion had been asked. Jeffery wasn't fond of Emily, but he retained enough family loyalty to be unhappy contemplating her cold-blooded murder. Staring into his empty glass, he wished miserably he'd never agreed to Ainsworth's terms and that he'd never invited the man to The Birches.

Aware that Jeffery was having second thoughts, Ainsworth said, "We only have to change our plans slightly. I don't want to waste any more time." He looked thoughtful. "In fact, I think we should quietly return to your house and spy out the lay of the land. It's possible that luck will be on our side and we can snatch your cousin without anyone ever realizing we have even been on the grounds." He smiled. "She'll just disappear . . . and later reappear as my bride." Jeffery didn't appear enthusiastic and, guessing that the murder of Kelsey had disturbed him, Ainsworth said with suspect sincerity, "I know what happened was a shock to you. . . . I'm sorry about Kelsey's death, but the fewer people that know about our being here, the better. With Kelsey, er, gone, we two are the only ones who know we have been here, and I'd just as soon keep it that way."

Ainsworth was wrong. Someone else knew that they were at the farmhouse—Sam Gates and his good friend, the cobbler's son, Billy Ford. The two boys, when able to escape from the parental eye, trampled at will through the country-side, and the stables at the abandoned farmhouse was a fa-vorite place of theirs to hunt rats with Billy's small terrier, Tiger. About midday when they'd slipped into the stables with the eager dog, they'd been astonished to find a pair of horses standing tied in the alleyway in the center of the building. Sam recognized the squire's horse, an elegant bay gelding with one white hind foot: his father had replaced a thrown shoe only a few days ago. A complete set of new shoes had been put on Ainsworth's dappled gray gelding the same day, so Sam had no trouble identifying the second horse.

Hearing the squire and Ainsworth's voices approaching, Sam and Billy grabbed Tiger and the two boys and dog scooted out the back of the stables through a loose board. The presence of the squire and his friend at the abandoned farmstead was notable and of a curious nature. Sam and Billy tied the dog a short distance away and returned to watch the two men. From their hiding place in a small patch of woods off to the side of the barn, the boys observed the squire and Ainsworth making several trips from the stables to the house carrying various items. After a while the boys grew bored and wandered back to the dog, deciding to ask the vicar if he would let them hunt in his stables. There wouldn't be as much sport since the vicar kept a half-dozen or so cats around the place, but they might be able to find an unwary rat or two.

It was late in the day by the time Sam made his way to The Crown where he knew that at this hour he would find his father enjoying a well-deserved tankard of ale. Entering the inn, he found his father sitting at a table with Jeb Brown and Mrs. Gilbert. At Sam's approach, knowing growing boys, Mrs. Gilbert smiled and said, "Go into the kitchen and have Flora or one of the girls fix you a sandwich."

Grinning, he said, "Thank you—I'm fair starved to death," and disappeared into the back of the inn. He reappeared several minutes later with crumbs on his chin and an impressive milk mustache framing his mouth, indicating he'd been fed well. As was his wont he sidled onto the remaining empty chair and half-dozing listened to the conversation of the adults.

Sam was almost asleep but he jerked wide-awake when Mrs. Gilbert said, "There's no telling what the squire and that unpleasant friend of his are capable of doing. At least we don't have to worry about them right now—when I saw Walker in the village yesterday, he mentioned that they were going to Newhaven today."

"But they didn't go to Newhaven," Sam said innocently. Three pairs of narrowed adult eyes swiveled in his direction. He swallowed and muttered, "Well, at least, they weren't there this afternoon. Me and Billy saw them out at the old Godart place earlier today."

"And what were you doing at the Godart place?" Caleb asked in a tone that told Sam he'd better have a good reason for having been at the deserted farmstead.

Earnestly, Sam said, "We were only going to hunt rats in the barn with Billy's dog."

Caleb grunted and Sam breathed easier.

"When did you see them?" asked Mrs. Gilbert, frowning.

Sam hunched a shoulder. "Don't know the time, but it was this afternoon—Billy had to work for his da until nearly noon and it was after that."

"That place has been standing empty for years," observed Jeb. "Can't imagine it would hold any interest for the squire and his friend. What were they doing?"

"I dunno," Sam said. "Their horses was in the stables and they had brought some things in their saddlebags that they took into the house." Apologetically, he said, "Me and Billy got bored watching them and so we walked on over to the vicar's and he let us hunt in his stables." His face brightened. "Tiger got three rats! Vicar was pleased."

Caleb, trailed by a lagging Sam, left a few minutes later. Alone at the table, Mrs. Gilbert looked at Jeb. "You still thinking of shoving off tonight after dark?"

"Barometer hasn't budged in a few days," Jeb admitted, "but my bad knee is starting to ache. Kept me awake half the night."

Jeb's "bad knee" had proven to be an excellent indicator of the weather in the past and knowing that if it was bothering him that there'd most likely be a storm blowing in before too many more days went by, Mrs. Gilbert nodded wisely. "Storm coming."

"Yep. I believe so."

"If you're sailing tonight, you'll have to see Miss Emily first. . . ." Mrs. Gilbert said, thinking aloud. "Might be a good thing," she added, "when you see her you tell her what young Sam just told us."

"Thought crossed my mind." His expression troubled, Jeb said, "I wonder what they were up to out at the Godart place. Seems suspicious like, them being there—especially since they're supposed to have been in Newhaven today."

"Which is why," Mrs. Gilbert said briskly, rising to her feet, "you'll tell Miss Emily when you see her."

Emily and Cornelia spent the afternoon packing what they would need for the first few days at Windmere. Emily was still resistant to the idea, unable to take seriously the notion that Ainsworth would substitute her in place of Anne. Every time she tried to renew the argument, Cornelia would stop her with a sharp look and the grim question: "Do you *really* want to take the chance?" Making a face, Emily returned to her packing, thinking that Cornelia was overreacting.

While the ladies were busy packing, Barnaby sent a message by Tom the footman to Windmere, stating that he and Lamb were returning home and requesting that his carriage be driven over to pick them up late that afternoon. To the stable at The Birches, he sent word to have his and Lamb's horses saddled and readied to leave.

Lamb had everything packed and the valises sitting by the front door within a matter of a few hours. Such was not the case with Emily and Cornelia. Since neither lady was confident that Jeffery wouldn't burn their belongings when he discovered they'd left, they ended up with considerably more things than originally planned.

With little to do but wait, Barnaby paced, impatient for the news that the women were *finally* packed and that the coach had arrived from Windmere. Jeffery and Ainsworth may have gone to Newhaven and weren't expected back until well into the evening, but Barnaby didn't want to take any chances on them returning unexpectedly. The sooner they were gone from The Birches and at Windmere, the better he would like it.

Emily and Cornelia managed to cram everything they could not bear to leave behind to Jeffery's tender mercies into two rather alarmingly large trunks and an equally large pair of bandboxes. Once the two trunks were muscled down the stairs into the entry hall and the bandboxes placed on top of them, everyone breathed easier.

With Lamb in the front of the house, on the lookout for the coach, Barnaby and the two women were closeted in the small green salon at the rear of the house. Conversation was sporadic and there were long stretches of silence; the three of them were waiting tensely for the news that the coach had arrived.

A tap on the door brought everyone to their feet, but

when Walker entered the room, he looked at Emily and said apologetically, "No, the coach has not arrived, but there is an, ah, friend of yours waiting to see you in the kitchen."

Emily immediately guessed the identity of her visitor and the reason for the visit. Blessing the coach's delay, giving Barnaby and Cornelia a quick smile, she said, "I'll only be a moment." When Barnaby looked ready to object, she added, "It is important. Walker will stay right by my side—I'll be quite safe."

Grabbing her blue-and-oyster silk-and-velvet reticule, she slipped into the hall. Shutting the door behind her, Emily asked, "Is it Jeb? He's going to sail tonight?"

Walker nodded, his face troubled. "And he was full of news of the squire and Mr. Ainsworth: they are not in Newhaven, but have been busy out at the old Godart place. Sam saw them there this afternoon."

Barely suppressing a gasp, Emily said, "So that's where they intended to take Anne!"

There was no time for further conversation and, with Walker at her heels, her fingers clutching the reticule, Emily sped toward the kitchen. This afternoon had been so frantic that it was only when she'd put the money for the next shipment into her reticule just before leaving her room to walk with Cornelia to the green salon had she given a thought to Jeb's impending trip, or the smuggling enterprise at all. Barnaby might have thought she was unduly quiet in the green salon, but Emily had been thinking hard about the ramifications her removal to Windmere would have on the smuggling operation. Mrs. Gilbert and the others needed to know what was happening.

Jeb's arrival tonight couldn't have been better timed and she was relieved that she could kill two birds with one stone: he'd have the money and he could tell Mrs. Gilbert of the removal to Windmere.

All of the servants knew what was going on, but they all

maintained the fiction that Jeb had merely come for a friendly visit with Jane, his niece, and lone remaining house-maid at The Birches. When Emily rushed into the kitchen, Jeb rose to his feet, kissed Jane on her cheek and said that he'd be off now—once he had a private word with Miss.

Daylight was fading as Emily and Jeb stepped out the kitchen door and hurried toward the stables where Jeb had left Caleb's horse. As they walked, their heads close to-gether, Emily brought Jeb current with the happenings at The Birches. Even though they were alone, they both kept their voices just above a whisper, always wary of being over-heard.

"Make certain Mrs. Gilbert knows that we will be at Windmere before you leave tonight," she ordered as they rounded a curve and the house disappeared from sight. The stables were hidden beyond another curve just ahead and at this particular stretch of road, between the two curves, they were out of sight from anyone at the stables or the house. Stopping in the middle of the narrow road she opened her reticule and hastily handed Jeb the small leather pouch. It disappeared inside his worn brown jacket.

"What if you're needed unexpectedly?" Jeb asked quietly, worry in his eyes. "How will we let you know? Can't have Sam slipping into the kitchen at Windmere with a message for you."

Emily considered his concerns. They were valid. Smug-gling was an uncertain business and beyond knowing the tides there wasn't ever any set timetable for Jeb's return and the unloading of the contraband goods. The only constant was that the smuggled items from France were unloaded on moonless nights or, to avoid the revenuers, in the midst of a storm—if possible. While still at sea, using a lantern, Jeb was able to signal his approach to Mr. Meek whose small cottage was situated on a chalk bluff above the pounding surf. Once Mr. Meek was alerted to Jeb's impending arrival, having acknowledged Jeb's signal with his own lantern, he hastened to The Crown and Mrs. Gilbert. She spread the word amongst the small crew that helped with the unloading and the transportation to London. As their leader, Emily was always there to lend a hand where needed. With the loyal band of servants at The Birches benefiting from the smuggling operation, it was simple enough for Sam to get her word that a landing was in the offing. But at Windmere . . .

Emily bit her lip. How was she to get word of a landing and, almost as important, slip out of the house in the dead of night and ride to the village?

"Do you know of anyone at Windmere we can trust?" she asked Jeb, keeping her voice low.

Jeb pulled on his ear. "Mrs. Spalding's sister, Mrs. Eason, is the cook there . . . I expect she knows how to keep her mouth shut and would help us."

Emily didn't like it but time was passing and she had to make a decision. As they stood there talking, a feeling of unease swept over her and she glanced around. There was the faintest breeze rattling the bare branches of the trees near the road, but even without leaves to obscure the view, the woods were full of shadows and odd patches of darkness. She saw nothing to alarm her, but unable to shake the feeling that they were being watched, she didn't linger and began to walk once more. When she spoke to Jeb, her voice was even lower than previously. "Explain it all to Mrs. Gilbert immediately," she urged, "and tell Mrs. Gilbert to talk to Mrs. Spalding—tomorrow. If they agree that Mrs. Eason will help us, Mrs. Spalding can see her sister and make the arrangements. If Mrs. Eason will do it, she can find a way to let me know."

"And if we can't trust her?" Jeb asked, keeping step with her.

"Then we'll have to think of something else," she admitted gloomily. "Hopefully, before your return, I will have discovered a way I can slip in and out of the house undetected."

She half smiled. "And stealing a horse from Lord Joslyn's barn shouldn't be beyond me. I'm sure they've had some of their animals 'borrowed' before this."

They continued walking, shortly rounding the curve that had hidden the stables from view. She noted the pair of saddled horses tied to the long rail in front of the stables, recognizing them as Lord Joslyn's and Lamb's horses. Several yards from the long building, Emily stopped and asked abruptly, "When you're in Calais have you noticed very many people trying to get out of the country?"

If he was surprised at her question, Jeb didn't show it. "I hear things . . . but I've never been approached."

Emily hesitated, then said in a rush, "Keep your ears open. Lord Joslyn has a half brother, Lucien, who is in France now and most likely will be trying to get out of the country. It's possible he could be at Calais."

Jeb looked thoughtful. "I know a few people. I can ask around."

"Oh, Jeb, you *are* a darling!" Emily exclaimed, beaming at him. "I know that Lord Joslyn will pay you well if you are able to bring Lucien back with you."

"*If* he's in Calais," Jeb warned. "There are other ports he might be in and I can't go looking for him."

Her smile fading, Emily nodded.

"Now I'll say good-bye," Jeb said gruffly. " I've got a ship and crew to get ready to sail with the tide."

She watched him disappear inside the stable and it was only when he reappeared, mounted his horse and with a wave rode off in the opposite way they had come did she turn in the direction of the house. Even though she knew she had been gone longer than planned, Emily's step was reluctant. She should have been feeling relieved, and in many ways she was—Jeb's timely arrival had solved quite a few problems for her. He now had the funds for more contraband and he would inform Mrs. Gilbert of her removal to Windmere. Tomorrow Mrs. Gilbert and Mrs. Spalding would put their heads together and hopefully Mrs. Eason would cooperate, but . . . She was, she realized, for reasons that escaped her, dreading the removal to Windmere and being indebted to Lord Joslyn.

She made a face. She was being silly. In minutes she'd be on her way to one of the most impressive homes in Britain, the guest of a man whose very look did peculiar things to her heart. Just about any other woman in the neighborhood, she admitted wryly, perhaps even the whole of England would be over the moon to be in her shoes.

Not one to repine, Emily straightened her shoulders and, her reticule in one hand, she picked up one side of her skirt with the other and briskly set out toward the house. Reaching that stretch of road hidden from both the stables and the house, she had not gone more than a dozen steps before her pace faltered. The back of her neck prickled, and despite the long sleeves and the warmth of the amber merino wool dress she was wearing, she shivered.

Scolding herself for being a goose, she took another step, but a sound behind her stopped her in her tracks. Spinning around, she looked in that direction as Jeffery, on his bay gelding, came crashing out of the forest and blocked the way to the stables.

Her first reaction was one of astonishment, although not as much as there would have been if Jeb hadn't told her that Jeffery and Ainsworth were seen this afternoon at the Godart place. In the flurry surrounding Jeb's arrival, she hadn't had time to think about Jeffery and Ainsworth not having gone to Newhaven, but assuming the two men were still at the Godart farm, she hadn't been concerned. She certainly hadn't expected Jeffery to suddenly appear before her.

Feigning innocence, she said, "Jeffery! What are you doing here? I thought you were going to Newhaven today."

Her cousin did not look well and his expression was sullen as he muttered, "Changed my mind."

Conscious of the fleeting minutes and of the need to tell Barnaby and Cornelia of Jeffery's return, she said, "Ah, well, I'll be on my way."

There was a rustle behind her and she whirled around, her heart leaping into her throat as Ainsworth, astride his dappled gray, stepped out onto the road, blocking her progress. It didn't escape her notice that she was trapped between the two men or that they were unobserved from either the stables or the house on this stretch of road.

Quelling the spasm of fear that clenched in her belly, reminding herself that they didn't know that Anne had escaped their clutches, her clear gray gaze fixed on Ainsworth, she said firmly, "You're blocking my way, sir. Please move your horse."

Ainsworth smiled nastily and something in that smile sent an arrow of fright shooting right through her. With all of Cornelia's dire warnings ringing in her ears, cursing herself for not paying more heed to her great-aunt's predications, Emily darted toward a thick patch of wood, hoping to lose herself in the tangle.

She was unsuccessful. Ainsworth's horse leaped forward and his arm closed around her waist, jerking her off her feet; her reticule dropped onto the road. Twisting and kicking, Emily was roughly hauled onto his horse in front of him. She clawed at Ainsworth's hand at her waist and he cursed as she drew blood.

One hand holding the reins of his dancing horse, Ainsworth grasped her hair with the other and pulled her head back until she thought her neck would snap. His lips next to her ear, he panted, "I like a woman with spirit, but save your strength for when I have you in bed."

Emily screamed with rage and, ignoring the pain, fought

to escape his vicious grip, her body thrashing about atop the horse. Unused to the unfamiliar weight and violent moments on his back, the horse snorted and half bucked and Ainsworth was nearly unseated. Forced to concentrate on his horse, his grip loosened on her hair.

Emily took advantage of the moment and sprang free. Her feet hit the ground and she stumbled into a run, but Ainsworth yelled to Jeffery, "Grab the reins, you fool!" and leaped from his horse right on her heels.

With one hand he caught her shoulder and spun her around, his other hand drawn back into fist. He moved so fast, she never even saw the blow that hit her. The last thing Emily remembered was a stunning shock of pain and then there was only blackness.

Chapter 13

Several minutes had passed and as Emily did not return, after looking at his gold pocket watch for the fourth time, not hiding his exasperation, Barnaby asked Cornelia, "What's taking her so long?"

Hiding her unease, Cornelia said, "She is probably just giving the servants a few last-minute instructions."

Barnaby looked at her incredulously. "Do you take me for a dunce?" Cornelia grimaced and he demanded, "Who is this 'friend' that it was so important she meet with right now?"

Cornelia considered the question, uncertain how much to reveal. Concluding that he could find out the identity of Emily's friend easily enough, she answered, "Most likely it is Jeb Brown."

"And what business would she have with a fisherman?" Barnaby inquired, his eyes narrowed and fixed on Cornelia's face. "And don't try to fob me off by telling me she's buying fresh fish for tonight's dinner!"

Cornelia hesitated. Shortly, she'd have Emily safely settled at Windmere and though aware that if things worked out as she hoped, Barnaby would have to know the truth eventually, she was still reluctant to expose Emily's smuggling. She eyed the dark, hard-faced man before her, wondering how he would react if she told him the truth. Cornelia trusted him else she would never have agreed to remove to Windmere; she suspected that his interest in Emily was more than just kindness and she'd been pleased with Emily's reaction to him, but that didn't mean she was ready to reveal all. It was too dicey, she finally decided, unwilling to risk a retraction of his invitation. She didn't think he would abandon them, in fact, she rather thought he'd take it in stride and never falter a step, but she wasn't willing to take any chances.

When Cornelia remained silent, Barnaby sighed. Sitting down beside her, he took her frail hand in his and said gently, "Suppose I tell you what I think is going on?"

"Suppose you do just that," she said, her intelligent hazel eyes intent on his.

"I believe that Emily has gone to meet Jeb because they are planning another run to a port in France to buy contraband goods for sale here in England," Barnaby said carefully. Noting that she had not hurled his words back in his face, he continued. "It's possible that Emily routinely goes about the countryside disguised as a boy and visits The Crown at odd hours of the night—as happened the night I first saw her, but I doubt it. I may be a newcomer to England, but even *I've* heard of the rampant smuggling that goes on along this stretch of coast. If she was involved in the landing of contraband goods, it explains why a gently born young woman was out at that hour of night garbed as a boy and at The Crown . . . the center of the, ah, smuggling ring."

"Quite a leap based on one event."

Barnaby grinned. "All right, I'll grant you that, but explain to me Jeb's presence in the Channel that night . . . in the midst of a storm—a time and condition I've learned is often chosen by smugglers to make a landing. No fisherman I've ever met would take that sort of risk and any fisherman worth his salt would have *known* the weather was turning ugly and would have made for port long before the storm hit."

Cornelia shrugged. "You may be right, but that doesn't mean he's a smuggler."

"No, but I'd like you to give me a good reason why he wasn't snugly in port that night . . . along with the revenuers."

"How should I know? I'm not a fisherman."

"That's true," Barnaby conceded. "It's also true that Mrs. Gilbert was particularly, er, reticent when I broached the subject with her that night. It was also clear she was hiding something—they all were. They could be involved in some other activity," he said slowly, "but my money is on smuggling." He studied her rigid features. "I am not your enemy, Cornelia," he muttered. "I'm on your side . . . but I cannot help you if I do not know what is going on."

"Just suppose you're right. . . . Why would you want to help us?" she demanded.

"I think you already know the answer," Barnaby said softly. At the gleam of satisfaction that leaped into her hazel eyes he smiled and added, "Yes, I mean to marry her—even if she is the Queen of the Sussex Smugglers." He scratched the side of his face and admitted wryly, "I'll admit that I'd prefer, as my future viscountess, that we end her smuggling days soon and decently bury that part of her past."

"She didn't want to do it," Cornelia confessed. "But Jeffery . . . Jeffery decimated the estate by his gambling and poor management and she felt she had no choice." She smiled sadly. "I didn't like my husband's nephew very much, but Emily's father was a damn sight better than that wastrel Jeffery. Emily's father looked out for his people and the village." She scowled. "When farms failed because of Jeffery's practices, many farmers and their families were forced to abandon their livelihood—which hurt the village. As money grew scarcer, Jeffery dismissed our servants with a pittance after they had served us well nearly all of their lives." Her eyes pleading for understanding, she said quietly, "Emily couldn't bear it. She had to do *something*."

Lifting up the hand he still held, Barnaby pressed a kiss onto the wrinkled surface. Smiling at her, he said, "I would have expected nothing less of her."

Cornelia's fingers tightened around his. "And you *do* mean to marry her?" she asked urgently.

"Try and stop me," he said, a crooked grin curving his lips.

Infused with new energy, Cornelia took her hand from his and, sitting up straighter, she looked around. "What is taking that dratted child so long?" she demanded crossly. "The coach will be arriving any minute." She waved a hand at Barnaby. "You best go find out what is keeping her."

Glad to have something to do, Barnaby hastened from the room. Entering the kitchen, and seeing no sign of Emily or Jeb there, a knife blade of foreboding slashed through him.

Astonished by his unexpected appearance in the middle of her kitchen, Mrs. Spalding looked up from the pot she was stirring and exclaimed, "Lord Joslyn! What brings you here?"

Walker, who had been sitting at the table drinking a cup of tea, surged to his feet. "Milord!" he cried. "Is something wrong?"

"Where is she?" Barnaby asked, his gaze hard on Walker's face. "And don't lie to me."

Walker swallowed. "Uh, I believe that she has walked to the stables."

"Alone?" Barnaby asked in a whiplash tone.

"Uh, no, her friend is with her."

"Which way to the stables?" Barnaby snapped.

"Follow me," Walker said nervously.

They stepped outside and Walker pointed in the direction

of the stables. "It's not more than an eighth of a mile past that bend."

Barnaby shot away from the house, his long stride eating up the distance. He had not gone more than a few yards when the sound of an approaching carriage spun him around. His coach had arrived.

At least that's one problem out of the way, he thought as he took off in the direction of the stables. He was nearing the second curve when he spied an object lying at the side of the road that he recognized immediately. The image of Emily grabbing the blue-and-cream reticule before she left the room to meet with her visitor sprang to his mind. Ice in his veins, he broke into a run, skidding to a stop before the feminine bit of silk and velvet. With trembling fingers, he picked up the reticule. It was Emily's and he could think of no good reason why it had been discarded here.

An excellent tracker, he scanned the road surface, spotting the recent prints of two horses. From the tracks it was obvious that the horsemen had come from the woods and that there had been a scuffle, but the many hoof prints made it difficult to tell. The tracks vanished into the woodland on the opposite side of the road.

Unable to form a clear picture in his mind of what had happened, but fearing it boded ill for Emily, with her reticule clenched in his hand, he ran to the stables. He prayed that she was there with Jeb and with a logical explanation why her reticule had been left on the side of the road, but in his heart, he knew he would not find her.

Rushing past the two horses he recognized as his own tied outside, Barnaby burst into the stables and seeing no sign of Emily or Jeb, the only occupant a towheaded stableboy of not more than twelve sweeping the main alleyway, he inquired sharply, "Where is she?" When the boy gaped at him, he added, "Where is Miss Emily and Jeb Brown?"

Confronted by a large stranger looking like black murder,

the stableboy gulped but held his ground. "And who might you be, asking for Miss Emily?" he asked before his courage deserted him.

"I am Lord Joslyn," Barnaby half growled.

The boy blanched and stammered, "L-L-Lord J-J-Joslyn! Forgive m-m-me, my l-l-lord, I didn't realize—"

Barnaby waved away his apologies. "Pay it no heed." In a kinder voice, he asked, "Has Jeb Brown been here?"

The boy nodded. "He was here about twenty minutes ago. Got on his horse and said he was leaving for the village."

Barnaby's heart contracted. "And Miss Emily? Did you see her?"

"No, my lord. Only Jeb."

Barnaby spun on his heel and headed out of the stable, calling over his shoulder, "I'll be taking the horses."

After mounting his horse, with Lamb's horse trailing behind him, Barnaby galloped to the house. Lamb and Walker met him in front of the house and, tossing the reins of Lamb's horse to him, he said, "Emily's missing. We have to find her."

Walker gasped, his face full of horror. "But she was with Jeb!" he exclaimed.

Barnaby cast him a cold glance and showed him the blue-and-cream reticule he'd stuck inside his jacket when he'd mounted his horse. "I found this on the road. There is no sign of Emily and the stableboy said that Jeb left twenty minutes or so ago."

"Those devils!" Walker burst out, incensed and clearly frightened. "They've taken her."

"If 'those devils' are Jeffery and Ainsworth, I agree, but unless we know their destination, the information does us little good—we do not know where they've taken her," Barnaby snapped, struggling to control the helpless rage coursing through him.

Walker's eyes lit up. "The Godart place!" he said eagerly. Babbling, he added, "Jeb just told us that Squire and Ainsworth had lied about going to Newhaven. Young Sam had seen both of them earlier this afternoon—at the old Godart farmstead. That must be where they've taken her."

Barnaby cursed his unfamiliarity with the area and bit out, "Where the hell is the Godart place?"

The directions spilled out of Walker's mouth faster than water bursting from a dam. With their destination clear, Barnaby and Lamb wheeled their horses around and disappeared down the driveway.

As he galloped away from The Birches, Barnaby didn't allow his mind to stray to what might be happening to Emily—that way lay madness. His one thought was simply to reach her before . . . Cursing and praying as he never had in his life, he concentrated grimly on the road before him. Like a beacon, the knowledge that Emily was in danger somewhere ahead drew him onward.

Dusk had fallen but they found the turnoff to the Godart place without effort and with hardly a check in their breakneck pace, their horses careened off the road and thundered down the twisting, overgrown track. A half mile in, there was a brief flicker of light as they followed the winding road, but it disappeared as they rounded another curve. Though it went against the grain, knowing they were coming up on the house, they slowed their horses, not wanting to alert the culprits of their arrival.

Arriving at the front of the shabby one-story farmhouse, they jerked their horses to a halt and swung out of the saddle almost in the same motion. In the deepening dusk, Barnaby studied the dark shape of the place, listening intently, searching for a sign of the faint light he'd glimpsed on the way in. From the front the building looked empty and deserted, but glancing down the east side of the house Barnaby spied the flickering light. It was coming from a room situated just about in the middle of the house. His heart beat thickly. Instinctively he knew Emily was in that room.

Returning to the front of the house, he whispered to Lamb, "I'll take the front, you the back."

Lamb nodded and disappeared like a shadow into the encroaching darkness.

Slipping his knife from his boot, Barnaby approached the house. The stout wooden door opened silently and, knife in hand, he stepped inside the house, taking a moment for his eyes to adjust to the interior gloom. A musty smell met his nose and from the faint light that remained outside, Barnaby saw that the room he'd entered was empty. He crossed the room, easing toward a shadowy area ahead of him. As he had guessed, the shadows gave way to a narrow hall that he suspected led to the kitchen, but it was the glimmer of light that came from beneath a door on the left side of the hall that was the focus of his attention.

Emily woke disoriented with her jaw aching. Groggy, she reached for her jaw but was unable to move her hand. It took her a moment to understand why she could not: she was bound spread eagle, her hands fastened to either side of the bedposts, her ankles strapped to opposite posts at the bottom. Snapping fully awake, she made the alarming discovery that her gown and chemise had been slit down the middle and lay in tatters on either side of her body, leaving her bosom and thighs naked.

Panic shot through her and she bucked and twisted against her bonds, the memory of Ainsworth's abduction rushing back. What a fool she had been, she raged, not to pay more attention to Cornelia's warnings. But why me? she wondered. It was *Anne* Ainsworth had wanted and if he had been gone to Newhaven all day, there was no way he could have learned that Anne had escaped his grasp. . . .

Fighting back the horrified hysteria that rose in her throat, Emily struggled to make sense of her situation. Concentrating on something else helped calm her and allowed her to ignore her own desperate straits . . . and what might be her fate . . .

It was apparent, she admitted bitterly, that Ainsworth and that weasel Jeffery had learned somehow of Anne's departure from The Birches. How? When? But none of that mattered right now, Emily told herself, battering back another wave of panic. What mattered was her escape.

In the light from the lone candle sitting on a short, battered chest of drawers against the wall, she studied her surroundings. Beyond the bed, the chest of drawers, a chair next to the chest heaped with a pile of men's clothing and a pair of gleaming boots on the floor beside the chair, there were no other furnishings—nothing that gave her any sense of where she was being held.

The room was small and under the overpowering scent of cinnamon and cloves that permeated the air, she caught the faint, musty odor associated with deserted, unused houses. From her position on the bed she could see that the ceiling and walls were roughly hewn—utilitarian and economical with no sign of style or elegance. Turning her head, she studied the bedposts to which she was tied. Made of good, solid English oak, they were square and without adornment. Like the chest and chair, practical and simple, they served a purpose, but no craftsman had ever touched them.

This was no gentleman's house and, turning over possibilities, she decided that most likely she was in an abandoned farmhouse. But where? And how would anybody find her before it was too late . . . before Ainsworth came and . . . The panic she had held at bay ripped free and even knowing it was helpless, like a vixen with her foot in a steel trap, Emily fought the bonds that held her so securely. It was a silent, desperate fight but futile, and after several minutes, her wrists and ankles torn and bleeding from her struggles, she collapsed exhausted against the mattress.

The room was cool and she shivered, unbearably aware of her nakedness. For just a moment, she let despair take her and tears leaked from the corners of her eyes. How arrogant she had been! And, oh, so damned, *damned* confident she had nothing to fear from Ainsworth.

Reflecting on her shortcomings accomplished nothing and, determined that Ainsworth would not find her cowering and broken, twisting her head brushed aside the signs of tears. Her mouth set. She didn't see a way to escape the fate that awaited her, but she wasn't going to give Ainsworth the satisfaction of hearing her plead or beg.

The door opened and she stiffened. Through slitted eyes she watched Ainsworth amble into the room. In one hand he held a candle and the other a snifter and a crystal decanter of amber-colored liquid she suspected was brandy—probably some she had smuggled in from France.

Ainsworth wore a dark blue silk robe with a gold thread running through it and her mouth went dry when she realized that it was his clothes on the chair and that he was naked beneath the robe.

Setting the candle, snifter and decanter down on the chest of drawers, Ainsworth walked back to the door and Emily heard the sound of a key turning in the lock. He returned to the chest of drawers and after pouring some brandy from the decanter into the snifter, he finally rotated in her direction and looked at her, his eyes traveling over her body.

Her flesh shriveled under that avid gaze, but she forced herself to give no sign of the revulsion roiling through her.

"Your charms are far more bountiful than I would ever have expected," Ainsworth said, crossing to stand beside the bed. He reached down and cupped one breast. "Now who would have ever thought that you had these charming little apples hidden away?"

Vowing not to give him the enjoyment of watching her struggle, she did not try to escape his touch—it would have been useless anyway. Ignoring the gorge rising in her throat while he fondled her breast, beyond the loathing glittering in her eyes, she betrayed nothing. When he trailed a hand down her thigh it took all the willpower she possessed not to give him the satisfaction of flinching and trying to jerk away.

His fingers returning to her breast, Ainsworth smiled. "Oh, lay there like a log if you wish, it matters not to me," he said. Something ugly moved in the gray eyes. "Because you see, my lovely, I can make you move if I want to." His fingers dug into her breast and in one swift movement he bent down and bit her nipple.

Pain and shock roared through her and she arched upward, screaming.

Outside in the hall, Emily's scream cut through Barnaby like a rapier. Fury and fear spurring him, he sprang forward, tried the doorknob and finding it locked used his shoulder as a battering ram. He hit the door and, propelled by his powerful assault, the wood splintered and the door burst open, banging explosively against the interior wall.

Barnaby charged into the room, the knife readied in his hand. It took him only a second to take in the scene, Emily's spread-eagle body on the bed and Ainsworth in the dark blue robe standing beside her.

At the sound of Barnaby's shoulder against the door, Ainsworth had straightened, but his fingers were still on Emily's breast and he stared at Barnaby in openmouthed astonishment. His gaze dropped to the knife and his hand slid away.

After that first, frantic glance at Emily, Barnaby halted a few feet from the bottom of the bed and kept his attention solely on Ainsworth. Grim-faced, the two men regarded each other across the small room, violence swirling in the air between them.

Despite the desperate situation, Ainsworth thought of a ploy that might save his life and allow him to snatch victory from defeat. Joslyn was making no attempt to attack him and gambling he could still turn this around in his favor and drive away the other man, brazenly, Ainsworth drawled, "I'm afraid you're too late." He smiled. "The deed is done. She is mine."

"He lies!" shouted Emily, straining against the bonds that held her, fury at Ainsworth replacing the sweet relief that had coursed through her when Joslyn had crashed into the room. Fixated on each other, neither man paid her any heed and desperately she cried, "He lies, I tell you! He is a lying serpent!"

His cold eyes watchful, Ainsworth said, "Well, of course, she would say that." Barnaby only stared at him with a predator's unblinking stare and Ainsworth added, "I'm sure she'd prefer a viscount to a mere mister, and your fortune to mine, but she'll have to settle for being plain Mrs. Ainsworth and be happy with what I can provide."

"I think not," said Barnaby softly. "When she leaves here tonight with me, it will be as my affianced bride."

Ainsworth nearly choked on the fury that spiraled up through him. To have come this close and failed. It was intolerable! His gaze strayed a second to his clothes on the chair just a few feet away. He carried a small pistol cunningly concealed in his jacket pocket, and if he could reach it . . . Sidling nearer the chair, he said indifferently, "The choice is yours . . . if you want another man's leavings."

"I don't believe you—and even if I did, it would make no difference," Barnaby said coolly. "I mean to marry her."

Emily gaped at Barnaby. Joslyn wanted to marry her? Absurd! His outrageous statement had to be a ploy to throw Ainsworth off guard. Joslyn couldn't want to marry *her!* Or could he? Heart thudding, her thoughts whirling, she could not tear her eyes away from that fierce, dark face.

"I'd heard that Americans had some odd habits, but I didn't realize that it included wedding damaged goods," Ainsworth sneered, moving imperceptibly nearer his clothes and the pistol.

Barnaby shrugged, not betraying by so much as a flicker of an eyelash the rage that coiled inside of him. His gaze fixed on Ainsworth, he waited with a skillful hunter's patience for the other man's next move.

Emily was bewildered by Joslyn's imperviousness to Ainsworth's taunts. Why didn't he *do* something? Ainsworth was unarmed and Joslyn had the knife. Why didn't he use it? She studied him, noting for the first time the vigilant yet apparently relaxed stance. He appeared in no hurry to strike, but there was no doubt in her mind that he had every intention of killing Ainsworth. Why the delay? Slowly it dawned on her that he was holding back for a reason, that he was enduring Ainsworth's taunts and deliberately allowing Ainsworth time. . . . But time for what? Why didn't he kill the bastard?

Like Emily, Ainsworth wondered why Barnaby had not gutted him in an instant—if positions were reversed, he would have . . . and enjoyed it. An Englishman, he thought contemptuously, wouldn't have hesitated—or endured the insults he had thrown at him. Convinced Joslyn was no danger to him, Ainsworth edged toward the chair. His leg brushed the edge of the chair and satisfaction flooded him. The pistol was inches away. . . .

Disdainfully, Ainsworth presented his back to Barnaby and reaching casually for his jacket, he said, "Since nothing I say appears able to dissuade you from this foolish course, I shall leave the pair of you to your fate." His fingers found the pistol and with the weapon firmly in hand, he whirled around, expecting Joslyn to still be standing by the bottom of the bed.

But Joslyn was no longer there. The instant Ainsworth turned his back, moving with the speed and grace of a hunting cat, Barnaby closed the distance between them and he was ready when Ainsworth swung around with the pistol in his hand. Only when Ainsworth faced him did he strike, and with one careless blow, Barnaby knocked the pistol from Ainsworth's grasp and drove his knife deep into Ainsworth's chest.

With disbelief Ainsworth stared down at the knife protruding from his chest. His eyes wide and astonished, he sank to the floor, gasped and died.

Barnaby's face expressionless, he reached down and pulled the knife free. Wiping the blade clean on Ainsworth's jacket, he turned around and stepping next to the bed, cut Emily free with swift, sure strokes.

Emily had never considered herself a watering pot, but the moment she was free, she sprang up and, kneeling on the bed, flung her arms around Barnaby's neck and burst into tears.

One hand gently caressing the back of her head, the other wrapped possessively around her slender body, he held her near. "Shush, now," he murmured. "Shhhh. I have you safe and you need never fear that craven again."

Once the first storm of weeping had passed, she lifted a tearstained face to his and asked, "How did you find me?"

"I found your reticule and at a *most* opportune time," he said, "Walker related to me the information Jeb had learned from Sam." He brushed a damp curl back from her cheek. "Do you know, I think we shall have to do something rather magnificent for young Sam—he is the hero of the piece."

Emily didn't deny the importance of Sam's part in her rescue, but in her heart, this big, tough American would always be her hero. At the moment she had needed him most, like an avenging god, he'd burst into the room and saved her from a horrid fate. Burrowed next to him, his arm firmly around her waist, he felt so warm, so large and solid that she never wanted to leave the protection of that strong embrace.

She sighed with pleasure and snuggled closer, the wool of his jacket scratching her bare breasts and belly. Suddenly aware that she was as good as naked and that she was clinging to him like a silly damsel in a Gothick novel, Emily froze. Her arms dropped from around his neck and, concentrating on her task, she dragged the remnants of her gown across the front of her body. Keeping her head down, she muttered, "I owe you more than I can say." Remembering his stunning announcement that he intended to marry her, hoping to set his mind at ease, she added hurriedly, "And of course I understand that you weren't serious about marrying me. I know you said that just to distract Ainsworth." She risked a glance at him and smiled nervously. "I will not hold you to it," she assured him.

Barnaby considered her tearstained features for a long minute. The silvery-fair hair hung in wild tangles about her pale skin, the thickly lashed gray eyes were dark with emotion and there was the slightest quiver to that tempting rosy mouth. She had never looked lovelier to him—even with an unsightly bruise forming along her jaw, and if he'd had any reservations about the state of his heart, they were settled.

He cursed the moment, aware that he could hardly declare himself when she had just endured a violent abduction, a near rape and a dead man lay on the floor just a few feet behind them. Sighing he said, "Thank you. That's very kind of you."

Emily didn't know whether she was relieved or devastated by his acknowledgment that he had not been serious when he had told Ainsworth he meant to marry her. Reminding herself that she didn't care, not *really,* she looked away and said, "I am indebted to you. If you had not arrived when you did . . ."

"But I did," Barnaby said, with an effort letting his arm drop from her waist. "And you owe me nothing."

Keeping her face averted, she pulled what remained of her gown tighter around her. "I *do* owe you," she insisted. "If not for you, he would have raped me." Her gaze lifted. "Thank you—you saved not only my honor, but perhaps my life."

"I think we're even," Barnaby said quietly. "Your Jeb saved me and now I have done nothing more than return the favor."

Emily started to argue the point, but decided it would be a poor way of showing her thankfulness. She forced a smile. "If you say so, but you will always have my deepest and most heartfelt gratitude."

Almost as if he had not heard her, his fingers gently skimmed the purple bruise he'd noticed earlier and he asked, "Did he do that?"

She nodded.

The black eyes hardened. "Then it's a good thing I killed him, isn't it?"

"I'm sure it's wicked of me," Emily admitted, "but I cannot help be glad that he is dead. He was a terrible man." Thinking back over those tense moments before he had killed Ainsworth, she frowned. "Why did you wait? Why didn't you attack him the instant you entered the room?"

When he made no reply, she didn't think he would answer her and he seemed far more interested in wrapping her in the sheet he ripped from the bed. Once she was swaddled in the concealing sheet, as if she was a featherweight, he swung her up into his arms.

Turning on his heel, with her cradled securely against him, he walked toward the door and it was then that he answered her. "Ainsworth spouted a great deal of nonsense, but he was right about Americans having some odd habits," he said evenly. "And one of those odd habits is a strong aversion to killing an unarmed man—I had to wait until he went for a weapon."

"But how did you know he had a weapon?" she asked, astonished.

Barnaby smiled and dropped the briefest kiss on her nose. "He was a snake, my love, and all snakes have fangs—I just had to wait for him to show them."

Chapter 14

Barnaby carried Emily swiftly through the darkened house. Reaching his horse, he tossed her lightly into the saddle. Leading the horse and heading toward the back of the house, he said, "Now let's find Lamb and discover what he has been up to."

When they arrived at the rear of the house, there was no sign of Lamb, but in the deepening darkness, Barnaby spied Lamb's horse tied in front of the old barn and a sliver of light peeking out from beneath the heavy doors. Motioning Emily for silence and handing her the reins, Barnaby crept to the barn.

He disliked leaving Emily alone, but he would have disliked her seeing her cousin's corpse even more. She'd seen enough violence tonight. Barnaby didn't regret killing Ainsworth; his only regret was that Emily had had to see it and he didn't want her to see another dead man, especially not one who was related to her.

Ear against the thick wooden doors, he listened a moment, frowning when all he heard was the sound of a man sobbing. Not Lamb.

Gingerly he opened the door and looked inside the building. A lantern hung from the center beam, illuminating the scene. His arms folded across his chest, Lamb leaned negligently against a post near the middle of the barn; slumped on the floor across from him was Jeffery . . . a Jeffery still alive. There was no sign of blood, but Jeffery was sniveling and wiping ineffectively at his nose.

Stepping into the barn, Barnaby asked, "What did you do to him?"

"Nothing," Lamb said disgustedly, glancing at Barnaby. "Is she all right?"

Barnaby nodded. "Shaken at the moment, but I expect she'll be her usual fractious adorable self by this time tomorrow."

"Ainsworth?"

"Dead," he said flatly.

Jeffery jerked around to gape at him. "You k-k-killed Ainsworth?"

"He's dead," Barnaby said in that same flat tone.

Jeffery sat up straighter, his tears drying. "And Emily? She's . . . safe?" He swallowed. "He didn't . . . ?"

"Let's worry about you and your part in this, shall we?" Barnaby replied, puzzled by Jeffery's continued existence. Why hadn't Lamb killed him?

"Me!" Jeffery said astonished. "I didn't do anything." Scrambling to his feet, he said earnestly, "This is all Ainsworth's doing. He *made* me help him. You must believe me!"

Barnaby looked at Lamb and Lamb shrugged. His gaze once more on Jeffery, Barnaby asked with morbid fascination, "If you had nothing to do with the abduction, why are you here?"

Jeffery tugged at his already disheveled cravat, his eyes sliding away from Barnaby's. "I'll not deny that I knew what he planned, but I could not stop him—he would have killed me, just like he did Kelsey."

"Kelsey? The fellow that ran Emily and Anne off the road that night?" Barnaby demanded sharply.

Jeffery nodded. "Yes. Kelsey knew we were, er, meeting here and he'd learned from that doxy of his that Anne had gone to visit my mother. He came to tell Ainsworth and extort money from him." Looking sick, he added, "Ainsworth paid him and then killed him—and forced me to bury Kelsey's body behind the stables."

"You want me to believe that your only part in this is that you helped conceal a murder and stood by helpless when he abducted your cousin? That you're as much a victim as Emily?" Barnaby growled, disgust and fury roiling through him. It took all his willpower not to leap on Jeffery and beat him into a pile of blood and bone.

Jeffery started weeping again and wiped at his nose. Hanging his head, he muttered, "I'm sorry. So sorry. I know I should have done something, but I swear he would have killed me."

"You sniveling coward," Barnaby snarled, and rage getting the better of him, he took a step nearer, the thirst for blood strong. "Rather than lift a finger to help her or tell others what was planned, you stood by and would have allowed Emily to be raped."

"Oh, it's better than that," Lamb said idly, calming some of Barnaby's rage. Lamb's icy blue eyes on Jeffery, he commanded, "Tell him why you're here hiding."

Jeffery risked a glance at Barnaby and flinched at what he saw in the other man's face. His voice barely above a whisper, he said, "Ainsworth likes . . . liked to hurt his women and I couldn't bear to stay in the house and hear her scream and cry for help, so I, uh, stayed out here."

"While his cousin is being subjected to a brutal rape, her charming relative hides in the stable, crying and feeling sorry for himself," Lamb commented without inflection. Straightening up from his position, he added, "He wants killing, but he's so pitiful and disgusting, I couldn't bring myself to touch him."

Revolted by Jeffery's actions, in spite of his rage, Barnaby could only agree with Lamb. It would have given him satisfaction to kill Jeffery, but the man was such a self-serving weakling that he could hardly bear to breathe the same air, let alone touch him. Emily was safe, he reminded himself, and because of that his fists unclenched and he swung away from Jeffery. Fighting down the revulsion that clogged his throat every time he thought of Jeffery cowering in the barn, leaving Emily to Ainsworth's attentions, Barnaby muttered to Lamb, "We'd best be on our way. Cornelia will be worried, and the sooner I have Emily at Windmere, the better I shall feel."

"But—but—what about me?" cried Jeffery, stumbling forward a few steps. "And what about Ainsworth's body?"

Barnaby flashed him a cold stare. "You seem to be able to dispose of bodies when it suits you—I suggest you take care of it."

"But *you* killed him!" Jeffery protested. "I didn't. I didn't have anything to do with his murder."

"And who says I did?" Barnaby purred. "As far as anyone is concerned, I was never here. Nor was Emily or Lamb." He smiled, his teeth bared. "I'm sure that your great-aunt and any number of other people will be willing to attest to the fact that we, none of us, ever left The Birches. While you . . . well, everyone knows that you've been gone all day with your good friend Ainsworth. . . ."

Leaving Jeffery gaping at him, thinking of Emily waiting for him, Barnaby stalked swiftly from the barn, Lamb following him. Shoving the door open, he nearly knocked down Emily.

Emily had been in the act of opening the door from the opposite side when he came storming out of the building. Catching her when she stumbled backward and noting the stout piece of wood she carried in one hand, he hid a smile. Spirited and resourceful, that was his woman. "What were you going to do?" he asked lightly. "Club him to death? Believe me, sweetheart, he isn't worth wasting your time on."

"I was coming to help you," she said stiffly, "but it took me a few minutes to find a weapon."

"We thank you, dear lady," Lamb said diplomatically from behind Barnaby, "but your assistance is unnecessary this time."

Emily sniffed, but dropped the improvised weapon and allowed Barnaby to escort her to his horse. Once they were mounted, Barnaby gulped in several breaths of fresh, clean air. "I don't mean to offend you, my sweet," he murmured into her ear, "but I'd prefer a night lost in a London sewer to spending any more time in the presence of your cousin."

Emily couldn't argue with that but she asked somberly, "Is he dead?"

Barnaby hesitated. He'd gone into the barn certain that if Lamb had not killed Jeffery that he would. "Will you be disappointed if I tell you we left him alive and feeling sorry for himself?"

Emily sighed and Barnaby felt the tenseness leave her body as she leaned more fully against him. "No," she admitted. "He is a pitiful creature and I loathe him, but I do not want him dead . . . at least not by your hand."

Barnaby dropped a kiss on the top of her head. "Then it's a good thing we left him alive, isn't it? Besides, he serves a purpose—we left the disposal of Ainsworth's body to him."

Emily caught her breath, all of tonight's events flooding over her. Full of remorse, she said in trembling tones, "I've made a terrible mess of everything, haven't I? Everything that Cornelia feared would happen happened and I've brought shame and disgrace on her . . . and put you in an invidious position." Head down, she muttered, "I shall say that

I killed him. No one needs to know that you and Lamb were even here."

Barnaby's arm tightened around her slender waist. "You have it half right, sweetheart. No one knows that *any* of us were here tonight."

She laughed bitterly. "And how do you explain my unexpected disappearance? And my return with you and Lamb?"

"You, my misguided darling, remembering one last thing you wanted to tell Jeb, hurried after him before he was out of sight. You took a shortcut through the woods, hoping to overtake him before he reached the main road."

"That's the most ridiculous tale I've ever heard," she said acidly. Curiosity had her asking though, "How do you explain my torn gown and why I was gone so long?"

"In the gathering darkness you fell, ripping your gown and twisting your ankle, which made it difficult for you to walk back to the house. Lamb and I, having set out in a gallant search for you, found you seated on a downed tree." He ended cheerfully, "And now we're bringing you home." When she remained silent, he added, "I think the twisted ankle is a nice touch, don't you? Of course, you'll have to limp for a few days but overall . . ."

"It might do," she said after a thoughtful pause. "Jeffery isn't going to want to reveal his part in what happened tonight. . . ." She tapped her lower lip with a finger. "Walker and the other servants will know otherwise, but they will say nothing." She brightened. "And if Jeffery is foolish enough to say anything different, it is really our word against his, isn't it?"

"Indeed," said Barnaby. "And who is going to believe that Viscount Joslyn, strange American though he is, and his manservant were involved in such sordid doings?"

For the first time since Jeffery and Ainsworth had burst out of the woods, Emily felt that last knot of anxiety loosen and disappear. Joslyn would bear no blame for tonight's doings and Cornelia would be able to face her neighbors with her head held high: her great-niece had not brought shame on the family.

Her cheek pressed against his broad chest, Emily listened to the steady beat of Joslyn's heart, gratitude tangling with another powerful, confusing emotion in her breast. He saved me, she admitted drowsily, unconsciously snuggling deeper into her secure embrace. Just before sleep took her, the stray thought crossed her mind that it was just as well he hadn't been serious about marrying her . . . although being married to him wouldn't have been so *very* bad. . . .

The removal to Windmere was not without conflict. Once Emily was at home and everyone assured that all was well, her ruined gown changed and her hair combed, feeling more like herself, she argued that there was no longer any reason for them to seek sanctuary at Windmere. She lost the argument, Cornelia siding with Barnaby.

"Ainsworth may not threaten us any longer," Cornelia agreed smoothly, "but I see no harm in accepting his lordship's very kind offer of hospitality for a few days." She beamed at Barnaby who lounged nearby. "We owe him a great deal and it seems a shabby thing to throw his generosity back in his face—all the more so when we are packed and the coach is waiting in the driveway."

Emily eyed Cornelia and Joslyn suspiciously. They were, she decided, far too cozy with each other for her liking. After Cornelia had seen for herself that Emily was indeed unharmed, she had left her to the care of Sally and returned to the green salon to join Joslyn. Emily would have given a small fortune to know what they talked about while she had been absent, and she couldn't shake the uneasy notion that she had been the topic of conversation. Still a bit shaky from

her ordeal, in the face of Cornelia's defection and the real
debt of gratitude she owed Joslyn Emily capitulated.

Waking the next morning at Windmere in the impressive
rose-and-ivory bedroom, for one terrible moment, not recognizing her surroundings, she lay there frozen with fear. Was
Ainsworth going to walk through the door and pick up
where he had left off last night?

Heart banging painfully in her chest, she jerked upright,
her gaze traveling over the elegantly draped rose-figured
ivory silk hung bed, the similarly hued rug on the floor and
the gracious furnishings, and she realized suddenly that she
was safe at Windmere. The home of Viscount Joslyn wasn't
exactly unknown to her, but her previous visits had only
been as a casual guest of the previous viscount: she'd never
stayed overnight at the magnificent house—or at the express
invitation of the owner. Her heart rate slowing, Emily pushed
back a heavy fall of silvery hair and, still slightly disoriented,
wondered what the day would bring.

Cornelia had been in her element when they had arrived
at Windmere last night and she had taken as her due the superior service of the various servants in green-and-wheat
livery who had wafted them from the coach and into the
mansion. Giving no sign that it was anything unusual for my
lord to return home with two female neighbors as guests,
Peckham, after removing their cloaks, had clapped his hands
and ordered their trunks and bandboxes carried upstairs.

Barnaby took one look at Emily's wan features and suggested that the ladies might wish to retire for the night. Smiling at the two women he said gently, "There is no need for
you to socialize with my cousins tonight. Tomorrow will be
soon enough."

Emily didn't know whether to be relieved or insulted that
she and Cornelia had been sent to bed like a pair of erring

children, but she didn't object. A cheerful, fresh-faced young woman had waited for her in the grand bedroom.

"Good evening, miss," the young woman had said. Dimpling, she had added, "I am Kate and will be your maid for your stay."

Normally having a stranger wait on her would have bothered Emily, but Kate was so quick and helpful and, realizing that she was wearier than she realized, Emily didn't mind Kate's assistance after all. When Emily was regally installed in the bed, with one last smile, Kate had disappeared.

Alone in the strange room, Emily had been afraid that after her ordeal, even with its near-miraculous outcome, she would not sleep, but such had not been the case. After a few restless moments, she had relaxed and sleep had come—no nightmares disturbed her slumber.

Feeling better than she thought she should, considering what had transpired yesterday, Emily slid from the bed. Her woolen robe lay nearby on an ivory damask-covered chair and slipping it on, she wandered into the adjoining dressing room. Pleased to find an ewer of still-warm water sitting next to a matching bowl trimmed in gilt and decorated with delicate pink rosebuds, she poured some of the water into the bowl and performed her morning ablutions.

Used to seeing to herself most of the time Emily never considered ringing for a maid and finding one of her better gowns in the huge mahogany armoire, she quickly dressed. Braiding her hair with a lavender silk ribbon that matched the stripe in her silk-and-wool gown, she fashioned the thick gleaming strand into a bun at the base of her neck.

She had just entered the charming sitting room adjacent to her bedroom when the door opened and Kate entered the room, humming under her breath. Seeing Emily, Kate stopped, surprised.

"Miss! I didn't expect to find you up and dressed already," she exclaimed. She smiled. "I was just coming to check on you, to see if you were awake and if the water I'd brought earlier was still warm."

Emily smiled at her. "It was. Thank you. And now I would appreciate it if you could show me to my aunt's room."

Kate did so and Emily wasn't surprised to find Cornelia up and dressed: both women were early risers. At Emily's entrance, Cornelia said, "Good! I was hoping you were awake. Shall we go downstairs and see if the gentlemen are up?"

Emily hesitated, not certain she was ready to face Joslyn or the curious eyes of his cousins just yet. Aware that she was only postponing the evil moment, she took a deep breath and nodded.

Peckham showed the two ladies into the morning room and Emily tensed when she saw that Joslyn and his cousins were there before them. The four gentlemen were scattered around the table, the remains of their meal littered across the pristine white tablecloth, and at the entrance of the ladies, they all rose politely to their feet.

From Mathew's pinched nostrils and the carefully controlled expression on Joslyn's face it was obvious that they had interrupted a disagreement of some kind. Mathew greeted them stiffly and Thomas, following his older brother's lead, did the same, but Simon bowed gracefully over Cornelia's hand and grinned and winked at Emily. Joslyn, an expression she found hard to read in the black eyes when he looked at her, escorted the pair of them to the table.

Having seated Emily to his right and Cornelia opposite, Joslyn returned to his place at the head of the table. "I trust you ladies slept well?" he asked, smiling.

Emily mumbled a reply and Cornelia replied in the affirmative. Glancing at Peckham hovering in the background, Barnaby said, "Serve the ladies, won't you?"

Little was said until the ladies were served and Peckham retired from the room. Too aware of Joslyn's big masculine form only inches from her, Emily kept her eyes on her plate and poked at her food as the conversation picked up around her.

Batting her still beautiful hazel eyes, Cornelia flirted outrageously with Simon and Barnaby; to Mathew and Thomas she was scrupulously polite—as they were to her.

From the chilly looks sent her way by Mathew and Thomas, Emily had a good idea that she had been the cause of both Mathew's displeasure and the look on Joslyn's face when she and Cornelia had entered the room. She frowned at her plate. What had caused the antipathy she sensed from Mathew and Thomas?

Thomas was seated on her other side and she glanced at him, groping for an explanation for the hostility she felt emanating from him. What had she ever done to him? She didn't particularly like him, much preferring Simon's easy manner, but there'd never been unpleasantness between them.

Feeling her eyes upon him, Thomas looked up and gave her a cool stare. With thinly concealed sarcasm he said, "The last time it was an overturned carriage. Tell me, Miss Townsend, what calamity brings you to Windmere this time?"

"Bats," answered Cornelia from across the table; the expression in her eyes as they fixed on him had Thomas sitting bolt upright and concentrating on the snowy tablecloth as if his life depended upon it. It probably did. She hadn't missed the unfriendly looks flashed Emily's way by either Mathew or Thomas, and she wasn't about to have Emily made the least uncomfortable by anyone, particularly not this impertinent, nosey stripling. "A whole swarm of them swooped out of a hole in the attics and roosted in our bedrooms," she went on coolly, her gimlet stare switching to Mathew. He paled as he came under the full power of that hazel gaze. "Walker should have them removed in a day or two and we will return home," she added carelessly. With a smile that dripped ice, she turned her attention back to Thomas and asked, "Does that answer your question, young man?"

Thomas muttered something and, satisfied he wouldn't dare risk her displeasure again, she said warmly to Barnaby, "And now, where were we, my lord?"

Barnaby hid a smile, but vowed never to give her cause to look at him as she had Mathew and Thomas. "I believe that you were telling me how charming you found my great-grandfather and how I seem to have inherited the same, er, incredible charm."

Cornelia cackled with delight and the awkward moment passed. Breakfast was eventually finished and while Peckham, at Barnaby's request, gave the ladies a tour of Windmere's famous conservatory, the gentlemen retired to Barnaby's study.

Barnaby's study was a handsome room in the oldest part of the mansion, the oak wainscot and the beautifully carved, coffered ceiling dating back to the days of the original castle. A rug in brilliant jeweled tones lay on the walnut parquet floor and chairs and sofas in fine fabrics and leather were spread about the big room; tables with marble tops were placed conveniently throughout the area. Books lined one wall, a massive desk and chair arranged in front of them; a huge black marble fireplace dominated the other wall and burgundy velvet drapes hung at the tall, narrow windows.

Barnaby sat in an oxblood leather overstuffed chair at one side of the fireplace; Mathew stood at the other end of the fireplace. A twin to the chair in which Barnaby sat was at the opposite end of the fireplace and Thomas had chosen to sit there. Not far, Barnaby noticed sardonically, from Mathew. Simon, on the other hand, was sprawled on a gilded wood sofa covered in a Beauvais tapestry centered in front of the fireplace, his long legs stretched toward the fire that blazed and crackled on the hearth.

As if there had been no pause, the moment the four men were settled, Mathew took up the argument that Emily and Cornelia's entrance into the morning room had interrupted.

"You cannot be serious about marrying her," Mathew said grimly.

"Of course, I am. You yourself have pointed out to me, among countless other things, that it is important that I marry." A mocking light in the dark eyes, he added, "I would have thought you'd be overjoyed that I am, for once, following your advice."

Mathew looked as if he would explode. Between clenched teeth he managed, "Yes, it's important that you marry, but it is equally important that the woman you marry equals you in rank and fortune." Taking a deep breath, he said carefully, "Miss Townsend is a delightful young woman and I am sure that she will make some man a wonderful wife . . . but not yours. I can name two or three young women who would be much more suitable—the Duke of Ashford's eldest daughter, for instance. She comes with an impressive dowry and her family is noble and well connected." When Barnaby merely stared at him, he went on almost desperately, "If she is not to your liking, there is the Earl of Mansfield's only child. She is not yet twenty, a pretty little thing and is heiress to thousands of acres of land and a handsome fortune in the funds. Either one would be far more suitable to be the next Viscountess Joslyn than Emily Townsend!"

Thomas entered the fray. "Miss Townsend is a charming young lady, no denying it," Tom said, "but good gad, she has no fortune to speak of, she is near as on the shelf as makes no matter and while her father was the local squire, she has no claim to noble blood. She is a nobody. You cannot marry her."

Barnaby's eyes narrowed on Thomas. "I would tread cautiously there if I were you—I don't recall that you have any say in who I marry or don't marry."

Tom flushed and muttered, "I merely meant that you have

not yet had an opportunity to meet other more eligible young women. As I said, Miss Townsend is charming, but I urge you to consider the great position she will hold as your wife."

Simon spoke up. A teasing gleam in the azure eyes he said, "My money is on Emily. She's a bruising rider and can birth a lamb as expertly as any shepherd." He grinned at Barnaby. "With your flocks that's a necessary virtue."

"But hardly," snapped Thomas, "an ability that the Viscountess Joslyn needs."

"I like Emily," admitted Mathew reluctantly. "Known her since she was a child, but she has spent most of her life buried here in the country and has little concept of the world and what being your wife would entail." When Barnaby remained unmoved, he burst out, "Damn it all, Barnaby! She is little more than a country bumpkin!"

Softly Barnaby said, "As I warned Tom, I would tread carefully—especially when speaking of the woman I intend to marry."

Mathew's lips whitened. "Your mind is made up?"

Barnaby nodded. "Telling you my plans was only a courtesy," he said, rising to his feet. "I don't need your permission, and while I understand your position, it does not change mine: I intend to marry Emily just as soon as I can arrange it." He smiled sweetly and murmured, "And now, if you will excuse me, I must go and see how my future bride is faring."

Barnaby found Emily and Cornelia in the conservatory, seated on a stone bench before a pool of water that swarmed with the brilliant gold and orange flashes of the darting goldfish amongst the artfully planted lily pads. Their expressions polite, the ladies were listening to Peckham as he pointed out the impressive variety of tropical plants before them. "This is but a small section containing vines and shrubs and trees from the tropics." Pointing, he said, "Those purple and white orchids you see on the other side of the pond were originally acquired by the sixth viscount and the banana trees next to the orchids actually bear fruit. We also have pineapples and an odd fruit called guava." He smiled proudly. "Our ferns are renowned for the many different species that have been collected over the years. If you would like, I can show—"

Barnaby's low cough stopped Peckham in midstream and, seeing his employer standing there, Peckham said, "My lord, I was just telling the ladies . . ."

"Yes, yes, I overheard you," Barnaby said hastily. "And a very good job you were doing. I'm sure they have enjoyed the tour immensely, but I can take over now."

Peckham bowed and departed, disappearing into the jungle-like growth. Smiling, Barnaby strolled over to the ladies. "Was he a dead bore?" he asked.

"Perhaps not *dead*," Emily replied, and Barnaby threw back his head and laughed. Aware of the rush of attraction she felt for him, Emily looked away, wishing that she didn't find him quite so appealing.

"Did you finish your business with your cousins?" Cornelia asked, eyeing him.

"Yes."

"And?"

Barnaby grinned at her. "And now if you'll allow me a few moments alone with your great-niece I'll settle things and we can all rest easy."

Openmouthed, Emily stared as Cornelia, looking very pleased, rose to her feet and said airily, "I am an old lady and need my rest. I think I shall go lie down." A moment later she was gone, the gently waving fronds the only sign of her passing.

Emily glanced up at Barnaby and her heart nearly leaped out of her throat at the intent expression in his gaze. Uneasily, she asked, "What is going on? Why did she leave us alone like this?"

Barnaby's mouth quirked. "Your great-aunt has merely given me the privacy I need to declare myself," he said gently.

Emily blinked at him. Her mouth dry, her pulse galloping, she said stupidly, "Declare yourself? What do you mean?"

Pulling her to her feet, he murmured, "Why, only that I am asking you to marry me." Drawing her into his embrace, he brushed his lips against hers. "Will you?"

Dazed, Emily stared up into those rough-hewn features, her lips tingling from that light touch of his. "But you said that you were not serious when you asserted to Ainsworth that you meant to marry me," she accused, her gray eyes nearly silver with the emotions swirling through her.

"No, *you* said that I wasn't serious," he said. "All I did was let you believe what you wanted."

Her fingers clenched the fine fabric of his dark blue coat and she gasped, "You want to marry me?"

He smiled and said softly, "No, I *mean* to marry you."

Speechless, she stared at him, trying to grab a coherent thought out of the chaos that whirled in her brain.

His lips found hers again, this time lingering, pressing warmly against hers, and delight shivered in her veins. Unconsciously, she strained nearer and Barnaby lost his head, his mouth hardening with passion, his tongue probing between her lips.

Emily had no thought to deny him and she shuddered in wonder at that first hungry invasion, his tongue sliding intimately along hers. With each hot thrust of his tongue, each slow, sensual exploration, he taught her the difference between kisses and kisses. . . .

Heat and hunger coiling low in her belly, when Barnaby

finally lifted his head she was warm and pliant in his arms, conscious of a clamoring in her body that was as foreign as it was unexpected. Had she ever felt the desire to lose herself in a man's embrace? Ever felt the yearning to cast caution to the winds and let herself be swept away by the sensations he aroused? With his mouth only inches from hers, his arms holding her close, Emily could not think, she could only feel—and she felt wonderful!

Breathing heavily, his eyes roamed over her dazed features. What he saw there must have satisfied him, because his head dipped and his mouth took hers again, this time hungrier and more explicit in its demand. He'd always kept his desire for her rigidly controlled, but he'd known from almost the first moment he'd seen her that he wanted her. He was unprepared, however, for the fierce exultation that thundered through him when she returned his kiss, her tongue slipping shyly into his mouth, her soft body pressing against him.

Crushing her next to him, his hands dropped to her hips and he pulled her closer to the swollen, aching length of him. In the grip of mindless desire, his hands closed around the sweet globes of her buttocks and he rocked slowly, intimately, against the notch between her thighs, letting her feel just how much he wanted her.

The world blurred and he lost himself in the heady sweetness of her. Having her finally in his arms, her mouth eager beneath his was addicting, and with his body begging for more, he nearly tipped her onto the floor and completed the union he so desperately wanted. But some sliver of sanity remained and to his regret, slowly but with increasing persistence, common sense won over the reckless urge.

Reluctantly he brought them back to earth, moving her tempting body away from his too-eager one. Allowing himself one last searing kiss, Barnaby lifted his head and stepped back from her.

"Unless you want me to ravish you here and now," he said huskily, "this must stop."

Emily blinked at him. With his mouth no longer seducing hers and his warm arms no longer keeping her in his embrace, lucidity rushed through her. Joslyn had asked her to marry him! Did she dare?

A thousand thoughts chased through her brain. Never mind the state of her silly heart, there were too many other things to consider. The smuggling. Anne. Cornelia. The smuggling. The investors who depended upon her. The smuggling. Walker and Mrs. Spalding. *The smuggling!* A hysterical bubble rose up in her chest. The Viscountess Joslyn, Smuggler Extraordinaire. Good God! It was bad enough she risked her own family's honor, she wasn't about to drag Joslyn into the same quagmire.

Barnaby knew the moment she had made her decision, and from the way her eyes slid from his, he knew her answer. The stubborn little chit was going to turn him down—and not because she wasn't attracted to him. Her response told him that she wasn't indifferent to him—quite the opposite. While not a vain man, he concluded that there could only be one reason for Emily's rejection of his suit: the bloody smuggling.

Not certain if he was offended, hurt or just annoyed, Barnaby jerked her into his arms. His dark eyes boring into hers, he growled, "If you dare try to refuse me because of some stupid idea that I'm going to be horrified to discover that you're involved with your own little band of smugglers, perish the thought." Ignoring her gasp, his hands tightened on her arms and he said, "I already know about it—Cornelia told me." He took a deep breath, admitting, "I can't say that having my wife running contraband under the noses of the revenuers is precisely the pastime I would have chosen, but once we are married, we shall find something less, er, illegal to occupy your time."

Emily stiffened and the gray eyes glittering dangerously, she asked sweetly, "Pastimes, such as filling your nursery?"

A slow smile crossed his face. "It's not out of the question. . . ." When she began to struggle, he pulled her resisting body next to his and, despite her efforts to escape him, his lips found hers and he kissed her.

With his mouth on hers, she fought against the overpowering tide of emotion that blotted out every emotion but the insidious demand of her heart and the drugging power of his kiss. Dizzy, unable to think, her arms crept around his neck and she lost the struggle to resist him. More than anything in the world, she realized giddily, this was where she wanted to be.

Feeling her mouth soften beneath his, he murmured against her lips, "Please? Please put me out of my misery and say you'll marry me?"

It was madness! Folly. But she could not help herself and, as if from a great distance, Emily heard herself say, "Yes, I will marry you."

Barnaby shouted and swung her up in his arms. Bussing her soundly, his eyes full of wicked amusement, he said, "Now let's go make the announcement to my family and watch Mathew turn purple."

Chapter 15

Despite her protests, dragging her willy-nilly behind him, Barnaby charged into the library where his cousins were gathered and announced cheerfully, "It's official. Emily has agreed to marry me."

Leaving his cousins to stare openmouthed, Barnaby whisked Emily away and went in search of Cornelia. Contrary to what she had said, Cornelia had not retired to take a nap. She was seated in a cozy room that overlooked a small garden, sipping tea and pretending to read from the novel she had brought with her from The Birches. The instant the door opened and Barnaby, with Emily in tow, strode into the room, she dropped the book and looked up expectantly.

Grinning, Barnaby brought Emily to his side and said, "It was a near thing, but she said yes."

Joy blazed across her great-aunt's face and stilled some of the turmoil in Emily's breast. Her hazel eyes bright with tears, Cornelia cried, "Oh, my dears! I cannot tell you how delighted I am."

Emily left Barnaby's side and sat down beside her. She searched Cornelia's face. "You are truly happy about this? And we have your blessing?"

Cornelia patted her on the cheek. "Indeed, I am and, of course, you have my blessing." She smiled. "From the moment I laid eyes on young Joslyn, I hoped that this would happen. I will admit, however, that I wasn't certain of the outcome. I feared you'd place all of us—me, Anne, Mrs. Gilbert, Jeb and the others, ahead of your own chance for happiness."

"I almost did," Emily admitted, looking troubled.

"Then it's a very good thing, isn't it," Barnaby said, "that your wise aunt told me all about your, er, hobby?"

Emily flashed him a hostile glance. "It is hardly a hobby," she shot back.

Barnaby threw up his hands. "Wrong choice of words, but it is hardly a pastime suitable for my viscountess." Her eyes narrowed and he added hastily, "I don't intend for you to abandon Mrs. Gilbert and the others, only that we will find another way to help them—something less likely to land us all in the gaol."

"Jeb sailed for Calais last night," Emily confessed. "I can hardly call him back."

Barnaby nodded. "I know that your entanglement cannot be ended overnight." A sparkle lit his eyes. "I may have to try my hand at smuggling a time or two before we are all safely away and everyone is secure. Running contraband goods ashore should prove quite an adventure."

Emily was aghast. Rising to her feet, she crossed to stand in front of him. Her hand resting on his arm, her eyes on his, she said urgently, "No! You dare not. What if you were caught? Think of the scandal. The Viscount Joslyn a common criminal."

Barnaby looked offended. "Now I resent that. I'm sure I'd make an *exceptional* criminal."

Cornelia snorted with laughter. "Indeed you would, my lord. Quite, quite exceptional."

"Don't tease," Emily begged, looking from one to the

other. "My involvement is bad enough, and if I could have found . . ." She stopped, made a face. "I'll just have to think of a way to disperse the group in a manner that doesn't cause them hardship."

Barnaby's hand closed warmly over hers where it lay on his arm. Smiling at her, he said, "*We'll* find a way. You're not in this alone anymore, sweetheart."

Emily looked doubtful and Barnaby's brow rose. "I think," he said in lofty tones at variance with the amusement glittering in his eyes, "that you forget that you now have call on the purse of a rich man. A very rich man according to my cousins."

"But Jeb and the others—they won't want charity," Emily objected.

"Do you know," Barnaby said, bored with the topic, "right now I don't give a damn what they want. We'll find a resolution, but may we please forget about them and simply enjoy our engagement?"

Guilt smote Emily. He could have offered for eligible young ladies with more beauty and fortune than she possessed, and yet for reasons that escaped her, he wanted to marry her. And what did she do? She fussed about a ragtag band of smugglers.

A rueful smile on her lips, she said, "You're right, of course—and I apologize."

"Apology accepted." He glanced from Emily to Cornelia. "So how soon can we arrange the wedding?"

A spirited discussion followed. Barnaby was all for riding to London and obtaining a special license and marrying Emily by the beginning of the next week. Emily was adamantly opposed and even Cornelia was hesitant.

Frowning, Cornelia glanced at Barnaby and said, "Your engagement to Emily is going to be a nine days' wonder." Barnaby shrugged and she went on. "You are an exceedingly eligible gentleman and there is going to be a bevy of disappointed, envious young ladies and equally disappointed parents when your engagement to the daughter of a mere country squire is announced. There is no cause to add fuel to the gossip by a too-hasty marriage." She grimaced. "Marrying as soon as the banns are called will still cause speculation, but much less than a marriage obtained by special license and performed before anyone is aware that your interest is fixed on Emily."

Feeling events were moving too fast for her, Emily asked, "Wouldn't it be better if we waited until spring or early summer to marry? Perhaps June?"

"No," Barnaby said flatly. "I want you out of that house and away from your contemptible cousin just as soon as it can be arranged."

"I am out of that house and away from him," Emily snapped.

Barnaby sighed. "And we both know that your visit here is going to create a great deal of talk—especially if it goes on for too long. We can brush by for a few nights, explaining that"—he looked at Cornelia and grinned—"out of deference to your great-aunt's age, it was decided that it would be less taxing on her, if during this exciting time, you both stayed here for a night or two."

"Now that's an excellent explanation," Cornelia said, nodding. "And one likely to be believed without question."

When Emily continued to argue for a summer wedding, Barnaby said, "If there is a long delay before we wed you cannot remain here. Even with Cornelia as chaperone, for you to live here for weeks, months on end would raise all sorts of eyebrows. People would wonder about Jeffery and be curious about why you aren't remaining in the home you have lived in all your life—a home that is only a few miles away from here."

"He's right," Cornelia admitted reluctantly. "And don't forget, no matter how this plays out or what story Jeffery concocts to explain it, there is going to be a devilish uproar over Ainsworth's death. I can't abide my great-nephew, but for your sake, for the sake of the family name, I don't want him exposed for the despicable scoundrel he is. If we remain here, there is bound to be talk." She looked grim. "Some of that talk will not be kind and some of those disappointed young ladies and their parents won't be above spreading spiteful gossip and innuendo."

Their arguments held weight and Emily gave in. "The banns it will be," she finally agreed with an unflattering lack of enthusiasm.

"Good!" said Cornelia. Looking at Barnaby, she ordered, "You can ride over to the vicar's today and tell him. The first calling of the banns can take place this Sunday and we can plan the wedding for the second week of February." Thoughtfully, Cornelia murmured, "I must write Anne and apprise her of events. Naturally, she and Hugh and his mother will attend the wedding and there will be time enough for us to order gowns from London." She smiled at Barnaby, her eyes dancing. "You'll have to stand the nonsense, I'm afraid—can't have your bride and her family appearing in rags. Once the banns are called, you should host at least one party, perhaps even a ball, and invite the neighbors, such as Lord and Lady Broadfoot, Sir Michael and Mrs. Featherstone and her brood. Oh, and naturally the vicar and his family. It's a good thing Mathew and his brothers are already here—they'll help even out the numbers." She grinned wickedly. "Your cousins can provide a nice consolation prize for those girls of Mrs. Featherstone's and Broadfoot's trio of daughters."

Upon further discussion, it was agreed that Emily and Cornelia would remain at Windmere one more night. "Tomorrow morning will be soon enough for us to return to The Birches," Cornelia decided. Tapping her finger to her lips, she said, "You know, after you've talked to the vicar this morning, it might be wise if you invite them to dinner tonight. Penelope Smythe is as kind a woman as you'll ever meet and despite having three daughters of her own to launch, she won't begrudge Emily's good fortune. With Penelope on our side, she'll be able to help smooth over any awkwardness." Cornelia's eyes twinkled. "And Christian lady though she is, she'll enjoy being the only lady of the neighborhood, besides ourselves, to meet you. It'll be a feather in her cap."

Amused, Barnaby said, "Since I have my marching orders, I shall leave you ladies for a few hours. If you need anything, ring for Peckham."

The small, hastily arranged dinner party that night went off very well. Mathew, despite his privately expressed disapproval of the engagement, closed ranks behind his American cousin and gave every appearance of a man well pleased with Barnaby's choice of a bride-to-be. Not surprising, Thomas copied his older brother's manner; Simon exuded nothing but goodwill and delight to everyone.

At the appointed time, the vicar and Mrs. Smythe arrived at Windmere with their three daughters and eldest son in tow. Since Mrs. Smythe was genuinely fond of Emily and Cornelia and had never given a serious thought to one of her daughters snaring the viscount, after her initial astonishment, she was, as Cornelia predicted, thrilled to meet the viscount and congratulate the newly engaged couple.

After dinner they all gathered in the grand gold-and-bronze salon. The Smythe girls, their brother and the Joslyn cousins were laughing and talking a short distance away; Barnaby, Emily and the vicar appeared to be deep in a private conversation in one of the alcoves created by a pair of bay windows that overlooked the front of the house. Her eyes on the trio in the alcove, Mrs. Smythe remarked to Cornelia, "They make a very handsome couple." Giving Cornelia an arch look, she murmured, "I suppose it goes without saying that you are very pleased with the match."

Cornelia nodded. "I cannot deny it." She looked meaningfully at Penelope. "But you know when the word spreads of the engagement that there is going to be a great deal of gossip."

The vicar's wife of nearly three decades was a tall, slender redhead who wore her forty-eight years well—despite the birth of six children before she was twenty-five. Even in her youth she had been only passably pretty, but she had kind brown eyes, a sprinkling of freckles across her nose that imparted a gamine charm and a vivacious smile. Seldom ruffled, Penelope Smythe adored gossip, was seldom unkind and could be counted on to keep a cool head in the midst of a crisis. Cornelia was very fond of her and in spite of the gap in their ages, counted on her as one of her dearest friends.

Penelope considered Cornelia's comment and agreed. "Yes, there's no pretending that there won't be a firestorm of gossip." Her gaze affectionate, she added, "You know the vicar and I will do our best to help quell the worst of it. Your Emily is a darling and I couldn't be happier for her . . . but there will be others who will suffer great heart burnings at her good fortune." She frowned. "If only there was a way that I could help defuse the worst of the dismay that certain ladies are bound to feel when they learn that the most eligible gentleman in the neighborhood is no longer available." She considered the situation a moment longer, and then an impish smile crossed her face. "I think I shall call upon Mrs. Featherstone tomorrow and perhaps Lady Broadfoot. After all, one might say, as the vicar's wife, that it is my *duty* to apprise them of this exciting occurrence. Much better for them to learn of the engagement from me than to hear of it out of the blue on Sunday."

Cornelia nodded her approval and Penelope went on. "Naturally, I shall let them know how much the vicar and I approve of the match—and remind them what a dear, charming young lady Emily is and how often they have expressed their fondness for her." Her eyes twinkled. "What else can they be but happy for her good fortune?"

Cornelia laughed. "I wonder if the vicar knows what a clever little minx he married."

"I think he suspects," Penelope admitted, smiling, "but I am very careful not to be *too* clever."

The two ladies were seated on one of the sofas near the fire that crackled on the hearth of the huge marble fireplace, and in perfect harmony, they sipped their tea, both of them satisfied with the plan Mrs. Smythe had put forth. Setting down her cup and looking toward the alcove where the vicar, Barnaby and Emily were still standing, Mrs. Smythe said, "After Mathew's unflattering description, I must say that Lord Joslyn is not at all what I expected."

Tartly Cornelia replied, "I'm sure that Mathew led you to expect a wild-haired barbarian wearing furs who eats raw meat with his fingers and wipes his nose on his sleeve."

Penelope smothered a laugh. "Something like that." Her expression serious once more, she added, "It was not very nice of Mathew, but one can hardly blame him for feeling rather hard done by. He'd been groomed for the title since he was a child."

Cornelia fixed a pensive gaze on Mathew where he stood at the edge of the group of younger people. He looked animated enough, she thought, as he smiled at something Esther, the eldest of the Smythe daughters, said. Watching him closely though, she detected just the faintest air of unhappiness around him. Something in his forced gaiety and the resentment she had noted in him sometimes when he was around Barnaby and thought himself unobserved told her that Mathew had not fully accepted his fall from grace. She didn't blame him. Only a saint would have accepted with equanimity the kind of loss Mathew had suffered.

Penelope echoed Cornelia's thoughts. "I'll have to give Mathew credit though for being here tonight. To be treated as a mere guest by the man who had taken away everything he had grown up believing would be his one day, can't be easy for him."

Barnaby laughed at something the vicar said and Penelope's gaze slid to him. "Particularly not easy when Lord Joslyn has such a winning way about him," she said. Her head tipped to one side, she studied Barnaby for a moment and added, "One cannot say that he is precisely handsome, but with those rugged features and broad shoulders there's no denying that he has great appeal for the feminine sex." Penelope sighed dreamily. "No wonder Emily agreed to marry him so quickly. Resisting all that dark virility would be near impossible."

"I agree," Cornelia murmured, a decidedly impure gleam dancing in her hazel eyes. "His great-grandfather was the same . . . and resisting him didn't cross my mind."

It wasn't very late when the party broke up and the guests departed. Emily and Cornelia did not linger long downstairs once the Smythes had driven away, and well before midnight, Emily was tucked up in her bedroom.

A candle flickered on the stand near her bed and finding sleep elusive Emily studied the intricate pattern of the silk canopy overhead. Throughout the day she'd had no private moment, no time to think about what she had done, but now alone for the first time, she grappled with the enormous changes that were going to take place in her life. Good God! She had agreed to marry Viscount Joslyn!

She wasn't completely certain of the state of her heart, but she couldn't pretend that she didn't find him fascinating.

Nor that she didn't find his company most exhilarating—when he wasn't being deliberately annoying. Ignoring his wealth and title, Joslyn appealed to her in a way no other man ever had, and there was no denying that he aroused the most delicious and exciting sensations within her when he took her into his arms. For just a while she lost herself in the memory of that demanding mouth on hers and the strength of those powerful arms as they had crushed her next to him. To her embarrassed astonishment, her nipples peaked and shuddery warmth cascaded through her body.

Her cheeks flaming, she buried her face in one of the pillows. He bewitched me, she decided not very happily, and like a feeble-minded twit I melted into his arms with nary a thought about anything but the wonder of his kiss. She snorted. Addlepated, that's what she was!

She rolled onto her back and stared again at the canopy as if the answer to her feelings and emotions were hidden in the complicated pattern woven in the silk. Was she regretting her acceptance of his proposal? Not exactly. But their courtship, if one could call it that, certainly had not followed the traditional path. A month ago Lord Joslyn had been an utter stranger, nothing more than a name to her, and yet now, a scant three weeks after that fateful meeting in the best bedroom of The Crown she had agreed to marry him.

He swept me off my feet, she acknowledged. There was much to admire about Lord Joslyn and he had proven himself to be an honorable man, a man who could be trusted and, don't forget, she thought with a wry smile, Cornelia approves of him.

Remembering the sight of him as he had burst into the room where Ainsworth held her captive, her heart swelled. He had looked like an avenging god, those black eyes blazing and that gleaming knife held in one hand; he had come to her aid at the time she had needed him most. He was many things. Fascinating. Trustworthy. Charming. Wealthy.

Kind to old ladies, she reminded herself, smiling. Don't forget that. And she suspected that she might very well be, if not in love with him, certainly falling in love with him. Of course she had agreed to marry him!

Emily frowned. Her reasons for accepting him were obvious, but why did he want to marry her? She had no fortune. She had no great, noble or titled family—quite the opposite, thinking of her cousin Jeffery. She wasn't a notable beauty or a scintillating wit. She sighed. There was nothing about her that she could see that would attract a man like Lord Joslyn. Her lips drooped. But if she couldn't name a reason why he would want to marry her, she could think of one very good reason why marriage to her would be anathema to a man like Joslyn: the smuggling.

Yet, incredibly, he had asked her to marry him. She sat up, hugging her knees to her chest. Indeed, he had seemed, she admitted, puzzled but pleased, determined to marry her. Who knew what he was thinking? She shook her head. It was all too complicated and she gave up trying to understand Joslyn's reasons and snuggled under the covers. A wistful smile curved her lips. Was it possible, she wondered, that he was as fascinated by her as she was by him?

All in all, as he lay in his bed, much later that evening, Barnaby was satisfied with the events of the day. Emily had agreed to marry him and tonight's dinner party had gone well. He liked the vicar and his wife and thought the daughters and son reflected laudably on their parents. A brief word with Cornelia before she had departed for her rooms imparted the welcome information that Mrs. Smythe would be cheerfully spreading the news of the engagement tomorrow. He smiled in the darkness. And, of course, from Lamb, he knew that the servant grapevine was already hard at work. By this time tomorrow night, he doubted there'd be anyone of high or low consequence in the area that wouldn't know that Lord Joslyn was to marry Miss Emily Townsend in early February.

For a second, Barnaby spared a thought for his younger sister, Bethany, an ocean away. She'd like Emily, he decided, and with the wedding soon to take place, he wished not for the first time that he had not given in to Bethany's pleadings and allowed her to remain in Virginia with their mother's brother and his wife as chaperones. His lips twitched. There was a great deal about his sister and his wife-to-be that was similar—they were a pair of stubborn, spirited wenches and he feared that he was as malleable as butter in their small, determined hands.

His smile faded as he considered the ominous clouds still on his horizon. Someone had tried to kill him, not once, but twice, and the unknown attacker, or attackers, remained at large. He rubbed the healing wound hidden beneath his thick black hair. The argument could be made that this latest attempt had been an accidental shooting by a poacher, but he dismissed that idea out of hand. He didn't believe in coincidences, and for him to have escaped death two times in less than a month beggared belief. It would have been comforting to think that whoever had tried to kill him would give up and accept defeat after two failures, but Barnaby doubted it.

It was possible, he conceded, that the attacks on his life had nothing to do with his inheritance, but it was difficult to come up with another compelling reason for someone to want him dead. He couldn't claim to be beloved by everyone he met, but neither could he come up with any reason *other* than the Joslyn fortune that would drive someone to want to murder him. Which left a very short list of suspects . . .

Mathew. Thomas. Simon. In various ways, they all stood to gain by his death. Mathew would inherit everything that he had always believed would be his; Thomas would become the heir apparent and while Barnaby admitted it was a weak reason for murder, it wasn't to be dismissed—what was one *more* murder when a fortune was at stake? As for Simon . . . Barnaby scowled. What would Simon gain? He couldn't think of any advantage for Simon beyond being one step closer to inheriting the title, but it seemed a weak reason. Killing three people in order to inherit seemed a bit extreme, but if he was willing to accept that Thomas might kill two people, then for Simon to kill three . . . The only thing Barnaby knew for certain was that *someone* wanted him dead.

Thoughts of death turned his mind to his half brother, Lucien. Emily's abduction yesterday had temporarily obliterated any serious contemplation of Lucien's fate, but with his own affairs well in hand Barnaby finally had a moment to consider Luc's situation. With the turmoil and savagery boiling through France these days, he wondered, with no little anxiety, if Luc was even alive. Barnaby had warned his half brother that this trip to France was folly, but Luc wouldn't listen to him—or Lamb—and had blithely sailed for the continent intent upon finding any surviving member of his mother's family.

The news of the death of Louis XVI had shaken Barnaby. France was a country about to explode into even greater violence and Luc was somewhere in the midst of the madness. Wearily, Barnaby ran a hand over his face, finally admitting that he had no choice but to go to France to try to find his half brother.

Tomorrow he would talk to Lamb about Luc and thinking of Emily and his own happiness, guilt clawed through him. How could he be happy knowing that Luc had need of him? How could he leave Emily behind at a time like this? But what choice did he have? He could no more ignore Luc's plight than he could have left Emily to Ainsworth's evil designs. He took a deep breath, aware of what he must do: just as soon as Jeb returned he'd have to talk to him about sailing back to France, this time with a passenger Jeb would be leaving behind. . . .

Barnaby grimaced and admitted that Mathew might be inheriting the title sooner than anyone expected, particularly if he should lose his life in France while on what might be a fruitless quest to find and rescue as thankless a scamp as ever lived. His heart ached at the thought of leaving Emily, but he could not abandon Luc. Blast him!

After tossing in the bed, he eventually gave up all pretense of sleep and, wrapping a dark blue robe around his nakedness, wandered to the other end of the cavernous room. A pair of overstuffed chairs with a low mahogany table situated between them was arranged in front of the massive fireplace and, selecting one of the chairs, he sat down. A fire glowed on the hearth and staring at the shimmering orange and yellow coals he tried to gain control of his unpleasant thoughts.

To no avail. No sooner had he pushed aside painful images of Luc's lifeless body or Emily standing over his own grave than the memory of Ainsworth lying dead at his feet popped into his brain. He frowned, wondering how he could have handled the situation differently. Leaving Jeffery alone with Ainsworth's body probably hadn't been the wisest thing he'd ever done, but the need to get Emily away from there and safely at Windmere had been his paramount concern. With the luxury of hindsight, he was aware that the decision to thrust the disposal of Ainsworth's body into Jeffery's hands could come back to haunt him.

The probability that he'd be awoken tomorrow morning with the news that he was being arrested for Ainsworth's murder was low, but Barnaby didn't trust that spineless cousin of Emily's not to make a muck of everything. On the other hand, he reminded himself sourly, Jeffery had a strong sense of self-preservation. . . .

Barnaby was still thinking about the Jeffery/Ainsworth problem when he arose the next morning. As Lamb helped him shrug into a jacket of russet superfine, Barnaby said, "We should have heard something about Ainsworth before now. A death in the country, especially one under suspicious circumstances, should have raised comment." He glanced at Lamb. "You've heard nothing in the kitchen?"

Lamb shook his head. "All anyone can talk about is your engagement. Everyone, except perhaps Peckham, is over the moon about your choice. Your Miss Emily is well thought of in the community and most people are happy for her." He grinned. "You have risen in the opinion of your staff. They're of a mind that having the good sense to choose Miss Emily for your bride that, despite being an American, you're a right good fellow, after all."

Barnaby chuckled. "Well, one does try to keep the staff happy at all costs."

"And you?" Lamb asked, his blue eyes searching Barnaby's face. "Are you happy?"

Barnaby patted him on the shoulder. "Yes, old man, I am happy." When Lamb just continued to stare at him, his brow raised, he asked, "Don't tell me you're in Mathew's camp and disapprove of my choice?"

Lamb smiled. "No. If she is the bride of your choice, then I cannot wish you anything but happy."

It wasn't quite the glowing acceptance Barnaby could have wished for, but it would do. He suspected that any reservations Lamb held had more to do with Jeffery than with Emily, and reminded again of the Jeffery/Ainsworth problem, he frowned.

Almost as if he read Barnaby's mind, Lamb said slowly, "I'm thinking it would behoove me to ride into the village and find out if there is any talk about Ainsworth or Jeffery. As you said, something should have surfaced by now." He

grimaced. "Unless Jeffery buried Ainsworth's body alongside of that other fellow's and is just going to pretend
Ainsworth rode away without a word to anyone."

"Surely, he's not that stupid!"

Jeffery wasn't stupid at all, as they were to discover.

With Barnaby's blessing, Lamb had ridden into the village to spend an hour or two at The Crown and to further his
acquaintance with Mrs. Gilbert and perhaps one or two of
her pretty daughters. There was, he told himself, as he tied
his horse to the rail in front of the inn, no reason not to com-
bine pleasure with business. Entering the main room, that
Saturday afternoon, he glanced around and was pleased to
see that except for a pair of old fishermen seated at one of
the tables and two of the Gilbert daughters behind the long
counter, no one else was inside the inn. He'd barely seated
himself in a quiet corner and been served a tankard of ale
by a smiling Flora, before Mrs. Gilbert appeared from the
nether regions of the inn and joined him. Seating herself
across from him, she said, "Terrible news about poor Mr.
Ainsworth, isn't it?"

In the act of sipping from his tankard of ale, Lamb set the
tankard down on the table and asked cautiously, "And what
news would that be?"

"Why only that it seems he and Squire imbibed too much
while in Newhaven on Thursday and lost their way home.
According to Squire, in the darkness and in a state of great
inebriation, he missed the road to The Birches. Seems they
ended up near the cliffs of the Seven Sisters and Mr.
Ainsworth, needing to relieve himself, dismounted his horse
and, despite a warning from Squire, wandered too near the
edge of the cliffs." Her voice bland, she continued, "Unfortunate man fell over the cliffs and was swept out to sea. Village
gossip has it that it was near three o'clock on Friday morn-

ing before Squire was able to make it to the constable's house and report the accident. Of course, a search was instituted, but . . . Constable thinks the poor fellow was killed by the fall from the cliffs and that there was nothing anyone could have done for him even if they'd found him right away." She shuddered delicately. "Ainsworth's body was discovered only this morning on a rocky stretch of beach not far away—they say that the ravages of the sea and rocks was something terrible to see . . . or so I hear."

Lamb's eyes met hers unflinchingly. "Now that's a tragic tale," he said slowly, thinking that Jeffery might be swine dung but the man obviously thought on his feet. Considering the situation, Lamb decided that it worked very well and also gave a plausible reason to explain why Emily's cousin hadn't been at Windmere last night. Lamb had assumed that the news of the engagement would have already reached the village, but it appeared he was mistaken. He rubbed his jaw. "It's a shame this had to happen at a most joyous time for Miss Emily."

Mrs. Gilbert's eyes sharpened. "What about Miss Emily?"

Leaning back, his azure eyes gleaming, he murmured, "Why, only that his lordship announced his engagement to Miss Emily last night at Windmere."

Chapter 16

Mrs. Gilbert let out such a whoop that all five of her daughters appeared from nowhere and rushed over to the table. Their pretty faces filled with anxiety, they crowded around.

"What is it, Ma?" cried Faith.

"Why, only the best news I've heard in a decade," Mrs. Gilbert exclaimed. Smiling at her daughters, she said, "Mr. Lamb just told me that Viscount Joslyn is going to marry our Miss Emily."

There were more whoops and laughter and, cheeks pink with pleasure, blue eyes dancing, they pelted Lamb with questions. Surrounded by a group of demanding women, Lamb did his best to comply, enjoying being the center of all that feminine attention. They were all so genuinely happy about the engagement and seemed to have a real fondness for Emily that some of his reservations about the Gilbert family faded. Perhaps Barnaby was right to trust them.

Lamb was feeling very pleased with himself when he rode home to Windmere an hour later. The news of Joslyn's engagement to Emily was spreading like wildfire, toppling the tragic death of Ainsworth as the main topic of conversation. He had to give Emily's cousin credit for concocting a credible explanation for Ainsworth's death and a reason for any signs of violence that might have been noticed. Except for the most discerning eye, or someone looking for it, the fatal stab wound would be lost amongst the other damage the body had suffered when it was washed up on the rocks.

Jeffery remained a problem, though, and Lamb fully expected him to try his hand at blackmail at the first opportunity.

Lamb was correct. While Lamb was loitering in the village, prior to escorting the two ladies back to The Birches, Barnaby was having a very cordial meeting with Cornelia and Emily in his office. The delicate business of money behind them, after Barnaby had written a note and sent it off by footman to London requesting his solicitor to draw up the necessary papers, they were ready to depart from Windmere. Once Emily and Cornelia were nestled in the coach, Barnaby astride Satan, a big black stallion that had caught his eye in the vast Windmere stables, escorted them home.

Walker met them as the coach halted in front of the house. His face giving nothing away, he apprised them of the shocking death of poor Mr. Ainsworth. "The master," he said expressionlessly, "is utterly devastated."

"Well, perhaps, our news will cheer him up," Barnaby said drily, as he followed the ladies into the house.

Walker glanced quickly at him. "News, my lord?" he asked.

Unable to help herself, Cornelia cackled. "Our Miss Emily is engaged to marry his lordship. They'll wed just as soon as the banns are called!"

Only years of training kept Walker from breaking into a

jig and whooping as had Mrs. Gilbert. The huge smile that
lit up his face told its own tale and his voice full of delight,
he said, "Congratulations, my lord, Miss Emily!"

"Thank you," Emily said, smiling. A twinkle in her eyes,
she added, "And yes, you have permission to tell the staff."

While Walker divested the ladies of their outerwear and
took Barnaby's gloves, a pair of brawny servants from Windmere unloaded the trunks and bandboxes from the coach and
hefted them into the entry hall.

Leading the way down the hall, Cornelia said to Walker,
"You can show them where those trunks belong." She grinned
at him and added, "And after that you may open some of that
champagne laid down in the wine cellar by the old squire
and bring it to us in the green salon." Wryly, she said, "I suppose you should let the squire know that we are home and in
the green salon."

They entered the green salon and Cornelia seated herself
on the celery damask settee, Emily taking a dainty gilt-and-
wood tapestry chair nearby. Barnaby stood at one end of the
fireplace across from where the ladies sat.

Barnaby frowned. "I know you had to come here, but I'm
not happy about it."

"You are fretting for nothing," Cornelia scolded. "It was
Ainsworth who was the dangerous one, not Jeffery. Emily
will be perfectly safe now that we no longer have to worry
about Ainsworth." Her eyes hardened. "Emily and I can handle my spineless nephew. Have no doubt of that!"

Barnaby didn't look convinced. Emily rose up from her
chair and came to stand in front of him, one hand resting on
his arm. "My great-aunt is right," she said, smiling at him.
"Since my father died, we have managed to rub along with
my cousin without killing each other—he is more bluff and
bully than anything else. Jeffery is an irritating nuisance, but
he is not dangerous."

"I sincerely hope you know what you are talking about,"

Barnaby muttered. His eyes caressing her face, he said, "If you have the slightest worry, send word to me immediately."

The door opened and Jeffery, having been informed of their arrival by Walker, walked into the room.

It was an awkward moment for Jeffery. Joslyn knew him for a craven and he winced, remembering his helpless blubbering in the barn. As for Emily and Cornelia . . . He swallowed. From the expressions on their faces, it was obvious that his female relatives despised him for what happened. Or nearly happened. But it wasn't my fault, he thought self-righteously. If Anne had proven more malleable or Emily hadn't been so cold to Ainsworth none of this would have happened. If anyone was to blame, he decided viciously, it was his mean-spirited great-aunt. She could have encouraged Anne to look favorably upon Ainsworth, or pointed out to Emily what a good match Ainsworth would have been, but had she done that? No! The old harridan had pitted both the younger women against poor Ainsworth. And Ainsworth . . . He shuddered, remembering the sight of Ainsworth sprawled dead and bloody on the floor of the farmhouse.

Thinking of the tactics he'd had to employ in disposing of the body, Jeffery swelled with injustice. To think that Joslyn and that oafish servant of his had just ridden away, leaving him there alone with the task of getting rid of the body! The straits he'd been put to! Loading a body onto a horse wasn't an easy task, he reminded himself, and then leading the skittish animal with its grisly burden into the night . . . He'd been terrified of discovery the whole time and the relief he'd felt when he'd finally dumped Ainsworth's body over the cliffs. . . .

He shot a resentful glance at Barnaby. It would have served Joslyn right if he'd ridden immediately to the constable's house and reported the murder. Bitterly, Jeffery admitted that if he'd thought for a moment that anyone would have believed that Viscount Joslyn had murdered Ainsworth, he would have pointed the finger at Joslyn, but greedy, self-serving and vain he might be, Jeffery wasn't stupid. Joslyn had the correct reading of the situation: no one would believe that the viscount had murdered Ainsworth and Jeffery might very well have found himself standing in the dock accused of the murder. It just wasn't fair.

"Ah, Jeffery," purred Cornelia, breaking into his thoughts, "how kind of you to join us." Her eyes bright, she said, "We have news for you."

Warily, Jeffery eyed her. "Oh? And what would that be?"

"Why only," Barnaby said, "that your cousin has done me the honor of agreeing to marry me."

"In three weeks—just as soon as the banns are called," Cornelia said happily.

Jeffery gaped. Emily to marry Joslyn! His wish had come true. Visions of Joslyn gold dancing in front of him, he cheered right up. "By Jove!" he cried, smiling. "This is indeed good news. My congratulations to the pair of you."

He wagged a finger under Emily's nose. "What a sly, clever little puss you've been," he said waggishly. "If I'd had the least idea that you and Joslyn . . . I never would have . . ." He stopped, recognizing the danger of continuing that train of conversation. "Well," he said somewhat lamely, "this calls for a celebration."

As if on cue, Walker knocked and came into the room with a silver tray containing two bottles of uncorked champagne and several crystal flutes. Leaving the tray on a small satinwood table near the door, the butler departed.

Champagne was poured and Jeffery and Cornelia toasted the engaged couple. Once the toasts were over, a small, uncomfortable silence fell. Though polite, it was clear that Jeffery's presence was only being tolerated.

But Jeffery wasn't going to be driven away by cold silence—not without having a word with Joslyn. By thunder! The man was in his debt. And he intended to collect.

Setting down his empty flute, Jeffery said heartily, "And now, my lord, if I may have a private word with you?"

Barnaby glanced at him. "Why? I don't believe that you and I have anything to say to one another that couldn't be said in front of the ladies."

It was not an encouraging reply, but Jeffery wasn't going to be put off. Not when money was at stake. Gamely, Jeffery said, "Now that you and my cousin are engaged, there are some, ah, business matters that must be taken care of. Settlements, pin money, that sort of thing."

"That won't be necessary," Barnaby replied. "Your great-aunt and I have worked out the settlements and whatnot to our satisfaction."

Jeffery choked. Looking from a grinning Cornelia to a stone-faced Barnaby, he snapped, "But—but that's impossible! I am the head of family!" Pointing at Cornelia he said, "She's an old *woman*. What does she know about finance and the like?"

"As a woman, I know *precisely* what is needed to ensure Emily's future—and keep her money safe from the likes of you," Cornelia said sweetly. "His lordship and I met earlier today and with Emily's approval we came to certain agreements." Her eyes icy, she added, "Emily will never have to worry that she will find herself helpless and penniless again—and you'll never get your hands on any of the money Joslyn has set aside for her."

His face white with fury, Jeffery demanded, "Is this true, my lord?"

"Yes."

His hands curled into fists and, quivering with rage, Jeffery declared angrily, "Very well! Let us have some plain speaking. I think you forget that I know you murdered Ainsworth." He tittered. "I wonder what the constable would say if I were to tell him what really happened at the Godart farm Thursday evening."

Barnaby looked puzzled. "The Godart farm? I don't believe I know of the place." He glanced at Emily and Cornelia. "Have you ladies ever heard of it?"

Smoothly Emily said, "Yes. I think it is an abandoned farm and part of the estate." She looked at Jeffery, contempt in her eyes, but her voice held only curiosity when she asked, "But why do you think that old place is of interest to his lordship?"

"You know exactly why!" Jeffery shouted. "You were there!"

"I think you are mistaken," Emily said gently. She flashed an intimate smile in Barnaby's direction. "I was too busy being courted by Lord Joslyn on Thursday to pay a visit to an abandoned farm." Her gaze returned to Jeffery's purpling face. "Everyone can confirm that his lordship and I were here until we departed for Windmere and that we were never anywhere near the Godart farm." Perplexed, she asked, "Are you certain the loss of your friend hasn't overset your mind."

"My mind," Jeffery snarled, "is not overset!" His fulminating gaze swept over them. "You're all lying! Pretending innocence."

"Prove it," Cornelia challenged.

He could not. Frustrated and angry, he muttered, "This is intolerable!"

"What is intolerable," Barnaby said levelly, "is that we have to endure your presence. If you want to survive the next few weeks, I'd suggest you learn to choose your words with care and that you stay out of my sight as much as possible." He strolled across the room, stopping in front of Jeffery. Softly he said, "If I hear one word, one hint that you have treated my bride-to-be and Mrs. Townsend with anything less than the greatest respect, I'll tear you from limb to limb." He smiled and Jeffery staggered back at the menace in the smile.

Turning on his heel, Jeffery stalked from the room.

Barnaby glanced at the two ladies. Brow raised, he asked, "Do you think he'll try something else?"

Emily made a face. "Once he gets over his anger, he'll start angling to get his hands into your pocket—one way or another." She frowned. "Jeffery isn't very inventive," she said slowly, "and I think that most likely he'll limit himself to trying to make you feel sorry for him—or obligated to him."

Barnaby smiled. "Reminding me that I owe him?"

Cornelia nodded. "Oh, you can be sure of that."

Her expression troubled, Emily asked, "Are you sure you want to marry into a family that has someone like him as a member?"

Barnaby turned and walked back to her and, lifting her hand to his lips, pressed a kiss onto the back of her hand. His eyes moving warmly across her face, he murmured, "Try and stop me."

The dinner with the vicar and his family last night had put paid to any scheme Mathew might have had of ending the engagement and accepting that only an act of God would prevent the marriage, after dinner Saturday evening, Mathew sought a moment alone with Barnaby. Finding his host thumbing through a book in the library, Mathew said stiffly, "Our visit has been eventful but after the calling of the banns tomorrow, Tom and I shall be returning to Monks Abbey. Naturally, we shall return for the wedding."

"Not Simon?" Barnaby asked with a lifted brow.

Mathew grimaced. "Simon is enjoying this whole spectacle and he sees no reason to leave."

Barnaby laughed. "Now why am I not surprised?" Sobering, he added, "You know that all of you are always welcome at Windmere and that there is no reason for you to leave if you don't want to."

Mathew studied Barnaby's face for a long moment, searching for signs of insincerity. Finding none, he said coolly, "You are a much better man than I. If our positions were reversed, I'd be wishing you to the devil."

"As I did you at first," Barnaby admitted, smiling, "but I've mellowed."

"Perhaps in a decade or two," Mathew said, "I'll be able to say the same."

Barnaby laughed. "Let us hope that it is sooner."

A glimmer of a smile in the azure eyes, Mathew murmured, "I wouldn't hold my breath."

Barnaby was thoughtful after Mathew left the room. He hadn't minded the visit from his Joslyn cousins, but he wouldn't be sorry to see them leave either—especially Mathew and Thomas. Their thinly veiled animosity was wearying. Simon seemed not to mind that his older brother had lost the title and a fortune, but Barnaby wondered about that. Was Simon all that he appeared? He liked Simon, but Simon's desire to stay behind raised a few questions in his mind. Was he remaining behind to keep an eye on him? Make another attempt on his life? Or simply to rile Mathew? Barnaby smiled. Probably the latter.

Later that evening, while they were alone in his dressing room, Barnaby asked Lamb, "Have you heard that Mathew and Tom are leaving after the calling of the banns tomorrow? And that Simon is staying?"

Lamb, in the act of hanging up Barnaby's plum jacket in one of the massive mahogany wardrobes, glanced over his shoulder and answered, "Yes. There was talk in the kitchens earlier this evening about it."

Barnaby expected as much—the servants probably knew of Mathew and Tom's plans before he did, he thought wryly. "Why do you think Simon is staying?" he asked, unraveling his cravat.

"My money would be on annoying his brothers," Lamb replied.

"My thoughts precisely," Barnaby said with a laugh. Laughter fading, he asked casually, "You don't think Simon might be behind the attacks on me?"

"Do you?" Lamb asked, frowning.

"No. It seems rather far-fetched, but I am curious about his remaining behind. Seems to me that the three brothers tend to act in unison."

"You're wrong there," Lamb said. "Servant gossip has it that Simon is seldom at Monks Abbey and that he is not often in the company of either brother." Lamb hesitated. "His valet, Leighton, is a likable young man," he said finally, "whose main fault is a fondness for the bottle and a loose tongue. According to him, the hostility between Thomas and Simon is very real—they can't abide each other."

"So Simon could be staying to annoy Tom as much as Mathew," Barnaby said.

"That would be my guess."

Barnaby agreed and, shrugging out of his silk waistcoat, he handed the garment to Lamb. His day had been full, and while he would have preferred to think about Emily's charms, Luc was never far from his mind. Undoing his shirt, he said carefully, "I've been thinking about Luc and what to do about him."

Lamb swung around to look at him, his gaze narrowed. "Now why do I have the impression that I am not going to like what you're going to say?"

There was no wrapping it in clean linen and Barnaby said baldly, "I have to go after him. When Jeb returns I'm going to speak with him about taking me to France."

His jaw clenched, Lamb growled, "Now that is the most asinine idea you have ever expressed. You do not have to rescue that young devil from a danger of his own making. Despite all the warnings and advice to the contrary he chose to go to France, and it is not up to you to save his neck."

"You'd abandon him?"

"Not if I thought I could save him," Lamb said tightly, "but we have no idea where he is in France or even if he is still alive. For all you know, he's already lost that handsome head of his to the guillotine."

Barnaby winced. "Thank you," he muttered. "I'll try to sleep after you've put such a delightful picture in my mind."

"I would remind you that you have other responsibilities," Lamb said, "other people dependent upon you—such as everyone on this estate. Would you desert them?" At the stubborn expression on Barnaby's face, he demanded, "What of Miss Townsend? What are you going to do? Marry her one day and sail for France the next, not knowing when or if you'll return?"

That was the sticking point, Barnaby admitted. When he considered leaving Emily behind, whether married or not, every fiber in his body rebelled. He owed Luc loyalty, but didn't he owe the woman he was to marry more? Pain in the dark eyes, Barnaby asked, "How can I sacrifice one for the other?"

"You're not sacrificing anyone!" Lamb snarled. "Luc *chose* to sacrifice himself—you had nothing to do with it—and you did your damnedest to stop him from going." Taking a deep breath, he added, "Though there are times I would like to throttle him myself, I am not without feelings for him—he's my nephew just as you are and we share the bond of illegitimacy." His face softened and he said quietly, "I would remind you that Luc wouldn't thank you for throwing your own life away. Whatever his fate—he'd want you to marry your Amazon and raise strapping sons and fierce-eyed daughters and he'd curse you for a fool if you don't do exactly that."

Lamb was right about that, Barnaby admitted, and he

could almost hear Lucien's voice chiding him for even considering such a reckless, foolish act. *"Mon Dieu!"* Lucien cried in his head, and Barnaby could see the azure eyes gleaming with mockery. "You left the arms of a beautiful woman to search for me? You are a fool, my little brother. A fool. Bah! I cannot believe that we share the same father. One of us is a changeling and it is not *moi!*"

Shutting out that mocking voice, Barnaby said to Lamb, "You win. For the present we shall just hope that Lucifer lives up to his name." Forcing a grin, he added, "And I shall keep my thoughts on my Amazon and those strapping sons and fierce-eyed daughters."

Upon returning home, Emily had no thoughts of strapping sons and fierce-eyed daughters; her thoughts were of more mundane things—such as her life regaining some semblance of normality. She assumed that she could simply slip back into her usual routine and she was unprepared for the furor her engagement to Lord Joslyn created all through the surrounding countryside. Once the engagement became public that Sunday morning at the calling of the banns, everyone of note simply *had* to call at The Birches and offer their congratulations—and of course, Barnaby rode over nearly every day, distracting her with stolen kisses and teasing looks. When Barnaby wasn't underfoot, her time was spent smiling and nodding at all the various, twittering ladies that came to call. Near the end of that first week, her face felt as if a permanent smile had been plastered on it. Many of the ladies were kind, but there were inquisitive stares and a few, their voices full of speculation, were bold enough to comment aloud at the suddenness of the engagement. Emily either ignored them or allowed Cornelia to give them a proper setdown—which she did with relish.

If Emily was not being teased and seduced by Barnaby or

badgered by the curious, she was being led away for another fitting of this gown or that gown. Having endured two Seasons in London, she was half prepared for the enormous amount of clothing being Joslyn's viscountess would require, but she hadn't realized the ruthless enthusiasm that would govern her great-aunt when it came to assembling a suitable wardrobe. Having free call on Joslyn's generous pocketbook had unleashed a hither-to-unknown desire in Cornelia to fill every wardrobe, trunk and chest in the house with fabulous garments for both of them for every conceivable occasion. The list of things Cornelia felt were absolutely necessary for Emily's elevated position, and her own, seemed endless. "After all," Cornelia commented with a wicked grin, "I'm as near a mother-in-law as he'll ever get, and you know the viscount wouldn't want me to appear in these old rags." A thought struck her. "Oh, and Anne! Anne must have some new gowns in time for the wedding, too."

During the past week there had been a series of letters carried back and forth between The Birches and Parkham House by the servants. With Ainsworth's death, there was no longer any reason for Anne to remain at Parkham House, but since Hugh and his mother would be attending the wedding, it was agreed that she would wait and return to The Birches with them. Hugh's mother settled the problem of new gowns by suggesting Anne use her seamstress. Informed by Cornelia of the situation, Barnaby dutifully saw that a generous sum of money was sent to Anne.

Amusement in his eyes, Barnaby said to Cornelia as he wrote out the instructions for the transfer of money, "Enjoying spending my money, are you?"

Cornelia twinkled at him. "Immensely!"

At Cornelia's urgent request, a notable modiste from London had arrived on the steps of The Birches—along with a coach full of materials. Martha Webber, despite her crippled hands, begged to be allowed to help with the sewing of dear Miss Emily's wardrobe and, helpless against the appeal in those faded eyes, what could Emily say? The old lady and her sister, Mrs. Gant, were installed in one of the bedrooms near the London modiste. The arrival of a pair of young seamstresses from London swelled the number of women working on the wardrobes.

Never mind that between the curious ladies and the fittings that her wedding loomed large on the horizon, or that Emily had her hands full with the day-to-day running of The Birches . . . and just never mind about anything to do with smugglers. . . . Lambing season hovered close and she'd already spent two nights until the early hours of the morning in the lambing shed with Loren. An older ewe and her breech big ram lamb they managed to save, but on a stormy Thursday night the last day of January, they lost a young ewe and the twins she carried. And then there had been the dinner party and ball planned by Joslyn on Saturday the second of February, where she made her first official appearance at Windmere as his bride-to-be.

After the second calling of the banns, Emily hoped that the novelty of her engagement would fade, but such was not the case. If anything, with the wedding approaching in ten days or so, the interest was even more intense. Every night of the next week it seemed that she and Joslyn attended a soiree or a ball hosted by the leaders in the neighborhood, each one trying to outdo the other.

On Friday evening, having escorted the two ladies home through a driving rainstorm from a ball given by Lord and Lady Broadfoot, after bidding Cornelia good night, Barnaby stole a moment alone with Emily. He'd noted the shadows under her eyes and the distracted air about her.

Determined to get to the bottom of it, he whisked her into the green salon and demanded, "What is wrong? Something is worrying you. Jeffery?"

Emily sighed and sank down onto the settee. She considered hedging but in the end she said simply, "Jeb should have returned by now. He's been gone two weeks." She bit her lip. "He's never been gone more than a week and the one time that he was delayed was because he'd had to replace a sail shredded in a storm."

Barnaby frowned. "Is there any way you can find out if he is safely in Calais or if there was trouble with his boat in the Channel?"

"Not without sending someone specifically to look for him," she admitted unhappily. "Jeb and his crew are experienced seamen," she added, as much to remind herself as Barnaby. "There was no storm the night they left, although the waters of the Channel can be rough even without a storm, so it is possible that there was some sort of trouble during the crossing." She sighed again. "I cannot imagine that he ran afoul of the port authorities in Calais, and if he fell into the hands of the revenuers, we'd know about it." She looked down at her fingers nervously pleating the spangled net overskirt of her pink silk gown. "Sometimes the people smugglers have to deal with would just as soon murder them and steal their money as sell them contraband."

"Do you think that is what happened?"

She shrugged. "It was riskier for us in the beginning because we didn't know who we could trust, but these days Jeb has only certain traders he deals with—men that won't try to cheat him—or at least ones that he hopes won't take advantage of him." She looked up at him, her gray eyes troubled. "Something is delaying him and I fear that it cannot be good."

Barnaby longed to comfort her, but smuggling and its associated dangers were not his forte. Beyond the most basic information, he knew little of smuggling . . . and of boats, he thought uneasily, remembering that desperate time he had fought for his life in the Channel.

Trying to come up with some logical reason for Jeb's

delay, and the memory of those angry waves vivid in his mind, he offered, "Perhaps the Channel crossing was indeed rougher than expected and there was some damage done to the boat and repairs are taking time."

"If there was damage done to the boat," she said grimly, "I'd put my money on sabotage by the Nolles gang."

Barnaby didn't like the sound of that and he reminded himself again that he needed to pay a visit to The Ram's Head and discover for himself just how much danger this Nolles and his gang represented. His eyes traveled over Emily's anxious features, his gaze lingering on the soft, enticing curve of her mouth. His lips twitched. He was alone with his bride-to-be and instead of sweeping her into his arms and showing her how delightful he found her, he was discussing smugglers!

Deciding that since he could not solve the problem of Jeb's absence, he could at least distract her, he sat down beside her. His fingers brushed against her cheek and he murmured, "Our wedding is in four days. Perhaps we could forget about everyone else for the moment and concentrate on ourselves. . . ."

Her eyes met his and her breath caught at the leashed passion she saw glittering in those dark depths. He'd kissed her several times during the past few weeks since the announcement of their engagement, and her body responded instantly to the knowledge of what was to come. Her nipples stiffened, desire quickened in her belly and her lips parted in anticipation of his kiss.

Barnaby did not disappoint. His mouth came down hungrily on hers and she moaned when his tongue thrust between her lips. She went into his embrace eagerly, her arms clasping around his neck, her bosom pressed against his broad chest.

During the days since their engagement, Emily had learned a great deal about her body and the response Barnaby evoked so effortlessly. She no longer fought against the attraction she felt for him, reveling in the heat and sweet power his kiss, his touch aroused and she returned his kiss with innocent fervor, her tongue sliding silkily against his and following his lead, dipping boldly into his mouth.

These all-too-brief moments when he had her alone were driving Barnaby mad, and every time he had her in his arms, his control slipped just a little and tonight was no different. Her generous response was all he could have asked for and his body demanding more, his hand dropped to her breast and he kneaded the soft flesh, his fingers plucking at the hard nub of her nipple. Heady with desire, he fought against the urge to take what was his. The knowledge that the wedding was so close made him reckless and he tipped her back against the settee, his hand fumbling with the net and silk that concealed what he desperately wanted to touch. He struggled against the urge to rip and tear the delicate material and he growled with satisfaction when at last his fingers found the naked warmth of her calf.

They had never been this intimate and Emily's heart galloped in her breast as his hand slid unerringly up her leg, lingering on her thigh before sliding unerringly upward. Emily stiffened, beset by frantic emotions—desire, delight, anticipation and fear of the unknown—and then his fingers found her. . . . She shuddered at the aching sweetness of his exploration, the sensation of his fingers moving so cleverly over her mound, clouding her brain.

Barnaby's lips hardened, the pounding demand to make her his, overpowering. His swollen rod was near-to-bursting from his breeches and the fierce need to seek relief was unceasing. She was warm and ripe before him and, gripped by blind desire, a question hummed dizzily at the back of his brain: what would be the harm?

His searching finger slipped inside of her and Emily arched up at the blunt invasion. Stroking inside all that silky heat, hearing her muted moans, his own body ready to explode, he balanced on the edge. Take her? Or not?

There was a rap on the door and the mood shattered. Simultaneously they were recalled to their surroundings and leaped apart like scalded cats. Barnaby sprang away from her and snapped at whoever was on the other side of the door, "A moment."

Emily jerked into a sitting position and her cheeks flaming, frantically pushed down the skirts of her gown. A quick tug and pull here and there and she looked demure as a nun as she sat on the green settee.

Seeing that she was in command of herself, Barnaby crossed to stand next to the fireplace. Placing one arm on the mantel and keeping his body partially turned to hide the state of his arousal, he called out, "Yes? Come in."

Walker rushed into the room. "Miss Emily," he cried, oblivious to any undercurrents, "you must come quick—there's been trouble. Jeb and the others were attacked as they were unloading on the beach."

Chapter 17

Emily leaped up from the settee. There'd been trouble? Pray God, no one had been hurt!

"Is anyone hurt?" she demanded. Her eyes flashed. "How could this happen? Why the devil didn't I know about the landing? I should have been there."

Unhappily Walker said, "You'd already left for the ball when Mr. Meek spied Jeb's signal. Everyone knew that the Broadfoot ball was tonight and that you'd be attending it. We were all aware that if Jeb chose tonight for a landing that there wouldn't be any way that we could get word to you— or that you could leave the ball." He looked apologetic. "We decided amongst ourselves that if Jeb *did* show up tonight that we'd handle the transport of the goods ourselves. There wasn't any other choice."

"He's right," Barnaby said. "You had to be at that ball tonight and no excuse short of being on your deathbed would have been acceptable for your absence."

Knowing that Barnaby was right didn't lessen her feelings of guilt, but in a calmer tone, she said to Walker, "Tell me."

Walker cleared his throat. "When Mr. Meek came to Mrs. Gilbert with word that Jeb was landing tonight she was pre-

pared to go ahead without you." Emily's lips tightened and
he added hastily, "This wasn't Jeb's first landing—you've a
good crew and everyone knew their task. Morning would
have been soon enough for you to hear that Jeb had returned." He hung his head and muttered, "No one was expecting the Nolles gang to be lying in wait."

Her face strained, Emily asked, "Jeb? Mrs. Gilbert? Are
they hurt?"

"There are some bloody heads and bruises, but no one is
in danger of dying," Walker admitted. "But come to the
kitchen—Jeb is desperate to talk to you."

Emily rushed past Walker, and with Barnaby and Walker
on her heels she ran to the kitchen. Though it was well after
midnight, the kitchen was filled with people.

Alice was busy wrapping a strip of clean linen around
Jeb's temple as he sat on a stool next to the scrubbed oak
table; Caleb, sporting an impressive black eye, stood beside
Jeb. Mrs. Spalding and Jane were concentrating on another
one of Jeb's crew slumped on the table at the opposite end.

At their entrance, Jeb struggled to his feet. "Lord Joslyn!
I didn't expect you here at this time of night."

"I escorted Miss Townsend home from the ball," Barnaby
said. Noting the bandage dangling down the side of Jeb's
face and the way Jeb gripped the table for balance, he said
gently, "Now sit down before you fall, and tell us what has
happened."

Gratefully following Barnaby's orders, Jeb sat back
down. Sending Emily a crooked smile, Jeb said, "We'll all
live, missy, so don't you start scolding."

Relief swept through her. "Oh, Jeb! I was so fearful!
You're sure you're all right? And everybody else?"

"We'll live, but no use pretending we're not bruised and
bloody. Those bullies of Nolles's are right handy with those
wooden clubs they carry and they outnumbered us. It's only
by grace and good luck that none of us suffered a broken

bone—or worse. Johnny Fuller was knocked out and gave us a scare until we had a chance to check his injuries. Mrs. Gilbert says he'll do fine. Faith took a nasty blow to her right arm, but nothing was broken; Mrs. Gilbert herself has a black eye to rival Caleb's and Ford has a split lip. Some of the others will have some aches and bruises—it could have been worse."

Sinking down onto a stool near Jeb, Emily asked, "How did it happen?"

"Been worried lately that they'd gotten wind of us," Jeb confessed. "I'd heard a whisper or two, but since we're small and not much competition, I thought they'd leave us alone." He sighed. "Near as we can figure, they must have been watching for my signal, or watching Meeks's house or mayhap The Crown and so they knew of the landing. They jumped us after we unloaded everything and had the horses packed and were leaving the beach."

"It wasn't enough that they used their clubs on us with enthusiasm," Caleb broke in angrily. "They stole the entire load of contraband and laughed as they left."

Emily took in a trembling breath. "At least you're all alive."

"Aye, that we are," Jeb said, "but what are we going to do now?"

"Nothing for the moment," Barnaby said, coming to stand beside Emily. One hand resting on her shoulder, his eyes on Jeb, he added, "I'm afraid that after tonight we're going to have to find a more respectable way for you to make a living."

Emily stiffened and would have risen, but Barnaby's hand kept her in her seat.

Jeb surveyed him coolly. "No disrespect, your lordship, but you'll not find many of us willing to take charity."

"Will honest employment be viewed as charity?" Barnaby asked.

Having a good idea what he was up to, Emily squirmed around in her seat and glared up at Barnaby. "Title and fortune you may have, but you cannot employ everyone in the county," she said tightly.

Barnaby smiled at her. "I don't intend to employ everyone—just the main characters involved in your, er, enterprise—they'll have to take care of the others." He looked across at Jeb. "I wouldn't have chosen now to bring this up, but I'll be replacing the Joslyn yacht. . . . It, uh, disappeared. Since I know little of sailing, I'll need a trustworthy captain and a small crew of his choosing. The wages would be fair and generous. Do you know of anyone who might be interested?"

Jeb nodded and rubbed his chin. "Think I'll be able to find a few able seamen who might do. Johnny Fuller is my first mate—he'd be a good man to have." He grinned. "And I know just the fellow to be your captain."

"I thought you might," Barnaby said, his dark eyes amused.

Emily didn't know whether to laugh or cry. Just that easily Barnaby had seduced Jeb away from her and onto his side. She tried to feel resentful about Jeb's defection, but she could not. Jeb wasn't a smuggler at heart—none of them were. Circumstances had forced them into the contraband trade and she admitted that she wouldn't be sorry to see the end of it. No doubt, she thought wryly, Barnaby already had plans for Mrs. Gilbert and some of the other investors.

Emily said to Jeb, "There is nothing more can be done tonight. Walker can find you places to sleep here tonight and have you gone before Jeffery or his valet is likely to stumble over you."

Jeb shook his head. "That won't be necessary. We're going back to The Crown just in case Will and his gang decides to inflict more damage tonight. I left Ford and Fuller and a few others with Mrs. Gilbert to keep an eye out for trouble, but Caleb and I need to be there if it comes to a fight."

"Do you think it will come to that?" Emily asked worriedly.

"No. Will and his boys got what they wanted and gave us a good trouncing in the bargain. I suspect they'll only go after The Crown if we don't heed their warning and continue to run contraband, but I don't want to risk being wrong again."

Her initial shock and horror at tonight's events fading, Emily was puzzled. She could have heard all of this in the morning, so why was Jeb here at this hour?

Almost as if he read her mind, Jeb said, "I suppose you're wondering now what was so important that I had to see you tonight." At Emily's nod, he looked sly and added, "Well, the answer is sitting right there at the other end of the table."

Almost as one, Emily and Barnaby swung around to stare down the length of the long table. The fisherman, a stranger to her, was no longer slumped facedown on the table, but was now propped up in the chair, his chin resting weakly on his chest. The bulky fisherman's garb hung loosely on his tall frame and he was slim to the point of thinness, the bones of his wrists jutting out. Heavy black hair framed his face and fell down in a wave across his forehead, almost obscuring his eyes; his complexion was pale, but whether natural or from some illness, Emily couldn't tell. He looked, she decided, like a man who had narrowly escaped death.

Barnaby stiffened, hardly able to believe his eyes. After a stunned moment, he rushed to the other end of the table and exclaimed, *"Lucien!"* Appalled by Luc's condition, he gently touched his half brother's bone-thin shoulder. "What the hell happened to you?"

Lucien stirred slightly and with an effort his head lifted. Dull, azure eyes met Barnaby's. "I diced with death one time too often, but thanks to your friend, Jeb, here, he managed to get me out of France."

"He was damn near dead when I found him," Jeb said quietly. "And that's what delayed us. Miss Emily had asked me to find out what I could about your brother when I was in Calais. As soon as we arrived in port I asked a few discreet questions, but learned nothing. Two days later, just as we readied to sail, word came from a . . . friend that she had an American who might be the fellow I was looking for." Jeb hesitated, then muttered, "He was in a, ah, brothel and Marie feared he might die. When I first laid eyes on him, he wasn't dead yet but damn near. We had no choice but to wait and see if he was going to live or not." He grinned at Luc. "The fellow decided to live so we brought him back with us."

Barnaby shook his head and, despite his concern over Luc's state, he muttered, "A whorehouse? Now why am I not surprised?"

Luc flashed him a shadow of his old mocking grin and murmured, "The ladies, you know, they adore me."

"But what happened?" Barnaby demanded. "How did you end up nearly dead in a whorehouse in Calais?"

"It was not easy," Lucien replied. The azure eyes lifted to Barnaby's anxious face and Luc said, "I should have listened to you and Lamb—it was a foolish task I set for myself and one bound to fail." Running a hand tiredly over his face, he continued, "I nearly lost my life and all I learned is that Maman's family are all dead, and to be in France these days—especially for a foreigner—is . . . unhealthy. Since last summer Danton and Marat have dominated the Paris commune and have taken over all police power and they use it at will. In November I was in Paris and, having finally accepted that none of the family survived, I was preparing to leave the city when someone reported that I had been asking pointed questions about the Gagnier family." A ragged smile crossed his face. "The police came to call and I'm afraid, I was not polite—I ended up in prison."

Mrs. Spalding interrupted the narrative by placing a mug

of steaming potage swimming with bits of beef and mutton and carrots, parsnips and cabbage in front of Luc and declaring, "Eat! You can talk afterward. Right now, you need this."

Glaring at Jeb, she said, "And the same goes for you and Caleb. It's a bitter, cold night out there and you're not leaving my kitchen before getting something warm in your bellies." A bit more politely to Emily, she asked, "Would you or his lordship care for something? I have a nice pot of tea ready and some cinnamon-and-raisin scones are about ready to come out of the oven any minute now. There's also plenty of that potage if you'd like some."

Emily and Barnaby meekly decided that a cup of tea and some scones would be appreciated. The others accepted the potage and the chunks of bread and cheese Alice and Mrs. Spalding put before them.

While the others ate, over the rim of her cup, Emily studied Barnaby's half brother. She could see little resemblance to Barnaby beyond a certain look around the mouth and jaw and, like Lamb, Luc had inherited the Joslyn blue eyes and aristocratic features; he would have easily passed for Mathew's brother. Though tall, even when he regained the weight he had obviously lost, Lucien would be a slim man, a rapier to Barnaby's broadsword.

As if feeling her eyes on him, Luc looked up and stared back at her. She flushed at the admiring smile that lit up his face and the speculative glint in that azure gaze as it traveled over her face and down to her bosom.

Seeing Emily's blush and guessing the cause, Barnaby sighed. Luc liked women almost as much as they liked him and even having just barely escaped death his half brother couldn't help flirting with the nearest attractive woman.

Glancing at Lucien, Barnaby said softly, "Leave her alone, Luc. I'm marrying her on Tuesday."

Astonished, Luc looked from Barnaby to Emily. A delighted grin flitted across his face. "*Mon Dieu!* Now this is wonderful news. It is very good that Captain Jeb found me in time to attend the wedding, *oui*?"

"Yes, it is," Barnaby agreed, "but you haven't told us how you ended up half-dead in a whorehouse."

Luc started to shrug, then grimaced and rubbed his right shoulder. "After nearly two months in prison as a guest of the French police, I knew I had to escape or I'd die either of starvation, disease or the guillotine. I was desperate, and when the opportunity arose to take part in a prison break, I took it." His lips twisted. "Unfortunately, I was shot during the escape. My, er, compatriots left me for dead and they scattered in all directions. With no money, surrounded by strangers and the French police looking for me, reaching the coast and getting aboard a ship headed for England was my only option. Under the cover of darkness I made my way on foot to the coast . . . stealing what I could as I traveled." He shot Barnaby a sardonic look. "If I had any luck at all during that cursed trip it was that upon my initial arrival in France, while in Calais, I made the, uh, acquaintance of the same woman Jeb knew—Marie Dupre. I hoped if I could make it to her place that she would help me." A disgusted expression crossed his mobile features. "I'd have been fine if the damned wound hadn't become infected. But it did and by the time I reached Calais and Marie's place, I was so weak and racked by fever I could hardly stand. If she hadn't taken me in . . ." He smiled crookedly. "If she'd turned her back on me, this story would have a different ending."

His voice thick with emotion, Barnaby said, "I warned you that it was a damned sleeveless errand. Christ! You could have died, Luc!"

Seated beside Barnaby, Emily placed her hand over his as it lay on the table beside his cup of tea and squeezed gently, her heart aching for him. His hand turned and his fingers tightened on hers and in that odd moment all doubts about her coming marriage vanished. Why, we *belong* together she admitted, staggered by the insight. Her gaze dropped to their hands. Just as our hands were linked in some indefinable way, she thought, dazed, so are our very lives unalterably melded together. Together they were stronger, more complete and in that instant, she realized why: she was in love with him. Stunned by the discovery, her thoughts in a whirl, her fingers clenched even tighter around Barnaby's.

His fingers gripping Emily's as if he'd never let them go, when Lucien remained silent, Barnaby said, "Go on. Finish it."

Toying with a small chunk of bread, Lucien said wearily, "When I first arrived in France, I stayed a few days in Calais and one night, I visited Marie's establishment. There was some trouble in her place that night. . . ." His face went hard, and he said, flatly, "I settled the problem—much to Marie's relief and gratitude. She swore she was in my debt and that if I ever needed a favor to call upon her." He shrugged. "So when I showed up half-dead on her doorstep months later, she repaid the favor."

Barnaby glanced at Jeb. "It seems that I am deeper in your debt than I realized. Thank you for saving his life and bringing my brother safely home."

Jeb waved a dismissing hand. "Miss Emily is the one you should thank. If she hadn't mentioned him to me, we'd have sailed from Calais with nary a thought of looking for Mr. Lucien."

His eyes on Emily, Luc said, "It seems, soon-to-be-sweet-sister, that I am in your debt. You saved my life—it is yours to command."

"Then I command you for your brother's sake to regain your health and *try* not to cause him further anxiety," Emily said with a glimmer of a smile in her fine eyes.

"Once you know him better," Barnaby said drily, "you will discover that the latter is beyond him. He is not called Lucifer for nothing."

"Pay him no heed," Luc replied airily. "My *petite* brother

fusses like a hen with one chick." He grinned. "It is good that his attention will now be shared between us. Keeping him distracted is a burden I will gladly share with you."

With Lucien's tale told, the group broke up, Jeb and Caleb leaving to return to the village. Shortly after that, having said a private good night to Emily, Barnaby bundled Lucien into the waiting Joslyn coach.

Sinking back against the luxurious padded dark blue cushions as the big coach lurched into motion and drove away from The Birches, Lucien shook his head. In the light created by the small candles burning in the four glass lanterns hung on either side of the coach doors, he regarded Barnaby seated across from him. Smiling faintly, he asked, "Your lordship? How the bloody hell did that happen?"

As the coach rumbled through the night, Barnaby gave an expurgated version of the events that had occurred during the seven months since they had last seen each other. "A viscount!" Lucien exclaimed when Barnaby was through. "And Lamb here with you." He shot him a teasing look from between thick, feminine lashes. "With your penchant for acting like a broody hen I'm surprised you let Bethany remain at home and didn't drag her to England with you."

Barnaby hunched a shoulder. "I didn't know what I was walking into here and she was adamantly opposed to leaving Green Hill. It seemed wisest to leave her behind for the time being."

Naming Barnaby and Bethany's uncle, Lucien said, "Fortier with her?"

Barnaby nodded.

Satisfied that all was well with his young half sister, and aware that there were some intriguing gaps in Barnaby's narrative, Luc said, "Now tell me how it is that the lovely, fair-haired Amazon you plan to marry is at home with a gang of smugglers."

Laughing, Barnaby said, "You and Lamb! He's called her my Amazon from the moment he first laid eyes on her."

"Lamb and I often agree about women," Lucien purred, "but I notice you're not telling me about the smugglers."

Knowing Lucien wouldn't give up until he had the whole story, reluctantly, Barnaby related the main points.

Lucien nodded several times and when Barnaby finished speaking, he grinned at him. "You know, I am liking this Amazon of yours more and more—I predict she will save you from becoming a stuffy old man. And Cornelia . . ." Lucien chuckled. "If she were fifty years younger she'd steal my heart."

"She will anyway," Barnaby said, smiling.

"So tell me more of our cousins, Mathew, Thomas and Simon . . . and the possibility"—Lucien's eyes narrowed—"that one of them is trying to kill my favorite brother."

"I'm your *only* brother," Barnaby reminded him drily.

"*Oui,* that is true," Lucien observed, "which is why you are my favorite and why I would prefer not to lose you."

The remainder of the drive to Windmere was spent considering the reasons and the identity of the person behind the attacks on Barnaby. "I think I liked it better," Lucien said as the coach pulled to a stop at the front of the mansion, "when Mathew and Thomas were at your house where you could watch them. Who knows what they are up to at this Monks Abbey."

"Not to worry," Barnaby said as he reached for the handle of the coach door. "They'll be arriving back here on Monday for the wedding on Tuesday. In the meantime you can meet Simon and take his measure."

In the darkness Lucien wasn't treated to the full magnificence of the house, but stepping inside the soaring two-story foyer and the rich furnishings, his eyes widened. "*Mon Dieu!* I begin to see why our cousin might very well wish you dead."

The tall, young footman, William Weldon, was there to greet them, and not as well trained as his butler, Weldon couldn't hide his flash of astonishment that his lordship had returned home with a scruffy fisherman by his side and one whose features bore the Joslyn stamp. Barnaby grinned, liking the honest reaction, rather than Peckham's expressionless features.

Upon reaching his rooms, Barnaby showed Lucien into the handsomely appointed sitting room adjoining his bedroom and rang for Lamb. He offered Lucien some liquor from the dazzling array of Baccarat crystal decanters that lined a mahogany sideboard on the far side of the room.

Lucien declined the offer, but sprawled gratefully on one of the sofas. "Nothing for me. I need a clear head," Lucien murmured, "to endure a fierce scolding from Lamb."

Lamb entered via the bedroom a moment later. At first he didn't notice Lucien on the sofa and, smiling, he teased Barnaby, "I see your Amazon did not keep you long."

"Which was probably just as well," Barnaby said wryly, thinking of those passionate moments in her arms and how close he had been to seducing Emily tonight. He waved a hand in Lucien's direction and added, "I've brought home a guest—you'll have to find him suitable rooms."

Lamb glanced at the bag of bones lolling on the sofa and froze. There was a second that Barnaby glimpsed the naked love and relief that sped across Lamb's face, before it was instantly masked. Betraying little emotion, Lamb stared at Lucien and said calmly, "I've seen you looking better."

"Indeed. I confess there are times that I have felt better," Lucien replied just as calmly.

Barnaby had never understood the relationship between these two. He never doubted that they loved each other, but too often they were at daggers drawing. He could not decide for the life of him if it was because they were too much alike or because of an innate competitiveness. His mouth twisted. And he was usually caught in the middle of it.

Ignoring the pair of them, he splashed some hock in a glass. He took a swallow of the pale liquid and realizing that conversation was up to him, he related the high points of Lucien's arrival.

When Barnaby finished speaking, Lamb quirked a brow and like Barnaby before him, he said, "A whorehouse? Now why doesn't that surprise me?"

Unlike his reaction when Barnaby had made the same observation, Luc bristled and replied curtly, "You know me—any port in a storm."

Barnaby stalled the sharp retort he sensed hovering on Lamb's tongue by saying hastily, "The point is he is home and safe. He's not fully recovered yet and the best place for him right now is bed."

Lamb studied Lucien's face and, not liking his color or the dull sheen in his eyes, didn't argue. On his way out of the room, he said over his shoulder, "I'll see to it immediately."

Lamb was as good as his word and within thirty minutes Lucien was installed in a superb suite of rooms just down the hall from Barnaby's. Lamb had assigned an eager young footman, Bertram Hinton, to act as Lucien's manservant until other arrangements could be made.

With Lucien, now wearing one of the nightshirts Barnaby routinely ignored, tucked into bed, before he left the room, Lamb looked at him and shook his head. "You do have the devil's own luck, you know—if you'd arrived only hours later . . ." Lamb's heart clenched at how close they had come to losing him. Struggling against the tide of emotion that flooded him, he said softly, "Welcome home, bantling—we were worried about you."

*   *   *

Barnaby looked up from the contemplation of his empty glass of hock when Lamb entered the room. "Is he all settled?" he asked as Lamb took the glass from him and refilled it.

"For now," Lamb replied, turning back with the full glass and handing it to Barnaby. "He's in the suite two doors down. I've assigned Hinton to act as his valet for now." For several minutes they mulled over Lucien's return as well as the attack by the Nolles gang tonight.

"It was only luck that Emily wasn't with Jeb tonight," Barnaby said, then added thoughtfully, "I'll have to do something about Nolles and his gang soon."

"But not before the wedding," Lamb warned. "You are going to stand hale and hearty before Vicar Smythe and marry the Amazon Tuesday morning if I have to shackle you to the bed until then."

Barnaby smiled. "That won't be necessary. Once the wedding is behind us will be soon enough to tackle the Nolles problem." Setting down the half-empty glass of hock, he asked, "All well here?"

Lamb rubbed his jaw. "There's something smoky about that butler of yours, but I can't put my finger on it."

"What makes you say that?" Barnaby asked. "Peckham seems competent enough."

"That may be, but I don't like him."

"Ah, well then, that explains everything."

Lamb shot him a look. "Blast it! This is no light matter. I tell you, he was up to something tonight, but damned if I can figure out what it was." He paused and said slowly, "Most of the staff had gone to bed by the time I started paying attention to Peckham. All evening he appeared to be waiting for something . . . or looking for something."

"Why do you say that?"

"Because," Lamb said impatiently, "he kept darting in and out of the kitchen like a damn rabbit from a hole and I finally got curious about what he was up to and followed him. When he headed to the cellar, I thought that he was helping himself to a nip of brandy or wine now and then and sure enough, he headed right to the wine cellar."

Barnaby shrugged. "I don't begrudge the man some wine—Lord knows there's enough down there."

"Problem is," Lamb said, "this time he was in the wine cellar a very long time. I got tired of waiting for him to return and decided to see what was taking him so long." His voice heavy with import, he said, "Barnaby, I know it's a big place—more like a cavern filled with rows of racks and barrels than a room, but I checked the area thoroughly and the cellar was empty—there was no sign of him."

Interested now, Barnaby sat forward in his chair. "Secret doorway? Someone mentioned something about tunnels or passageways under the older parts of the house. Perhaps he's found one of the entrances."

"That's my guess. I looked for it, but I couldn't find anything that might be a hidden spring or handle."

"What about when he came back? Did you ask him about it then?"

"The thing is," Lamb said heavily, "he hasn't *come* back. He's disappeared."

Barnaby stared at him. "Er, you mean like forever?"

"I don't know. I just know he went into the wine cellar and I haven't seen him since."

A huge yawn overtook Barnaby. Shaking his head, he said, "Since it appears he disappeared on his own, I'm not about to wake the household and institute a search for him. The morning will be soon enough."

When Lamb entered Barnaby's room that Saturday morning the first words out of his mouth were, "Peckham's back." Grimly, he added, "Fellow was in the kitchen this morning as bright and cheery as a canary, acting as if nothing happened—and for all I know, nothing did."

"But he did disappear—he went somewhere," Barnaby reminded him as he left his bed and threw on the robe Lamb held out for him. Barnaby walked into the dressing room and after completing his morning ablutions, as he dried his hands on a towel made of fine Russian toweling, he said, "We'll have to examine that wine cellar. If there is a secret door or doors, I want to know where they are and where they lead."

It had become Barnaby's routine, after breakfast and a meeting with Tilden, his house steward, who also acted as his secretary and his bailiff, to ride over to The Birches. A few weeks ago, Jamieson, his head stableman, had shown him a shortcut between Windmere and The Birches and Barnaby no longer bothered taking the public road when he went to call upon Emily and Cornelia. With Lucien's arrival, he was later than usual getting away this morning, but finally just before noon, he was able to head for the stables and his horse—the spirited black stallion, aptly named Satan.

The day was gray and drizzly as a few dark-bottomed clouds, left over from last night's storm, scudded across the sky, but eager to see Emily, Barnaby wasn't about to allow a light shower to stop him. His thoughts were turned inward as Satan, eager to run, galloped over the by-now-familiar route to The Birches.

Barnaby reflected on his visit with Lucien this morning. Lucien looked better this morning, although he knew it would be weeks, perhaps months, before his half brother was fully recovered, not only from his time in prison, but the wound and infection that had nearly killed him. Peckham's odd activities last night nagged at the back of his mind. Where had the butler disappeared to and why? And then there was the Nolles gang. . . .

Deep in thought, by the time he crossed onto the lands owned by Emily's cousin, Barnaby wasn't paying attention to the rolling countryside. One second he was riding along, lost in his thoughts, and the next Satan screamed and went down.

Barnaby catapulted over the horse's head and slammed into the ground. He hit hard, his head taking the brunt of the fall. Dazed and dizzy he lay there, the breath knocked from his body. His vision swam when he raised his head to look around. Blurry-eyed, he saw Satan struggle to his feet and limp to the side of the trail. The world went black but a second later he was back lying on the road, staring up at the gray sky. Aware he was fading in and out of consciousness, he tried to concentrate, tried to make sense of what had happened to him. The bleating of sheep in the distance filtered through his foggy brain and, groaning, he lifted his head once more. Fighting the dizziness, he looked around, but saw nothing beyond the stallion, his head hanging low, standing nearby.

Noticing a taut thin cord stretched across the lane behind Satan, he frowned. He stared stupidly at the cord, his befuddled thoughts trying to make sense of what he was seeing. Distracted and barely conscious, he didn't hear the rustling in the bushes next to the road and was unaware of the shadowy figure slipping onto the pathway.

A voice, familiar and yet not familiar, floated in the air somewhere above him. "Damn you! Why the hell won't you die?" snarled the voice. "You should have broken your bloody neck, but since you didn't, isn't it a good thing I stayed to make certain this time?"

Barnaby's gaze jerked upward just as excruciating pain exploded in his head and this time the blackness stayed.

Chapter 18

When Barnaby regained consciousness a wrinkled male face that he vaguely recognized was staring down at him, the pale blue eyes anxious. The smell and bleating of sheep surrounded him and he risked turning his head and stared into the brown faces of half a dozen placidly chewing ewes. A shepherd, he decided. A shepherd had found him. Loren? Yes. It was Loren, Emily's head shepherd.

At the first sign of returning life from Barnaby, Loren cried, "Milord! Thank God, you're alive! Gave me a fright, you did, when I topped the rise and saw you lying here, like one dead." And when Barnaby tried to sit up, Loren pushed him gently back down. "No. No. Lay there—you'll most likely be sick if you try to get up. You've an ugly gash across your forehead where you hit your head when you fell."

Ignoring Loren's advice, Barnaby sat up and was instantly, violently sick. When he stopped retching, Loren handed him a rag. After Barnaby had wiped away all signs of his bout with nausea, from one of the voluminous pockets of his old jacket Loren brought forth a leather-covered flask that he thrust into Barnaby's hand. "Drink this," Loren said.

Gratefully Barnaby did, not surprised that the flask contained some of the finest French brandy he'd ever tasted. Probably from one of Jeb's runs, he thought ruefully. When the brandy stayed down and the world no longer tilted, he cautiously looked around. To his relief Satan hadn't wandered off, but when the big stallion attempted to walk, Barnaby's heart sank: there was blood on the horse's front legs and the stallion clearly didn't want to put any weight on his right leg.

With Loren's help Barnaby struggled to his feet, swaying as the world spun around him. Hanging on to Loren he managed to stay upright and after a minute, things stopped spinning. Loren helped him to the side of the road and leaning against a sapling, Barnaby said, "I'm fine for the moment. See to the horse. Tell me, if you can, if the leg is broken."

Satan wasn't fond of strangers and snorting, the big stallion, favoring that front leg, awkwardly tried to turn and run when Loren approached, but Loren snatched up one of the fallen reins and the horse halted. A tense few minutes later, Loren said over his shoulder, "He's got cuts on both legs, the worst is the right knee—that leg appears to be badly sprained but I don't think it's broken."

Relieved, Barnaby watched as Loren tied Satin to a low-growing bush. Walking back, Loren said, "Took a spill, did you, milord?"

Barnaby's gaze slid to where he'd seen the cord stretched across the road. The cord was gone, but then he hadn't expected it to still be there. Unless he'd dreamed that voice in his head, whoever had spoken to him, had taken the cord with him. He touched his forehead, wincing at the stab of pain. His mouth tightened. Whoever it was, must have given him a good whack, hoping to kill him before removing all signs of the cord that had been used to trip Satan. There was one good thing about this latest attempt on his life, he thought grimly: he no longer had any doubt that someone *was* trying to murder him.

He asked Loren, "Was there anyone else around when you found me?"

Loren started to shake his head, then paused. Fingering the side of his jaw, he said slowly, "Well, now that I think of it, there was a rider cutting across that field behind you." Loren's blue eyes sharpened. "Strange the fellow didn't offer help."

"Perhaps he didn't see the accident," Barnaby muttered.

Loren nodded and said, "Could be. Now how do we get you to Miss Emily?"

Confident his attacker wouldn't return and with Satan unable to be ridden, and not precisely certain of his equilibrium, Barnaby said, "I'll remain here while you get help. Leave that flask of brandy with me and take your sheep and go to the house. Tell Walker what happened and have him send the gig for me."

Left alone at the side of the road with the flask and Satan, Barnaby sank to the ground. Sprawled at the side of the pathway, a few nips of brandy warming his stomach, he replayed the events in his head. Someone had definitely tried to kill him. Someone had stretched a rope across the shortcut between Windmere and The Birches—a route he was known to ride nearly every morning. And someone had remained hidden amongst the shrubby brush and straggly trees that edged the road in this section, watching to see if success had been achieved this time. When he hadn't been killed by the fall, someone had left the hiding place and struck him a vicious blow to the head, hoping to finish him off.

He touched the gash again, his fingers coming away stained with blood. Gingerly resting his head back against the sapling and swallowing another slug of brandy, he decided that he was getting dashed tired of these attempts. More importantly, his luck was bound to run out sooner or later—which meant he'd better identify his would-be murderer and prevent another, perhaps successful, attack.

It helped to know that there was no longer any question about his series of misfortunes being "accidents." Someone was trying to kill him.

The sound of a fast-approaching vehicle made him smile. He'd lay odds that Emily was the whip and that she was coming to rescue him posthaste.

Barnaby was right. A moment later, a galloping horse, pulling the gig, topped the rise and sped toward him.

Yanking the horse to a stop, Emily scrambled from the gig, the young footman, Tom, following her, a small valise in his hand. Gray eyes dark with worry, she sank to the ground beside him, the skirts of her blue gown fluttering around her. Tom stood behind her.

With gentle fingers she explored the broken skin across his forehead. "What happened?" she asked tightly. "All Loren would say was that you had fallen from your horse."

Tom's presence prevented Barnaby from telling the truth, but he wasn't so certain he would have even told the whole story without the footman being present. He hadn't had time to think things fully through, but he saw no reason to alarm Emily. Lamb and Luc could be told the truth, but he'd just as soon Emily remain in the dark—for now.

Smiling wryly, he said, "Loren's correct and it's my own fault. Satan is a handful and I'm afraid my thoughts were on you, not the stallion, and we came to a parting of the ways." His smile fled. "Loren says that beside the cuts on Satan's legs and knee that the stallion's leg is only sprained, not broken. I'm sorry for that."

Emily eyed him suspiciously and he suspected that she knew he was spinning her a Banbury story, but she only sniffed and examined him more closely. Deciding the cleaning of the gash could wait until they were at The Birches, she said, "Tom, we won't need the things in the valise. Put it back in the gig and help me get his lordship into the gig."

Barnaby was dizzy by the time he was in the gig, but he

hadn't passed out or thrown up again. His head ached, but it was nothing compared to what his head had felt like when he'd been shot—or nearly drowned. The next time Lamb called him a hardheaded jackass, he thought amused, he'd remind him that thanks to that hard head, he was still alive.

Seeing the flask he still gripped in his hand, Emily plucked it out of his fingers and said, "I think you've had enough of this for now." Tossing the flask onto the floor of the gig, she glanced at Tom and said, "You might as well unsaddle the horse and let us take the saddle with us." That task accomplished, leaving Tom to follow along on foot, leading the limping Satan at a pace the stallion could sustain, Emily and Barnaby drove away.

At The Birches, Barnaby was solicitously escorted upstairs into the room he had occupied when he had been "accidentally" shot hardly two weeks previously. That wound had barely healed and now he was sporting a hard-to-miss gash across his forehead. The gash wasn't deep, more broken skin than anything else, but there was going to be a devil of a bruise—which was going to look wonderful, he admitted, when he and Emily married on Tuesday morning.

A note to Lamb at Windmere along with a request for a carriage was sent off with Alice, the scullery maid, and while he waited, having refused the services of a physician, Barnaby submitted to Emily's doctoring. She was, he decided, every bit as competent as Lamb.

Once the cut had been cleaned to her satisfaction, Emily leaned back in her chair and stared hard at Barnaby. Cornelia sat nearby, frowning.

"You still insist that you fell," Emily said for the sixth time.

"Yes," Barnaby replied as he had the previous five times. He cocked a brow. "Haven't you ever fallen from a horse? It happens to the best of riders."

"You appear to be a bit accident-prone, wouldn't you

say?" Cornelia remarked, those sharp hazel eyes not moving from his face. "You're found half-drowned in the Channel—a boating accident of some sort; then a poacher 'accidentally' shot you and now you've 'accidentally' taken a spill from your horse. Odd, don't you think?"

Barnaby hunched a shoulder. "Unfortunate, a string of bad luck."

Emily's gaze never left his face. "Someone's trying to kill you, aren't they?"

Now why, he wondered bitterly, had he fallen in love with an intelligent woman? At the moment, what he wouldn't give for Emily to be a biddable little thing with nothing in her head but frivolous yearnings for gowns and gewgaws. And Cornelia, he added, seeing the speculation in those brilliant eyes of hers. Of course, if they weren't so smart, they'd have bored him to death . . . and he wouldn't have fallen in love with Emily—and the formidable great-aunt.

Forcing a laugh, he said, "Come, come now, don't be ridiculous—I fell off my horse. Nothing else. No one wants me dead. No one is trying to kill me. Why would they?" He waggled his eyebrows at Emily. "You of all people know how charming I am."

Emily could have hit him, and from between clenched teeth, she got out, "And how infuriating! This is no jesting matter. Someone has tried to kill you three times."

"That many?" he teased. "If that's true it's certainly an inept would-be murderer, wouldn't you say?"

So angry she could hardly see straight, Emily jumped up from her chair and, crossing to the marble-topped bureau that held the supplies she'd used to clean and patch Barnaby's wound, she threw down the damp cloth. Perhaps his would-be killer was inept, she thought furiously, but the person was equally persistent and sooner or later . . .

Barnaby wasn't, she decided slowly, a stupid man. He had to know that someone was trying to kill him. That his life was in danger. So why was he pretending otherwise? Her breath caught. Of course—the idiot was *protecting* her. A warm tide washed over her. It had been so long since anyone had tried to protect her from anything that she was touched . . . and furious. He probably, she thought acidly, wasn't telling her the truth because he didn't want her to worry. Her heart twisted. Didn't he know that not knowing the truth was far worse?

A militant gleam in her eye, she swung around. Even with the gash on his forehead already turning an interesting shade of purple, he looked so dear, so beloved sitting there, that her anger ebbed and she was only aware that she loved him more than anything else in the world. He smiled sunnily at her and despite herself she smiled back at him. Damn him.

Barnaby knew he'd handled the situation badly. I should have told her, he thought, as he rode home in the carriage with Lamb an hour later. But what good would it have done? She'd only have worried . . . but I should have told her.

Seated across from him, Lamb said, "You know, I can't remember the last time you were unhorsed." He sent Barnaby a look. "May I assume that there is more to the tale than what you told Miss Townsend and that you're about to tell me the truth?"

"Yes," Barnaby said, and as the coach rolled homeward, proceeded to tell Lamb the exact sequence of events.

Lamb nodded several times and when Barnaby finished speaking he said, "Well, at least now we know that someone is definitely trying to kill you and that nothing has been an accident."

His gaze on the passing countryside, Barnaby asked abruptly, "Do you think that Simon could be behind the attacks?"

Surprised, Lamb questioned, "Simon? Now why has your fancy hit upon him?"

"Because Mathew and Thomas are not in the area— they're at Monks Abbey several hours away and not due to arrive at Windmere until Monday. Simon, I would remind you, is still at Windmere, roaming freely about."

"Yes, but . . ." Lamb frowned. "It's possible . . . he did go for a ride this morning. . . ."

His face grim, Barnaby said, "Find out, discreetly, what time my dear cousin Simon left for his ride this morning, the direction, if possible, and when he returned."

They rode in silence a bit, then Lamb asked, "Are you going to tell Luc?"

"Yes. It's only fair and it will be comforting to have another pair of eyes watching my back." Barnaby grimaced, thinking of Emily. Why was it fair to tell Luc, but not Emily? Was he being fair to her, keeping the truth from her? I should have told her, he thought again, conscious of the hole he had dug for himself. Recalling the militant look in her eye, he sighed. She hadn't believed him anyway, and unless he missed his guess, his prevarication had been for naught.

Peckham was horrified by Barnaby's pink-and-lavender-hued forehead when he arrived back at Windmere, but Barnaby brushed aside the butler's sympathy as he ascended the stairs to his rooms.

Simon appeared concerned when they met that afternoon but Barnaby caught him looking at him with a queer expression in his eyes when Simon thought himself unobserved. Guilty conscience? Astonishment that he was still alive? Or genuine puzzlement? Perhaps even worry? But why would Simon worry if he believed it was only an accident?

*   *   *

Anne, Hugh and Mrs. Althea Townsend arrived at The Birches late Saturday afternoon and Emily hadn't known how much she had missed her stepmother until Hugh helped Anne down from the big old traveling coach. Anne embraced her and whispered in her ear, "Oh, Emily, my dear! I could not be happier for you."

Althea Townsend was just as always, sweet and easygoing, her blue eyes as beautiful as they had been when she had been a girl of twenty. Over the years, her once glorious golden hair had faded to a lovely champagne color, but her delicate figure was only a little rounder than it had been the day she married Jeffery and Hugh's father, Emily's father's younger brother. Emily always thought that Aunt Althea, with her champagne curls, blue eyes and pink cheeks, resembled a big, china-faced doll. Cornelia routinely dismissed Althea as a pretty pea-goose but she was very fond of her and no one could deny that Althea was as kind as she was silly.

Once she had been helped from the coach by Jeffery, Althea, with those blue eyes full of affection and pleasure, had hugged Emily and congratulated her on her coming wedding. Tucking her small hand under Emily's arm, she breathed, "My goodness! It has been an exciting few weeks, hasn't it? Now you must tell me all about Joslyn. I hear he is very large and not very handsome and speaks a strange sort of English."

Smothering a laugh, Emily patiently tried to explain Barnaby to her aunt—especially the soft, Virginia drawl that marked his speech. After Althea had greeted Cornelia in the foyer, Emily guided her upstairs to the room Althea would use during her stay at the house. It was the same room Barnaby had used only hours earlier and Emily was relieved to see that Walker and Jane had removed all signs of that brief occupancy. There was even a large bouquet of gay, welcoming daffodils placed on the small table near one of the windows. Althea was charmed.

With his mother present and aware that he had no allies in the house, Jeffery was graciousness itself. He welcomed Anne back profusely, greeted his brother with a hearty smile and proceeded to dote on his mother. His attentiveness to Althea was so marked, especially compared to his usual indifference, that as he solicitously escorted her to the green salon after dinner that evening, she peered up at him and asked, puzzled, "My dear, are you feeling quite the thing?"

Hugh and Cornelia had gone ahead, and Anne and Emily, following behind Jeffery and Althea, overheard the question and convulsed with laughter. Althea, even more puzzled by their laughter, looked back at them. "What?" she demanded. "Surely you have noticed that he is not acting like himself."

When Anne and Emily only shook their heads, she turned to Jeffery and murmured, "I think the approaching wedding has made everyone giddy."

Jeffery shot the two younger women a murderous look, but then smiling benignly down at his mother, he said jovially, "I believe you are right. We are all of us excited and silly with delight. Just think, our sweet Emily, a viscountess!"

Sunday, at the third and final calling of the banns, Barnaby, with Emily at his side, his forehead now an eye-popping purple, ran the gauntlet of shocked well-wishers, deftly turning aside anyone who probed too closely about the circumstances of his accident. After the service, by mentioning to several people his delight at the sudden arrival of his half brother, Lucien, Barnaby was able to accomplish two things: deflect interest from his accident and smooth the way for Luc's appearance at the wedding. His brother, he added somberly, couldn't be here this morning because he was recovering from a debilitating fever contracted while traveling on the continent. It was hoped Lucien would be well enough to attend the wedding.

At Windmere that evening there was a small dinner party and the guests, all family members, except for the vicar and his wife, tactfully ignored Barnaby's bruise. If anyone doubted that a fall from his horse had been the cause, they were all too polite to say so.

While Luc had not attended church, he did make an appearance at the dinner party, and except for his slenderness and extreme pallor, looked extremely handsome as he was introduced and bowed elegantly over the ladies' hands. There had been no time to obtain suitable clothing for him and only Barnaby knew his half brother was tricked out in some hastily cut down clothing of Barnaby's.

Luc's illegitimacy alone would cause gossip enough and his unexpected arrival only added to the curiosity about him, but there was no help for it. Deciding that the sooner Luc was introduced to the country society the better, Barnaby had suggested that his half brother join them that Sunday evening. Since it was primarily a family party, except for the vicar and his wife, it seemed an ideal time for Luc to make his first appearance.

His eyes twinkling with amusement, Barnaby presented Luc first to Cornelia, who was looking very regal in a gown of amber shot-silk and her steel-gray hair piled high on her head, diamond-and-topaz earrings dangling from her ears. Luc bowed gracefully and took Cornelia's hand in his and pressed a kiss on her wrinkled skin. From the sparkle in her eyes, Barnaby knew she was pleased.

"Very prettily done," she murmured, when Luc released her hand and straightened. "Your great-grandfather couldn't have done it better."

A teasing gleam in the azure eyes, Luc replied, "Surely, such an attractive lady as yourself is far too young to have known my great-grandfather."

Cornelia chuckled, liking him, and tapped him on the cheek with her painted silk-and-lace fan. "Doing it up too brown, my boy."

"You wound me, madame," Luc cried, clutching his heart, though his eyes danced.

Cornelia snorted, but there was laughter in her voice when she said, "Well, take your wounded self across the room and share your charm on someone who's not old enough to be your grandmother and might actually believe you."

After introducing Luc to the assembled guests, Barnaby returned to Cornelia.

"Well, what do you think?" he asked.

"I think that he's going to cause havoc amongst the ladies," she said. Smiling, she added, "Which is just as well, since you've been taken from the field, but we'll have to do a little spade work to ensure that he is welcomed everywhere."

Barnaby didn't doubt that Cornelia would do her best to quell the worst of the gossip about Luc and she assured him that Penelope Smythe could be counted on to lend a hand.

"Penelope knows everyone in the area," Cornelia told him. "And she adores intrigue. Under the guise of spreading gossip, she will be able to present your half brother in the best possible light—and stop much of the speculation before it starts." She grinned at Barnaby. "Actually the timing of his arrival couldn't be better—everyone is so excited about the wedding on Tuesday that I suspect no one will pay him much heed." Her gaze slid to Luc. "Besides, he has the devil's own charm and with very little help from us, he'll do just fine."

Watching Luc moving about the room, smiling and talking animatedly with Simon, Hugh and the vicar and then a few minutes later charming Anne, Penelope Smythe and Althea Townsend, Barnaby decided that Cornelia might be right. Luc would be fine.

Feeling he had done what he could to smooth Luc's way, Barnaby set about pleasing himself. Unfortunately, beyond exchanging glances with Emily during the dinner that followed, it wasn't until after the meal and they'd all gathered in the gold salon for tea and coffee that he was finally able to have a private word with her. Cutting her deftly away from the ladies, he walked her to the edge of the room for a few minutes of low-voiced private conversation. Glancing down, he murmured, "Ah, alone at last."

Emily smiled and with a hand she indicated the room full of guests. "Alone?"

Barnaby sighed. "Well, as alone as I can arrange things right now."

Which was just as well, Emily thought, remembering how close she had come to surrendering to him two nights ago. Thinking of those passionate kisses and his hand on her breast sent a warm thrill through her. If Walker had not interrupted them . . . She swallowed, wondering where calm, levelheaded Emily had gone. In Barnaby's arms she forgot everything but the delight of his kiss, his touch . . . A flush stained her cheeks when she felt her nipples tighten.

Seeing her blush and having a good idea what she was thinking, he muttered, "If I had you alone, our lips would be very busy, but we certainly wouldn't be *talking.*"

"Talking is exactly what we should be doing," she said, determinedly thrusting aside the vivid thoughts of Barnaby's lips moving over her body.

He grimaced. She was right, of course. This was torture, having her so close and yet unable to touch and caress her as he longed to do.

Taking a deep breath, he said, "I think we have events well in hand, don't you?"

Grateful for a safer topic, she replied, "I agree. When one thinks how things could have turned out, we do, indeed, have events well in hand . . . for the moment."

"For the moment," Barnaby agreed, not having forgotten about the Nolles gang or that someone was trying to kill him. Despite his good intentions, he couldn't help his gaze from lingering on her, thinking that she looked particularly lovely this evening with that glorious mane of fair hair tamed into soft ringlets that framed her face and wearing a gown of lavender satin and an overskirt of pale green gauze. Of course, what interested him more was all the warm, silky flesh hidden beneath the gown and, remembering the sensation of his hands sliding over that sweet skin, heat flared in his groin.

Smothering a groan, he dragged his eyes away from Emily, concentrating instead on stifling a certain part of his anatomy that had no sense of timing. What he wouldn't give, he thought, for the wedding to be behind them and to know that when they retired tonight it would be to each other's arms and he could slake the hot ache for her that seldom left him these days.

Peckham appeared and walked quickly over to Barnaby. Bowing, he murmured, "My lord, Mr. Mathew and Mr. Thomas have arrived unexpectedly." He coughed delicately. "I've had their luggage taken up to the rooms they used during their previous stay. I trust that meets with your approval."

"Do whatever is necessary to make them comfortable," Barnaby said. Mathew and Thomas had not been expected to return to Windmere until tomorrow night and he wondered idly what had prompted their earlier arrival. He smiled without amusement. It certainly wasn't a fondness for his company.

Glancing at Peckham, Barnaby asked, "Are they going to join us?"

"If that is your wish, my lord. They're aware you have guests . . . they did not wish to intrude."

"They're my cousins," Barnaby said. "They could hardly be called intruders. Show them in when they're ready."

Five minutes after Peckham had departed the salon the butler returned to announce Mr. Mathew Joslyn and Mr.

Thomas Joslyn. Barnaby left Emily with Cornelia and Anne and walked over to greet them, prepared for their reactions to the gash on his forehead—and the magnificent bruise that surrounded it.

Mathew's eyes widened when he caught sight of the bruise and the alarm on his handsome face seemed genuine. "Good God!" Mathew exclaimed, as he stood in front of Barnaby. "Simon wrote that you had taken a spill, but he made no mention of the lasting effects." Shaking his head, he added, "Seeing for myself the results of your accident, I understand Simon's anxiety and why he wrote me. Dash it all, Barnaby, you could have been killed!"

"Simon wrote you?" Barnaby asked, honing in on the only part of Mathew's speech that interested him.

"Yes," Tom said quickly, stepping next to Mathew. "A messenger delivered his note explaining your unfortunate accident to us last night at Monks Abbey. This morning we decided that nothing would do but that we see for ourselves the extent of your injuries."

Simon strolled up and, sending his brothers a sharp look, he said, "I think we should discuss this privately—after the guests have left."

"Yes, yes, of course," Mathew said hastily, recalled to their surroundings. The two new arrivals knew everyone present except for Luc, and from the shock on their faces when Luc was introduced to them, it was obvious that in his note Simon had failed to mention Luc's sudden appearance at Windmere. Simon's actions in sending a note posthaste to his brothers perplexed Barnaby and made him wonder precisely what was going on. Was it possible that all *three* brothers were involved in a plot to kill him and Simon had written to warn them that the latest attempt had failed?

The vicar and his wife had been on the verge of taking their leave when Thomas and Mathew arrived, but they remained several minutes longer to visit with the newcomers.

After the vicar and his wife finally departed, it wasn't long after that the Townsend coach was called for and the entire group, escorted by Barnaby and the other Joslyn men, gathered at the front of the mansion.

Barnaby sighed as he helped Emily ascend the coach, regretting that there would be no stolen kisses tonight. Pressing a warm kiss onto the palm of her hand, he said, "I shall see you tomorrow afternoon."

Worry in her eyes, she said, "Only if you bring Lamb or one of your cousins with you."

Since he doubted Lamb would let him out of his sight, Barnaby graciously agreed. A crooked smile on his lips, he said, "As you wish, my love."

Once the coach lights had disappeared into the darkness the men walked together back into the house. Luc looked exhausted and Barnaby whispered to him, "Shall I make an excuse for you?"

Luc shook his head and muttered, "And leave you alone with the enemy?"

As they crossed the huge foyer, Mathew suggested that they retire to Barnaby's study and shrugging, Barnaby agreed. In his study, the three brothers arranged themselves at one side of the room; Mathew remained standing, while Thomas and Simon seated themselves in a pair of leather chairs. Barnaby and Luc took the opposite end of the room, Barnaby taking up a position near the fireplace, Luc sinking down gratefully onto the sofa.

"I suppose you are wondering what this is all about," Mathew said heavily.

His eyes on Simon, Barnaby said, "I assume it has to do with Simon's note."

Simon flushed. "I'm no tale bearer, but your latest 'accident' worried me and I felt Mathew should know about it."

"A fall from my horse? Now why should that worry any of you?"

"Because, dash it all, since January, this is the third time you've suffered a serious *accident*," Mathew snapped.

Barnaby stilled. "The third time? I know of only two accidents."

Mathew made an impatient movement with his hand. Angrily he said, "Don't play me for a fool! There was always something smoky about the yacht disappearing like it did and then about the time the yacht vanishes, you're suddenly bedridden at The Crown. You were in rude health when I saw you the previous morning before you left London, yet you turn up at The Crown so ill that you had to remain the night at the inn—when Windmere is only miles away." Mathew snorted. "What happened? Did you sink her and nearly drown in the process? Another accident?"

"So you know what happened to the yacht?"

Mathew sighed. "Not all of it. I always suspected that you had something to do with its disappearance; the timing was too coincidental. But if you didn't want to admit you'd sunk her in the Channel, it was none of my business." Mathew shot him a level look. "Servants see things, and though Lamb was discreet, someone noticed that after you arrived, he left your room once with some bloody bandages, a clear indication that in addition to your illness you suffered a wound of some sort."

Barnaby didn't believe that Lamb had been so foolish and he was convinced that "someone" had done some serious snooping or already knew about the wound. . . .

"Suppose you're right," Barnaby said slowly. "Suppose I was on the yacht when it sank. Suppose I did get a blow to my head and nearly drowned. And suppose I have suffered a few accidents since then. What does it matter to you?"

His eyes bleak, Mathew declared bluntly, "Because I don't want your death on my conscience. My brothers and I are convinced that someone is trying to kill you."

Chapter 19

Of everything Mathew could have said, nothing could have astonished Barnaby more. He and Luc exchanged glances and it was clear that Luc was as astounded as he was by Mathew's words.

His voice carefully neutral, Barnaby said, "Unfortunately, if someone is trying to kill me, you have the best motive."

Mathew's eyes flashed. "Don't you think I know that!" He sent Barnaby a hard look. "If someone is trying to kill you, I don't appreciate being set up to take the blame for your murder." He threw out a hand and said passionately, "You may find it hard to believe, but the last thing I want is to inherit a title tainted by the suspicion that I murdered the previous holder to gain it." He glanced around at his brothers and both Thomas and Simon nodded, their faces grim and set. Looking back at Barnaby, Mathew said quietly, "None of us do."

Barnaby studied Mathew. The man sounded sincere and his reaction was exactly what Barnaby would have expected of him—he would have felt the same. His eyes moved slowly over Thomas and Simon. The animosity between Thomas and Simon was well known, but both of them ap-

peared to hold their eldest brother in high esteem—even if
Simon couldn't resist poking at Mathew now and then.
Would their love and affection for their brother drive them to
murder for him? It seemed far-fetched to think so, yet someone had, indeed, tried to arrange his death on three separate
occasions and the obvious motive was the inheritance of the
title. If not the title then why, he wondered, puzzled, would
someone want him dead?

He and Luc exchanged glances once again. Luc spread
his hands and shrugged.

Mathew's protestation of innocence could be a ruse to
gain Barnaby's confidence, but it didn't feel like it. Mathew's
words rang true . . . but then his cousin could be a great
actor. Barnaby sighed. He had a decision to make: did he
trust Mathew and his brothers or didn't he?

Deciding to gamble—and trust his own instincts, he said,
"Someone did try to kill me yesterday—I heard the culprit
say so and curse the fact that I survived the other two attempts on my life."

"He spoke to you?" demanded Mathew, excited. "Did
you see him?"

Barnaby shook his head. "No, I didn't see him. I only
heard his voice." At Mathew's eager look, he said, "And no, I
didn't recognize the voice. It sounded familiar, but I could
not place it."

"What do you remember?" Tom asked, frowning.

Barnaby relayed the facts, including his memory of the
cord stretched across the road. "Of course, the cord was
gone when I regained consciousness," he finished drily.

"This Loren fellow," Mathew mused. "Could he have
been hired to kill you and been your attacker? He might have
been pretending to have just found you."

"If that was the case," Barnaby replied, "he could have
finished the job while I was out cold." He smiled slightly.
"Even when I came to, I was disoriented and would have

been easy prey. If he'd wanted to, it wouldn't have taken much for Loren to give me another whack or two, making certain that I never woke again."

"What about the horseman that Loren spied riding away?" Simon inquired, bending forward. "Could he identify him—or the horse?"

Again Barnaby shook his head. "No. Loren admitted he paid the horseman little heed, all his attention was on me." He rubbed the back of his neck. "He admitted that it was strange the horseman hadn't stopped, but beyond that, he could add nothing." Barnaby grimaced. "Believe me, before I left The Birches, I questioned him closely. As did Miss Townsend. There was nothing about the horseman or his horse that stood out to Loren."

"So all we really know," Mathew said dispiritedly, "is that you have an enemy who has made three attempts on your life."

"Unsuccessful attempts," Luc said quietly.

His frown deepening, Tom asked, "But why would someone want you dead?"

Barnaby shrugged. "If we eliminate you and your brothers, while you may find it hard to believe, I can't think of anyone I've offended or annoyed to such an extent that they would try to murder me."

Interjecting a light note, Luc grinned and murmured, "I will confess, *mes amis,* that he has driven me often to think fondly of murdering him, but I assure you in this case, I am innocent."

There was a general laugh, but soon enough the conversation turned serious again. Mathew and his brothers peppered Barnaby with questions about the other attempts and he answered them as truthfully and completely as he could. Eventually interest returned to the sinking of the yacht—it being the most risky and elaborate of the "accidents." He told them what he remembered, glossing over any references to smuggling and smugglers and did some tricky dancing around his actual rescue from the Channel.

"And when you woke at The Crown you had no idea how you got there? Or who brought you there?" Tom questioned closely, his eyes fixed on Barnaby's face.

"None," Barnaby said cheerfully. Noting Luc's drooping eyes and deciding that they had wasted enough time discussing the attempts on his life, he said, "And now, gentlemen, I think we should call it a night." He smiled. "I have been living with this for several weeks, but you have much to think over. Perhaps in the morning, you will have come up with some ideas to unmask whoever is trying to kill me."

The following morning when the gentlemen met in the morning room, no one had any ideas to add from the previous night's discussion. Barnaby wasn't much interested anyway—the wedding was tomorrow morning and his thoughts and energies were on his bride and his marriage.

With the faithful Lamb riding alert and eagle-eyed beside him, Barnaby rode over to The Birches that afternoon. Laughter and excitement filled the air at the old manor house and the ladies were much too busy with the packing of Emily's things and some last-minute fittings to allow his bride more than a few minutes private conversation with Barnaby. Taking his leave of Emily after a frustratingly short visit, Barnaby muttered, "At least this is the last time I have to say good-bye to you here. By this time tomorrow we shall be man and wife."

Emily's heart thumped at that knowledge and the tiniest quiver of uncertainty went through her when she looked up at his dark face and took in again that big, powerfully muscled body. This man would virtually *own* her by this time tomorrow—and he wasn't a man to be trifled with or easily deceived or ignored like Jeffery. The image of him as he had stood before her in the Godart farmhouse, his face full of terrible resolve, the knife in his hand as he confronted Ainsworth, blazed through her mind. If she dared to defy him there would be consequences, possibly dangerous ones. . . . But I love him, she reminded herself, and if he doesn't love me, he has affection for me. Surely he would never treat me cruelly.

Sensing her fears, he kissed her fingertips and murmured, "Emily, I swear to you that I will be a good husband to you and never mistreat you." He grinned at her. "Although I am sure that you will madden me from time to time—as I will you."

Unable to resist that oh-so-beguiling grin, she smiled back at him. "Indeed, my lord, as far as the latter is concerned, I suspect you are absolutely correct."

The wedding day dawned sullen and gray, a storm hovering on the horizon. Despite the storm, which by midmorning was snarling its fury overhead, the pews of the village church were packed with friends and family of the bride and groom.

Looking impressive and every inch the aristocrat in a plum tail coat, the lace frill of his shirt spilling across the dark material, and fawn satin knee breeches that hugged his muscular thighs, Barnaby's voice rang out emphatically as he repeated his vows. Emily's response was less forceful, but everyone agreed that with her silvery fair hair arranged in clusters of ringlets embellished with small sprays of pink rosebuds she made a lovely bride. Everyone, especially the ladies, agreed that her gown of rose-and-cream striped silk, lavishly trimmed with lace around the square neckline and at the wrists of the long sleeves was everything a bride could have wished for.

Only the storm marred the perfection of the day. When a

bolt of lightning struck nearby and lit up the inside of the church like a thousand torches, just as Emily said, "I do," she tried not to think of the storm as an omen for her life with Barnaby.

A wedding breakfast was planned at Windmere and even the storm couldn't dampen the spirits and pleasure of the guests who followed the newlyweds back to the mansion. It was an eclectic group of people who gathered to celebrate the marriage of Lord Joslyn to Emily Townsend. Eclectic the guests might be, but Barnaby preferred to think of them as a democratic group where Mrs. Gilbert easily rubbed shoulders with Lord Broadfoot and his lady and the other leading landowners of the area. Jeb Brown and Caleb Gates, both looking very spruce in their best jackets and boots, could be seen conversing with Mathew and Simon and three of the Gilbert daughters were laughing as they clustered around Luc and Thomas. Flanked by Althea and Anne, Cornelia held court in one corner of the room, where one and all came to pay their respects—and compliment her on her looks and indeed, she was in high fettle at seeing her dear Emily so successfully settled. Hugh, it was noted by several, was never far away from sparkling-eyed Anne. Jeffery wandered from one group to the other accepting as if it were his due, the congratulations on Emily's advantageous marriage. The vicar and his wife drifted about the room, lingering to visit with Cornelia and later, Mrs. Featherstone, who was there with her daughters, and as soon as the Gilbert girls had moved on, immediately set her sights on Luc and Thomas.

Once everyone had enjoyed a dizzying array of food prepared by Mrs. Eason and toasted the newlyweds, except for members of both families, the guests trickled away and headed into the storm for their homes. Dusk was falling when the Townsend group finally braved the weather and departed for The Birches, leaving Emily alone with her husband . . . and his relatives.

Watching Cornelia and the rest of her family drive away in the lumbering Townsend family coach, Emily was aware of feeling abandoned to strangers. Oh, to be sure, her very new husband wasn't a stranger to her, but there was much about him that she didn't know. Staring down at the wide gold band upon her finger, she realized with a start, that from the moment she had first set eyes on Barnaby that night at the inn that not even two months had passed. And now she was married to him, she thought breathlessly, their lives forever entwined—as their bodies would be tonight. . . .

Rather than going away for a few days to begin their life together, Emily and Barnaby had chosen to remain at Windmere and originally, Mathew and his brothers had planned to depart for Monks Abbey after the wedding breakfast, but the storm made that impractical. Conscious that this was Barnaby and Emily's wedding night, Mathew, Thomas and Simon made plans to be gone for the evening—they were, Mathew explained, braving the storm and riding into the village to sample the entertainment to be found at The Ram's Head. Luc mentioned tactfully that he was looking forward to a quiet dinner and evening in his rooms.

With the guests all departed, Emily bid the gentlemen good evening and walked to the bottom of the graceful swooping double staircase, intending to escape to her rooms. At the base of the left staircase, she stopped, realizing that she had no idea where her rooms were. Peckham startled her when he suddenly appeared by her side. Bowing low, he murmured, "I don't believe that you have had a chance to inspect your suite yet—it is in a different wing than the rooms you stayed in previously. If you wish, my lady, I can show you to them."

Emily nodded and said, "I would appreciate that."

He coughed delicately. "Since you didn't bring a maid

with you, I've taken it upon myself to select someone from the staff." He looked unhappy. "Under normal circumstances, my lady, I would never allow such a young and untrained female to serve you, but unless she displeases you, Kate, who waited on you previously here at Windmere, will act as your personal maid. She has unpacked your things that arrived from The Birches this morning and will assist you in any way you desire. If you have the *slightest* complaint you must notify me at once and I shall immediately rectify the problem."

Emily might have been more impressed by his words, if she hadn't gotten the distinct idea that he would enjoy "rectifying the problem" far too much, and she vowed that the butler would never hear a complaint from her about any of the staff.

As they walked up the staircase toward the upper floors, Peckham said, "There was no time to redo your rooms prior to the wedding, but I'm sure that you will find them more than satisfactory—everything at Windmere is of the highest quality." A sly glance drifted her way and he added, "Of course, you will no doubt be changing things to suit yourself."

Not certain if she had been insulted or not, Emily held her tongue, but she decided that she didn't much care for Barnaby's butler. Continuing on their way, she listened with an interested expression on her face as he pointed out first one and then another grand room and found herself longing for Walker's amiable presence and the comfortable familiarity of The Birches.

Keeping pace with Peckham's measured tread through the meandering candlelit hallways, Emily was certain that, left to her own devices, she would have surely lost her way. She was right. When he eventually stopped and swung wide a pair of double doors and urged her to enter, she was thoroughly disoriented and she had the suspicion that he had deliberately taken her on a circumambulating route. The candles had all been lit earlier and, having meticulously shown her around the sumptuously appointed suite, consisting of sitting room, bedroom and dressing room all decorated in shades of pearl, moss and rose, Peckham departed.

After Peckham left, Emily looked around the sitting room, deciding that the butler had been right about one thing: everything at Windmere was of the highest quality. A lovely rosewood desk and a chair covered in a rose-and-ivory tapestry sat invitingly beneath one of several long windows adorned with moss silk drapes. A thick woolen rug richly woven in shades of amber, pink and pearl lay upon the floor. Satinwood tables and chairs upholstered in moss and gold-striped velvet and a pair of settees were scattered tastefully about the room; tall cabinets of fine marquetry flanked the doors that led to her bedroom. A fireplace with an ancient, intricately carved oak mantel dominated the far wall and with the storm outside, Emily was glad of the yellow and orange flames dancing on the hearth.

Sitting down on one of the settees, Emily forced herself to relax. Who would have known that getting married was so exhausting? she thought, kicking off her silk slippers and absently pulling the flowers from her hair and dropping them beside her on the settee. She looked around the room again. This was now her suite. She wasn't here as a guest. She *lived* here—in this huge, enormous mansion—and she couldn't help thinking of the shabby charm of her former home and everyone that she had left behind. She would never again be plain Emily Townsend of The Birches, she realized with a pang. She was now Lady Joslyn—mistress of Windmere and responsible for overseeing the army of servants, many whose names she didn't even know, and for making certain that Windmere remained in immaculate condition.

Her lips drooped. A wave of loneliness swept over her as she pictured Anne and Cornelia returning home to the comforts of the familiar, where dear, smiling Walker would be greeting them and Mrs. Spalding would be cooking something delicious for the evening in the big, old kitchen at The Birches.

Disgusted with herself, she shook herself and stood up. Good heavens! She was married to a wealthy, exciting man—and here she was moping about as if she had been cast up helpless on some nameless shore. Barnaby's dark, intent face leaped to her mind and thinking of the coming night, her whole body responded in a way that excited and flustered her. Her breasts tingled, heat flooded her lower body and her pulse beat madly at the thought of what would come.

Seeking escape from the lurid and undeniably arousing images in her brain, she hurried out of the sitting room and into the bedchamber and, catching sight of the moss and gold damask bed hangings that draped the massive bed, she jerked her gaze away. Picturing Barnaby naked in that big bed certainly wasn't helping calm her galloping imagination and almost desperately, she sought distraction.

Hearing sounds of movement in the dressing room, Emily peeked around the doorway. Kate, the young maid she'd met during her previous stay, was smiling and humming to herself as she placed a pitcher of warm water upon the mahogany-and-marble washstand in the corner of the spacious room. Since Kate hadn't been there when Peckham had shown her the rooms, Emily assumed the maid had entered via the servants' staircase.

Catching sight of Emily out of the corner of her eye, Kate squeaked and jumped. Recognizing her mistress, she flushed and hastily curtsied. "Oh, my lady, I didn't see you there."

Smiling, Emily entered the room. "I'm sorry. I didn't mean to startle you."

Emily wasn't certain how she would deal with a lady's

maid all her own, but she discovered that Kate was a gem. Not only was the young maid cheerful and friendly, she was in direct contrast to Peckham's irritating, polite behavior.

While she'd been getting married and entertaining guests today, the trunks from The Birches had arrived and Kate had unpacked and put everything away. Like a puppy accepting praise, Kate fairly quivered with pleasure as Emily complimented her on a task well done.

After asking Kate to arrange a bath, Emily wandered back into the bedroom, her gaze lingering on the tall, carved oak door on the far wall that Peckham had pointed out led to the viscount's rooms. She swallowed. Any time he wished, Barnaby could enter her room and take her into his arms and kiss her and . . . Warmth rushed through her and she hastened into the sitting room, embarrassed by her fixation on Barnaby's kisses and . . . other things.

Seating herself on one of the rose damask-covered settees, she glanced around the area again thinking that four of her bedrooms at The Birches would have fit in the sitting room—with space left over. Her eyes dropped down to the ring on her finger. She was married—to Barnaby. And tonight when he took her into his arms . . . She trembled, knowing that tonight there would be no barriers between them and that when he kissed her and touched her, there would be no interruptions, no stopping him from taking what was now, by law, his. Her heart thumped and she didn't know whether she was excited or afraid. She bit her lip. She didn't fear Barnaby, so she must be excited, she decided, remembering other times and all those incredible sensations he aroused within her.

Filled with anticipation and not much caring whether it was immodest or not, Emily thought the time would drag until she saw Barnaby again. She was astonished to discover that by the time she had bathed and changed into a simple blue gown and Kate had brushed her hair until it cascaded in near-silver curls down her back, that the hour was just a few minutes shy of eight o'clock.

She was halfway across the candlelit room, when the door connecting her rooms with Barnaby's opened and Barnaby sauntered into the room. At the sight of him, looking so big and virile, her heart gave that funny little thump she was beginning to expect whenever she saw him.

Like her, he had changed and this evening wore far less formal clothes. His cravat was smaller and there was no lace fall at his neck; his dark blue coat and pale gray breeches, though expensive and expertly tailored, were of less costly materials. Eschewing the usual queue, Barnaby had left his heavy black hair loose and it fell in luxurious waves to his shoulders. With all that black silk hair framing his face, it brought attention to the broad cheekbones and intensified the darkness of his complexion, making his Indian ancestry very apparent.

Spying Emily, Barnaby stopped as if hit with a sledgehammer and any thought of the quiet, polite dinner he'd ordered served in her sitting room, followed by a gentle seduction vanished. His eyes narrowed and fastened on her half-parted rosy mouth, the blood roaring in his head as the memory of those tempting lips crushed under his swept through him. To his damnation, he was instantly hard and ready to rip those clothes from her body and take what was his. He struggled against his most basic instincts, fighting back the urge to toss her on the bed and discover all the charms he knew lay beneath that charming blue gown.

Emily took a half step back at the expression on his face, even as her body responded to the hungry desire she saw there. Her nipples peaked against the thin silk of her gown, her legs went weak and the anticipation of his touch, of his mouth on hers, stilled further retreat.

Barnaby's gaze dropped to her nipples pushing impudently against the blue fabric and he muttered something between a curse and a benediction and in two long strides was before her, dragging her into his arms. For a second, their eyes met, the fierce hunger blazing in his meeting the uncertain eagerness of hers and then with his hands tightly gripping her upper arms and holding her against him, his mouth came down hard and demanding on hers.

That first kiss was not gentle—he couldn't control himself, his lips and tongue plundering at will—but as the seconds passed, despite every urge to the contrary, he was able to regain some sanity. This was *Emily*. His wife. His bride!

Breathing as if he'd run a race, he slowly gentled his touch, his tongue seeking and meeting hers, twining and tasting, luring her deeper into desire. His mouth seducing hers, his hands left her arms and slid to her hips, jerking her snugly against the rampant rod between his thighs.

Emily's arms clasped his neck and she reveled in the force of his kiss and the feel of that muscled body pressing against hers. Ardently she returned his kiss, shivering with delight when his big hands gripped her hips and brought her to that rigid length of flesh that told of his arousal.

Kisses soon weren't enough and, groaning, Barnaby swept her up into his arms and half stumbled to the bed. His mouth never leaving hers, he followed her down onto the bed, need and desire dictating his every move. Together they sprawled there, their mouths locked together, Barnaby's body half covering hers, one thigh lodged between her legs.

As driven as he, Emily kissed him back passionately, gasping when his thigh rubbed insistently against that part of her lower body that burned and ached for his touch. Her hands clutched his shoulders and she twisted beneath him, her legs tightening around that intruding thigh, holding him there where all sensation seemed centered.

His hand moved to her breast and he shoved the material lower, baring her breasts, and those hard, masculine fingers cupped and caressed all that warm flesh he had laid bare. Trailing nipping kisses along her jaw, down her throat and across her chest, his lips traveled to her breasts and closed hungrily around her nipples. The touch of his mouth, the feel of his teeth and the laving of his tongue across those sensitive buds sent a flash of heat searing through Emily and she arched up, offering him all that he would take.

She was fire and satin beneath him and with the small part of his brain not clouded by desire, Barnaby fought to control the clawing hunger that demanded the joining of their bodies. Trembling on the knife-edge between sanity and primitive instinct, he slid between her legs, rocking his swollen manhood against the softness at the junction of her thighs. Pleasure erupted through him when her arms tightened around him and her hips rose up to meet him. Struggling not to give in to the violent need to bury himself deep within her, he tore his lips from her breast.

Beset by sensations and emotions that destroyed coherent thought, Emily cried out when that sweet suckling mouth left her nipple. Dazedly she stared up at the dark, fierce face above her, her eyes smoky and mysterious in the flickering light of the candles, her mouth rosy and swollen from his kisses and her cheeks flushed with desire.

Barnaby had never seen anything lovelier . . . and she deserved better, he thought angrily, than a brutal mating with a rutting boar. Yet when he started to lever his body away from hers, Emily's arms tightened and she breathed, "No. Don't leave me this way. I need you."

Her words inflamed him, but he threw off the powerful urge to sink back and seek his own pleasure. Forcing a smile that was as tender as it was strained, he muttered, "Emily, love, if you don't let me put some space between myself and your tempting self, I'll not be able to control my baser instincts." He ran a caressing finger across her mouth. "When you are in my arms, I lose my head and all I can think of is possessing you." He swallowed. "Your first time should be gentle."

Her body on fire, aching, burning for him, she didn't give a damn about gentleness. Wanting him so badly she was certain she'd die if he didn't end this delicious agony soon, she said, "Perhaps I don't want gentle right now . . . perhaps I just want you to do with me as you will."

Barnaby hovered on the edge and then his eyes dropped to her naked breasts and he lost the battle. Brushing his lips across her, his hands fastened on her gown. "If that is your wish, madame wife," he said huskily against her ear, "never let it be said that I disobeyed. And the first thing we need to do is get rid of these clothes."

He proved exceedingly adept at stripping her out of her gown, and it took him only a few seconds longer to rid himself of his own clothes. In the dancing candlelight they regarded each other, Barnaby, big and dark and muscular; Emily, pale as alabaster and despite her slimness, seductively curved. Both were mesmerized by what they saw and like a fire stoked anew, the flame between them flared higher.

They met as one, lips and tongues desperately seeking, limbs entwining and bodies entangling. Ignoring promptings to the contrary, Barnaby lingered over the enchanting length of her, sampling again the honey of her breasts, his fingers drifting over the yielding form before him. As much to please her as himself, he managed to rein back his own desire and learned the curves and hollows of her body, those big, warm hands wandering down her back to her buttocks, squeezing the firm cheeks before slipping around to the front.

Each new caress heightened the ache, the melting dampness between her thighs and she moved restlessly beneath his touch, wanting, wanting, wanting. . . . He overpowered her, his taste upon her tongue, his scent in her nostrils and his skin warm and rough under her drifting hands. His mouth sought hers again, the blunt demands of his kiss heightening the pressure building within her, and when his fingers found her and parted the damp flesh between her thighs, Emily twisted in shocked delight.

His touch was knowing and gently, persistently, he teased her, pulling at the folds, lazily exploring before slipping one and then two fingers into her. She gasped at the new sensation, each thrust of those invading fingers sending waves of urgent yearning spiraling through her body. Dizzy, helpless under the onslaught of the simple, basic clamoring of her body, fevered and wild, she bit his lip, her fingers clawing at his back.

"Please," she moaned against his mouth. Her arms tightened around his neck and her rising hips met the thrust of his fingers. *"Please!"*

His breathing ragged, his shaft swollen to the point of exploding and devoured by lust such as he had never known nearly choking him, her plea ripped through the last remnant of his restraint. Shaking with the power of his need, he knelt between her parted legs, his engorged member pressing against the nest of tight curls at the junction of her thighs. Lips and tongue explicit in their demand he found her mouth and slowly lowered himself onto her, pushing deeper and deeper into the hot sweetness of her body.

Emily gasped at the size and heat of him as he filled her and she knew a second's panic when he met resistance and the brief spasm of pain dimmed her pleasure. Aware of the change in her body, he stilled, but wrapping her legs even more securely around his, she murmured, "No. Please. Don't stop—it, it didn't hurt very much at all."

Half buried within her, surrounded by her satiny, slick heat, Barnaby doubted he could have stopped if she had asked it of him. Thickly, he said, "I swear to you that from this moment on, there will only be pleasure in our marriage bed."

Her lips slid across his. "Show me," she breathed, her eyes drowsy with desire.

Goaded by her words and the seductive allure of her body, he groaned and plunged fully into her. He tried to be gentle, tried to prolong the sweet agony, but his body was in the grip of a primitive emotion bordering on ecstasy that stripped him of everything except the basic impulse to lose himself within her.

Emily was prey to those same instincts and with every heavy thrust of his body into hers, she hurtled toward the same pinnacle he sought. His fingers dug into her hips and he moved on her with increasing desperation, the friction of his body surging into hers, sending a frantic need flooding through her. She wanted, she wanted, she wanted . . . *this,* she thought giddily, as her body quaked and sudden, powerful pleasure swamped her and she drowned in ecstasy.

Feeling her body convulse around him, Barnaby groaned, thrusting even more frantically into her until at last, he, too, found that sweet oblivion.

Chapter 20

As the days of February drifted by, prodded by the execution of Louis XVI in Paris, England and her allies declared war on France. The war cast a pall over the entire country, but as February gave way to March and a hint of spring teased the air, Emily marveled at the unexpected path her life had taken. Her marriage to Barnaby had been a monumental upheaval in her life but there had been additional changes in the neighborhood since that stormy February morning they had exchanged vows.

When Barnaby had reluctantly left Emily's bed that first morning after their wedding, ridding his house of all the extra guests had been on his mind. Just the sight of her flushed and drowsy-eyed as she snuggled deeper under the blankets sent a surge of lust through him, and it was all he could do not to sink back into bed beside her and awaken the passionate creature who had taken him to heaven last night. He sighed. The further discovery of his bride's many delights would have to wait. First he had to convince Mathew and his brothers that there was no reason for them to remain at Windmere waiting for another attack on him.

The two men met in Barnaby's study and when Barnaby

told Mathew that he and his brothers should return to Monks Abbey, of course, Mathew objected. "Have you forgotten that someone is trying to kill you?" he demanded, his jaw tight, his eyes bloodshot from a night of carousing at The Ram's Head.

Barnaby shook his head. "No, I haven't, but I don't believe that being constantly in the company of you and your brothers is going to prevent another attempt. Dash it all—I was shot with Emily riding right beside me!" Grimly, he added, "If the would-be assassin is as determined as I fear he may be, your presence will be for naught."

"Yes, but—"

"But nothing," Barnaby interrupted. "I appreciate your concerns, but you cannot remain indefinitely at Windmere waiting for someone to take another stab"—Barnaby winced—"at me." When Mathew looked mulish, Barnaby said persuasively, "Thanks to the last attack, I know that there is someone who wants me dead and that none of these 'accidents' were accidental. My guard is up—I'll not be caught napping again. Lamb and my brother will provide the extra eyes that I need." He smiled. "And I have an even greater reason for wanting to stay alive now—Emily. I will take care to keep breathing, I assure you."

Mathew didn't like it, but in the end, he reluctantly agreed that he and his brothers would leave for Monks Abbey that afternoon. Before they left Barnaby's study, he shot him a hard look and said, "I would remind you that I am on your side in this. If you have the slightest need of me—send word." His lips thinned. "I do not wish to inherit a title with your blood on it." Barnaby nodded and they parted. With that problem solved, Barnaby was able to return to his bride with the happy news that their guests would be gone in a matter of hours.

Mathew and his brothers departed as promised and Luc, who remained discreetly out of sight, allowed the newlyweds the privacy they craved, but by the first week of March, there was a new occupant at Windmere—Cornelia.

If Emily hadn't already been in love with Barnaby, he would have stolen her heart when before the wedding he'd made it evident that he wanted Cornelia and Anne living with them at Windmere. "God knows the place is big enough to house an army, and the addition of two women won't make the least ripple." Caressing her cheek, he'd added, "I know that they are very dear to you and that you would worry about them if we abandoned them to your cousin." He paused, made a face and admitted, "I'm not saying they should move in immediately—I'd like us to have a few weeks to ourselves. But after that, I'd be most happy to have both ladies in residence—and whatever staff they wish to bring with them."

Pride had made Emily hesitate and Barnaby had taken her into his arms and shook her gently. "I'm a wealthy man," he said bluntly. "You will be my wife in a matter of days. Let me do this for two members of your family—both of whom I have grown very fond." When she'd have protested, he'd put a finger against her lips and muttered, "And I don't want to hear one word about charity. It's my bloody money and I'll spend it how I see fit." He'd grinned at her. "Better I spend it seeing to their comfort than throwing it away on the gaming tables. Take your choice." There was no choice, as Emily had known full well the moment he'd brought up the subject.

When the idea had been presented to her, Cornelia accepted Barnaby's offer with brazen glee, but Anne, approached by Emily the day before the wedding, had hesitated. After a moment, her brown eyes full of anxiety, she asked, "Would you be wounded or think me ungrateful if I refused your very kind offer?" Emily shook her head, already half prepared for Anne's reply. In a rush, Anne said, "I didn't want to say anything until after the wedding, but dear Althea has begged me to make Parkham House my home and I think I shall do very well living there." Quickly, Anne added, "If Cornelia was remaining here, I would never desert her but with you married to Barnaby and Cornelia moving in with you"—she blushed— "I can please myself."

And so by the nineteenth of March, Anne was nestled at Parkham House and Cornelia was reigning over her splendid suite of rooms at Windmere: Agatha had come with her mistress to Windmere.

As Cornelia had been moving in, Luc had been moving out. Finding him his own place had been accomplished easily. The Dower House, situated a scant mile from Windmere, was sitting empty and, God willing, not likely to be used any time during the next thirty or forty years. Like everything else connected with the estate, the Elizabethan manor house had been kept in immaculate condition and was ready for occupancy if Luc found favor with the suggestion. Luc did. Barnaby could even supply an exceptional butler and cook for him: Walker and Mrs. Spalding. These days Luc was happily settled in at the Dower House, with Mrs. Spalding, aided by Alice, the scullery maid, bustling about the kitchen and Walker overseeing Tom, the footman, and Jane, Sally and another pair of housemaids taken from the staff at Windmere.

While Luc was willing to allow Barnaby to house and care for him at the moment, it was understood to be a temporary arrangement. Barnaby was aware that once Luc was fully recovered that he would chafe at being dependent on someone else and that it would be only a matter of time before Luc would seek his own fortune.

Having arrived in England penniless and half alive, Luc had no choice but to accept Barnaby's generosity in providing for his care, but he balked when Barnaby mentioned settling a small fortune on him.

His azure eyes blazing in his thin, pale face, Luc declared roundly, "I know that I am in no condition—or position—to refuse your help, but damn it, Barnaby, I am quite capable of making my own way—with no help from you . . . or anybody else! I cannot and will not turn into a parasite living off my rich relative. Keep your blasted money! I'll make my own way."

Unperturbed by Luc's outburst—he'd been expecting it—Barnaby murmured, "I know you will. Let us consider it more of a loan." He grinned at Luc. "Admit it—you'll need a stake and I'm willing to provide it. You can pay me back, with interest, when you have the funds—which I know will be soon enough once you reach London and the gaming tables."

Luc laughed reluctantly. "Damn you! Must you always get your own way?"

Barnaby smiled and the matter was settled. There was never any question that Luc wouldn't repay the debt or the manner in which he would earn the money to do so. Luc had earned his nickname because he did indeed have the devil looking out for him when it came to most things—witness his escape from France. And at the gaming table, well, there was many a fine gentleman who rose from the table with a much lighter purse swearing he'd played against Lucifer himself.

For the past fortnight, Jeffery had been king at The Birches—as he'd plotted and planned, he finally had the house all to himself. The Season was due to start in a few weeks and with his financial affairs in shambles, it was impractical to invite any of his rakish cronies to visit. This winter, he swore, would be different. He'd fill the house with knowing gamblers, hard drinkers, neck-or-nothing riders and men of the world like himself. Naturally there would be a few dashing widows and ladies of questionable reputations amongst the guests. Without his great-aunt and his cousin's disapproving looks, he could please himself—and he intended to.

Emily's marriage to Joslyn, while leaving him in sole possession of the house, had done nothing to improve Jeffery's money woes, and he drank and brooded over the unfairness of it all. He'd had one stroke of luck though—the day after Ainsworth's death, he'd rifled through the man's belongings and found the vowels that his late friend had held over his head. He promptly destroyed them. Telling himself that Ainsworth no longer had any need of it, Jeffery also pocketed the tidy sum of money Ainsworth had left behind in his room on that fateful day. After that, he'd ordered Ainsworth's valet to pack up everything and depart for London.

Jeffery was not destitute, but his lack of money greatly curtailed his activities and prevented him from living the life he wanted, the life he had *expected* to live when he had inherited from his uncle. What had seemed like an immense fortune in the beginning had disappeared at an astonishing rate through his careless fingers and, besides raiding the money set aside for Cornelia, Anne and Emily, he'd put nothing back into his estate and drained every penny to support his extravagant ways in London.

Another man would have seen the ruin facing him and set his mind to shoring up his estate and abandoning, at least for the time being, London and the dangers that lurked there, but not Jeffery. He brooded over ways to get his hands in the pockets of Emily's husband, the very, very wealthy Lord Joslyn. All he had to do, he decided, gambling with funds he did have and drinking himself into a stupor at The Ram's Head night after night, was to come up with a plan, an idea to part Joslyn from his money. . . .

* * *

Emily never gave Jeffery a thought. And while Barnaby
had cleverly managed to provide employment for many of
the people dear to her, Emily worried about the fate of Mrs.
Gilbert and the others in the village.

"I can't just abandon them," Emily said unhappily to Cornelia this unpleasant March day when they met in the morning room. It had stormed most of the previous night and
even now, rain beat against the windows and a blustery wind
battered the house. Barnaby had eaten earlier and a few minutes ago, after dropping a kiss on his wife's forehead, had
left the ladies for a meeting in his study with his business-
man, Worley.

Picking at the plate of coddled eggs and minced ham before her, she muttered, "I know that Barnaby is seeing that
Jeb and his crew are employed, but what about everyone
else?" Pushing around the eggs, she said, "Finding positions
for Walker and the others was a stroke of luck enough and I
know that Barnaby has spoken to Loren about coming to
work for him after all the lambs have arrived. . . ." She
snorted. "My husband was too noble to steal him from Jeffery
at the height of lambing season, but Loren will soon take up
his position as head shepherd at Windmere, yet what of Mrs.
Gilbert and Caleb and Miss Webber and the others—what is
to be done about them?" Putting down her fork, she picked up
a Shrewsbury cake Mrs. Eason had baked this morning and
Peckham had placed in the center of the table not five minutes
previously. Emily topped her round, caraway-seed-flavored
cake with raspberry jam; Cornelia preferred red currant jelly.

Cornelia nodded as she finished slathering jelly on the
warm cake. "I agree it is a problem." She sent Emily a troubled look. "While you may want to, you may not be able to
save everyone, you know."

Emily's mouth tightened. "I have to try. I cannot simply

abandon them now that my own need is no longer great."
Her voice hardened with resolution. "Something has to be
done—and Barnaby cannot hire everyone in the village to
work for him."

"True," Cornelia said, "but your husband can't give that
stiff-rumped Peckham the boot soon enough to please me."

Distracted by that enchanting picture, Emily giggled. "Oh,
I so agree. He's insufferable and condescending, isn't he?"

Cornelia's brows rose. "I thought he reserved that treat-
ment especially for me." Sending Emily a stern look, she
said, "You are mistress of Windmere. If Peckham displeases
you, send him on his way or tell your husband how you feel
about him."

Emily frowned. "I don't think Barnaby likes him very
much either, but I have the impression that for some reason
he's willing to put up with him for now."

Emily was right. Barnaby didn't care much for Peckham
but for the present he wanted the man where he could keep
an eye on him. Lamb reported this morning that the slippery
fellow had disappeared again last night—just as he had during the first week of March, little more than a fortnight ago.
The fact that, as on the previous two occasions, there had
been a storm hadn't escaped Barnaby's notice and with his
knowledge of the smugglers' preference for stormy nights to
land their contraband, it wasn't such a leap to connect Peckham's vanishing act with the landing of smuggled goods. It
was too much of a coincidence that the butler only disappeared on the same stormy nights when smugglers were
most likely to run their goods ashore.

Only half listening as Worley gave his report, Barnaby
considered Peckham's behavior. If Peckham *did* have deal-
ings with any smugglers in the area, he concluded that it
would have to be the Nolles gang. His eyes hardened. He

had a score to settle with Nolles and his men and, reminding himself that he had yet to pay a visit to The Ram's Head, he wondered if today would be as good as any.

After Mr. Worley gathered up his papers and departed, Barnaby continued to sit in his chair, his thoughts unpleasant. The knowledge that someone wanted him dead intruded into his mind. He'd taken what precautions he could to protect himself, remaining securely within the confines of Windmere, but he realized that all he was doing was stalling. Sooner or later, he'd have to expose himself to whoever had tried three times to kill him and he acknowledged he was weary of hiding. His eyes narrowed. Perhaps more than one thing could be accomplished by a ride to the village.

A plan forming in his head, Barnaby went in search of his wife. The word "wife" lingered sweetly in his mind and he decided that it was a fine word, a word of which he was growing increasingly enamored. Just as he was with his wife, he admitted with a cheerful grin and a tingle of lust.

The meeting with Worley had lasted longer than he'd expected and Emily and Cornelia were no longer in the morning room: Cornelia had returned to her rooms and Emily had retired to an informal room nearby that she liked for its bright pink chintz and leaf-green decorations. When he entered the room, Emily was going over the day's menu with Mrs. Eason. Normally, the butler oversaw anything to do with food and drink, but Emily had instituted the routine that Mrs. Eason confer with her over the menus rather than with the butler.

At Barnaby's entrance, Mrs. Eason bobbed a curtsy and after a final word from Emily, the cook walked out of the room. Alone with her husband and seeing the sudden intentness in his eyes as his gaze traveled over her as she sat demurely on the sofa, her toes curled in pleasurable anticipation and beneath her gown of mulberry Bombazine her nipples peaked.

He'd had no intention of making love to her when he entered the room. He'd come to tell her he was going to ride into the village, not, of course, mentioning he would be paying call at The Ram's Head, but just the sight of her distracted him and the knowledge of what lay beneath that charming gown aroused him. Painfully. Frantically. The need to lose himself in the hot silk of her body drove all thoughts but making love to her from his mind.

Locking the door behind him, Barnaby dragged her into his arms and kissed her as if it had been days instead of hours since he had last touched her. Her arms closed around his neck and she returned his kiss fervently, moaning when those knowing hands fondled her breasts.

Emily had been stunned to discover how very much she enjoyed the marriage bed and her husband's lovemaking. Barnaby had only to look at her and she went weak with wanting and this morning it was no different. She'd known as soon as she caught the expression in his eyes and noted the carnal curve of his lips that he wanted her . . . as she wanted him.

Her body already aflame for him, she made no protest when he pulled her bodice lower and bared her breasts. His hot mouth tasting her sent a delicious shudder through her and she pressed closer to those marauding lips, her breathing quickening.

She was honey and heat beneath his mouth and Barnaby lost himself in her sweetness. Full of the same desire and yearning that had Emily warm and willing in his embrace, his lips found her mouth once more and he kissed her with increasing urgency.

The brush of her body against his was more than he could stand and Barnaby fumbled at the fastening of his breeches and a second later his member, engorged and rigid, sprang free. Emily's fingers slid along the smooth width, teasing him, making him groan before her hand tightened around him and her hand began to move in the motion he had taught her.

His mouth lifted from hers and his eyes glazed with desire, he muttered, "I didn't mean to go this far, I really only meant to kiss you. . . ."

Her lips red from his kiss, she murmured, "It was only to kiss me that made you lock the door, hmmm?" Her fingers tickled the swollen knob and he shuddered beneath her caress.

"God, no!" he admitted thickly. "I have visions of making love to you in every room in the place and since we're here . . ."

His hands moved beneath her skirts, sliding upward until he found the welcoming dampness between her thighs. His fingers parted the pale gold curls and she clung to him as he stroked that soft flesh until she was writhing and mewling in his arms.

Breathing harshly, Barnaby backed her to the wall and, lifting her, he panted, "Wrap your legs around me." She did so, gasping when he lowered her onto his shaft.

Their mouths met and, locked together, he drove into her again and again, each violent pump of his body into hers tumbling them closer to the edge, until at last they plummeted into the abyss.

Small tremors still pulsing through her body, Emily leaned weakly against the wall, hardly able to stand when Barnaby finally moved and her legs slid to the floor. Only his arms wrapped securely around her kept her upright and prevented her from sinking into a damp puddle of ecstasy at his feet.

His forehead resting against hers, his lips brushing hers, he said huskily, "That's why I locked the door—wouldn't want to shock the servants."

Recalled to her surroundings, Emily giggled, blushed and pulled her gown back into position. Shaking out her skirts she was embarrassingly aware of a damp trickle between her legs. Good heavens, what had she been thinking? Suppose *Peckham* had knocked on the door? Her cheeks grew even hotter and she wondered if the day would come that making love to her husband whenever and wherever she wanted would seem commonplace. She doubted it.

Seating herself on the pink chintz sofa once more, she pushed into place the few strands of hair that had come loose from the cherry-and-black plaid silk ribbon Kate had wound through her curls this morning. Feeling more composed, she watched as Barnaby, who had already rearranged his clothing, walked over and unlocked the door.

Joining her on the sofa, he took her hand in his and, gently kissing it, he murmured, "I find you far too ravishing for my own good. I didn't mean to fall upon you."

She smiled at him. "I can't recall, but did I scream for help or ask you to stop?"

Barnaby threw back his head and laughed. "Now I know why I love you."

Emily's smile faltered and uncertainty in her eyes, she asked softly, "And do you? Love me?"

His hand tightened around hers and dark eyes glittering now with a different emotion, all signs of laughter gone, he said, "It is why I married you . . . because I love you and couldn't imagine life without you."

Her heart leaped and a weight she hadn't even been aware of slid away. She'd have to have been blind not to know that he had affection for her, and while she knew the state of her own heart, she had never been sure of his. That he had a gallant and generous nature was obvious and the worry that it was those very traits that had prompted their engagement nagged at the back of her mind. A strong streak of chivalry ran deep within Barnaby and, confronted with her situation, it would have been the most natural thing in the world for him to want to rescue her. She smiled tenderly. And Cornelia, Anne, Walker, Jeb and all the others. The niggling fear that pity and kindness had been at the root of his determination to marry her vanished and her fingers clung even more tightly to his. He loved her, she thought giddily. He'd just said so.

Hugging the moment to her, Emily's gaze dropped to their hands, his so big and dark, holding her much smaller and paler one. *He loved her!*

Barnaby tipped her chin up and, staring down into her eyes, he asked quietly, "What are you thinking, my love?"

So filled with love for him, she could barely speak, she said thickly, "That I am so very lucky that you love me . . . and that I love you more than life itself."

A light blazed across his face and in a shaken voice he said, "I hoped you did, but I was never certain—and it worried me."

She stared at him dumbfounded. "You worried?"

He smiled and dropped a warm kiss on her nose. "I did, indeed. I was marrying an Amazon—most men would have been worried." Giving her a little shake, he added, "Of course I was worried. I knew you found me attractive and that you responded to my advances, but you were never very forthcoming about your feelings. I couldn't help wondering if you were marrying me just to provide security for Cornelia and all the rest of your vulnerable chicks."

Emily's mouth fell open and she gaped at him. "But—but," she spluttered, "I thought you might be marrying me because you felt sorry for me."

"Sorry for you?" he said, and burst out laughing. Pulling her onto his lap, he kissed her soundly and said, "Sweetheart, if I felt sorry for anyone, it was my own besotted self. I was mad for you almost from the moment I laid eyes on you, and all you did was keep me at arm's length and act as if you found me a bearable nuisance."

"I did not!"

"Yes, you did." His eyes warm and caressing on her face,

he murmured, "You're going to have to make it up to me by loving me until the end of our days."

Her heart melted, her arms encircled his neck and she replied demurely, "Well, since I have no other choice, I shall do my best." Her arms tightened and she cried, "Oh, Barnaby, I *do* love you."

"And I, you, sweetheart," he swore softly. "Always and forever."

They kissed and for a long time, while the storm churned outside, in that charming pink chintz room, there were only the murmurings between lovers.

Barnaby's step was light when he finally tore himself away from Emily's beguiling presence. He was a happy man. His passionate, beautiful wife loved him and he thanked the fate that had brought him to England and Emily. Possessing a magnificent fortune, he thought, after ordering his horse brought up from the stables, was a splendid thing, but having Emily love him . . . He grinned; he couldn't help it—even if it caused Peckham, who was crossing the entry hall, to stare at him strangely. Having his Amazon love him, Barnaby decided, now *that* was a most splendid thing!

Mindful of the previous attempts on his life, Barnaby didn't, as he would have normally, ride alone to the village. Lamb was at the Dower House and knowing that there would be hell to pay if he didn't take either Lamb or Luc with him, a trip to the Dower House was in order. To pick up my nursemaids, he thought wryly.

Mounting his horse, a lively brown filly with a pair of high white stockings on her rear legs and a big blaze running down her face, Barnaby set out for the Dower House. The day was cool, the wind blowing and a light rain falling, but he was too happy to let sullen weather ruin his mood. He let the filly, Glory, have her head the first half of the ride and she pranced and cavorted unfettered in the cool, damp air, but the last quarter mile he reminded her of her manners. A few minutes later they were trotting sedately up to the front door of the Dower House.

Walker met him at the door and, bowing low, murmured, "My lord. It is good to see you."

"Settling in, are you?" Barnaby asked as he handed Walker his gloves and hat. Having placed the hat and gloves on a narrow marble-topped table in the alcove entry, Walker moved quickly to help him out of his greatcoat. "My brother not being too demanding?"

Walker grinned. "Oh, no, my lord, Master Luc is very easy to serve. As long as Mrs. Spalding keeps him stuffed with her veal patties and gammon steaks on toast—of which he is particularly fond—and I see to it that the wine and brandy decanters are full, he is a happy man."

Barnaby laughed. "That sounds like Luc. Show me to him."

Luc was in a pleasant room with wainscoted and green figured silk walls at the side of the house. A Turkish rug in vivid shades of amber, gold, sapphire, emerald and ruby lay on the floor and green velvet drapes hung at the windows. A welcoming fire burned on the hearth of the faded brick fireplace in the corner.

Luc was sprawled in a chair near the fire, studying the cards laid out on the table before him; Lamb, looking very much at home, sat across from him. Hearing the door open, both men looked up and a welcoming smile lit Luc's face when he saw Barnaby.

Rising to his feet, he clasped Barnaby's hand warmly and exclaimed, "*Tiens!* I certainly didn't expect to see you today." Luc glanced at the rain spitting against the window. "In case you haven't noticed it's filthy outside. Little Lamb nearly drowned on his way over here."

"I noticed," Barnaby said, "but I have a desire to visit The

Ram's Head." He shot Lamb a glance. "And since I am under orders not to stray from my nursemaid's watchful eye, I came in search of him." He grinned at Luc and added, "I'd be happy to have you join us—if you don't think you'll melt."

"Try and stop me!" Luc said, the azure eyes gleaming with enthusiasm. "Perhaps I shall find someone to give me a good game—Lamb has no head for gambling. He has lost at least two fortunes equal to yours to me already today."

There were little signs of the invalid that Jeb had brought back to England just over a month ago. Luc's build was deceptively slender and he was still a little thin, although Mrs. Spalding's cooking seemed to be taking care of that. The sunken look around his eyes was gone and his skin had lost that unhealthy pastiness. His color was good these days and the mocking light was back in those brilliant eyes.

Ignoring Luc's barb, Lamb scowled at Barnaby. "You just can't resist poking at a hornet's nest, can you?" he growled.

"You know me so well," Barnaby returned, smiling sweetly.

Luc had been made privy to all that had occurred before he arrived in England so he understood the exchange. He'd been too ill in the beginning to do more than speculate about who was trying to kill Barnaby and how to deal with the Nolles gang, but that time was past and he was eager to lend his half brother aid. Besides, he had had his own reasons for wanting to observe Nolles—no more than Barnaby did he appreciate the attack by the Nolles gang the night he landed in England.

Brushing aside Lamb's words, Luc said, "Bah! Little Lamb, you act like an old woman, sometimes."

"At least I'll be *old*," retorted Lamb. "Unlike a certain pair of devil-may-care scamps I could name."

Luc and Barnaby grinned.

Lamb was not amused. His gaze fixed on Barnaby, he

said, "I would remind you that right now might not be the best time to tackle Nolles and his gang."

Barnaby looked innocent. "Who said anything about tackling Nolles?"

Lamb snorted. "I know you." His fist hit the table. "Blast it, Barnaby! You have a wife to consider now. What the devil are you thinking of by gallivanting off to the village and stirring up God knows what sort of trouble?"

"You have no need to remind me of my responsibilities," Barnaby shot back. "I cannot remain hiding at Windmere for the rest of my life. At some point, I will have to leave the haven of Windmere. A trip to the village—accompanied by two stalwart protectors—doesn't seem an unreasonable first step."

"He's right," said Luc. "There has been no sign of this would-be assassin—perhaps, he has given up."

Lamb eyed Luc disgustedly. "I should have known you'd side with him—you're so bloody wise, you nearly lost your life on a fool's quest."

Luc's fists clenched and he started forward. Lamb rose from the table, looking as pugnacious as Luc. As he had so often in the past, Barnaby quickly stepped between the two of them.

A placating note in his voice, Barnaby said to Lamb, "If I thought I was in any danger today, I swear, I'd follow your advice. I don't believe my would-be killer has given up, but who knows how long it will be before he strikes again? Am I to remain a prisoner forever?"

Something in Barnaby's voice caught Lamb's attention and his eyes narrowed. "You're not just going to the village to see Nolles—you're also hoping to draw out whoever is trying to kill you!"

The guilty look that flitted across Barnaby's face was answer enough and Lamb swore low and viciously.

"*Mon Dieu!*" cried Luc, realizing Lamb spoke the truth.

342   *Shirlee Busbee*

Grabbing Barnaby's shoulder, he shook him. "Are you mad?"

"No," said Barnaby, shrugging off Luc's hands. "But if I stay secluded at Windmere, sooner or later, this killer will be forced to strike, and I'd prefer Emily and Cornelia nowhere around when he does." When Lamb and Luc remained unconvinced, Barnaby said wearily, "May I remind you both that we know nothing about this man? Not who he is, where he is or even why he wants me dead. We're unlikely to learn anything as long as I stay confined at Windmere. Despite the danger, at some point, I have to resume some semblance of my life." He took a deep breath. "He has to be drawn out and the only way I can do that is to give him an opportunity to kill me."

"And it has to be today?" snarled Lamb.

"If not today, then when?" Barnaby asked. "Tomorrow? Next week? Next month?"

Thoughtfully, Luc said, "Unless we have very bad luck, it is doubtful that this mysterious fellow will even know that Barnaby has left Windmere to visit The Ram's Head."

"My point exactly," said Barnaby. "I should be safe today. The danger will be greatest once I return to a more regular routine."

Lamb wasn't happy about it, but in the end he agreed that for *today* Barnaby's ill-advised trip to The Ram's Head should be without peril. "That is," he grumbled as the three men mounted in the light rain and prepared to ride to the village, "if the pair of you don't get up to any of your tricks." He bent a fierce eye onto Luc. "Especially you! Barnaby's in enough trouble without having to risk his neck pulling your chickens from the fire."

Offended, Luc glared back at him. "I am perfectly capable of taking care of myself—and I outgrew the need of your scolds long ago."

Barnaby sighed. It was going to be a long ride.

Chapter 21

The Ram's Head was a handsome brick-and-timber build-ing built within the last half century situated at the edge of a country lane that led to the intersection of two main roads—one leading to Brighton, the other to Tunbridge Wells and from there to London. The tavern was easily twice the size of Mrs. Gilbert's establishment and there was none of the shabby charm of The Crown; no shutters hung crookedly at lace-edged windows and no door dark with age guarded the entrance; Barnaby hated the place on sight.

From the raucous sounds that spilled from inside out onto the road, it was obvious that The Ram's Head did a rousing business. There were several horses tied to the oak rail in front of the inn and, along with Lamb and Luc, Barnaby dis-mounted and tied his horse.

Entering The Ram's Head they were assaulted by drunken laughter, loud conversation and a film of smoke drifted above the crowd, the scent of tobacco, spirits, brandy and ale and other less identifiable odors hung in the air. Despite the hour, early afternoon, the main room was packed with men of all stripes—fishermen, farmers, common laborers and a few leading landowners. Barnaby spied Sir Michael and a pair of gentlemen he recognized sitting at a table near the massive stone fireplace on the other side of the big room. He also saw a pair of the neighborhood's young bucks leaning against the long oak bar at the rear of the room, ogling the buxom young women scurrying around carrying trays covered with overflowing pitchers of dark ale and heavy, pewter tankards and mugs dripping with froth.

Barnaby's entrance, flanked by Lam and Luc, created a stir and conversation ebbed for a startled second, before rising again with renewed vigor. Lamb leaned near and murmured, "How much do you want to wager that we, mainly you, are the topic of conversation?"

Barnaby shook his head, smiling wryly. A commotion near a door at the side of the room caught his attention and he glimpsed a tall, broad-shouldered form rising from a table half-hidden by shadows and disappearing through the door. Thomas? Simon?

Luc asked softly, "Did you see that? I could have sworn one of your cousins just bolted out that door over there."

"Did you recognize him?" Barnaby asked, his gaze on the door.

"Thomas or Simon," answered Lamb, "but I couldn't tell which one for certain."

"Neither could I," muttered Luc. "I'd swear though that it was one of them."

From that same discreet table by the door a slim, smartly garbed gentleman stood and sauntered over to Barnaby. Stopping in front of him, he smiled and bowed.

"Lord Joslyn, this *is* a pleasure," purred the gentleman. "I have long hoped that you would sample the charms of my humble establishment. I am Will Nolles."

Barnaby hadn't known what the vicious leader of a notorious gang of smugglers should look like, but he would never have connected Will Nolles with such an ungenteel enterprise. Nolles's luxurious ginger hair was worn in a queue and confined with a black silk ribbon, much like Barnaby's, and his dark green coat of superfine and buff pantaloons could have been made by the same Bond Street tailor Barnaby favored. There was a hint of the dandy in Nolles's stiff collar points, gaily-embroidered white waistcoat and the striped hose he wore with his black kid pumps—the heels higher than fashion demanded to give him some much-needed height: the top of his head barely reached Barnaby's shoulders.

"Thank you for the welcome," Barnaby said with a cool smile. He glanced around. "You appear to have a fine place here . . . quite popular, I see."

Nolles nodded. "Indeed, we are reputed to be the finest tavern in the area." A sly expression in his pale green eyes, he added, "I trust you will find The Ram's Head far superior to . . . other inns and taverns you have visited recently." Radiating complacency, he continued. "If you haven't already, you will discover that all the gentlemen, in fact, anyone of note in the area, prefer what we have to offer over the, ah, rustic charms to be found elsewhere."

Barnaby didn't consider himself a violent man, but he was fighting hard not to punch Nolles in the face. Smug bastard.

"I find that I like a certain rustic charm, and whether your establishment lives up to *my* expectations remains to be seen, doesn't it?" Barnaby replied.

Nolles's thin lips tightened and he murmured, "Indeed, it does, my lord." The pale green eyes speculative, he asked, "Would you prefer a private room or will you allow me to escort you to a table here in the public area? Of course, your first round of drinks will be at my expense—a welcoming gift as it were."

"No private room for us—we'll be quite happy with a

table out here." Not wishing to be beholden to Nolles for anything, Barnaby said, "It's kind of you to offer us free refreshments, but it isn't necessary."

Nolles smiled. "Oh, but it will be my pleasure, my lord."

"Then thank you," Barnaby said, giving in gracefully.

Nolles paraded them across the room and settled them at a large, round oak table not far from where Sir Michael and his cronies sat. After asking their choice of libations, Nolles said, "I shall see that your refreshments are served promptly." Those green eyes fixed on Barnaby's face, he added, "We are noted for our service, and of course, if there is any complaint, please do not hesitate to make your concerns known to me." He bowed again to Barnaby and said, "I shall leave you to enjoy yourself, my lord . . . for what I hope will be the first of many visits."

Watching Nolles mince away, Barnaby said slowly, "Fellow reminds me of a coral snake. Small, dainty, lovely to look at . . . and deadly."

Lamb agreed. "I think he could smile, not even breaking into a sweat while he cut out your liver."

Luc nodded. "A most dangerous man our Will Nolles. He leaves one feeling in need of a bath, *oui*?"

Catching Sir Michael's eye, Barnaby smiled and nodded. As his gaze moved around the room, he acknowledged a few other men he'd met, aware that Luc and Lamb's presence with him was sure to cause talk—the neighborhood still wasn't easy with Lamb and Luc's obvious illegitimacy or how to treat them. Barnaby's casual acceptance and warm relationship with both men puzzled nearly everyone regardless of wealth and rank, but while people like Sir Michael appeared to accept it, there was no escaping the whispers and raised eyebrows. Barnaby grinned. Bugger 'em.

The three men said little until after their tankards of ale had been served by a dark-eyed wench whose low-cut bodice gave an enticing view of her impressive bosom. Placing down a pitcher full of rich, dark ale, a saucy smile on her lips, she said, "If there is anything else you wish, my lord . . . you have only to ask."

Barnaby would have had to be dead not to admire the seductive sway of her hips as she ambled away, but after an appreciative glance, deciding he much preferred his wife's trim little buttocks, his eyes turned to Lamb and Luc.

Leaning back in his chair, Barnaby said, "Interesting that we interrupted a meeting between one of the cousins and the smooth Mr. Will Nolles, isn't it? Tends to make one think the mysterious London backer might just be one of them. Even more interesting is the fact one of my esteemed cousins is in the area, but has neglected to pay a call at Windmere. I wonder why?"

"Curious that he scooted out the door the moment we entered the room," murmured Luc, sipping from his mug.

Lamb scratched the side of his face. "Be interesting to be privy to what they were talking about over there in that private little corner . . . and why he didn't want to be seen by you, us."

Barnaby nodded, his glance moving around the room. There were not many people he recognized, as much from being new to the area, as the fact that the majority of the inhabitants were not likely to be found in the sacred precincts of Almack's or any of the gentlemen's clubs along Pall Mall favored by the *ton*. These were common laborers, farmers and fishermen with a scattering of the wellborn and wealthy amongst them. Spotting a pair of uniformed customs men at a table with three other men, their heads close together, Barnaby's brow rose. The revenue men appeared to be right at home in the tavern. The three other men at their table could have been honest fishermen, but there was a furtive air about them that made Barnaby suspect they were smugglers. Part of Nolles's gang? he wondered. If so, the gossip and Lieutenant Deering's suspicions that Nolles bribed the very men that were supposed to stop the smugglers appeared to be true.

Barnaby recognized no one here that he'd ever seen at The Crown and he thought it odd that with Mrs. Gilbert's tavern closer to the waterfront that more of the fishermen wouldn't have patronized her place rather than traveling the extra miles out to The Ram's Head. Recalling that Mrs. Gilbert's husband had died after a visit to Nolles's establishment, he frowned. Perhaps, Nolles had given the community a good reason for avoiding The Crown.

Barnaby, Lamb and Luc relaxed around the table, drinking their ale, talking in low tones. After a moment, Luc nudged Barnaby and tipped his head to the left. "Do you see what I see through that doorway over there, brother mine?"

Barnaby looked in the direction Luc motioned, noticing for the first time an opened door in the far wall. Across a hallway, another door stood half open and Barnaby saw what had caught Luc's attention. From this narrow vantage, he couldn't see very much, but he realized that the room he was looking into was set up for gaming. More interesting, while he didn't recognize one of the men playing cards, he knew the other one very well: Jeffery Townsend. One of the barmaids came out of the room where Jeffery sat and shut the door behind her, closing off the view.

Barnaby looked at Luc and asked, "Do you mean to try your hand?"

Luc shook his head. "Not today." He smiled. "But perhaps some other time."

Unobtrusively, the three men continued to assess and track the area. Most of the patrons they dismissed as being precisely what they seemed—gentlemen of leisure or honest hardworking men enjoying a tipple or two on a rainy afternoon. But eventually, Barnaby's gaze fixed on a group of tough-looking brutes hunched over a table across the room. More members of Nolles's gang, he decided, noting the way the other men in the room gave that table a wide berth—that and the covert, hard glances those brutal-faced fellows slid his way now and then.

About the same time, Lamb murmured, "Over there on the far side, at the second table from the end."

"They've been studying us," Luc said, "since the moment we sat down."

Barnaby nodded and finished his ale. Setting down his tankard, he said, "I think our time here is over. We've met Nolles—our main purpose—and we will recognize some members of his gang should we come across them again." Rising to his feet, he muttered, "I don't know about you, but I've had about all I can take of Nolles's hospitality. Let us be off."

Taking his time, stopping to chat for a moment with Sir Michael, Barnaby wasn't surprised that before he reached the doors at the front of the room, Nolles materialized at his side. "Leaving so soon, my lord?" Nolles asked. "I trust everything was to your satisfaction?"

"I found no fault," Barnaby said, continuing on his way. A touch stopped him and he looked down to see Nolles's dainty, white hand on his arm.

"Perhaps you will come again soon and stay longer," Nolles said. "The Ram's Head has much to offer a gentleman wishing to while away an afternoon . . . women, gambling . . . whatever you wish. Having Viscount Joslyn frequent my establishment is good for business." His hand tightened on Barnaby's arm. "Your, ah, preference for a different tavern has cost me a few patrons." Nolles smiled thinly. "You'll discover that I don't like losing."

Barnaby considered the small, slim man before him, reminding himself that this man had ordered the attack on Emily's intrepid band of smugglers. The Nolles gang had brazenly stolen the contraband Jeb, Mrs. Gilbert and the others had worked so hard to land and had visited violence upon them. Luc had been with Jeb that night and anger simmered within him at the notion that this same, dandified little creature could have caused Luc's death. A terrifying thought occurred to him. Only by the grace of God Emily hadn't been on the beach that night. . . .

Glancing down at the hand on his arm, Barnaby said without heat, "If you don't remove your hand from my arm immediately, I'll break every bone in your body." Nolles's hand disappeared as if by magic. A dangerous gleam in his black eyes, Barnaby snarled softly, "And threaten me . . . or anything of mine again and I'll stuff your ballocks down your throat."

His face pale with rage, Nolles cautioned, "You're making a mistake, my lord. I make a far better friend than I do an enemy—as others have learned to their cost."

"Have you forgotten already what I just explained to you about threats?" Barnaby inquired silkily, the expression on his face warning that it wouldn't take much for him to implement his threat.

Nolles stepped away from Barnaby. His eyes bright with fury, Nolles said, "We understand each other, my lord. I trust you won't regret the choice you have made."

Barnaby smiled, something in that smile making Nolles back up even more. "Regret? Doubtful." Barnaby said. "As for understanding each other . . . indeed, we do, Mr. Nolles. Indeed we do."

A misty rain was falling and a chilly wind whistled around the building as the three men walked out of the tavern and mounted their horses. Shoulders hunched against the weather, they rode away from The Ram's Head, Lamb observing sourly, "Well, that went well. So much for just spying out the lay of the land."

Barnaby grimaced. "Not very diplomatic of me, I know,

but it was either that or tear that simpering creature from limb to limb."

They were riding abreast, with Barnaby boxed in between Lamb and Luc. From his other side Luc said, "Barnaby may have thrown down the gauntlet, but we learned a great deal this afternoon. Nolles is a viper and that Jeffery enjoys the gaming tables Nolles so kindly provides. Oh, and, of course, that one of your cousins was visiting with Monsieur Nolles."

"But which one?" Lamb grumbled. He glanced at Barnaby. "What are the odds when we return home we discover that one of your cousins has come to visit?"

Barnaby's lips twitched. "I may not be the gambler Luc is, but even I know when not to bet against a sure thing."

Prepared to find his home invaded by one or all of his cousins, after parting with Luc at the Dower House, when Barnaby and Lamb arrived at Windmere it was to discover that no guests had arrived in their absence. Learning that Emily and Cornella were enjoying a visit from the vicar's wife, Penelope, Barnaby, with Lamb at his heels, retired to the study.

While Lamb stretched out in a chair by the fire, Barnaby paced the room, a scowl on his face. "You'd think," he complained, "that whichever of my cousins was meeting with Nolles this afternoon, he'd have had the decency to show his face here so we could identify him."

His booted feet inches from leaping flames, Lamb grinned. "Bloody inconsiderate of the fellow, I agree."

Barnaby threw him a look. "Dash it all! Waiting around to be killed is devilish unpleasant business, I can tell you."

Lamb sobered. "I agree. But how do you know that identifying Nolles's visitor will help you unmask whoever is trying to kill you? Even if it was one of your cousins, there could be an innocent explanation—being at the tavern doesn't mean he is Nolles's London moneyman. Even his abrupt departure doesn't mean much—perhaps his visit was over and he didn't notice your arrival."

Barnaby snorted. "Having met Nolles, after today, I don't believe in anything 'innocent' in connection with him." His jaw clenched. "And I don't believe in coincidences either." Lamb watched him pace for several more moments. Stopping in front of Lamb, Barnaby said slowly, "I believe there is a connection between the attempts on my life, Peckham's disappearances and now today, Nolles's mysterious visitor—and if I'm right, I know what it is that connects them all together."

Lamb looked doubtful. "One of your cousins sneaking back into the area, I can connect with the attempts on your life, but it could just have been a coincidence that he was visiting with Nolles this afternoon. And Peckham? What part does he play?"

Barnaby turned away and, staring at the fire, he said, "I know it sounds far-fetched, but . . ." He glanced back at Lamb and said, "There are some things we know to be true. One of them is that Peckham's three disappearances have all occurred on nights favored by the smugglers to make a landing. The second thing we know is that Nolles is reputed to be the biggest smuggler in the area—and I'll wager my last pound that Peckham is working with Nolles."

Lamb didn't look convinced, but he nodded. "Go on."

His hands resting on the mantel, Barnaby stared once more into the fire. "Nolles was just another fisherman, and occasional smuggler, until about a decade ago, and then almost overnight, he expanded. The size of his gang increased as did the frequency and amount of contraband smuggled ashore; about that same time Nolles purchased the old tavern, The Ram's Head, and renovated it, making it the headquarters for his gang." Barnaby looked at Lamb. "Obviously, someone invested a lot of money in Nolles's gang—the mysterious London backer. I'm convinced the moneyman is someone who has ties to this area, a wealthy man who knew Nolles." Barnaby made a face. "Which could include Lord Broadfoot or any number of wealthy landowners, but the timing is what caught my attention. If it was someone local funding Nolles, such as Broadfoot, he'd have been doing it for decades, not just the past ten years or less. So who came into money around ten years ago with connections to this area?" Barnaby pulled on his ear. "That's about when Mathew and his brothers came into their majorities . . . and inherited their various fortunes."

An arrested expression on his face, Lamb sat up straighter. "You're thinking that Nolles's backer is one of your cousins, aren't you?"

"It makes sense."

"Even if one of them is Nolles's backer, what does that have to do with Peckham and more importantly, killing you?" Lamb demanded. "You haven't gone back to thinking that Mathew is behind the attacks, have you? That he wants the title at any cost? And if not him, what? Thomas is willing to kill you and his older brother to gain the title? Or Simon is willing to kill you and both brothers to inherit? That's madness!"

"Yes, I agree," Barnaby said. "But suppose the title isn't the *only* reason behind the attacks on me? Suppose the other reason has to do with Peckham . . . and Windmere itself?"

Lamb stared at him, turning the idea over in his head. "If Windmere is at the root of it, there must be something here that is useful to the smugglers," he said thoughtfully, "and it has to be connected to Peckham's disappearances. . . ."

Barnaby knew the moment Lamb made the same connections he had. Lamb's eyes widened and he jerked upright, exclaiming, "Tunnels! Secret passages!" Excited, he bent forward. "Of course. Landing large amounts of contraband requires a safe place to conceal the goods until they can arrange transportation to London."

"Peckham is in on it," Barnaby said. "I don't know his role, but I suspect he guides the smugglers in and locks up securely after them. I'm sure if we examine the wine cellar, looking for a secret door or lever or whatever, we'll find how he's been disappearing—and proof of our suspicions."

"But why kill you? Why not just continue as they have been? You're not likely to be snooping around in the bowels of the house."

"They can't afford to take the chance that I won't be," Barnaby said. "I'm the new owner, a stranger to the area. Why wouldn't I want to inspect everything? I already know about the tunnels. Odds are I'm going to see them sooner or later."

"You're thinking the previous viscount knew about the smuggling? Condoned it? And if you were dead that Mathew would follow in his footsteps?"

"Something like that. I don't know if the old viscount knew about the smuggling—I suspect he didn't—but he certainly wouldn't be poking about in some old, half-forgotten tunnels beneath a house he'd lived in all his life. Why would he? The same could be said for Mathew. Even if Mathew's not involved in the scheme, he'd be unlikely to pay any attention to the tunnels—they're only a fond memory from childhood for him. With Mathew at the helm, the smugglers could continue to hide their goods without interference."

"And if he's part of the operation," Lamb added, "there'd be no reason for him to do anything different than he's already doing."

Barnaby nodded. "Precisely. And if it's not Mathew it has to be one of his brothers. They all know about the tunnels—they've mentioned playing in them as children—as did Emily. With Mathew living at Windmere oblivious to what was going on under his nose, Thomas or Simon could contihue the operation unhindered. Even if Mathew discovered what they were about, he wouldn't expose one of his brothers," Barnaby smiled grimly. "I was the unknown quantity, but with me dead, Mathew would inherit as everyone had assumed he would in the first place and everything would have gone on just as it always had."

They stared at each other, considering all angles. A few minutes later, Lamb sighed. "It hangs together and explains a great deal."

Barnaby agreed. "The only question now is—which brother?"

"Finding Peckham's secret door might be helpful," Lamb muttered. "It would confirm our suspicion."

"Much as I would like to, we can't just go charging into the wine cellar and start probing for a hidden entrance. The moment we do that, Peckham will raise the alarm and they'll know we've tumbled onto their scheme," Barnaby said. He looked thoughtful. "Unless, of course," he murmured, "I send Peckham on an errand that ensures his absence from the house for several hours . . . perhaps even overnight." He shot Lamb a keen glance. "What about the other servants? How trustworthy are they? Do you think any of them could be part of it?"

Lamb grimaced. "Anything's possible." He smiled at Barnaby. "Most of them are becoming used to me, but I am still a stranger to these people, and since I am neither fish nor fowl, that only adds to their wariness around me. I think the majority of your people are just what they seem to be— honest, hardworking folk." He paused. "Some of them probably have ties to the smuggling community, but as for any actual participation . . ." He shook his head. "No."

"Luc has to be told," Barnaby said. "He'll have some thoughts on the subject."

"I'm sure he'll have several and won't hesitate to share them with us," Lamb said drily. Rising to his feet, he added,

"I intended to ride over to the Dower House later and see him anyway. I can tell him then."

"Checking to make certain your chick suffered no setback after this afternoon?" Barnaby asked with a grin.

Lamb reddened. Stiffly, he said, "It isn't so long ago that he rose from his sick bed—remember he could have died. I don't think there's any harm in checking that he didn't overtax himself today. It *was* the first time he's been on a horse in weeks."

Barnaby considered teasing Lamb further, but decided to have mercy on him. "Of course," he said. "Excellent idea."

Lamb eyed him suspiciously, but when Barnaby made no other comment, he said, "What are your plans?"

Barnaby rubbed his neck. "I'll have to think of an errand for Peckham before we check for a hidden door." He scowled. "And it will have to be soon—if there was a landing last night, the tunnels will be filled with contraband right now, but they won't remain that way for long." Struck by a thought, he added, "A run last night would explain why one of my cousins was meeting with Nolles this afternoon and lends credence to our theory."

Lamb agreed. A few more minutes' conversation and Lamb departed for the kitchens to ferret out anything that would bolster their suspicions.

Alone in his study, Barnaby wandered around the room, seeking any holes or discrepancies in his theory. He found none, but any way one looked at it, it was all speculation. It was one explanation, but he had absolutely no proof of any of it. It would have been nice, he mused, if when he had returned home, one of his cousins had been waiting for him. Then I'd know which one of the bastards is behind this, he thought harshly. My enemy would have a face. . . .

Whether to tell Emily and how much to tell her preyed on his mind. She wasn't, he reminded himself repeatedly, a hothouse flower, likely to faint at the idea that smugglers were using her home as a hiding place for smuggled goods. He grinned. More likely she'd think it a capital idea and admire their enterprise. He had yet to admit to her that someone was trying to kill him, but he suspected Emily had already come to that conclusion herself and, knowing his wife, she wouldn't take kindly either to the notion that someone wanted him dead. He sighed. She was his *wife*. He wasn't comfortable with not telling her, nor was he convinced that keeping secrets from her was wise. So how much did he tell her? All? Nothing? Or something in between?

Barnaby still hadn't made up his mind when he walked into Emily's rooms to escort her downstairs for dinner. The skirts of her green watered silk gown spread out around her, Emily was seated on the sofa, leafing through a ladies' magazine when he strolled into the room.

She glanced up at his entrance, her heart giving that familiar little thump at the sight of him. He looked very handsome tonight in a burgundy jacket and pale gray knee breeches.

He bowed before her and, an appreciative glint in his eyes, he murmured, "I have never seen you look so beautiful . . . except perhaps when you are as bare as nature made you." Lifting her fingers to his lips he pressed a kiss to them. "And I hope to see you that way before the evening is very much older."

"Am I allowed to eat first?" she asked, twinkling up at him.

Barnaby would have preferred to continue flirting with his wife, but the compulsion to tell her what he had been about this afternoon and the conclusions he had come to nagged at him. Deciding that now was as good a time as any, he sat beside her on the sofa.

Taking her hand in his, he said, "Lamb, Luc and I rode into the village this afternoon . . . to The Ram's Head. I met Nolles."

Emily's eyes widened and her fingers tightened on his. Anxiety and unease mingled in her voice, she asked, "And why did you do that?"

Barnaby made a face. "It was time. Almost from the moment I heard his name, I've wanted to meet him, but . . ." He smiled crookedly. "But with one thing and another, you, marriage, Luc and a few accidents to name the most compelling, the moment never seemed right."

She couldn't argue with him about that—the past few months had been eventful, and since he had taken Lamb and Luc with him, she couldn't even scold him for venturing into the village, but the idea of Barnaby confronting Nolles, even politely, was worrisome. She trusted Barnaby's abilities to take care of himself, but Nolles was not to be trifled with— he was vicious and cunning. Ambush was his favorite means of attack and neither her husband's title, position nor wealth would mean a thing to him should Barnaby run afoul of him. Emily sighed, not optimistic about Barnaby treading carefully around Nolles. Her troubled gaze on Barnaby's dark face, she asked, "How did Nolles react?"

Barnaby smiled. "Politely. He even bought us a pitcher of ale to welcome us. It was an enlightening afternoon."

Casting him a sharp look, she demanded, "What happened?"

Playing with her fingers, his gaze dropped and he said, "It's rather a long story."

"Dinner can wait. Tell me."

He did. Holding nothing back.

When he finished speaking, angry, intrigued and dismayed all at the same time, she stared at him, turning his words over in her mind. Since she already suspected the accidents were not accidents, they were the least interesting part of what he told her. Frightening, but not such a surprise. The incident with Nolles disturbed her and the news that one of Barnaby's cousins may have been visiting with Nolles lent credence to the rest of the story.

Taking in a deep breath, she said calmly, "I agree—it *was* an enlightening afternoon."

He smiled. "No scold?"

"Would it make any difference?" she asked with an arched brow.

"No, but you might feel better."

Emily snorted. "The only thing that will make me feel better is identifying which one of your cousins is behind this and putting an end to it." A thought struck her and she murmured, "Of course, being rid of Peckham will be a nice bonus." She lowered her lashes. "And if you'd told me about Peckham in the first place, I could have shown you the entrance into the tunnels from the wine cellar ages ago."

"You know where it is?" he demanded, excitement gleaming in his eyes.

"Yes—the entrance and most of the tunnels." She looked thoughtful. "I haven't been down there since I was a child, but I'm sure I'll remember the layout. There's more than one tunnel, some are smaller than others and they angle off in all directions—one of the reasons, as children, we liked to hide and play in them." She flashed him a mocking glance. "Local legend has it that the tunnels were constructed by one of your ancestors early in the last century and that the Joslyn fortune is based on smuggled goods." But he wasn't to be drawn and she went on. "They would certainly be a perfect place to store contraband." She tapped her lips. "As I recall, there used to be other entrances scattered about the countryside, but most of them had been filled in or forgotten . . . but

I know where one of them is—it's located in one of your barns near the main road leading to the village. We used it as children."

He shook his head, smiling ruefully. "I should have told you before now. If only I had I'd have known all of this weeks ago. . . ."

She kissed his nose. "And let that be a lesson to you."

Most evenings Cornelia ate with them, but upon occasion, and tonight was one of them, she preferred dining in her rooms. Since both Barnaby and Emily felt it was ostentatious to dine in the huge, formal dining room, they often ate a simple evening meal in the morning room.

With Peckham hovering about they didn't discuss the topic uppermost in their minds, but after the meal, with the table cleared, they lingered over coffee. They were just preparing to rise when Peckham walked into the room. Bowing, he said, "My lord, your cousin has arrived."

Barnaby's and Emily's eyes met.

"Show him in," Barnaby murmured, elation surging through him. At last, his would-be killer would have a face.

But for all his elation, his heart sank when Simon, a teasing smile lurking on his lips, strolled into the room.

Chapter 22

Emily gasped in shock. Suspecting one of Barnaby's cousins wanted to murder him had been bad enough, but for it to be *Simon!* Devastated, she could hardly look at him, this friend of her childhood, this *beast* who had tried to kill her husband.

Barnaby was equally shocked and aware of a bitter disappointment. He'd *liked* Simon. But for the culprit to be the youngest Joslyn cousin shouldn't have been a surprise. When his two brothers had returned to Monks Abbey, Simon had remained behind at Windmere . . . to kill him. He and Lamb had discussed the possibility that it could have been Simon that had laid the trap for him the morning Satan had been tripped, but dismissed it. Because, Barnaby admitted savagely, I didn't want it to be him. I *liked* him, he thought again, a mixture of rage and sorrow twisting his guts.

Simon sensed something was wrong and his smile faltered. Halting abruptly a few feet away, he said, "Have I arrived at a bad time? I know I should have written first, but something came up and I . . ." He smiled uncertainly. "I can stay in the village if it is inconvenient for me to be here right now."

Rising to his feet, Barnaby shook his head. "No. No. Nothing is wrong. We were just surprised to have a guest arrive this late." Meeting Simon in the middle of the room, he shook his hand and, indicating a place at the table, said, "Please, come join us. Have you eaten? Shall I ring for Peckham to bring you something?"

Barnaby's manner eased the awkwardness and Simon said, "No, that it isn't necessary—I've already eaten . . . at Lord Broadfoot's." He grinned at Emily as he took a seat and added, "Laugh if you will, but I came to see him about a horse."

Trying to react naturally, she exclaimed, "Never say so! You know he is not reliable when it comes to horses."

Simon chuckled. "I know. I know. But I was in the market for a new pair and he wrote me, extolling the virtues of a stunning pair of chestnuts he has for sale and I thought I'd take a chance that for once he had actually gotten his hands on something worthy. I rode over this morning from Monks Abbey." He sent Emily an apologetic glance. "The moment I arrived at Broadfoot's I should have had him send one of his servants over with a note. I apologize for not doing so."

"Oh, pay it no heed," Emily said. Infusing warmth into her voice, she added, "Of course, you're always welcome at Windmere. We are family, after all."

"And Broadfoot's horses?" Barnaby asked. "Did the pair live up to his praises?"

"Well, they are evenly matched, all right," Simon replied with dancing eyes, "and both of them tied at the knees and unable to do more than a polite shuffle."

Emily and Barnaby laughed politely. Toying with his empty cup, Barnaby said, "I'd have been happy to check them out for you first and saved you a trip."

"Simon should have known better," Emily muttered. "Broadfoot is the worst judge of horseflesh I've ever known—everybody who knows him, knows it."

"You're right—I should have known better," Simon admitted, "but there was always the chance . . ." He shrugged. "Nothing ventured, nothing gained."

Emily managed to keep her emotions in check, smiling when necessary and acting as normally as possible, but all the while, fury and disbelief raged in her breast. She'd known Simon since childhood: he'd always been kind to her, protecting her from bullying from his older brothers and making her smile with his silly teasing and yet it seemed that he was also capable of cold-blooded murder. Of her husband, she reminded herself fiercely. Unconsciously her fingers curled about a bread knife still on the table and she fought against the urge to hurl it right into Simon's smiling face.

An hour later, with Simon safely shown to his rooms by Peckham, and Emily and Barnaby retired to her sitting room upstairs, she confessed, "It was all I could do not to take that knife and . . ." She took a deep breath and a note of pain in her voice, she said, "Oh, Barnaby, that it is Simon is unbelievable! He is the last person I would have suspected."

Barnaby nodded. "I'm having trouble believing it myself, but it has to be him. I'm convinced it was one of my cousins who was meeting with Nolles this afternoon—and there is no sign of Mathew or Thomas." He grimaced. "Like it or not, Simon is here and they are . . . not."

Sinking down onto the sofa, Emily kicked off her satin slippers and said, "What a devious character he is—writing to Mathew, claiming to be worried about you, pretending to be concerned for you, when he is the very one trying to kill you!"

"He's clever, I'll grant you that."

"But what are we going to do about him?" Emily asked,

watching Barnaby pacing restlessly back and forth in front of her.

Barnaby had no answer for her. He didn't see much would be gained by confronting Simon with his suspicion— he had no proof, and Simon would most likely brush it all aside and prove to be even wilier. Nor could he go to Mathew with those same suspicions. Even if Mathew was entirely innocent, Mathew's first instinct would be to protect his brother. He sighed. They'd have to devise a plan to catch Simon in the act. . . . Not a pleasant thought, when the "act" meant his life would be in peril, he admitted.

Yet, as he considered the situation, a simple idea occurred to him. If tomorrow afternoon he and the others went boldly into the tunnels, perhaps, even with the young riding officer, Lieutenant Deering, and trumpeted their discovery of, hopefully, a large stash of contraband, wouldn't that solve everything? If the reason behind the attacks on him was to prevent discovery of the use of the tunnels by the Nolles gang, wouldn't that reason have disappeared? And once the use of the tunnels became known to the revenuers, wouldn't the smugglers be forced to find a new place to hide their contraband?

Sitting down beside Emily, he put forth his ideas for ending the situation.

Emily wasn't happy about any of it. Bluntly, she said, "Acting as bait to draw him out is foolish. Even with all of us shadowing you, there is every possibility that Simon still might be able to kill you—and it will do us no good to know your murderer if you are dead." Her lovely eyes full of anxiety, she said, "I love you . . . I don't want to become a widow within weeks of having become a bride."

Taking her into his arms, Barnaby sought to reassure her. He kissed her tenderly and, lifting his lips from hers, he said, "And I love you—I want to grow very old with you by my side and our children and grandchildren gathered around us. Sweetheart, I'm not about to take unnecessary chances."

"Offering yourself as bait isn't taking chances?" she asked sharply.

He shrugged. "Perhaps a little, but if Simon couldn't kill me when I had no idea who it was behind the attacks, what makes you think he'll be successful now that we know who he is?"

"I don't like it," she said, her expression tight and unhappy.

"I'm not particularly keen on it myself," Barnaby admitted, "but if we don't expose him and simply find the contraband and dutifully turn it over to Lieutenant Deering, Simon, Nolles and even Peckham will escape justice. They'll just set up their operation somewhere else in the county." His jaw tightened. "Of course, Peckham won't be our butler anymore, but being let go without references doesn't seem quite punishment enough for my liking."

Emily made a face. "I agree, and while I don't like it that Simon and his cohorts would escape punishment, I much prefer that to having you murdered." Her fingers traced his jaw. "Having you dead would make me dreadfully unhappy."

He kissed her fingertips, a wave of love flooding him. The last thing he wanted was to die, and he didn't plan to do so, but he couldn't dismiss Emily's fear lightly—if he offered himself as bait, there was always the chance that something would go wrong and Simon would kill him. And then there was Emily herself . . .

Keeping her safe and out of danger was his paramount concern, but his Amazonian bride, he admitted torn between pride and dread, was hardly going to loiter about while Simon attempted to kill him. Barnaby wanted her out of it, but at the moment, he didn't see any way that could be accomplished.

Abruptly, he said, "We can accomplish no more tonight. We have to talk to Lamb and Luc."

* * *

Barnaby informed Lamb of Simon's presence in the house late that evening when Lamb returned from visiting Luc. Like Emily and Barnaby, Lamb initially had trouble believing the person trying to kill Barnaby was Simon, but he accepted the idea more readily than had Emily and Barnaby.

Helping Barnaby out of his jacket as he prepared for bed, Lamb said, "It makes sense, if you think about it. Simon's the youngest of the brothers and his fortune would have been the least of them all. He'd have inherited enough though to finance some smuggling, and if his profits were managed wisely, he could turn a small fortune into a very large one."

"I'm not arguing with you," Barnaby said, ripping off his cravat and tossing it on the chair. Glancing at Lamb, he asked, "Will you go to Luc tonight?"

Lamb shook his head. "Too many people might wonder why, having just returned from the Dower House, I suddenly need to return. I'll see him in the morning." He looked at Barnaby, frowning. "She absolutely has to be part of this?"

Barnaby grinned at him. "If you remember, you're the one who named her 'Amazon.' Do you really think we can keep her out of it?"

Lamb grimaced. "Probably not."

It was afternoon when Barnaby and Emily met with Lamb and Luc at the Dower House. Cornelia had been delighted by Simon's visit and neither Barnaby nor Emily had the heart to tell her the truth. Cornelia's presence, however, helped Simon's stay seem normal, but by the time Cornelia disappeared upstairs for her afternoon nap and Simon had ridden off to the village, Emily was exhausted from smiling and pretending everything was fine.

Being greeted by Walker at the Dower House lifted her spirits and she was smiling when she and Barnaby walked into the burgundy-and-gray sitting room where Lamb and Luc awaited them. Once Walker left the room and Emily had taken a seat in a figured gray velvet chair by the fire, Luc said, "What a devilish coil!" Looking at Barnaby who had taken up a position just behind his wife near the fire, he asked, "How do you intend to flush him out?"

Barnaby sighed, knowing Emily wasn't going to like the plan that he'd finally thought best. Letting Simon and Nolles walk away didn't set well with him. Not looking at Emily, he said, "I see only one way and that is for me to exhibit myself like a piece of raw meat before a tiger and hope he takes the bait." He smiled at Lamb and Luc. "And once he has me between his claws, that you, my two stalwart fellows, pounce on him before he does me very much damage."

His wife looked at him as if he had lost his mind. "That's the very *worst* idea," she said tightly, "I've ever heard."

"Actually," Lamb said, rubbing his chin, "Luc and I discussed something similar this morning. Of course, we could just tell the authorities, but I mislike letting rats scamper free." Avoiding Emily's glare, he said, "We might not be able to catch Nolles in our net, but if we catch Simon, Nolles will have lost his big London backer, which will hurt him—that and the loss of the Windmere tunnels." He eyed Barnaby. "But in order to catch Simon, we have to draw him out someway and you're the only thing he wants."

Outraged, Emily snapped, "Easy for you to say—it's not your life at risk."

"This is true," Luc said, "but Simon doesn't want Lamb, he wants your husband—better we control the situation than allow Simon to do so."

Her head down bent, Emily said in a small voice, "I don't want them to escape unscathed either, but I want my husband alive more than I want them to suffer retribution. There *has* to be another way."

Barnaby came around and sat a hip on the arm of her

chair. Forcing her chin up, his eyes on hers, he said, "I'll take all the precautions I can—remember we have an advantage. We *know* who is trying to kill me and we know why Simon wants me out of the picture."

She didn't take much comfort from his words and she demanded, "Is there nothing I can say that will dissuade you?"

His heart ached for causing her distress, but Barnaby shook his head. "Not unless you can come up with a better idea."

She couldn't and though she listened intently as they discussed plans to keep Barnaby safe, adding her own biting comments from time to time, she wasn't reassured. The only thing she agreed with was that they explore the tunnels as soon as possible and discover if the smugglers were actually using them.

"The tunnels should be entered through the old barn," Emily said. "That way we avoid Peckham or any of the other servants wondering why we're interested in the wine cellar. If the smugglers are using the tunnels, the contraband will be stored in a place that provides the easiest entrance and exit—the old barn. The tunnel was widened at the end and, as I recall, there's a large cavern—perfectly suitable for storing a large amount of contraband." Her jaw set, she glowered at Barnaby and continued. "There's no reason for all of us to go trooping through the tunnels. Obviously, I need to go but I only want one other person with me . . . and that person will *not* be you. Lamb or Luc can accompany me."

Barnaby would have argued, but the glitter in her eyes told him she would not back down from her stand and further comment would be useless. "Very well. Who do you want to go with you?"

Without hesitation, she said, "Lamb."

Luc looked disappointed, but her choice made sense. If he was going to be poking about in a tunnel with the possibility that he might come face-to-face with a smuggler, he'd prefer Lamb at his side rather than a man who had just risen from his sickbed not many days ago.

"When?" Barnaby asked, not happy with his wife risking her neck while he remained safely behind.

"Now," she said, rising to her feet and shaking out the skirts of her indigo velvet riding habit. "It is the middle of the day and none of the smugglers will be about. Simon is in the village and Peckham is at the house. Our horses are saddled and ready. Lamb and I should be gone less than an hour."

Barnaby looked at Lamb. "Bring her back to me safe and sound."

Lamb nodded.

Watching Emily and Lamb walk out of the room was the most difficult, painful thing Barnaby had ever been forced to do. Every instinct demanded that he stop her from leaving, the need to protect her, to keep her safe clawing at his vitals. He fought down the frantic urge to call her back, but he knew it would be futile—just as he would not be prevented from offering himself as bait, so would his wife not be diverted from her task. He scowled. Sometimes, he decided bitterly, they were too damned much alike for comfort.

There was only one exchange between Emily and Lamb as they mounted their horses and prepared to ride away from the Dower House.

Eyeing her closed expression, Lamb said, "You're angry."

She flashed him a look that scorched his bones and retorted in a voice that did not invite further conversation, "No, I'm not, angry. I'm *furious*."

Pointing to a track through the woods that avoided the main drive and would give them cover, Emily kicked her horse into a canter and Lamb meekly followed. Brave he might be, but not even he was prepared to take on a blazing-eyed Amazon.

Twelve minutes later, Emily turned her horse off the narrow path they'd been following around the bottom of a series of sloping hills. She guided her horse several yards into a patch of trees that crowded along the side of the path before halting. Dismounting, she said, "From here we are hidden by those hills over there, but as the crow flies, we are less than an eighth of a mile from the house. The barn is about fifty yards ahead, through that stand of beeches. Tie your horse and follow me."

Lamb admired her coolness and the silent way she slipped through the woods. The Amazon knew what she was about and he decided that if his back was against the wall, he'd be honored to have her at his side. The woods thinned and the barn came into view. Emily examined the area carefully and then leaving the cover of the trees hurried across an open expanse and sidled up next to the rear of the old wooden barn.

Looking over her shoulder at Lamb she said softly, "The main opening faces the road, but around the corner from us there is a smaller door—we'll enter that way."

A moment later, they were inside the barn, both noting that the door opened easily—perhaps a little too easily for an old seldom-used building. It was gloomy inside the structure, the scent of hay and livestock filling their noses. Emily took a moment for her eyes to adjust to the dim light and then she moved forward purposefully. A row of sagging stalls stood along one side of the building and on the other, bundles of hay and straw were piled high, leaving a wide aisleway running down the middle of the barn.

Dust motes floated in the air—kicked up from their feet as Emily, followed closely by Lamb, crept forward. Their progress was careful in the dimness of the interior, all of their senses alert for the presence of others. They did a hasty reconnoiter, determining at the moment that they were the only inhabitants. Stopping in the middle of the barn, Emily stared at the thick carpet of hay and straw strewn across the floor.

Softly she said, "If anybody looked, the hay would hide any signs of their activity."

Lamb nodded. "Probably laid down on their way out after unloading the contraband." He looked around. "Where's the entrance?"

"Over here," she said, moving away. Halfway down the row of stalls, she stopped and, throwing open the heavy stall door, with Lamb at her heels, she stepped inside the stall. The ease with which she had opened the door to the stall told its own story, and a quick examination of the catch and hinges revealed that they had been well oiled. The floor of the stall was heaped with straw, but it took only a moment to kick it aside, exposing a trapdoor. Lamb grasped the handle hidden in the straw and lifted. The door opened soundlessly. A black hole yawned at their feet, the tip of a ladder showing at the edge of the darkness.

Lamb cursed under his breath. "We didn't bring a lantern."

Emily grinned at him, the ride to the barn having banished most of her fury. She edged around the trapdoor and reached into the manger filled with hay. Triumphantly, from beneath the hay, she pulled a small lantern and a piece of flint.

Lantern lit, after a short argument over which one should go first, Lamb descended the short wooden ladder. Clutching the skirts of her riding habit, Emily scrambled down behind him.

Lamb hoisted the lantern and, staring at the piles and stacks of contraband pushed against the walls of the big cavern he was standing in, he whistled. Together they walked along the rows of goods, barrels and tubs of overproof brandy and gin, ropes of tobacco, bolts of silk and velvet and packets of lace and fine thread, among other things.

"Merciful heavens!" Emily exclaimed, awed. "This isn't just from one run. It's a storehouse of contraband—they can supply anyone with anything at any time."

"I agree," Lamb said. "We've found what we're looking for. We need to leave."

Though the impulse to explore further was strong, beyond showing him where the tunnel narrowed and would lead to the house, Emily didn't argue. Within minutes, they were out of the cavern, the lantern doused and, once cooled, hidden under the hay in the manger. The trapdoor was shut and the straw scattered over it. Careful to leave no sign of disturbance, they exited the barn and hastened to their horses.

Rushing into the room where Barnaby and Luc waited, her face bright with exhilaration, Emily launched herself into Barnaby's arms and cried, "We were right! We found a *mountain* of contraband. There's enough goods stored in the tunnel to supply half of London for six months."

Clutching Emily to him as if he would never let her go, Barnaby glanced over at Lamb, who followed her into the room. Smiling, Lamb nodded. "They're not only using the tunnel to hide their contraband, they're using it to warehouse the goods. They can go weeks without making a run yet still keep their buyers supplied." His smile faded. "I'm not surprised that Simon wants you dead—there's a bloody fortune involved. This is no small smuggling operation by a band of desperate fishermen—it's huge and worth killing for."

The mention of Simon's lethal designs on her husband shattered Emily's exhilaration. Even with his arms cradling her close, a chill slid down her spine. Forcing herself to leave behind the comfort of his warm body, she made one more attempt to change Barnaby's mind about placing himself in danger. "Revealing the whereabouts of the contraband to Lieutenant Deering would be devastating to the smugglers," she said. "They'd lose their warehouse and the contraband. Simon would have no reason to try to kill you."

Barnaby shook his head. "I don't want to simply take away Simon's reason for wanting me dead: I want him and the Nolles gang destroyed. Yes, losing the hiding place and the goods would be a massive blow, but it wouldn't stop them. The contraband would be in the hands of the authorities, but everyone connected to the smuggling operation would remain untouched." When Emily started to argue, he warned, "Remember, all we'd be giving Deering is the location and the smuggled goods—we have suspicion aplenty, but we have no proof of Nolles and Simon's participation. We can tell Deering what we suspect, but without proof he can't touch them. I'll wager that within a matter of months, perhaps, weeks, with Simon's backing, Nolles would be in business again. Mayhap, not on the scale they are now—at least not right away, but in time, they'd reestablish themselves. All Deering will do is eliminate one hiding place and deal them a financial blow, but nothing else. The gang, the contacts, the routes and the bribed revenue officers will all remain." A grim smile flitted across his face. "I'm sure Simon is clever enough to find another place to safely warehouse the enormous amount of contraband he's moving regularly from France to London now. It might not be as convenient, but I'm sure it exists." He frowned, struck by a thought. "In fact, I wouldn't be surprised if he already has a site selected. He's not a stupid man—he'd have considered all angles."

Gloomily, Emily conceded that Barnaby was right. Blast him! Simon and Nolles had to be destroyed once and for all.

It was difficult for her to greet Simon in her usual friendly manner that evening. She smiled and laughed at the appropriate times, but her heart wasn't in it. Cornelia was in fine form flirting with both gentlemen and Barnaby appeared to have no trouble conversing amiably with a man he knew had tried three times to kill him and would, most likely, try again. Emily was grateful for their contributions because she could barely bring herself to speak to Simon. While the conversation ranged around her, from beneath her lashes Emily studied Simon, wondering how he could be so dastardly, wondering how she could have misjudged him so badly. How could he accept Barnaby's hospitality and act as if he enjoyed his company, yet all the while plan to kill him? Her lips thinned and rage billowed through her. He was a black-hearted beast, she thought savagely, glaring at him over the rim of her wineglass. By God, she'd like nothing better than to run him through.

Simon's eyes met hers and fear rushed through her. Praying to God that he had not glimpsed her rage, she forced a smile and glanced away. After that, to her unease, she caught Simon staring at her from time to time, his expression puzzled. She wasn't, she decided, very good at deception.

Emily got through the long evening and she was thankful when Cornelia bid the gentlemen good night. Knowing that Simon wouldn't be so foolhardy to attack Barnaby in his own home and that the watchful Lamb would be nearby, Emily joined her great-aunt, leaving Barnaby and Simon to amuse themselves.

Walking up the stairs, Cornelia glanced at her and asked, "Do you want to tell me what Simon has done to be in your black books?"

Emily's step faltered, but recovering, she sent Cornelia what she hoped was an innocent look. "Simon? In my black books? Why, whatever do you mean?"

Cornelia's magnificent eyes narrowed. "You never were a very good liar and you have not improved with time."

She sighed. Cornelia was right: she wasn't a very good

liar—and there was no need to lie to her great-aunt. She and Barnaby hadn't intended to hide anything from Cornelia— there just hadn't been time to tell her. As they reached the landing, she asked, "The hour isn't late. Shall I join you in your room for a chat?"

Cornelia stared at her a moment. "Yes," she said. "I'd enjoy that."

Arriving at Cornelia's rooms, the minute the door to her sitting room shut, Cornelia said, "All right. Tell me what is going on."

Emily did, leaving nothing out.

When she finally stopped speaking, Cornelia snorted. "You're fair and far off if you think that Simon Joslyn is a smuggler and trying to kill Barnaby. The boy doesn't have it in him—and you should know it. My money's on Nolles— he has as much reason to want Barnaby dead as anyone." Her brow arched. "After all, he is the smuggler. Why does he need anyone else to do his dirty work for him?"

Emily stared openmouthed at her for a moment. Was it possible that Nolles was acting on his own? It made sense. Then she remembered the London backer and her lips snapped shut. Shaking her head, she said, "You're forgetting whoever is backing the operation. That person certainly isn't Nolles."

"You're right," Cornelia said slowly. Unhappily, she looked back at Emily. "I just can't believe that Simon would align himself with smugglers and involve himself in murder." Her lip curled. "If you'd mentioned Jeffery's name, now *that* I'd have no trouble believing."

Emily smiled wearily. "Jeffery doesn't have any money. He could never finance the sort of operation Nolles and his men are running."

"I cannot believe that it is Simon," Cornelia said bluntly. She wagged a finger at Emily. "But if you're going to persist

in this folly, you're going to have to be a better hostess than
you have been so far if you don't want him to become suspicious."

Simon *was* suspicious. He knew Emily too well not to
know that something was up. His lips quirked. From her
glances tonight, he feared she'd separate his head from his
shoulders, but rack his brains though he did, he could think
of nothing he had done to offend or upset her. Remembering
the hostile gleam in her eyes, he shook his head. She looked
at him as if he were an enemy. . . . Barnaby had hidden his
reactions better, but there was something in the way his host
looked at him. . . .

Alone in his rooms he stalked restlessly around the gracious sitting room, pondering the problem. Barnaby's watchful reserve hadn't escaped his notice either. He dismissed the
notion that they were annoyed at his unexpected arrival.
Barnaby had waved aside his offer to stay in the village, so
that wasn't the cause of their reactions to him.

When last they'd parted, they had all been on the same
side, united against whoever had tried to kill Barnaby. That
whoever wanted Barnaby dead hadn't struck again had been
encouraging, but while Tom thought they were overreacting,
he and Mathew weren't betting that the problem had simply
evaporated. Simon had come to look at Broadfoot's chestnuts, but that, he admitted, had just been an excuse to call
upon Barnaby and Emily. He'd wanted to see for himself that
all was well at Windmere and Mathew had agreed that a
friendly visit wouldn't come amiss.

Something was going on, that much was obvious: Emily
and Barnaby didn't trust him any longer and he needed to
know why. He sighed. And Mathew needed to know.

Chapter 23

Within minutes the next morning of a Windmere servant departing for Monks Abbey, Lamb relayed the news to Barnaby that Simon had sent a note to Mathew. Lamb would have given much for a glimpse of the contents of that note. Barnaby expressed a similar thought.

"I wonder what was so important that Simon felt the need to write his brother," Barnaby mused, sipping from the cup of coffee Lamb had brought with him.

Despite the early hour—a pink-and-gold dawn was just spilling over the horizon—Barnaby was already up and garbed for the day. He preferred mornings, but his wife . . . A private smile curved his lips. His bride was still sweetly asleep after a night of passionate lovemaking.

Lamb shrugged at Barnaby and offered, "Reinforcements? The possibility has always existed that we have fallen into a nest of snakes and that more than one brother is involved."

Barnaby nodded. Knowing the size of the smuggling operation, it wasn't inconceivable that more than just Simon was behind the Nolles gang. It was even possible that all three brothers were filling their purses with gains from the smuggling. Their fortunes were reputed to be large—had that largeness come from contraband?

A discussion followed that left them no wiser. Setting down his empty cup, Barnaby said, "Enough. We are accomplishing nothing."

Lamb made a face. "I agree. I'll see Luc later this morning and tell him about the note to Mathew." He grinned at Barnaby. "And you'll tell your Amazon—perhaps she will see something we have missed."

Preparing to leave, Lamb said, "What are your plans for the day? Should Luc and I be ready to accompany you anywhere?"

Barnaby shook his head. "No. I have meetings with Worley again and several of my tenants throughout the day. I'd like to convince a few to experiment with crop rotation and increased fodder production, as well as suggest that they consider diversifying instead of relying almost exclusively on sheep. Windmere and several of the farms could run substantially larger herds of cattle than they do presently."

"What you're saying," Lamb murmured with a grin, "is in spite of your title, that you're a farmer at heart and instead of tobacco and sugar, your worries are now sheep and cattle."

Barnaby laughed. "Don't forget crop rotation."

When Barnaby informed Emily of Simon's message to Mathew, she frowned. They were in her sitting room, preferring its privacy to the morning room and Peckham's ubiquitous presence. She might not have risen before dawn as had her husband, but Emily was no lie-abed. The time was not yet eight o'clock in the morning and wearing a finely woven woolen gown in a charming shade of mauve, her fair hair caught up in a neat chignon at her neck, she was ready for the day.

On a nearby table, a silver tray bearing the Joslyn crest

held the remains of her breakfast—toast, coddled eggs and some strawberries from one of the Windmere hothouses, along with coffee. Pouring herself and Barnaby a last cup of coffee, Emily absently stirred cream, fresh from the herd of dairy cattle on the estate, in her cup, thinking over the implications of Simon's actions.

"That can only mean one of two things," she said finally. "Either Mathew is involved and Simon wants his help, or Simon is innocent and wants Mathew's help."

Barnaby hadn't considered the latter conclusion. It was his turn to frown and he said slowly, "I suppose that is possible. After the last attack on me, Simon wrote to Mathew that time, too." Nettled, he muttered, "Blast it! Perhaps all of our thoughts are wrong and none of my cousins have anything to do with the smuggling—everything could be Nolles's doing."

"Cornelia thinks we are wrong about Simon," Emily said uneasily. "And she did suggest Nolles. . . ." Her lips twisted. "And Jeffery, except we all know he doesn't have any money."

Barnaby half smiled. "Your cousin is capable of many things, but this operation took money and brains and it's my observation that Jeffery is sadly lacking in both."

Emily sighed. "I don't disagree." She looked over at her husband. "So what are we to do?"

"Until we come up with some other plan, all we can do is go about our day as normally as possible."

"And wait for Mathew's arrival," she said drily. "Whatever his reasons for doing so, I think we can safely assume he'll come in answer to Simon's note." Putting down her cup, she asked, "How soon do you think it will be before he drives up to the front of Windmere?"

"Late this afternoon at the earliest, but before noon tomorrow at the latest."

*   *   *

Barnaby spent the majority of the day in his study as planned, but in the afternoon, he and Lamb couldn't resist a stealthy visit to the wine cellar to look for the hidden door. They both felt the timing was propitious. It was Peckham's half day and the butler was gone from the house until late that evening; Simon was visiting Luc at the Dower House and Emily and Cornelia were busy at the vicarage, helping prepare baskets of food for the needy in the area. After ascertaining that the other servants were busy about their tasks, Lamb and Barnaby slipped down the stairs to the cellar. The occasional torch hung on the stone walls created small pools of lights within the darkness and guided their steps.

They'd thought they'd escaped detection, but as they entered the wide hallway of the lower regions of the house that led to the wine cellar, they met Tilden exiting the room, a pair of bottles of burgundy in each hand.

"Milord!" he exclaimed, startled to see the viscount in the cellar.

"Ah, good afternoon, Tilden," Barnaby said, cursing their luck. Eyeing the bottles, he added gamely, "Resupplying the liquor cabinet, I see."

Tilden smiled and nodded, though still puzzled by Barnaby's presence in the nether reaches of the house.

Lamb spoke up smoothly. "I was telling my lord about the extensive and varied collection of spirits that had been laid down by the previous viscount." Lamb chuckled. "I spoke so highly of it, he wished to see it for himself."

Tilden's face cleared. "Of course! I am surprised that Peckham has not given you a tour of the wine cellar before now. It is his province and he guards it jealously." He grinned and held up the two bottles. "Only when he is away do I dare invade it."

"Well, then, if that is the case, in the interest of keeping peace," said Barnaby, smiling, "my visit today shall remain a secret between us."

Tilden grinned. "As you wish, my lord." And went on his way.

Entering the darkness of the wine cellar, Barnaby said, "I could have wished he hadn't seen us, but I think we can trust him not to prattle."

"I agree," Lamb said, as he quickly lit one of the torches just inside the doorway. "Even if he were to say something to some of the other servants, Peckham is not well liked and I doubt word would get back to him of our little foray."

After Barnaby had taken down a torch from the walls inside the wine cellar and lit it, guided by the flickering light, even knowing what they were looking for, it took them several minutes before they discovered it. The door was concealed in the far corner of the room behind a tall rack full of bottles of brandy, hock and Madeira. Upon closer examination they found the catch on the rack that allowed it to swing out and away from its position.

Only a blank corner met their gaze. A careful examination revealed that the adjoining racks covered the seams of the door, and after a further search, Barnaby spied the small handle hidden behind a bottle of burgundy. He gently pulled the handle and magically a large doorway appeared in front of him. A worn stone staircase led downward.

In the light of their torches, the two men descended and studied the walls, eventually finding the mechanisms that worked the door and corner rack from inside the tunnel. Eyes glittering with excitement, Barnaby had to see for himself how well it worked. Leaving Barnaby behind, grumbling, Lamb stepped back into the wine cellar.

With Barnaby standing on the stairs, Lamb watching, Barnaby pulled the lever on the wall and the door slid shut. A moment later the corner rack swung smoothly, silently back into place, leaving Lamb staring at a rack full of bottles of spirits. A moment later, the movements were reversed and Barnaby reappeared.

"So now we know," Barnaby said as he stepped into the wine cellar, "how Peckham disappeared." He glanced back at the doorway. "By Jove, but I'd like to do more exploring—actually follow the tunnel to the other end."

"You need your wife for that," Lamb said drily. "She said that there are other tunnels but only one leads to the old barn—the last thing we need is to get lost and suffer the humiliation of being rescued by your wife."

Barnaby winced but continued to look longingly at the beckoning doorway. Almost to himself, he said, "I'll wager the tunnel Peckham is using is well marked and that we could follow it with no trouble."

"No doubt, but do you want to face the wrath of your Amazon," Lamb asked, the azure eyes smiling, "should you do so without her?"

"Excellent point," Barnaby said absently, staring mesmerized by the darkness beyond the range of their torches. "But since she's going to be mad as fire," he murmured, "with our antics today as it is"—he glanced back at Lamb and grinned—"I've a mind to go exploring. Are you with me?"

"I'm sure as the devil not going to let you go disappearing down here by yourself," Lamb said, an answering grin curving his mouth.

Both men were aware of the reasons why exploring the tunnel would be unwise, but the lure proved irresistible. Like two schoolboys in search of adventure, after closing the secret door, their torches lighting the way, they set off.

The tunnel was not large. In several places, their heads brushed the ceiling. The tunnel was narrow, hardly wider than their shoulders, and thinking of the endless buckets of dirt and rock dug out by pickax and shovel and hauled to the surface, Barnaby wasn't surprised. The tunnel in which they

walked would have taken months, perhaps years to con-
struct. Some oak beams for support had been added, but
stopping to examine some of them, it was apparent they
were very old—older than the last century when legend had
it that his ancestor had constructed the tunnel to hide his
smuggling practices. No, the tunnel had been dug out long
before that and Barnaby suspected his ancestor had only re-
opened an existing tunnel.

Lamb echoed his thoughts. "You'll never convince me
that someone spent the time, money and manpower to build
something like this for the purpose of hiding and moving
smuggled goods. I'll wager it was constructed when Windmere was a fortified castle and was built to move troops
around out of sight of the enemy."

Barnaby agreed. "That makes far more sense than the
smuggling legend—but like most legends it appears that
only part of it is true."

As they explored, they passed two openings leading off
from the main tunnel, but a quick glance with their torches
revealed that while these other tunnels might have been
passable once, they had caved in and were no longer usable.

The tunnel traveled fairly straight, only curving when the
makers had hit solid rock and had been forced to change direction around it. The two men pressed onward, noting periodically torches hanging on the walls. Examining one of
them, Barnaby smiled grimly. "This is no ancient torch—
and it's been used recently."

"Probably during Peckham's last trip down here," Lamb
replied.

The first signs of the smugglers' activities came into view
when they spied several ropes of tobacco piled along the
edge of the tunnel near their feet.

"How much farther to the end do you think?" Barnaby
asked, staring at the tobacco.

"Not far," Lamb said. "Your wife indicated yesterday that

as the crow flies, the barn is less than an eighth of a mile from the house. Unless I miss my guess, we've come nearly that far already."

Edging past more stacks of contraband, they rounded a bend and stepped into the cavern Lamb had seen with Emily yesterday.

Astonished by the size of the area and the rows, stacks and piles of smuggled goods before him, Barnaby whistled. "What do you want to wager that it was the creation of this cavern that gave rise to the legend that our ancestors built the tunnels in the first place?"

"You're most likely right."

Aware that smuggling activities commonly took place under the cover of darkness, Barnaby hadn't been worried about stumbling across any smugglers this afternoon, yet as he stood at the edge of that large cavern, a feeling of unease swept through him. His head lifted and like an animal scenting danger, his gaze raked the area in front of him. The wavering light of his torch caused shadows to slide and jump over the stacks and barrels of contraband, but he saw nothing to alarm him.

Still, as he stepped out of the tunnel and into the cavern, he whispered to Lamb, "Keep your wits about you."

Lamb muttered, "I'm not likely to let them stray down here."

The two men edged cautiously toward the center of the cavern, stopping when they came to a cleared space that contained a chair and a wooden table; several pieces of paper scattered across the scarred surface. As if hastily thrown down, a quill lay amongst the papers, a pewter ink holder and a small lantern sat off to one side of the table. In the light of his torch, Barnaby saw the wet gleam of ink on the quill and the hair on the back of his neck rose. Someone had been down here using the quill not long ago. . . .

Cursing himself for blundering, he took a quick step

away from the table. His eyes met Lamb's and he hissed, "Douse your lantern! Someone is here."

But it was too late. Even as he reached to kill his torch, a half-dozen figures appeared from behind the stacks of contraband and surrounded them.

"We'll take the torches," said Tom Joslyn, as he stepped forward, the pistol in his hand pointed at Barnaby's heart.

Within minutes Barnaby and Lamb were stripped of their torches and securely tied up. Arms fastened behind their backs, their ankles roped together, they sat on the ground, shoulder-to-shoulder, their backs against a stack of barrels of brandy. Full of rage at his own stupidity, Barnaby stared at Tom's smug features, his agile brain considering and discarding a dozen different means of escape.

Barnaby knew that Lamb would be doing the same thing. And if he had to fight for his life, then he couldn't ask for a better companion at his side than Lamb. He glanced around, recognizing Peckham standing beside the table and realizing after a closer look that the other men were some of the brutes he'd seen at The Ram's Head.

The situation wasn't as desperate as it appeared. He had Lamb at his side . . . and though their pockets and the inside of their coats had been searched for weapons, the knife inside his boot had not been discovered, nor the equally dangerous blade Barnaby knew Lamb carried. The smugglers should have known better, but they'd been looking for pistols, not concealed knives. . . .

The lantern on the table was relit and Tom Joslyn seated himself on a corner of the table, a satisfied smile on his lips. Looking at Barnaby and Lamb trussed up like a pair of Christmas peacocks before him, Tom said, "To think that after all my scheming you simply wander into my hands like, ah"—he grinned—"lambs to slaughter."

"That remains to be seen," Barnaby said in a bored tone. "You've not managed to kill me yet."

Tom's face darkened. "That may be, but I'm afraid this time your luck has run out." He leaned forward. "Matt should have been Viscount Joslyn," he snapped. "All his life he was groomed for the title—it was his and you stole it from him!" Hatred glittered in the azure eyes. "Bah! Every time I look at you I am reminded of a pig dressed up in silk." His voice shook with emotion and he spat, "Every time I've had to bow and call you 'my lord' the words burned like acid in my mouth and I dreamed of the day you'd die and Matt would take his rightful place."

His gaze watchful, Barnaby said, "Ah, so your desire for my death has nothing to do with keeping your connection with Nolles and his gang a secret?"

"I'll admit your death will be killing two birds with one stone," Tom answered. "Matt inherits the title and Windmere and I no longer have to worry that you'll poke your nose where it doesn't belong." A smile tugged at his lips. "Your death will be my noble deed for my brother—giving him all that was meant to be his from birth."

"Don't delude yourself," Barnaby growled. "You're not killing me for Mathew, you're killing me to hide your lucrative arrangement with Nolles."

Tom smirked. "Well, there is that. Even if Matt were to discover the source of my fortune, he'd not betray me." For a moment, something vicious flashed in Tom's eyes, "Now Simon . . . Simon would turn me over to the revenue service in the blink of an eye." Looking thoughtful, he rubbed his chin. "I fear that my younger brother may suffer a fatal accident a few months from now." He smiled at Barnaby. "Of course, should that cow of yours be with child, I'll have to take care of her first. Such a tragedy it will be. First you and then your wife and her unborn child. . . ."

Barnaby surged forward, murder blazing in his eyes. Tom laughed and, standing up, kicked him in the head. Barnaby saw stars and sliding sideways, fought against the blackness that threatened to overtake him.

From beside him, he heard Lamb ask calmly, "Tell me, did you enjoy torturing kittens as a child? Or was it puppies? Certainly it had to be something defenseless, because you're too much of a coward to offer a fair fight. I wonder if his hands were untied if you'd dare touch him."

"Shut your filthy mouth!" Tom snarled, striking Lamb in the face with his fist. Turning to Barnaby, he prodded him with his foot. "Who knows you're down here?"

Fighting off the dizziness, Barnaby struggled into a sitting position. "You expect me to tell you? And if I don't, what will you do?" He grinned. "Kill me?"

Annoyed, Tom said, "It doesn't matter. By the time your disappearance is discovered, it'll be too late for you." A cold smile curving his lips, he said, "This time when you end up in the Channel there'll be no escape."

It was late afternoon when Emily and Cornelia returned home. Greeted by a smiling Tilden in the black-and-white tiled foyer as she handed him her gloves, Emily asked, "My lord? Is he about?"

Tilden hesitated. "I saw him earlier this afternoon with Lamb, but I've not seen him since."

Emily smiled at him. "He's probably in his study—or at the Dower House visiting his brother. Will you find him and tell him that we are home and that once my aunt and I have freshened up that we will be in the blue-and-silver salon and would like him to join us?"

Several minutes later, when Emily and Cornelia entered the salon, Emily was surprised to find the room empty. "I suppose he is at the Dower House and hasn't returned yet," Emily said, wandering around the room. She and Cornelia were very pleased with their afternoon's work at the vicarage and she'd been looking forward to relaying to Barnaby the difference his very generous donation had made to the poor in the area.

She and Cornelia spent a pleasant half hour discussing their accomplishments and future plans, but as time passed and there was no sign of Barnaby, Emily began to fidget. Where was he? She wasn't worried yet, but unease fluttered in her chest. Telling herself he was probably delayed by business, she chatted away with Cornelia, but her ears were pricked for the sound of his arrival.

Aware that Emily was only half listening to her, Cornelia said bluntly, "Ring for Tilden and ask him to find out what is delaying your husband. And stop fretting—nothing's happened to him."

Looking somewhat harassed, Tilden appeared in answer to her pull of the velvet bell rope in the corner. When Emily asked after Barnaby, Tilden muttered, "Uh, we cannot find him."

The unease in her chest bloomed into near panic. "What do you mean, you cannot find him?" she asked in a surprisingly calm tone. He's fine, she told herself. I am fearful for no reason. He's here in the house . . . somewhere.

Tugging at his cravat, Tilden said, "When I did not find him in his study or the library or any of the rooms where he would usually be, I sent one of the footmen to inquire if he was at the Dower House." He shook his head. "He was not there." Almost ringing his hands, Tilden cried, "We have searched everywhere, but there is no sign of him . . . or Lamb."

Lamb! If Lamb was with him . . . Her fear eased back and her eyes narrowed. "You said you saw him and Lamb earlier—where?"

Tilden's face cleared. "Of course. They must still be in

the wine cellar." He laughed nervously. "Milord must have decided to sample a few bottles and hasn't realized the time."

"I wouldn't bet on it," Emily said under her breath as she rushed from the room. Tilden was at her heels when she entered the wine cellar and his eyes nearly popped out of his head when she walked right over to the corner wine rack and a moment later the secret door opened. There was no sign of their passage, but she was as certain as she was standing here that Barnaby and Lamb hadn't been able to resist the opportunity to explore the tunnel on their own. Ignoring the panic nipping at her ankles, telling herself that at any moment she'd see the flicker of light that would herald their return, she stared into the darkness, willing Barnaby and Lamb to appear. But they did not.

Whirling around to look at Tilden, she demanded, "When did you see them? How long ago?"

"Um, it was hours ago—early afternoon." Pointing at the secret doorway, he asked, awed, "How long has that been there?"

Shutting the door and returning the wine rack to its customary place, she said, "Probably since Windmere was first built." She didn't have time to know if she'd been wise or incredibly stupid by showing Tilden the secret door, but the damage was done. Fixing him with a look, she said, "I trust you'll keep this to yourself?"

"Oh, indeed, milady," Tilden promised earnestly.

Her thoughts churning, she hastened to the main part of the house. Stopping to look back at Tilden, she said, "Send someone to the stables and have a horse saddled for me. Tell my aunt I'll be joining her in a few minutes."

Emily had no clear plan as she mounted the stairs to her rooms. If Tilden was correct, Barnaby and Lamb had been missing for hours. There had been time aplenty for them to have done their exploring and returned. . . . Charging into her rooms, she ran across through the sitting room, across her bedroom and into her dressing room.

Throwing wide the doors of one of the wardrobes, wild conjecture tumbling through her brain, she poked around looking for the bundle of clothes she'd brought from The Birches. If they hadn't returned, something, or *someone* had delayed them.

Frightened as she had never been in her life, she concentrated on the task at hand. Finding what she was looking for, she scrambled out of her gown and into the male attire she'd worn that first night she'd met Barnaby. Attire, she admitted grimly, she'd never thought to wear again. She snorted. That was a lie, else why had she brought it with her? Had she sensed she might have need of it?

After slipping a pistol into one pocket of her coat, she slid her knife into the other. Armed, she dragged out a black cloak from another wardrobe and whipping it around her shoulders, headed downstairs for the salon where Cornelia awaited her. Reaching the bottom of the stairs, she paused, struggling to compose herself and to make sense out of the chaos spinning in her brain. Just because Barnaby and Lamb couldn't be found didn't mean they were in danger. There could be a reasonable explanation for their absence, she reminded herself, and that reason would have nothing to do with secret tunnels, smugglers or the fact that someone had made three different attempts on her husband's life. Except she didn't believe it. She was certain that Barnaby and Lamb had gone exploring and that, somehow, they'd ended up in the hands of the Nolles gang. She swallowed painfully. Barnaby could be in the hands of whoever was trying to kill him. Had, perhaps, already killed him. . . .

Eyes silver with panic, the cloak flying out behind her, Emily burst into the salon and skidded to a stop when she saw Mathew, still wearing his greatcoat, smiling and talking with her aunt. They both looked up astonished at her impetuous entrance.

Cornelia's breath caught at the sight of Emily's garb, recognizing the significance of it. Her hand at her throat, she cried, "My dear! What is it?"

Emily hesitated. Just because Mathew was here now didn't mean he didn't know where Barnaby and Lamb were. Or their fate.

Her hand slid in the pocket of her jacket and closed around the pistol. Eyes hard on Mathew, she demanded, "Why are you here?"

Thoroughly taken aback, not only by her dress, but her manner, Mathew stared at her as if she had gone mad. "I, ah, I was, er, in the area," Mathew stammered, clearly thrown off stride.

"You're lying," Emily said. "Simon wrote you."

Mathew's lips thinned. "What if he did? He's worried about your husband. Someone's tried to kill him, remember?"

"You?" She hurled the accusation at him like a spear.

His fists clenched and he took a threatening step toward her, the azure eyes blazing. "By God! If you were a man, I'd knock you down for that. For the last time. I. Do. Not. Want. Your. Husband. Dead."

Quietly, Cornelia said, "I believe him. I told you that you're wrong about Simon and I'm telling you now you'd be wrong not to trust Mathew. I've watched both boys grow up into fine men and I trust them as much as I do Barnaby."

"Barnaby's life may hang in the balance," Emily warned with a desperate glance at her great-aunt's face.

"Which is why you have to trust Mathew. Whatever has happened—and something obviously has—you cannot save him by yourself," Cornelia said softly.

Emily bit out a curse. Feeling time spinning away every moment she hesitated, she made a decision. And God help her if it was the wrong one.

Concisely, she told him what she and Lamb had discovered yesterday at the old barn, ending with Barnaby and Lamb's disappearance. She didn't have to explain herself twice. Mathew grasped the situation immediately.

His eyes as hard and grim as hers, he said, "You think they stumbled onto something they shouldn't have and that they've been captured by the smugglers—and the man who has tried to kill your husband."

She nodded curtly. "There's no point in following the tunnel from this end—if they have them, they'd have to move them out from the barn entrance." She smiled, as lethal a smile as Mathew had ever seen. "And I'll be waiting for them."

Mathew's smile matched hers. "No, my dear. *We'll* be waiting for them."

Chapter 24

U nwilling to waste the time alerting Luc at the Dower
House, Emily sped from the house, not caring if Mathew
followed or not. He did.

Twilight had fallen and despite the questions he obviously had, Emily and Mathew rode in silence through the
purpling darkness. Leaving their horses tethered some distance from the barn, they approached the building warily,
moving silently together as if they'd always been a team.
Sidling up to the barn, they stopped, listening intently. Reaching the same door she and Lamb had used the previous day,
Emily stopped, transfixed by the faintest glimmer of light
peeking from beneath the bottom of the door. Someone was
in the barn!

Emily didn't know whether to be elated or terrified at
having her suspicions confirmed. The certainty that Barnaby, alive or dead, was on the other side of the door solidified
deep within her. Hope and fear tangling in her heart, she
sank to her knees and hardly aware of Mathew leaning over
her shoulder, eased open the door a crack.

A lightning glance burned the scene in her mind. Two
lanterns hung at the far end of the barn spilled a soft glow

over the front area where four or five men moved about, the wide aisle between the hay and the stalls filled with several carts and horses. Smuggled goods lay heaped on the floor ready to be piled into the carts. She watched breathless as a cart loaded with contraband was driven out of the barn through the doors at the front of the building and, on its way to London, vanished into the night. Two burly men burdened with barrels of brandy on their shoulders caught her attention as they swaggered out of the stall that contained the hidden entrance. The barrels loaded into a cart, they disappeared back into the stall again.

It was Mathew who spied the two human forms flopped on the ground near the pile of hay. His hand fastened like an eagle's talon on her shoulder and when her head jerked up, he murmured, "Over there, lying against the hay. Look in the shadows across from the last stall."

She peered in that direction and her heart nearly leaped out of her throat when she saw Barnaby and Lamb . . . alive! Both men were securely bound, but from their occasional movements, it was apparent they were alive. Her mouth tightened. Until I get my hands on the pair of them, she thought.

Carefully shutting the door, she and Mathew retreated to the woods.

"We are too few," Mathew whispered. "We need more men."

Emily shook her head. "No. By the time you leave and return with help, Barnaby could be dead." Through the darkness, she glared at Mathew. "I'm not leaving him."

Mathew sighed. "Then what," he asked reasonably, "do you propose we do? We can hardly storm the barn. They outnumber us three or four to one." Fortunately for Mathew's continued existence, left unsaid was, "And you're a woman."

Emily frowned, listening as the jingle of harnesses and the creak of wooden wheels drifted through the air. Another

cart meant another driver had left and that meant one less
smuggler inside the barn. . . .

"If every time a cart leaves, another man leaves with it,
we have only to wait and watch until the odds in our favor
are better before we attack," she said slowly.

It wasn't much of a plan and Mathew didn't like it, but he
had to agree she was right. They crept back to the barn and
dared another look inside. This end of the barn was deep in
shadows and she risked a longer look, counting five remaining carts and noticing for the first time, a pair of saddle
horses tied to a center post.

Shutting the door again, and leaning against the side of
the barn, she whispered, "There's at least seven men inside
right now—not counting Barnaby and Lamb. Five carts. Two
saddle horses."

Mathew nodded. "And if the carts continue to leave one
at a time . . ."

Emily grinned in the darkness. "Odds increase in our favor."

But Emily was worried and as the minutes passed and
two more carts rumbled into the night, waiting outside didn't
seem such a wise option. Barnaby and Lamb were inside,
helpless and vulnerable, and while she and Mathew waited
outside for the odds to change, anything could happen. Her
stomach dropped away. Barnaby could be shot and killed before she knew it. She had to be inside that barn where she
could react immediately if needed and not just risk a glance
inside now and then. Too much could happen between one
glance and the next.

Leaping to her feet, she said, "I'm going inside." Not giving herself a chance to consider the wisdom of her actions,
before Mathew could react, she opened the door and slid inside the barn.

Cursing under his breath, Mathew grasped his pistol and
braced himself to charge into the barn. Cracking open the
door a narrow sliver, he glanced inside, expecting a cry of

alarm when Emily was discovered. To his profound relief all appeared normal. A swift look around and he spied Emily concealed from the smugglers behind the bundles of hay and straw.

The remaining smugglers, Mathew noted, were busy at the far end of the building as another cart prepared to roll through the barn door and out into the dark. Taking a deep breath, his heart pounding like a battle drum, Mathew stepped quickly through the door and dashed to Emily's side behind the piles of hay.

"You're mad," he hissed when he knelt down beside her.

"You followed me," she pointed out with a grin. "What does that make you?"

"Mad as a hatter," Mathew muttered, shocked and a little embarrassed to discover he was *almost* enjoying himself. If Barnaby's and Lamb's lives weren't at risk, he admitted ruefully, he'd think this a great lark—and by far the most exciting time he'd ever had in his staid, respectable life.

Emily had been right, he conceded, for them to be inside the barn. Outside they'd been blind except for the occasional glance, but now they were positioned to strike in an instant should it prove necessary. Unfortunately, Emily wasn't content to simply watch and, to Mathew's horror, just as his heart began to beat normally, she whispered, "I'm going to work my way around to Barnaby and Lamb and cut them free."

Instinctively, he tried to stop her, grabbing for her booted foot as she slithered away, but she was moving too fast and he missed. Mathew swore and scrambled after her. Christ! She was going to get them all killed.

Emily had no intention of getting anyone killed, but she wanted her husband safe. By her estimation, there were four or five smugglers still in the barn, and during the next few minutes, one of them would be driving away, leaving only three or four men behind—good enough odds for her. Barn-aby and Lamb were on the other side of the mound of hay and straw where she lay hidden, and if she was going to make a move to free them, now was as good as ever. The loose bundles and piles of hay and straw gave her perfect cover and, focused on reaching her husband, she winnowed her way through it toward him.

Barnaby's head throbbed and his shoulders ached from the hours his arms had been brutally tied behind his back. He didn't allow himself to consider that he might die . . . and Lamb with him. His thoughts were all about escape and re-turning to Emily's sweet, warm embrace.

Since their capture, he and Lamb had been under the eye of one or another of their captors and there had been no op-portunity for either one of them to help the other one reach the knives they both carried. During the last few minutes as the barn emptied out and no one seemed to be paying atten-tion to them, he and Lamb had wiggled deeper into the shad-ows. They knew that time was running out for them and that if they were to make an escape, it had to be soon. Barnaby eyed the small door set in the back wall. Their best chance would be out that door.

Of one thing, Barnaby was certain. Tom would wait until the last cart had been driven away before disposing of him and Lamb. When their bodies were found, that Tom had mur-dered them would become legend in the smuggling commu-nity, but the man wasn't stupid enough to kill them in front of witnesses. But kill them he would—the only questions were when and where.

Tom and Peckham were still below in the tunnel keeping track of the goods selected for this particular run to London, but Barnaby knew they wouldn't remain there much longer.

He considered the two smugglers at the other end of the barn. They'd finished with the one cart and were busy loading the last of the contraband in the final cart.

Assuming the two carts would depart together, leaving he and Lamb with Tom and Peckham, Barnaby murmured to Lamb, "Can you get your hands in front? They tied my arms as well as my hands and I can't move them."

The smugglers had only tied Lamb's hands behind his back, not roping his arms to his body as they had with Barnaby. "I've been trying for the last five minutes," Lamb growled, "and in just a minute . . ."

Beside him, Barnaby felt a violent movement and heard Lamb grunt.

"Ah, that's much better," said Lamb, his bound hands finally in front of him. "Now where's that knife of yours?"

"We'll use mine," Emily said softly from behind Barnaby, jolting both men.

A dozen questions floated in the air between them, but there was no time. Once they were safe would be soon enough for explanations. And tongue lashings, Emily thought grimly. Tongue lashings that would strip hide off of both men, but only when she had them safe.

Her knife sliced through the ropes around Barnaby's arms and a moment later his hands were free. Reaching for the knife in his boot, he said, "How did you guess?"

Busy cutting Lamb's hands free, Emily said calmly, "Once I knew you'd gone down the tunnel and hadn't returned, looking for you here seemed logical."

"Logical and utterly mad," muttered Mathew, crawling up beside Emily.

Barnaby stared incredulously at him, barely able to make out his features in the shadows. "How in the hell . . . !"

"Cornelia vouched for him," Emily said simply. "I told him everything." She reached into her pocket and handed Barnaby the pistol. "If we have to fight our way clear," she whispered, "you should have this." A grin flashed across her face. "I'm sure you're a better shot than I am."

Barnaby's fingers tightened on the pistol, his heart suddenly so full of love for her, he dare not speak. Lamb was right. She *was* an Amazon. And she was his.

The second cart loaded, one of the smugglers reached up and blew out the lantern near the middle of the barn, deepening the shadows where Barnaby and the others crouched.

"It looks like they're getting ready to leave," Mathew said. "I suggest that we get the hell out of here and alert the authorities to what is going on."

Barnaby and Lamb's eyes met. "Ah, I don't think that would be wise," Barnaby said, fumbling for words. He wanted Tom Joslyn stopped, but he saw no good reason why Mathew and Simon should suffer the public humiliation and scandal that would accompany their brother's exposure as an active participant and the moneyman behind a vicious gang of smugglers. Tom had already revealed that Mathew had nothing to do with the attempts on his life or any part of the smuggling, but how would Mathew feel if forced to take sides? Would his affection for his brother pit against them?

A commotion near the carts caught their attention. A newcomer had arrived and in the faint light of the remaining lantern, Barnaby recognized the dainty figure that strolled into the barn, leading his horse behind him. Barnaby swore. "Nolles."

"The odds just went up," Emily murmured, "but we can still take them."

Barnaby shook his head decisively. He'd relish a fight, eager to mete out some justice of his own, but not when it placed his wife in danger. He already felt like a fool blundering into a nest of smugglers like a green boy and he wasn't going to add to the feeling by increasing the risks Emily had already taken.

Tonight's events weren't a total loss, he reminded himself. He now knew the identity of his would-be killer and Nolles's London backer; a report to Lieutenant Deering would end the use of the Windmere tunnels as a hiding place for contraband. Though it gnawed at his vitals, he had to face the fact that Nolles and Tom Joslyn would escape retribution tonight. This wasn't the outcome Barnaby wanted, but it would have to be enough . . . for now. He and Lamb were safe and Emily was by his side. Yes. It was enough.

Lamb glanced at him, reading the decision in Barnaby's face. "There'll be another time," Lamb promised softly.

Taking one last quick look around, Barnaby stiffened as two figures exited the stall and walked over to meet Nolles. Tom and Peckham. Unless he missed his guess, sometime in the next few minutes, Tom would be showing off his captives to Nolles.

Lamb spotted Tom and Peckham at the same time Barnaby did and as one they dived under the bundles of hay and straw, joining Emily and Mathew. "Go! Go! Out the back door," Barnaby said urgently, hustling Emily deeper into the hay.

Puzzled, but hearing the sharp command in his tone, she didn't argue and like an eel she tunneled through the hay, stopping only when she reached the back wall. With Barnaby and the others at her heels, she scrambled toward the back door.

A shout froze them in their tracks. "The prisoners," yelled Tom. "They've escaped! Find them, you bloody fools. Find them now!"

Fueled by fear, Emily sprang forward, her fingers scrabbling at the door before finding purchase and flinging it open. Barnaby shoved her out the door and into the darkness as another shout, "Over there! The door!" rang out and a shot shattered the night.

Seeing that Barnaby and the others had reached the door, Lamb circled back, thinking to launch a rear attack: Barnaby and Mathew, pistols readied, whirled to confront the danger. The sole lantern still lit was at the front of the barn but with the light behind them, beyond height and breadth the three men rushing toward Mathew and Barnaby were unrecognizable.

Already knowing who they were, Barnaby easily identified Tom by his height and Nolles by his shortness. Of medium stature, Peckham was in the middle of the other two men, Tom in the lead, Nolles hanging back—of the other two smugglers there was no sign. Peckham's arm flew up, getting off a shot at them, and Barnaby fired back. The butler crumpled to the ground. Tom halted and loosed another shot in their direction.

A bullet whistled by Mathew's head and, throwing himself to one side, he returned fire. His target cried out and clutching his chest fell facedown onto the barn floor.

After one terrified look at his fallen comrades, Nolles scampered to his horse. Lamb stormed after him, but he was too late. Catching a glimpse of Lamb bearing down on him, Nolles squeaked, threw himself on his horse and spurred the animal out of the barn.

"I nearly had the strutting, little rooster," he said disgustedly as Barnaby came to stand beside him. "One more minute . . ."

"It doesn't matter," said Barnaby. "We've pulled his fangs tonight. He'll grow another pair, but I'll wager he'll never be as dangerous as he was."

Emily hurtled back inside the barn, running to her husband. Barnaby's arm closed around her, pulling her tightly to his side. Brushing a kiss across her forehead, he said, "You very likely saved my life tonight, my love. Thank you."

She should be furious with him, she told herself, but he was alive and safe and she was too happy to hold a grudge. Besides, she was woefully aware, had positions been reversed, she wouldn't have been able to resist the lure of the tunnel either. Remembering the night he'd rescued her from Ainsworth, she hugged him back and smiled up at him. "I think we're even."

Sitting on a bundle of hay, Mathew stared dazedly around him. He understood the art of dueling, he understood the manners of war but the sort of violence he'd faced tonight was beyond his ken and he was shaken by his part in it. He looked at the two unmoving forms on the floor of the barn, knowing they were both dead, knowing he'd killed one of them. He'd killed a man tonight, he thought stupefied. He looked down at the pistol in his hand, appalled and awed by its lethal power.

Lamb walked over and sat down beside him. "First time?" he asked gently.

Mathew glanced at him, startled. He swallowed and nodded. "I've acted as second in a few duels, and have fought one or two myself, but no one ever died." He forced a smile. "Killing someone isn't easy, is it?"

"Not for a man of honor."

Mathew's gaze slid again to the bodies on the barn floor. "Do we know who they are?"

"We know," said Barnaby. With Emily locked at his side, he walked over to where Mathew and Lamb sat. "One of them is the man who has been trying to kill me—the other is my butler, Peckham."

"Peckham!" Mathew cried, diverted. "Your butler? But Tom hired him. He swore to me that Peckham was above reproach. My word, this is—!" He shook his head. "This is just simply too incredible. And the other man?"

Barnaby and Lamb looked at each other. The muscle in Barnaby's jaw bunched and he said in a voice that felt like he'd swallowed rusty nails, "I'm sorry, but it's Tom."

Mathew stared at him. "Tom?" he echoed, starting to his feet. "My brother, Tom?"

Emily gasped, looking in horrified dismay at the body on the floor of the barn.

Full of angry disbelief, Mathew snapped, "I don't know what sort of a game you're playing, but it's a damned cruel one."

"No game," Barnaby said.

"I don't believe you!"

Mathew brushed past Barnaby and Emily and stalked over to where the taller body lay. Kneeling, he hesitated and then, breathing deeply, he gently turned the still form over and stared down into his dead brother's face.

With Barnaby and Lamb astride the saddle horses from inside the barn, it was a silent, somber quartet that rode away from the scene of death. There'd been little talk between them, but it was decided that Lamb would tell Luc and Simon of tonight's events and have them join the others at Windmere. At a divide in the lane, Lamb left them, heading for the Dower House.

Arriving at Windmere, the subdued trio dismounted and after a low-voiced exchange with Tilden by Barnaby, they retired to Barnaby's study. Notified by Tilden of their return, Cornelia joined them. Shortly, Lamb, Luc and Simon walked into the room, their faces grave.

Simon went immediately to where Mathew sat like a stone-faced statue. His hand was gentle when he placed it on his brother's shoulder. Mathew jerked and, looking up at him, said thickly, "I killed him, Simon. I killed Tom. I killed my own brother."

Simon nodded, anguish for Mathew knifing through him. He was unsure of his own emotions about Tom's death. They'd never been close, had actively disliked each other, but the man had been his brother. . . . And a smuggler, he reminded himself savagely. A would-be murderer. If not stopped, Tom would have cold-bloodedly killed Barnaby and Lamb to protect his smuggling activities. Mathew had killed Tom, but unknowingly, and to protect his own life and that of the others. To Simon's mind, Mathew was a hero and bore no blame for Tom's death.

Simon knew that the days ahead were not going to be easy for any of them, Mathew most of all. His heart ached for him. In a short span, Matt had seen the title and fortune he'd assume he'd inherit stripped away from him, and now he had to live with the terrible burden of having killed their brother—and the ugly scandal that was about to erupt.

Looking over at Barnaby slumped on the sofa, next to Emily, Simon asked, "When will you notify Deering?"

"Within the hour," Barnaby said flatly. Picking up a snifter of brandy from the table at the end of the sofa, he took a hefty swallow. Setting down the snifter with a thud, he added, "Lamb and I will ride into the village and explain to Deering precisely what happened." His eyes on Mathew's face, he said slowly, "Deering will learn from us how it was that Tom came to me late this afternoon with the news that he had discovered that the smugglers were using the tunnels beneath Windmere to warehouse their contraband." Barnaby paused, frowning. "I think"—he began, putting it together as he spoke—"that I asked Tom to inspect the old barn for me to see if he agreed with me that it should be destroyed." Barnaby straightened. "Yes, that would work . . . and it was while he was there . . . remembering from childhood, the tunnels, he decided to see if the hidden entrance was still usable. He was horrified when he found the contraband."

Mathew stiffened, staring hard at Barnaby. Barnaby's gaze never wavering from his, he said, "Of course, once we were over our astonishment at his news, we thought it was most exciting and like the blundering amateurs we are, we had to see it for ourselves. Peckham, uh, accompanied us.

Unfortunately, we stumbled into the smugglers moving their contraband. We were fired upon and in the exchange that followed, tragically your brother and my butler were killed."

There was silence when Barnaby finished speaking, but Lamb and Luc were nodding their heads in agreement and Emily and Cornelia were staring at Barnaby with awed respect.

Cornelia thumped her cane on the floor and exclaimed admiringly, "You're a very good liar. I like it!"

Looking at Mathew, Simon said quietly, "Matt, I think it would be best if we allowed Barnaby and Lamb to explain to Deering what happened."

"I'm to hide behind a pack of lies?" Mathew cried.

"No," said Barnaby coolly. "We're *all* hiding behind a pack of lies, but I would remind you that this pack of lies will protect the family from scandal and allow the public to think that your brother died a hero. We know the truth. There is no reason to wash our dirty linen in public."

"What of Nolles?" Emily asked. "Won't he refute your story?"

Barnaby smiled grimly. "Nolles dare not say a word, else his part would be exposed."

No one had anything else to say and after a moment, Barnaby rose to his feet. "Unless there are objections, Lamb and I shall be off to see Lieutenant Deering."

Barnaby's eyes met Mathew's. They stared at each other a long moment and then slowly, almost imperceptibly, Mathew nodded.

When Barnaby and Lamb's tale of the events at the old barn became public it created a nine days' wonder in the neighborhood. Deering was delighted by the amount of contraband recovered from the tunnel and, as Barnaby had predicted, Tom was hailed as a hero. With his grieving relatives standing at his graveside, Tom was buried at Monks Abbey. Nolles, unfortunately, escaped unscathed, appearing as he swaggered around The Ram's Head to be amazed as anybody by the discovery of a huge store of contraband in the tunnel.

All in all, Barnaby was satisfied with the outcome, but there was one last task he needed to complete before he could put the matter behind him. A week after Tom was laid to rest, Barnaby oversaw the dismantling of the barn and the filling in of the tunnel entrance with boulders brought in by estate carts.

Emily stood at his side as the last cart rolled up and the boulders were muscled into place. Where the barn had once stood, there was only an open space, a mound of rock and boulders marking the spot where the entrance to the tunnels had been.

"I'm a little sad to see it destroyed," Emily said, her hand resting on Barnaby's arm, "but at least Nolles won't be using it anymore."

Barnaby nodded. "We'll have to do something about him eventually . . ." He grinned down at her. "But not for now. For now I'd like to live a rather mundane existence. No more smugglers underfoot . . ." He cocked an eyebrow at her. "Your little band as well as the Nolles's gang, and no more attempts on my life."

She dimpled up at him. "Won't you be terribly bored?"

Barnaby laughed and, heedless of the workmen still about, swung her into his arms and kissed her. Emily responded sweetly and he was breathing hard when he finally lifted his lips from hers. "Bored?" he asked smiling at her, his heart overflowing with love. "Married to an Amazon? I sincerely doubt it."

If you enjoyed RAPTURE BECOMES HER,
don't miss Shirlee Busbee's

FOR LOVE ALONE.

Turn the page for a special excerpt.

A Zebra mass-market paperback on sale now!

The elegant rooms were packed with gaily dressed ladies and gentlemen, the sound of their laughter and chatter almost overpowering. From the size of the glittering crowd, it appeared that Lord and Lady Denning's at home was going to receive the highest accolade possible from the members of the ton. It was indeed a dreadful squeeze.

Having found a small, quiet alcove in which to observe the activities, Viscount Harrington viewed the swirling mass with a jaundiced eye. To think that this was the height of ambition: to be packed into overheated rooms like raw recruits in the hold of a ship on their way to dreaded India; to see and be seen and to waste one's time prattling complete nonsense to vaguely familiar acquaintances, before departing and hurrying to the next social engagement. He shook his head. It was madness. Dashed if he wouldn't rather face a charge of Napoléon's finest cavalry than be subjected to another night like tonight.

So why was he here? Because *I have to find myself a bloody wife!* Ives thought irritably, as he stared out at the shifting crowd of women in their expensive high-waisted gowns of pastel silks and spangled gauze. The gentlemen were also garbed in the height of fashion; pristine white cravats, formfitting coats, embroidered waistcoats and black knee breeches.

It was almost incomprehensible to him that he found himself in this position. Less than fifteen months ago, he had been a carefree bachelor, marriage the farthest thought from his mind. He had a position that he enjoyed—a major in the King's Cavalry—and with the war against Napoléon still raging, there was every possibility of rapid advancement. He had certainly never expected to find himself inheriting his uncle's title and fortune and being placed in the position of needing to beget an heir.

A shaft of pain went through him. Could it have been just fourteen months ago that he had learned of the tragedy that had overtaken the Harrington family? Fourteen months ago that he had found himself devastated by the news that his father, uncle and two cousins had drowned when his uncle's yacht had gone down in a sudden squall? In one fell swoop, Ives had found himself the sole male survivor of the branch of the family which bore the proud Harrington name. Aunt Barbara's two sons, John and Charles, bore her husband's name, so that left them out. Clearly it was his duty, he thought morosely, to find a wife and replenish the Harrington blood. He owed it to his dead father and uncle and cousins to make certain that the proud name of Harrington continued—to ensure that there *was* a twelfth Viscount Harrington to inherit.

He sighed. I really *would* prefer to be fighting Bony, he mused unhappily. Complex battle maneuvers he understood. Women were something else again entirely. Not that there had been no women in his life. There had been quite a few. But he'd had only one use for them. And certainly there had never been any gently reared virgins among them! His women had known what they were doing, why they were in his bed, and what he expected from them. He grimaced. It sounded bloody cold when he thought of it that way. But it hadn't been. He had also known what he was doing, having learned long ago that there was much pleasure to be gained from giving pleasure, even if he was paying for the woman's favors.

Ives glanced around the room. He wondered how some of the young ladies parading here tonight would react if he made a straightforward proposition: Marry me, give me an heir, and I shall see to it that you never want for anything again. You shall be a viscountess, live in a fine home, and have a tidy fortune at your dainty fingertips. Once you have given me my son, we shan't have to bother with each other very much. We shall live separately and what you do with your life will be your business—provided you are discreet and do not besmirch my name. So? Is it a bargain?

He scowled as he realized that what he proposed was not a great deal different than most of the marriages contracted in the ton. And he admitted sourly that he did not want a marriage like the one that had befallen his father. He definitely didn't want *his* wife running away with another man and leaving him with two sons to raise. Bloody hell, no!

A soft giggle interrupted his unpleasant thoughts, and his gaze fell upon a young lady, not more than eighteen, who had been angling for several minutes for his attention. The bleak expression on his bold-featured face and the dark emotion roiling in his devil green eyes made her blanch and scurry away. Viscount or not, she suddenly wanted nothing to do with him.

Ives was amused by her reaction, and a singularly attractive smile transformed his features. That it had often been compared to a brigand's smile did not detract from its impact. He knew that he was not *un*handsome, but he would freely admit that his nose was too large, his cheekbones too prominent, and his mouth too wide for true male beauty. But as several women had told him, there was something about him. . . . Whatever it was, when he flashed that smile, women responded—as did the young lady he had just sent into flight. She glanced back, and, seeing the change in his expression, her step slowed, and she dimpled and demurely lowered her eyes.

Ives nearly laughed aloud. Little minx. His thick black hair, coupled with heavily browed green eyes, skin far darker than was fashionable and a body of a Greek athlete had served him well with the opposite sex. The fact that he now came with a title and a fortune only made him that much more desirable. He grimaced, suddenly feeling rather vain.

"Charming though little Felice Alden may be, she is far too young for a dangerous rogue like you, my dear fellow," drawled a familiar voice. "I beg you, for her sake, do not raise her hopes."

Looking at the speaker who strolled up to stand beside him, Ives grinned. "Percival! What the devil are you doing here? I thought you never attend this sort of boring affair."

Percival Forrest, a willowy fop just a few years younger than Ives, made a face. "M'father's sister. She came up to town for a few weeks and I was not quick enough to escape her clutches when she came to call. Insisted that I escort her here tonight." A sly smile crossed his sharp, attractive features. "No need to ask why you are here. How is the bride-hunting coming along?"

Ives shrugged. "Let us just say that the announcement of my nuptials is not in imminent danger of appearing in the *Times*." He jerked his head in the direction of the young damsel, who was still hovering in the vicinity. "And if the Alden chit is a sample of the majority of the prospects to bear my name, I fear that it will be a *very* long time before an announcement does appear."

The two men exchanged an amused glance. Percival had been a lieutenant under Ives's command until nearly five years ago, when he had unexpectedly inherited a comfortable fortune from his great-uncle and had sold out and returned to England. Ives had been sorry to see him go but pleased for his friend's good fortune. They had known each other all their lives—the Forrest estate lay near the Harrington family home, and they had been particular friends in the cavalry. Having grown up with him, Ives knew that beneath Percival's foppish exterior lay a fearless heart and a clever mind.

Ives had always enjoyed himself in Percival's company, and, upon his return to England last year, Percival had been one of the first people to call upon him. Their shared military background made a further bond between them. Unlike Ives, who would have preferred to bury himself in the country, Percival had taken to the ton like a duck to water. Since his arrival in London a month ago, Ives had relied increasingly on Percival's wickedly piercing insight into the antics of the ton to help him in his reluctant search for a wife.

They talked for a few minutes about a horse they had both liked at Tattersall's but that neither had decided to bid upon. From there the conversation drifted onto the exciting news that had arrived in London only days ago of Lord Cochrae's destruction of the French fleet at Aix. From that victory, it was an easy jump to Sir Arthur Wellesley's recent arrival in Portugal.

For the first time that evening, Ives was thoroughly enjoying himself. He was deeply immersed in conversation with Percival, when something—a laugh?—caught his attention.

Like a tiger scenting prey, his head lifted. The crowd before him parted suddenly, and there she was.

Gripping Percival's arm, he demanded, "Who is she?"

Percival, in the midst of discussing a complicated military maneuver, looked nonplussed for a second. When his gaze followed Ives's, he groaned.

"Oh, absolutely not! Of all the women here tonight, *she* arouses your interest?"

When Ives remained unmoved, his gaze fixed intently on the scintillating creature at the center of a circle of admiring males, Percival sighed. "Oh, very well, if you must know. She is Sophy, Lady Marlowe, the Marquise Marlowe to be exact."

Ives was stunned by the sensation of dismay that filled him. "She is married?"

Percival sighed again. "No. Widowed."

Ives's face brightened, and, with renewed intensity, his eyes wandered over her. She was like a butterfly. A lovely, golden butterfly. From the crown of her golden curls to the glimpse of her golden slippers beneath the hem of her golden gown. Her bare shoulders even gleamed like palest gold in the light from the many crystal candelabra gracing the high ceiling of the large room. And when she laughed . . . when she laughed, Ives was aware of an odd thrill going through him. She was, he thought dazedly, absolutely the most exquisite creature he had ever seen in his life. Tall and slender, she looked as if the slightest puff of wind would send her drifting away, and yet there was an air of strength about her. The profile turned his way was utterly enchanting.

"Introduce me," he commanded.

"Dash it all, Ives! Did you not hear a word I just said? She is a widow—a widow with a nasty past, believe me."

Ives glanced at his friend. "What do you mean?"

Percival grimaced. "Do you even know who Simon Marlowe was?"

"I seem to recall my father mentioning his name once when I was home on leave, but no, I do not know him."

"Which is just as well! He was by all accounts a nasty

piece of work. *Not* a gentleman, despite his title—and certainly not a man any self-respecting family would wish one of their daughters to marry."

Ives frowned. "Are you saying that her family is not a respectable one?"

"Not exactly. Her father's family is exemplary." Percival looked uncomfortable. "It is her mother's family . . ." He cleared his throat and fumbled for words.

He had Ives's full attention now. "What about her mother's family?"

Knowing from long experience that Ives was not going to give up until all his questions were answered to his satisfaction, Percival muttered, "Damn, I had hoped your paths would not cross and that. . ." He took a deep breath, and blurted out, "Her mother was Jane Scoville."

Ives stiffened as a new, dangerous element added to the intensity of his gaze which was still fastened on Lady Marlowe's profile. "The same Jane Scoville that charmed my brother, Robert?" he asked in a deadly tone.

"The same," Percival admitted uneasily. "Now do you see why she is absolutely the last woman you would be interested in? And the identity of her mother is aside from the fact that there are rumors that Lady Marlowe murdered her husband."

A silence fell between the two men, Ives hardly hearing Percival's last sentence. Jane Scoville, he thought, his hands unconsciously clenching into fists. The heartless, silly jade who had beguiled Robert, until he had been mad with love for her. So besotted that he could not accept the news of her engagement to the Earl of Grayson. So very mad, so despondent, that on the day she had married the Earl, he had hanged himself in the main stables at Harrington Chase. Ives had just turned ten years old at the time, but it was as if it had all happened yesterday. He had adored his brother, twelve years his senior, and he had been the one to find Robert's body.

"And how is dear Jane these days?" Ives asked grimly. "I must pay her a call if she is in town."

"She's dead, Ives. She died several years ago." Percival looked thoughtful. "You could, I suppose, defile her grave if you think it would make you feel better."

A reluctant laugh was dragged from Ives, and he relaxed slightly. "No, I'll not stoop to that." He jerked his head in Lady Marlowe's direction. "But I might be tempted to extract a little revenge from her daughter."

Percival shook his head vehemently. "Did you not hear what I said about her? *She murdered her husband.* She is not a lady, I, for one, would care to trifle with."

"I thought you said it was only rumors."

Percival looked annoyed. "So you were listening to me, after all! The official verdict is that he died in a fall down the stairs, but I was there that night—and I think she killed him." When Ives cocked an inquiring brow, Percival added, "I fell in with Marlowe's crowd when I first returned, which is how I know so much about his reputation. I do not want to make excuses for myself, but I had just come home after years of fighting in the wars and had seen and done things that were undoubtedly the substance of the most terrifying nightmares imaginable. Suddenly I had a great deal of time and money at my disposal. Marlowe and his friends were just the sort of wild and randy fellows to appeal to someone like me let loose in London, looking for adventure. It took me a while to realize that there is a great difference between wildness and wickedness. Marlowe was a downright nasty fellow, his friends not much better." Percival took a deep breath. "I am not proud of my actions that first year or two when I returned to England . . . but that is all behind me now."

"If the official verdict is accidental death, why do you still think she killed him?" Ives asked idly.

"Marlowe was drinking heavily that night, but I know that

he was not *that* foxed. And, there had been a terrible argument between them only minutes before he fell to his death. It was well-known amongst us that he had been denied his wife's bed. He complained bitterly about it when in his cups. And it was equally well-known that his wife despised him *and* his friends."

"And that is the basis of your belief that she killed him?" Ives's incredulity was obvious.

"Of course that is not all!" Percival replied testily. "Not only had they just had an ugly row, but she had shot at him."

Ives's brow rose. "And naturally all this occurred in your presence?"

"No, it did not! But we all heard the shot, and Sir Arthur Bellingham and Lord Scoville—" At Ives's expression, Percival looked uncomfortable, and muttered unhappily, "Yes, Jane's brother was part of the same crowd. He and Bellingham, being Marlowe's closest friends, went to see what was amiss. Marlowe himself told them that his wife had just shot at him. Scoville wandered back and told the rest of us. He was quite proud of his niece's marksmanship. And that was not a half hour before Marlowe's body was found."

"She shot him?" Ives asked, more intrigued than scandalized.

"Yes—the bullet hole was in the shoulder of the jacket he was wearing when he died. Naturally the officials investigating his death wanted to know how it came to be there, and Lady Marlowe was quite open about it when they questioned her. She admitted that she had shot at him and she made no attempt to hide the fact that she utterly despised her husband. She was *not* a grieving widow."

"If her husband was the blackguard you claim him to have been, perhaps he deserved to be shot."

"Are you defending her?" Percival demanded, the expression in his blue eyes clearly aghast.

Ives smiled and shook his head. "No. I am just saying that

there might have been a good reason for her to have taken a shot at the departed Marlowe."

"Well, that may be," Percival replied, slightly ruffled by Ives's reaction to Lady Marlowe's sins, "but surely you see why she is not a woman that you would care to know more intimately."

At that moment, almost as if she sensed that she was the topic of the conversation taking place in the small alcove, Lady Marlowe glanced in their direction. As her clear, golden stare moved curiously over him, Ives felt as if he had been struck by a thunderbolt. Every nerve in his body tingled as their gazes met and held.

She was exquisite. Her features had been fashioned by a master hand, the tip-tilted nose, the high brow and delicately sculpted mouth blending perfectly with the determined little chin and stubborn jaw. No simpering damsel here, he decided, as he stared boldly back at her. Not with that jaw and chin. Yes, he could believe that she had shot at her husband. Might even have murdered him, if Percival was to be believed. And she was Jane's daughter.

His reasons for being in London, for being here tonight instantly vanished. He was after something else at the moment. Something that had waited a long time. Something that had eaten at him and fashioned him into the man he had become. Even after all these years, the hunger for revenge for Robert's suicide was not dead in his breast. It did not matter that she was merely the daughter of the woman who had caused the death of his brother. What suddenly mattered was that Jane was beyond his reach . . . but her daughter was not.

And if her past was anything to go by, she was not going to be the type of weak, innocent creature who might cause him guilt for what had just occurred to him. He was, he admitted unashamedly, going to thoroughly enjoy wreaking vengeance on the already infamous Lady Marlowe.

His fierce gaze never dropping from hers, Ives touched

Percival's arm once more. "Introduce us," he said again, the note in his voice making Percival glance sharply at him.

"Oh, no," Percival said, "I am not going to be a part of seeing you make a fool of yourself. Find somebody else to help you make a cake of yourself."

Ives's eyes dropped to him. And he smiled, a smile that made Percival distinctly uneasy. "I have no intention of making Lady Marlowe my bride. But I suddenly have a yearning to meet this remarkable young woman . . . dear Jane's daughter."

Percival jerked and stared at him appalled. "You mean to punish her for what Jane did?" When Ives's dark head dipped arrogantly in assent, Percival said, "That is the most ridiculously idiotic idea you have had in a very long time. I hold no fondness for her or her mother, but *she* is not responsible for what happened to Robert."

Ives sent him a bland look. "Indeed not," he agreed, "but there is an interesting passage in the Bible, something about 'the sins of the fathers being visited upon the children'—or in this case, the sins of the mother. Now are you going to introduce me to her, or must I find someone else to do it?"

"Oh, damn and blast! I knew I never should have allowed Aunt Margaret to bully me into coming here. Come along then, if you are determined to make a fool of yourself." Percival shook a finger at Ives. "Just do not blame me for what happens."

Sophy was enjoying herself, or enjoying herself as much as she did at any of these gatherings. She had not wanted to come tonight, but Marcus, unexpectedly in the throes of his first calf love, had begged her to accompany him so that his attendance at such a stuffy event would not be so obvious. She smiled. At nineteen, Marcus had grown up into an extremely handsome and personable youth. His title and fortune only added to his appeal, and Sophy was just a little concerned about his current infatuation. She wanted to assure herself that the young lady was suitable. Not that she cared about fortune or breeding. What Sophy worried about was that the young lady's affections were for *Marcus*—not his title and wealth.

This was Sophy's first trip to London since her husband had died and she had gone to live with Marcus and Phoebe at Gatewood, the Grayson family estate in Cornwall. In the years since Marlowe's death, they had lived very quietly in the country, as much because it was their choice as the fact that their uncle continued to make inroads into the family's wealth. Despite the enormity of the Grayson fortune, funds had not been flowing with any regularity or generosity.

Fortunately, Sophy's monies were hers to command, and she had seen to it that they all three lived comfortably at Gatewood. A season in London was an expensive proposition, and she had not wanted to spend much needed gold on something so frivolous when there was still so much to be done at Gatewood. But this year, Lord Scoville had experienced a particularly good run of luck. Prompted as much by Sophy's increasingly angry demands for what was due her siblings, as by a sudden prickle of conscience, Baron Scoville had handed over a lavish amount of money for their use.

Marcus, restless and eager to see London, was determined to gain some "town bronze" and join his friends in the city. He had begged that they come to London. Phoebe, only weeks away from turning fifteen, had unexpectedly added her entreaties. Her big golden brown eyes full of pleading, she had breathed, "Oh, please, Sophy. Do let us go! I would ever so much like to go to Hookham's Lending Library and Hatchard's bookstore. My friend, Amanda, says that they have a simply *vast* selection of books."

"Books!" Marcus had exclaimed with great disgust. "I swear, Phoebe, all you care about is books. I want to go to

Weston's to buy some really fashionable garments. And to Manton's to shoot. And Tattersall's, to look at horses. And—"

"Yes, yes, I understand," Sophy had interrupted with a twinkle in her eyes. "You wish to make a dash." She smiled lovingly at Phoebe's young face. "And you wish to bury your nose in as many books as you can find. Very well, if you both want to go, we shall!"

"And you, Sophy? What will you do while we are in London?" asked Phoebe.

"I shall go to the British Museum and perhaps Westminster Abbey," Sophy stated calmly. The look Marcus and Phoebe exchanged made her laugh aloud.

The decision made, it did not take the siblings very long to set their plans in motion. They had arrived in London in March and had been settling very nicely into the Grayson town house on Berkeley Square. Marcus had already paid several visits to Weston's for his new wardrobe; Phoebe had been transported with delight over the number of books to be found at Hatchard's; and Sophy had found the British Museum positively fascinating. There were, of course, other entertainments that they had attended, either together or separately, and all three were feeling rather pleased with this first sojourn in London.

Despite her preference for quieter entertainment, Sophy had attended a few routs and balls during the past weeks and, to her astonishment, had thoroughly enjoyed herself. It was true that her path occasionally crossed that of her uncle and that there had been stiff, uncomfortable exchanges between them. There had also been unavoidable meetings with several of her late husband's friends, and the rumors about her part in Simon's death continued to be whispered about behind her back now and then. But all in all, she thought the trip to London had been a success; the ton had readily accepted them, and, though there were still a few raised eyebrows, most people had been surprisingly kind.

Edward's presence and the meetings with Simon's more disreputable friends were, at present, the only blights on her horizon. And since an "at home" was not the kind of entertainment which would normally appeal to Edward or Simon's other friends, she was fairly confident of enjoying the fifteen minutes allotted for this sort of entertainment without meeting any of them.

The circle of gentlemen presently surrounding her was mainly comprised of her brother and his friends. Two of them, Thomas Sutcliff and William Jarrett, she knew rather well—they lived in the vicinity of Gatewood and had grown up with Marcus. Since her return to Cornwall, she had become very used to them constantly being underfoot. At twenty-two, Thomas was the eldest and the acknowledged leader of the trio. Since this was his third London Season, he considered himself quite the man about town. Andrew, a year younger than Thomas, was affable and too easygoing for his own good. They were basically nice young men, and Sophy did not worry about Marcus when he was in their company.

Her gaze fell on another member of the group around her, and a faint ripple of unease dimmed her smile. Sir Alfred Caldwell was a new acquaintance of Marcus's, and Sophy could not say that she cared for him. At thirty-five, with a decided air of dissipation about him, he was much older than Marcus and his friends, and she worried that Sir Alfred's reasons for attaching himself to a green youth like her brother might not bode well for Marcus. Telling herself that she was being overly protective, she promptly put her concerns away. Thomas and William would keep Marcus from falling too deeply under Caldwell's influence.

There was one other member of the group surrounding Sophy, and she was not certain how she felt about him. One of Simon's more respectable acquaintances, Richard, Lord

Coleman, had come to call at the Grayson town house within days of their arrival in London. He had been extremely polite and had proved himself to be very helpful. It had been Lord Coleman who had advised Sophy where to hire the extra servants they needed; Lord Coleman who had gone with Marcus to his first sale at Tattersall's; Lord Coleman who arranged a delightful outing at Astley's Royal Amphitheatre for the entire family; and it was Lord Coleman who frequently accompanied Sophy about town. He had never acted anything but polite and proper, yet Sophy could not forget that he had been part of Simon's cortege and that he had been at the house the night Simon had died.

She did not know why he had attached himself to her side, but she suspected that, like her first husband, he had reached an age where the production of an heir was beginning to prey upon his mind. He had not yet reached forty, but she guessed he was not very far from that age, and she rather thought that he was angling for a wife.

A distinctly cynical smile curved her mouth. No doubt he thought that having been married to one roué she might be agreeable to marrying another. Her fingers unconsciously tightened around her gold-spangled fan. She would die before she married again! And certainly never to a man of Coleman's stripe or one whose only use for her was that of broodmare! *If* she ever married again, and she sincerely doubted that she ever would, it would be for love alone.

Suddenly, she felt that she was being watched. When they had first arrived in London, there had been a lot of stares and whispers when she entered a room, but most of that had died away by now. This felt different. She felt almost as if she were the object of some large predator's assessment.

Casually, she looked around, her gaze locking almost instantaneously with that of a tall, hard-faced gentleman standing in the small alcove to her left. A jolt of something she could not define flashed through her as their eyes remained fixed on each other. Fear? Excitement? Anticipation? Or dread?

She could not look away from him, the impact of his bold stare so overwhelming that she simply stood there helpless, unaware of anything happening around her. It was only when his gaze dropped to the man standing next to him that she was able to jerk her eyes away and became aware of Marcus laughing at something Andrew had said.

Shaken, she forced a smile and tried to pretend the odd moment had never happened. It was only by the greatest effort that she kept herself from looking again in the stranger's vicinity.

"Oh, I say," Lord Coleman murmured from where he stood at her side, "here comes Percival Forrest. Did not expect to see him at this sort of affair."

"Who is that big, bruising-looking fellow with him?" asked Caldwell. "I do not believe that I have met him before."

Percival advanced upon them before Caldwell's question could be answered and, bowing gracefully before Sophy, said, "Lady Marlowe, how delightful to see you again. How have you been?"

Sophy made some reply, unbearably aware of the tall, intimidating stranger at Percival's side.

"Lady Marlowe, allow me to introduce my friend Viscount Harrington," Percival went on smoothly. "Like you, this is his first London Season."

Coolly acknowledging Lord Harrington, Sophy thought her heart would literally stop when her eyes plunged once again into the depths of his devil green stare. He smiled at her, a smile that made her heart kick into a mad gallop, and she did not know if that smile was the most exciting thing she had ever seen or the most terrifying.